JULIE COOPER

This is a work of fiction. Names, characters, businesses, places, events, locales, and incidents are either the products of the author's imagination or used in a fictitious manner. Any resemblance to actual persons, living or dead, or actual events is purely coincidental.

Edited by Jan Ashton and Kristi Rawley

Cover Design by Crowglass Design

ISBN 978-1-951033-50-7 (ebook) and 978-1-951033-51-4 (paperback)

To Sarah
Such a quaint and tranquil name for such a dazzling force of nature.

Prologue

May 1808

He scoured the surrounding countryside, his vision obscured by the blinding afternoon sun. His sight was much better at night—of course—but so too would be Wickham's, and he was arrogant enough to believe his daylight skills significantly superior. Though he was the younger, he spent far more time than Wickham in pursuits designed to build strength, discipline, and endurance. In short, if an activity was less than pleasurable, Wickham was less than interested. Still, it would be a mistake to underestimate him; too many had done so to their ruin, and since last they met, Wickham's opportunities to improve in these areas had increased markedly.

Such was the reason Fitzwilliam Darcy found himself in the wilds of Hertfordshire. Those in authority searched London for the villain, calculating that in his current weakened condition, he would stay near the ready means of feeding available in the teeming city. Darcy disagreed—not with their logic, but with their conclusion. Wickham had planned this escape for long years; he would *count* on his enemies searching town. Instead, Darcy tracked the man's former paramour, Mary Younge, currently residing in Cambridge and luring young men more interested in hedonism than scholarship. Darcy judged Wickham to be making his way to her, and from thence, to Norfolk and the coast. He was certain he was on his trail, though the criss-crossed route in obscuring patterns made for interminably slow progress. Wickham's gifts did not extend to animals, and horses instinctively feared and hated him, becoming almost impossibly wild in his presence unless he spent months in training. Of course, normally the rogue could travel like the wind on foot; only the severity of Wickham's injuries left him so vulnerable and sluggish—thus too weak to attempt riding crazed steeds.

Remembering these vulnerabilities, Darcy forced himself to renewed attentiveness. Bright sunshine, unobscured by clouds, had a tendency to increase daylight's usual fatiguing effects, so he intensified his attentiveness to combat it. Even so, he nearly missed the slight burst of unholy glee emanating from a clearing some ways ahead. Then, that too was gone.

He bid his horse to remain still—Darcy had worked extensively on *his* skills with the animals—and swiftly, silently made his way to the woodsy glade. What he saw halted him in his tracks.

Wickham was feeding. In his clutches was a young girl—her features delicate, her skin pale, her long, dark curls caressing the forest floor as though spread upon a lover's pillow; he gorged upon blood directly from her chest.

Wickham's uncanny sense of self-preservation functioned as perfectly as ever, however, despite his weakness. His eyes lit on Darcy from across the clearing and he grinned, taking another pull from the poor chit before withdrawing slightly to speak. "Darcy, my brother. I admit to some surprise. I thought you in Italy."

"I came to England as soon as I heard of your…departure from your accommodations."

Wickham's grin turned bitter. "They kept me starved, Darcy, chained in silver. You try existing that way and see if alternatives do not become attractive."

"You wish my pity? I thought it a punishment of undeserved generosity. Another few decades and you would have been free to pursue those alternatives. Now, your life is forfeit."

"Only if I am caught."

"Consider it done."

"Ah. I suppose one could view it thus. Unless, of course, you wish to save this." He flicked a hand towards the body beneath him in a careless gesture.

"She is already gone."

Wickham cast him an odd glance. "No. She is close, certainly. You astonish me. Slipping in your dotage?"

Deceit was second nature to his opponent. If the girl lived, her force of life would tell him so, as it would any of their primeval species. The least amongst his breed could track a human—their powerful nose and keen hearing made them unsurpassed hunters to any mortal prey, and beyond that, every human bled something of itself in a subtle beckoning any predator recognised. But Darcy's talents were yet more acute. Even unconscious, the essence making her *herself* would call to him, even *shout* to him. It was both his gift and his curse that emotions—most especially those of mortals—were open to him. Even if she lay dying, he would hear...and he heard nothing.

"You lie. She is dead."

Wickham's expression changed to one of deep interest. "You cannot sense her. Incredible. Her heart has stopped, but her mind should still be salvageable." He peered down at the girl's chest.

Faster than the eye could see, Darcy made his move. Wickham bolted. Despite his recent feeding, Wickham was still weak; retribution was within Darcy's grasp. But he could not help sparing a glance at the dead girl before following. And to his astonishment, she gasped for breath.

He had only seconds to make his decision. Wickham was purely evil; allowing him escape could mean the death of many, including cruelties of unconscionable measure. Not to mention his own avowal of vengeance, an oath sworn upon his father's grave. The sacrifice of this one mortal in the face of such an outcome meant little. It was unlikely he could save her; truly, he scarce believed she lived. But he made the mistake of looking into her face and, though he did not often require breath, was unable to prevent the quick inhale.

She was the loveliest creature he had ever laid eyes upon.

She was only a child.

He let the scoundrel go.

One

October 1818

Fitzwilliam Darcy surveyed the crowded assembly, an expression of unmitigated boredom etched upon his handsome features. He had perfected this countenance, hiding, as it did, his deep unease in the midst of suffocating emotions breaking over him in wave after wave of excruciating perception. One would think, after more than two hundred years of practise, he would be accustomed to the sensation. One would be wrong.

His current position was annoyingly near a row of wallflowers, their hopeful despair leeching at his nerves, like cloying scent attempting to conceal the odour of sweat. It was a relief when Bingley came near—forthright, good-hearted Bingley, whose only emotions were positive ones. While his constant cheer could be provoking to one so wholly committed to dispassion, at least his company was bearable.

"Come, Darcy," Bingley implored. "Would it not be better to dance? You had much better dance than stand about stupidly. The exercise alone is a worthy distraction."

Not this again. "Doubtlessly, since *you* have managed to claim the attentions of the prettiest girl in the room."

"I agree. However, her sister is lovely, too. Do let me ask my partner to introduce you."

As if he would stand for *more* besieging emotions from strangers, exuding the stench of fright, avarice, or distasteful lust! "Do you think I want your leavings? I have endured the notice of every girl here and found not one tolerable enough to tempt me."

Behind him, he heard a startled gasp. Odd. He had sensed no one near enough to hear their murmured conversation.

Abruptly he turned.

She was tall for a female. Her hair was dark and full of curls in what had probably once been an elegant coiffure. They fell artlessly, framing her heart-shaped face and determined chin, giving her an almost fey appearance. Her figure was perhaps more, ah, rounded than was currently fashionable, and the gown did not flatter. Her large eyes—obviously her finest feature—flashed with anger.

He had been boorish and she was angry—he could plainly see it. But he could not feel it. Amazing.

It was *her*.

This night was proof of her destiny, Elizabeth Bennet decided. She had been resisting the notion that she was on the shelf. As evidence, she could point to the fact that beautiful, gracious Jane—who was everything lovely and kind and a year her senior, at four and twenty—could certainly not be considered spinsterish. It seemed likely that under the right sort of circumstances—sadly lacking in Meryton, of course—the two Bennet sisters might be *awash* in offers. For eight long years of dances, assemblies and parties, she had been clinging to this premise.

The company from Netherfield, however, sadly disproved her theory.

Not about Jane, of course. Her sister's charms were quickly apparent to the handsome party from London, most especially the estimable Mr Bingley. No, her mistake had been to include herself in Jane's worthier sphere. No longer could she pretend.

She walked along the perimeter of the room, feigning inattention to Miss Long and Miss Watson's giggles. "If she grows any taller, her hair will be in danger from the chandeliers!" Their laughter followed her, but she kept her head high.

If only, if only. If only the four-and-twenty families constituting

Meryton's best were not so sadly skewed towards the feminine gender. If only Papa would take them to London for a season, or allow Uncle Gardiner to introduce them to his admittedly lower but definitely more abundant prospects. With five daughters to marry off, one would think Mr Bennet slightly more interested in providing opportunities to show them to advantage.

But Mr Bennet adored his little kingdom, complete with five adoring devotees—at least one of whom could usually be found to wait upon him on those rare occasions he required an audience. If his wife was not one of his loyal subjects, he did not appear to notice. Nor did he discern that at least three of his daughters had passed the age when they should have begun realms of their own.

Tonight, Elizabeth had been hopeful: if they could not go to London, London had come to them. This night could be different. It could prove that in a different place, with different people, she would be—*would have been*—special.

Jane *had* proven it. Sadly, the same thing could not be said of herself. Evidently, she—and the rest of the young females here—were merely 'leavings.' The scrapings at the bottom of the barrel. Intolerable.

The man discourteous enough to call attention to her deficiencies turned at her gasp. Elizabeth took an involuntary step back. Up close, he was larger than she first thought, lean but long-limbed with broad shoulders framed to advantage in an elegantly austere black coat. It was his eyes, though, that struck her; they turned from an almost surreal green to fathomless black. It momentarily distracted her from the shock of his discourtesy.

"Your eyes are very unusual," she said without thinking. Then, embarrassed at having spoken her thoughts aloud and angry at her embarrassment when *he* was the offending party, she stiffened.

"I suppose I ought not to have mentioned it," she said pointedly. "It seems to be the night for saying aloud what is better left unsaid. I hope you know I meant nothing mean-spirited by *my* thoughtless remark. Please excuse me." She dropped the barest curtsey and turned away, disappearing into the crowd.

Darcy stood looking after her, his mouth open.

"You gape like a beached fish," Bingley commented. "I say, Darcy, why did you let her keep that memory? Dashed ill-mannered, you sounded. And she is Miss Bennet's sister. You might have made things right. I would like to leave a good impression."

Darcy forced his mouth shut. "I did try," he replied. "My efforts had no effect upon her."

It was Bingley's turn to gape.

Idly, Elizabeth studied the 'Spinster's Corner', wondering whether there was room for one more. Charlotte refused to take a seat there, but that was just pride. Why not relinquish hope and take her place? Announce to all and sundry the death of her expectations. Of course, her mother would have a fit. She sighed.

"Surely you do not consider donning a lace cap?" a low voice murmured directly in her ear.

She startled, her eyes widening as she recognised the speaker: the loutish gentleman from Derbyshire. But Mr Bingley pushed forward in front of his friend, casting him a look of some asperity as he did so.

"Miss Elizabeth—please allow me to introduce my friend, Mr Darcy. Darcy, Miss Elizabeth's family resides on the estate just to the north of Netherfield's eastern boundary. Longbourn, is it not?"

"It is indeed," she replied, without acknowledging the introduction.

But Mr Darcy refused to take offense. "I owe you an apology, Miss Elizabeth. I allowed ill temper to influence my conduct."

Elizabeth inclined her head, hoping it would be taken for a gracious reply. Mr Darcy, though perfectly tailored, wore his hair a little too long and his expression a little too sharp. He made her nervous, a truth she was loath to admit to herself, and ruining any interest she might have had in extending the conversation.

"Would you honour me with the next set?" he asked her, unfortunately not taking the hint.

"Yes," she answered baldly, not having the wherewithal to form a prettier reply, and gave a mental shrug. A dance was a dance, even one given for apology's sake, and she would not surrender an evening's entertainment for the sake of snubbing an oaf.

Heads turned as he led her onto the floor. Hers was the signal honour of being the only lady not of his party to claim a dance from the illustrious Mr Darcy, and of course no one understood he was simply being polite. Her neighbours looked on with interest and speculation. Uncomfortable, she raised her chin, meeting his steady gaze. His eyes were purely green again, puzzling her, and she glanced at the chandelier, wondering at the oddity of the light creating the effect.

But he was an admirable dancer, so light on his feet and quite graceful for a man so tall and with such breadth of shoulder. After a few minutes, Elizabeth submitted to the enjoyment of dancing; even the arrogant stranger could not ruin it. As her partner did not attempt conversation, she lost herself in the rhythm and steps, taking pleasure in making the patterns meet, divide, and re-form once more. Always, always, Mr Darcy matched her steps in harmonious accord—almost an extension of herself. There was something deeply satisfying in the way their rhythms aligned so perfectly; it had never happened with any other partner.

There were many challenges to his vampyric nature, but Fitzwilliam Darcy faced the most difficult of them as he danced a quadrille with the lively Miss Elizabeth Bennet. His brain had firmly and logically decided on Caroline Bingley as the answer to the dilemma of his needs. Caroline held only two emotions of any potency—greed and lust. The greed was easily satisfied with baubles, the lust more easily sated still. For a man—and Darcy still considered himself one, despite all evidence to the contrary—with his gifts and afflictions, such a personality as Miss Bingley's was ideal. No overwhelming grief or despair when he disappointed her, no unplumbed depths to worry and annoy and assault his peace of mind. The fact she already understood his nature and the secret of his existence was a bonus nearly carrying the day.

The rest of his person, however, had proven singularly uncooperative towards his brain's choice of companion. Whereas Caroline never roused much beyond a slight appreciation for face and figure, every bit of his primitive attention riveted on the lovely picture Miss Elizabeth made as she twirled and dipped in time to the music. He might not even be in the room for all the attention she gave him, her happiness in the dance having naught to do with her partner. He could almost feel her joy—and *only* with his nascent 'human' senses.

Her aura gave nothing away. The years since he had seen her had done nothing except redouble his interest. In fact, he had been able to dismiss her ten years before *only* because of her extreme youth, blaming her near-death and the subsequent protective feelings as an anomaly. He had thrust her from his mind. From his soul.

But now, with the clarity of hindsight, he could see that—all unknowing—she had become his standard for beauty, a measure by which he judged perfection. With disquiet, he now saw Caroline passed muster only because there was some similarity in colouring and hair. *Devil take me.*

He could almost *feel* the blood rushing in his veins, tingling in his gloved hand every time it met hers. As the exercise caused her heart to beat faster, an answering rhythm from his own matched it—territorial and primal—from a part of himself he had believed extinguished. He had known desire countless times; this was nothing like it, his instinct urging him to sweep her off her feet, to cart her away from this simple country dance with its simple country society and claim her as his own. Neither did his instinct much care what Miss Elizabeth might have to say about the matter, though his brain lodged several fervent reminders. Not since he first reached maturity—struggling to conquer the inherent, overwhelming hungers of a blood-born male vampyre—had he experienced such a detachment between mind and body, the beast and the man.

There was only one thing to be done: depart from this assembly—from this country—as quickly as possible. But when the dance was over, Miss Elizabeth safely restored to her sister's company, he did not leave.

Instead, he watched her, seldom able to look away. Unfortunately, his notice caused an unwelcome effect; suddenly, a dozen eligible males eyed her with new attention. He could not resist aiming his will upon each one, learning what they felt for her. In some, he sensed mild interest and typical male appreciation. Some felt curiosity—directed, he supposed, at his reasons for pairing with her. The last one, though, a man every bit of sixty years, oozed a filthy comingling of lust and craving, his beady eyes straying where no gentleman's ought. Darcy felt his own eyes going dark.

Not a sensible idea, his brain reminded.

The devil with sensible, his instinct answered, just before the fellow tripped over his own feet and fell hard to the ground, screaming.

"Poor Mr Goulding," Jane said sadly. "Mr Jones said his ankle is almost certainly broken. What very bad luck!"

The two girls were snuggled in their cosy bed, but sleep would be a long time coming. Tonight, there was much to discuss.

Elizabeth rolled her eyes. "Perhaps if he paid more attention to his feet than to my bosom, he would not have stumbled."

"Oh, Lizzy...surely—"

"Jane Bennet, you know he is a horrible old reprobate. Fate delivered exactly what he deserved tonight. Admit it."

A little giggle answered her, and Elizabeth smiled. It was not easy for Jane to acknowledge the flaws in others. Fortunately, this worked to her own advantage, for Jane was also very slow to recognise Elizabeth's less than admirable qualities.

"This night was entertaining for both of us, do not you agree?" Jane asked quietly.

"For you, dearest sister. Most definitely you are proven a diamond of the first water."

"What of Mr Darcy? You were the only girl he danced with not of his party."

Elizabeth sighed, explaining the situation to Jane. "Do not tell Mama, though. He did apologise, and though I still think him unbearably arrogant, I suppose he has some excuse for it. Anyone who looks as he does must naturally grow jaded, and if the rumours of his wealth are true—well, I suppose if all look upon him in the predatory manner Mr Goulding did me, the company of strangers would indeed become tiresome."

She pressed Jane on the subject of Mr Bingley with some force, but her naturally modest sister would not admit his attention meant anything special.

"I hope, dearest Jane, the events of this evening merited at least a mention in your diary?"

"Naturally I recorded my thoughts tonight—which I do every night, as you well know."

"I only wonder whether Mr Bingley earned a mention by name, or if you merely refer to him as 'one of the party from London'?"

"Oh, no, my clever Miss Lizzy. You shall not trick me into revealing anything more. 'Tis far too soon to say aught of the Londoners in our midst. And speaking of London, I noticed Miss King's new wardrobe has arrived. Was her gown not lovely?"

Elizabeth smiled and allowed her sister to change the subject. It was a long while before either girl slept.

Available amusements in the neighbourhood consisted, for the most part, of gatherings such as this one at Lucas Lodge. It could not have been more tedious; the curiosity of strangers clawed at Darcy, scratching at his consciousness as lice in a hair shirt. That was, until the moment Miss Elizabeth made her appearance. Being near her was akin to basking in a cool calm—the peace of it was almost more attractive than the pleasing figure hidden beneath yet another ill-fitting, ugly dress.

He had resisted coming at all, but Bingley was anxious to continue his acquaintance with Miss Bennet, his desire to see her again almost disquieting in one normally so mild. Perhaps she truly was 'the one'—he knew Bingley was anxious for such to be the case. Besides, as long as Netherfield remained a base of operations in the hunt for Wickham, it was as well they not appear odd to the community. Maintaining appearances was his sole impetus; the hope of furthering an acquaintance with Miss Elizabeth did not enter in.

Upon seeing her, however, he knew he had deceived himself. Wild to capture some sort of notice from her, he willed her to walk in his direction with a force that should have pulled the pictures from their frames—and yet she only glanced his way once, her expression mildly annoyed. Did she deliberately snub him?

Aggravated, he forced himself away, soon finding himself drawn into conversation between Miss Bennet, Bingley, and Lady Lucas. That good woman gushed with social triumph and nearly as much curiosity as her husband, punctuating each remark with aggressive expressions of inquisitive agreement. Miss Bennet smiled serenely at Bingley's descriptions of a rout in town, saying little. Was she merely polite, or genuinely interested in his friend? Darcy turned the power of his attention upon her.

Interesting. Beneath a deep layer of poise, the girl reacted with flickers of emotion every time Bingley offered a thought. At Lady Lucas's comments, she varied between indulgent patience and an easily interpreted mild embarrassment. Jane Bennet was one of those whose human company he could tolerate very well—she kept herself to herself. Probing further when Bingley spoke next, he felt Jane's blushing, maidenly awakening deep within.

He withdrew immediately, hating this, the inherent dishonour of being party to feelings perhaps hidden even from their source. Still, his loyalties did not lie with Miss Bennet. Against his better judgment, he answered Bingley's longing look of inquiry with a half-nod. Bingley's already warm gaze bloomed. Miss Bennet blushed.

Feeling decidedly *de trop*, Darcy pursued again the object of his desire, telling himself he was only disturbed by Miss Elizabeth's reasons for ignoring him. Though leaving the area soon, he must at least attempt a correction of his initial unpleasant first impression. He would not want her to think him ungentlemanly.

He timed his approach to intercept her as she passed near the voluble Sir William Lucas. Immune to his gifts Miss Elizabeth might be, but he would wager half his fortune Sir William was an easy mark. Darcy directed a single thought towards that worthy gentleman, and was not disappointed.

"Mr Darcy, you must allow me to present this young lady to you as a very desirable partner. You cannot refuse to dance, I am sure, when so much beauty is before you." Taking Miss Elizabeth's hand, he would have given it to Darcy, who—not at all surprised—waited to receive it. Instantly however, she drew back, saying with some discomposure to Sir William, "Indeed, sir, I have not the least intention of dancing. I entreat you not to suppose I moved this way in order to beg for a partner."

Darcy, with grave propriety, requested the honour of her hand, but in vain. Miss Elizabeth could not be manipulated or manoeuvred; nor did Sir William at all shake her purpose by his attempt at persuasion. Miss Lucas and her brother beckoned her over to settle some friendly dispute, and his opportunity was lost. Darcy seethed with frustration.

Miss Bingley found him brooding. "I can suppose how you must suffer amongst the insipidity and noise of this witless crowd," she said, trying to create an air of intimacy between them. As usual, the simplicity of her emotions was easily borne. Though females like the Bennet sisters might be more agreeable, their kind also had expectations—love, tenderness, even virtue—he could never provide. Caroline's affections were reserved for her own self, requiring nothing truly intimate and certainly nothing virtuous. But the appeal to him of only a few days past now felt repellent; the thought of spending even a brief mortal life span with such a small-minded female, insupportable. Thus, though she blathered on with her usual vapid condescension, Darcy ceased hearing a single word. Rather, he used her presence as a shield against other intrusions so his real attention might remain fixed. He would lie to himself no longer: unless he exercised the severest restraint, Miss Elizabeth Bennet would be his prey. Only someone as self-absorbed as Caroline Bingley could have missed it.

"Caroline, invite Miss Bennet for dinner, will you not? As soon as may be."

"La, Charles, you cannot be serious about the girl," she replied indolently. "Consider what a mother you would have on your hands—and on my nerves! Such a relation would always be mortifying, and you surely could not expect her to keep her own counsel." She cast a pointed look towards her brother-in-law, who snored softly on the settee.

"*That* remains to be seen. What is certain is that you shall issue the invitation."

Caroline turned at once to Darcy for support, but he disappointed her. "Do as your brother asks, Caroline. For once."

Fortunately, Caroline had little patience for prolonged argument, especially when thus encouraged by the man she expected to marry. She wrote out the invitation, and Darcy only just caught her air of satisfaction as she sealed it. He looked at her carefully, eyes narrowed.

"Bingley," he remarked, "Send our regrets to Colonel Forster, for your sister has invited Miss Bennet to dine on the very same date he expects us."

"Caroline," Bingley snapped, "enough of your games." The siblings' clashing waves of annoyance were enough to disturb Darcy's peace of mind, and he shortly thereafter excused himself.

"Now see what you have done," he heard Caroline complain after his departure.

"He can hear you, Caroline. Pretend to have a soul," her brother replied, his boredom evident.

Darcy smiled. Bingley was growing up.

Miss Bennet arrived on the appointed day, soaked to the skin from a sudden downpour. While Caroline took her upstairs to dry, Bingley looked at him askance.

Darcy laughed. "I assure you, Bingley, I am no Romanov Master, with power over weather. Still, this will be convenient as she may be a bit sleepy and perhaps feverish for some brief while afterward. We can blame her soaking."

"I say, you do think it right, Darcy? It all seems rather," he said, hesitating over his choice of word, "...unsavoury."

Darcy stiffened. "Of course, if you prefer, I shall not look at all. I looked for your father and his father and his father before that, at their request. I do it in honour of the loyalty your family has shown me and mine, not for my own amusement. Say the word and I gladly withdraw my offer."

"No, no, of course not," Bingley protested. "I pray you take no offense. 'Tis only...I believe perhaps...no matter what you see...I think I would take her regardless."

Darcy's brows rose. Undoubtedly, Bingley's forebears would never have been indifferent as to whether or not their intended bride was barren. Still, this was Charles Bingley, and he was as unlike his forebears as could be. A competent, complex man, cheerful, kind-hearted and gentle yet with the manipulative skills of Machiavelli. He had fallen in love prior to this, certainly—even nearly come to the point of asking Darcy's assistance once or twice. Always before, however, he noted the opinions of others on the matter. Caroline was unlikely to approve of anyone who might displace herself as mistress of her brother's household until she secured a grander one of her own, while Louisa always followed Caroline's lead. Darcy—with his innate knowledge of the darker side of human nature—had never been impressed with his choices. But this time, Bingley gave any disapproval the equivalent of a shrug of supreme indifference. Miss Bennet had captured him as no one ever before. Darcy felt a deep stirring of some undesirable emotion; it took him some moments to recognise it as envy and for once, not from Caroline.

He envied Charles Bingley. Why? Perhaps because he was free to pursue his love, while the best Darcy could hope for was a brief, shallow flirtation. He might, eventually, persuade Miss Elizabeth to dance again, but that was the extent of his prospects. Unable to touch her mind, he could not engage in any behaviour leading to expectations on her part. If he kissed her, he might erase all memory of indiscretion from the entire village...but could not, apparently, do so for her. Much less could he taste the sweetness of her essence, her delicate lifeblood, and then expect her to forget it. Ah, yes, he had cause for jealousy.

"It is entirely up to you. I am yours to command," he managed gruffly.

At this, Bingley's usual affable grin returned. "Pish, Darcy! As if, eh?" His brow furrowed again as he considered, then straightened in decision. "I *do* want you to look. It will help me to plan for the future. If she is barren, I shall have to push Caroline to marry elsewhere for an heir. I daresay she would love to take hold of the Bingley reins, however the means."

"I will not argue with you on that score."

Simultaneously, they both gave a small shudder at the thought of Caroline Bingley as any young child's mother. And yet...this had always been Darcy's plan. He shook off the sudden misgiving, knowing first-hand a child could survive a terrible parent. In fact, he knew himself to be alive today because he had been raised amongst treachery. Survived it. Conquered it.

"Brandy?" Bingley offered.

"No point," Darcy replied dourly. It was a dashed shame that liquor could not dull his sense of revulsion, as it would for Bingley.

❧

Jane nodded, smiling politely at Mrs Hurst's remarks—the other woman's conversation was not of the sort requiring response. She cast a covert glance at Mr Bingley, sitting at the table's head. He looked at her—as, indeed, he had done for most of the evening—but his expression was not a particularly happy one. Was there something wrong with her gown or, heaven forbid, something caught in her teeth? Miss Bingley was reserved as well, while Mr Darcy hardly spoke a word. Perhaps they regretted the invitation?

At last, the ladies departed for the parlour. Jane took note of small details of the furnishings which would interest her mother and youngest sisters, trying not to wish that the gentlemen would join them soon. Fortunately, they appeared shortly thereafter, Mr Bingley taking the place beside her on the settee, while Mr Darcy seated himself in the chair directly across from her. There came a breathless silence, as though the room awaited something.

"Miss Bennet," Darcy spoke for the first time that evening, "have you ever visited Derbyshire?"

"No, sir. I have not had that privilege."

"Lovely country," he said quietly. He began a description of the countryside where he made his home.

Unusual, she thought, *that he does not speak more often. His voice is so soothing...almost...comforting...and there is something about his eyes...*

❧

Breakfast was scarcely finished when a servant from Netherfield brought word to Longbourn from Jane.

My dearest Lizzy,

I find myself very unwell this morning, which, I suppose, is to be imputed to my getting wet through yesterday. My kind friends will not hear of my returning home till I am better. They insist also on my seeing Mr Jones—therefore do not be alarmed if you should hear of his having been to me—and excepting a headache and slight fever, there is not much the matter with me. I simply do not feel quite myself.

Yours, &c.
Jane

Elizabeth could scarcely bear listening to her father's sarcasm and mother's glee. She set off at once, ignoring the mud in her haste to attend her dear sister.

❧

Netherfield maintained a 'keep up appearances' protocol whilst Miss Bennet resided in a guest chamber. Despite being almost unaffected by sunlight, Darcy seldom graced the breakfast table under usual circumstances—he was, like all vampyres, a creature of the night. Thus, the early hour, the scattered, anxious peppering of emotions by Louisa Hurst, and Bingley's needless concern over Miss Bennet's response to entrancement all contributed to his foul mood. Everything changed, however, when Miss Elizabeth was shown into the breakfast parlour. He stood at once, hearing Caroline's barely veiled criticisms with only half an ear.

She was magnificent. Cheeks flushed with exercise, eyes wide with concern, her hair flowing freely over her shoulders in wild disarray—all he could think of was his pleasure in seeing her, and how he might capture for himself some of that bewitching interest she bestowed so fiercely upon her sister. Louisa led her away, chattering on about poor, dear Miss Bennet's ill luck in being caught out in yesterday's downpour, and taking his happiness with her. Only when she was gone did he recognise he had not said a word to her, had missed his opportunity. *Damnation.* Which was, surely, what he courted now.

❧

Darcy paced the library, the room least likely to be invaded by either Caroline or Louisa. Of course, his own chambers were truly the safest place—far from the family wing with the privacy he craved, where no one would ever dare intrude. But it was *too* far, too insulating. He could almost laugh at himself for this madness. Almost.

He could pinpoint each body in the house except for *hers*. The best he could do was to stay attuned to Miss Bennet and assume she was near her sister, envisioning her there, her hands gentle upon her sister's fevered brow, lavishing tender, loving care. He cursed his sentimentality.

Perhaps her immunity to his gifts increased her allure, providing a brief respite from hitherto incurable ennui. Or perhaps he only responded to the remembered taste of her blood as he healed her wounds all those years before, feeling part of himself flowing through her veins.

She had been so young, not quite to her thirteenth year, not yet a woman grown. That was important. It meant he could try to heal her without ruining her young life with the burdens of immortality. He replaced what she had lost with his own, stronger, more savage blood, which both healed and stimulated her heart into working order, sealing up wounds in her flawless skin, leaving it unscarred, ensuring the infusion did not overwhelm her weakness. She had tasted of springtime, of his mother's roses—forgotten for well over a century, now. Her essence was innocent and perfect, with a spice of mischief preventing a surfeit of saccharinity.

And yet, there was something even then...something odd, calling to him.

Oh, he had wondered at the time, of course. Why could he not sense her life essence? Was she simple? Soulless? Mad? How he had wished her eyes would open so he could judge! He had carried her to the nearest home—they had known her—and resisted asking questions to satisfy his curiosity...simply because he burned to know the answers. After trancing the family into believing they discovered her themselves after she fell from a tree, he had forced himself to leave the area.

After all, there was no point in remaining. Wickham knew his pursuer now and would go to ground, putting himself into a grave-like state. Even in his weakened condition he could exist for many, many years deep within the earth—untouchable and untraceable until he decided to move again. Thus, Darcy departed, setting watchers about the countryside to alert him if the scoundrel showed signs of reviving—as indeed, they had recently done.

He had shoved the memory of the girl into the furthest recesses of his mind. Forgotten her, he thought.

Except he had not. Ten years was a goodly period of time, but not so much as a blink when measured against his vast life span, and though he marvelled at seeing her again, he felt no astonishment, no surprise. It felt like returning to Pemberley after a fifty-year absence. Like home, as nowhere else could ever be.

A pity, then, that he could only walk away.

Three

Once Jane slept peacefully, Elizabeth sought out the library—finding several books she had never had the opportunity or pleasure of reading—and was just stretching for one on a high shelf when a deep voice startled her.

"Miss Elizabeth—allow me to reach that for you."

She stepped back immediately, blushing; her choice was no mind-improving history, but a novel. Mr Darcy's height allowed him to easily procure it—and, naturally, he abandoned delicacy in favour of comment upon her selection.

"*Belinda.* I see you have a taste for the scandalous, Miss Elizabeth."

"How ungentlemanly of you to notice. I suppose you think I ought to have chosen the Fordyce."

"Only a very dull gentleman would expect such a thing. I simply find your taste in literature unexpected. I presumed you leaned towards the more...scholarly."

She turned away from him, partly chagrined, partly annoyed he thought her a bluestocking. "My father's library is full of the...scholarly. I only sought the entertainment of a novel to pass the hours. I did not know I selected one so shocking or indeed, that Mr Bingley would own anything that could be labelled thus."

His voice came from directly behind her, appallingly close to her ear. "I very much doubt Bingley has any idea what his library contains. He is no great reader. I believe his sisters are responsible for many of the selections."

For some reason, having her reading preferences compared to Miss Bingley's did not improve her mood. She stepped closer to the window, hoping he would take the hint and withdraw. He did not do so.

"I regret to have disappointed," she said in discouraging accents.

"I have insulted you. 'Twas not my intention." His arm snaked towards her, and for a moment her heart went to her throat. Would he attempt a rogue's embrace? A large hand briefly encompassed her clenched fist, and she wondered if anyone would hear her if she screamed.

But he only gently pried her fingers apart enough to slip the novel within them, immediately stepping back. "I have read it, and found the heroine admirable enough," he said softly. "You will enjoy it, I believe."

Feeling a bit foolish, she seated herself with the novel, attempting to read, hoping to prove herself unintimidated by either his opinions or his presence. But while she turned a page every now and again for effect, she could not fix upon a single word; he *loomed*, though not interrupting her self-imposed silence. After a full thirty minutes she gave in, looking back at him—only to find he had somehow departed without a sound.

Darcy had to flee. His vaunted self-control was suddenly a flimsy, insubstantial thing, hardly worthy of his race. He was a Master, even one whom other Master vampyres feared, the head of a great House; yet when her blush plumped her skin with rosy heat, his attention was immediate and fiercely insistent. Worse still, only one word echoed in his thoughts, demanding utterance despite his fervent rejection of its meaning: *Mine.*

It had to be simple animal spirits. There were logical reasons for his species to mate, and mortal females were adequate receptacles for vampyre creation. Female vampyres—if one discounted Medici myth —never reproduced. Even so, human-vampyre pregnancy was sufficiently rare, their mortal mothers dying in over half the cases. The progeny of such unions was always vampyre—considered 'full-blooded' due to their significantly stronger gifts and abilities—but most Houses consisted entirely of the Made.

His own blood-born status required of him at least an effort to procreate. It was safer for him, and for the child and mother, if he legitimately married the woman involved so that he assumed rights of ownership over both. Indeed, had he not decided upon marriage to Caroline Bingley? A union with her would satisfy his nature and never leave him vulnerable when, inevitably, she succumbed to death centuries before he could follow.

A vague predisposition towards mating, strengthened by a strong physical attraction to Miss Elizabeth, created novelty. It had nothing to do with overwhelming possessiveness and primitive longing. It had nothing to do with a desire for intimate connexion to one so completely inappropriate, a female whose motivations he could never trust, whose heart would remain forever a mystery. Nothing at all.

Sighing deeply, he recognised all of the signs. He lied to himself once again.

❧

The evening meal was a quiet one. Mr Hurst dug in with enthusiasm, not offering any conversation beyond an interest in having his glass refilled. Mr Bingley voiced his deep concern for Jane's recovery. Elizabeth had the feeling most of his thoughts fixed upon the sickroom; it was a hopeful indication in Jane's favour but regrettable for mealtime pleasantries. Caroline had insisted on taking a turn at Jane's bedside —surprisingly, she genuinely seemed to care for her, finding every opportunity to spend time with her. Mrs Hurst, to her right and in the absence of her sister, seemed far more cognisant of her husband. There was something inexpressibly sad in the way she followed his every movement whilst he ignored her completely.

Mr Darcy, to her left...brooded.

It was the only word for it. He met no one's eye, his expression reflecting scarcely concealed discontent. What was odd was how completely the rest of the table disregarded him—while *her* eyes wandered in his direction constantly. Since he disregarded all her attempts at conversation, she resolved to wholly ignore him.

Except she could not. His presence was like a wintry spectre in the room, a ghostly demand for her attention, compelling her to notice...well, *everything*. His long fingers as he cut his meat, his throat — hidden beneath the folds of an exquisitely tied cravat—as he swallowed. Even the harsh lines cutting his forehead and bracketing his mouth drew her to wonder what dire events of the past shaped such severity of expression. His dark coats emphasised his silhouette, denoting strength or perhaps its uglier cousin, brutality. Though his valet turned him out perfectly, a lock of hair fell over his forehead, as if to emphasise he could not be completely tamed. While beautiful, his was the dangerous beauty of a serpent, a weapon or a tool to be used.

He was intimidating, so *considerable* a presence. Does prey find its hunter appealing? Abruptly, she grew annoyed with herself and him. She was no Lydia, to be lured by appearances, and there was something sinister about him that no female ought to overlook.

If her flaw was a shortage of disinterest, his was a surplus of it. What must it be like, to have his gifts and yet hate everybody?

Darcy willed her to look away as aggressively as he formerly attempted to attract her attention. Any other being—be they vampyre or human—would likely be in the next county by now. Certainly, he existed for no other person at the table. Yet she persisted in casting him those occasional long looks beneath thick lashes. He forced himself to a frozen calm, pretending she did not call to the beast within, grunting boorishly at her polite comment upon the number of dishes served. Worse still, he might be unable to sense a single thought from that pretty head, but he was no stranger to the blush of an interested female, her cheeks pink with attraction. His nostrils flared, his canines lengthened.

Imagining her away was futile and pretending Caroline in her place, impossible. His animal nature overrode his will, repelling any female except the one whom, yet again, ignored his repeated signals to look away. This was not what he planned. The very opposite. It had all the makings of disaster.

History repeating itself in the worst possible way.

The following day, Elizabeth strolled the Netherfield garden paths. The day was chill, but a weak sun shone and her brisk pace—as well as mortification over her mother and younger sisters' gauche behaviour during this morning's visit—kept her warm. She stumbled in surprise when Mr Darcy abruptly joined her, seemingly appearing out of nowhere.

"Mr Darcy!" she exclaimed, as he took her elbow to steady her. "You are so abominably quiet on these gravelled paths! I wish you would not startle me!" Blushing at her clumsiness, she snapped at him in her embarrassment.

"My apologies, Miss Elizabeth," he replied gravely.

She said nothing more for some moments as they strolled side by side, until she sighed deeply. "I have been thinking disparaging thoughts of my own relations, only to be discourteous to the first person I meet. I should not have blamed you for my inattention."

"I ought to have announced myself sooner. The fault was mine."

She laughed. "Oh no, that will not do. We shall blame your valet for his inattention to your wardrobe. Reprimand him for failing to attach bells to your boots. Or were you ignorant of our country traditions?"

"No. However, I foolishly believed them only for cows."

In the face of his good-humoured acceptance of her feeble joke, she felt somewhat shrewish about her earlier critical thoughts. In the bold light of day, even her fanciful thoughts over last night's dinner seemed farfetched. He was, no doubt, a perfectly civil gentleman, if an excessively brooding one, and she felt a bit foolish.

"Your visit with your family...it was unpleasant?" he probed, interrupting her thoughts.

"Yes," she said honestly, before thinking. She sighed again. "My sisters...not much of excitement happens in Meryton. They plagued poor Mr Bingley until he agreed to host a ball."

"I would not think it took much encouragement," he said. "Bingley loves to entertain."

"Had it been his idea...but they were awful, and he was polite. Mama urged Mr Bingley almost as boldly as the girls. It was humiliating seeing their actions reflected in Miss Bingley's eyes. They earned every one of her nasty sneers." She clapped a hand over her mouth. "And now I have belittled her as well. I do apologise. I am not fit company."

He shrugged. "You need not ask my forgiveness. Pray do not allow Miss Bingley's disapproval to sour your afternoon. She is not known for her benevolence under the best of circumstances."

"Oh, I understand that," she answered candidly. "But they made it so easy for her to find reasons to despise them. And Jane did so want to make a good—"

She blushed again at her indiscretion. When had she become such a gabblemonger?

I complain of my family, and then demonstrate the very faults for which I blame them. Enough! Firmly, she owned her mistake. "Well, Mr Darcy, I suppose *you* have never revealed more than you wished to strangers." She pasted a smile on her face, resolved to say not another word.

"It has been the study of my life to avoid such weaknesses. Thank you for allowing me to join you on your stroll," he muttered, bowing stiffly. "I bid you a good afternoon." He turned on his heel and walked away.

Finding herself suddenly alone, Lizzy blinked. "I have done it," she said aloud. "I have lost his good opinion forever!"

And she laughed aloud at the absurdity of the notion that *she* should care, or *he* have any opinion of her at all.

"I have done it!" Bingley burst into Darcy's rooms on a wave of jubilance. It was a sign of his complete and utter elation that he failed to knock first, disregarding a lifetime of training. He was not precisely a servant of Darcy's, in the way a solicitor was not precisely the servant of his client. Still, a solicitor could be fired and replaced. The bonds connecting these two men were of a more permanent nature, of a type that death could not sever and payment did not mitigate. Obligations and commitments, created centuries past, preserved unbreakable loyalty.

Darcy looked up with brow raised. He held up a hand with his usual imperiousness, halting his ebullient companion. He traced the household's occupants, ensuring there were no witnesses to this conversation. With a sigh, he admitted to himself that Miss Elizabeth could be lurking beyond his chamber door and he would not know it unless she were singing in the corridors. He laughed humourlessly, and Bingley's brow knit with confusion.

"Make certain no one lingers," he said quietly, pointing towards the door.

"You cannot hear?" Bingley asked incredulously.

"Not if it is Miss Elizabeth who lingers, if she is quiet about it," Darcy replied. "These walls are thick." He kept no secrets from Charles. Well, very few.

Dutifully, Bingley turned back and carefully assured their privacy. "All clear," he announced upon returning. "Though I fail to see why she would be skulking about," he muttered.

Darcy ignored this observation. "Thank you. Now if you would be so kind, tell me what has you so, ah, enthusiastic."

"The proof of discretion, of course! I despaired finding time alone with Miss Bennet in order to say *anything* to her," Bingley said, pacing the room. "She is completely recovered, and it has taken considerable effort to convince her to stay under my roof. I almost resorted to asking you to mesmerise her into remaining! I am convinced Miss Elizabeth suspects my intentions, for she has been most useful in preventing her sister from bolting. What surprises me is that Caroline also seems to have taken a liking to Miss Bennet. She is as solicitous as I have ever seen her—to another female, that is."

"Yes. I find it deeply suspicious," Darcy muttered. He would lay money Caroline was plotting, but as yet he could not see her game.

"Perhaps she sees my choice of a sister for her is an excellent one and that we could do no better."

"Perhaps. Excuse me if I remain mistrustful."

Bingley shrugged. "Mrs Bennet and her two youngest daughters called. I say, Darcy, you would not believe the difference between the two youngest and two eldest in that family. Almost as if they had two different upbringings. They quite embarrassed Miss Bennet and Miss Elizabeth. The mother did naught to discourage their high spirits. In fact, she was nearly as unrestrained."

Darcy was completely uninterested in tales of Miss Elizabeth's family failings, having seen far too much over the course of the last centuries to bother about a few harmless if silly mortals. "You were saying you found a private moment with Miss Bennet?"

"Oh, yes, of course. After Mrs Bennet was reassured as to Miss Bennet's health, agreeing she should not return home for another few days, she took her leave. Caroline and Miss Elizabeth walked them all out, leaving me alone with Jane." He pronounced her name with daring affection. "We began conversing—she is deuced easy to speak with, by Jove."

"Where was Caroline during the discreet portions of this conversation? She could not have taken overlong to say farewell to the Bennets."

"She did not. She joined us after a very few moments, saying Miss Elizabeth had retired upstairs. But directly after, Lucy entered to say Cook threatened to leave again because Mrs Nicholls refused her order of mutton with the butcher. Caroline was needed to resolve the disagreement immediately."

Everyone knew of the longstanding disputes between Cook and the housekeeper. It was unsurprising they should come to a head today.

"Caroline left with Lucy and I shut the door behind them, using the excuse of keeping the fire's heat in the room so Jane might not catch a chill." Darcy raised a brow at this impropriety but did not interrupt. "We spoke of many things while I tried to introduce some daring secret into the conversation, but Jane is not much for gossip. She genuinely seemed interested in...well, me...my family and history and such. Then she asked me a question about our future plans—yours and mine. Almost without consideration, I put you in Kent a month hence, saying you considered establishing an alliance. A formal alliance with Anne de Bourgh." Bingley grinned widely at the expression of disgust on Darcy's face.

"Of all ill-begotten untruths!" Darcy nearly spit with displeasure. "No one who knows me would believe it."

"Of course. Which makes it perfect. Besides, you needn't fret. Miss Bennet is the soul of discretion."

"This was unwise. I have reason to believe Miss Elizabeth is not... indifferent to me. Should she confide that interest to her sister, Miss Bennet may feel duty bound to warn her away. You might force a choice between her discretion and her loyalty to her sister."

Bingley appeared troubled. "Really? You are certain Miss Eliz—er, I thought her closed to you?"

"There are other senses. Yes, I am certain." Catching the feelings of surprise, he gave his friend a quelling look. "And Miss Elizabeth's behaviour is all that is proper."

Bingley grinned ruefully. "I have seen more than one sensible woman misplace her dignity in your presence. But do you wish to *encourage* Miss Elizabeth? Is it possible you care whether or not she is...warned away?"

"I refer mostly to the likelihood Miss Bennet might feel some sisterly obligation to speak, when her natural inclination would be to keep silent." Darcy continued to contemplate Bingley's question for some moments, his countenance darkening. "I believe Miss Elizabeth and I have a mutual...fascination. I briefly considered... But no. Her mind is completely closed to me. There would be no way to undo this if she were revolted by my true society. Still, I would rather Miss Elizabeth not be troubled by cares of another attachment on my part."

Bingley's forehead wrinkled as he considered his confidence in his beloved. After a moment, his brow cleared. "No. I asked Miss Bennet to give me her word she would say nothing to anyone, as your future was undecided. She will keep her promise, and we all will be assured the family's secrets remain safe in her care."

Darcy sighed. There was truly nothing to be done about it now. With any luck, his friend's intuition regarding his would-be bride was correct. Jane Bennet did seem to possess a great deal of discretion. After some moments, he realised Charles was still speaking.

"So, what do you plan to do?"

"Do?"

"Regarding Miss Elizabeth? I must say, Darcy, 'tis unlike you to take up with an innocent."

"Is this your tactful way of reminding me the girl is possibly to be your sister? Well then, let me assure you—*again*—I plan *nothing* in regard to Miss Elizabeth. Nothing whatsoever."

Bingley's concern remained. "I say, this *fascination* is dashed unusual for you. Might it not be worth the risk to simply marry her? After all, she did not hesitate to march alone across the countryside to nurse her sister. Shows a lot of pluck, by Jove."

Darcy's jaw firmed. "I cannot. What I am requires full disclosure *before* marriage, for there is no hiding our differences if our union is blessed with a child. I shall not take the risk of its mother looking upon it with abject horror."

They were both quiet for long moments—Bingley in silent sympathy, Darcy in painful memory. When it became apparent

Darcy would not speak again, Bingley turned to leave. He paused with his hand on the door.

"At the risk of incurring your displeasure, I urge you to reconsider. I have never known you to express an opinion regarding a female and I hear more in your voice when you speak of Miss Elizabeth than you probably would wish. Caroline has never been your only option for a mate, just the most convenient one. And you have always been more than what you eat."

Caroline Bingley did not feel anger. Her brother's commitment to a union with this-this *nobody* was revolting, but she refused to allow the reasonable expression of indignation. Instead, she channelled fury into useful action. She could stop this.

For a family such as theirs, committed to the service of the Darcy line, the first requirement of any potential spouse was discretion. Any who could not keep mouths shut—and often eyes and ears—was disaster waiting to happen. After neglecting to do so for the Hurst union, with its subsequent catastrophe, Jane Bennet's discretion *would* be tested. And she *would* fail.

Caroline was certain of it.

Darcy wanted her for his own. Remembering their walk in the garden together, the lightness of her laughter and the sparkle in her eyes, ignited dangerous impulses and forbidden ideas. The heady thought that she might not entirely reject a kiss nearly overwhelmed him. He'd had to take himself away, riding his horse at breakneck pace across the countryside, allowing the late fall chill to do what it could to dull the fires of yearning. Almost, he could laugh at himself for his foolish behaviour. Most of his life he had held his father responsible for the deceit at the foundation of his son's misery; only now did he begin to understand the compulsion leading to it.

And because he did not want to remember, he forced himself to.

A pale, scrawny youngling—perhaps eight years—he delayed feeding an impossibly long time for one of his youth. The coldness had settled into a place deep inside, making him shudder with every breath of arctic air. Though the cellar was dark, he could see perfectly...the moisture coalescing on the walls into little drips he now followed with hypnotic fascination. An old wardrobe sagged against the wall, tilting drunkenly to one side. In his fading sensibility, it began to list back and forth in a peculiar new gravity, as though perched upon the waves of the seaside where his father had once taken him. This cellar room, deep in the bowels of Pemberley, had no particular purpose beyond storing discarded furnishings. Perhaps he could be discarded as well...allowed to fade.

The stone floor pillowed his head now. Odd, he did not remember lying down. He must have dozed...but what wakened him? Gradually he realised the floor echoed, a peculiar sound...a new wave, other than those upon which the wardrobe floated. With a sinking feeling of despair, he recognised his father's power. Reaching out...discovering him...it was never any use hiding from George Darcy. Heavy footfalls sounded shortly thereafter; a barred door could never stop him. And then Father was inside, finally discovering the small heap on the floor that was his child.

His father's despair flooded the room as surely as high tide swamped the beach near Ramsgate, a drowning sorrow of love and misery, saturating his young son. Carefully, he was lifted in strong arms and carried up long flights of stairs. Though no longer in the frigid cellar, and wrapped in a man's greatcoat, he yet shivered and trembled. The next thing he knew, he was in the warmth of the nursery, his father gently slapping his cheeks. He felt Mrs Reynolds hovering just out of sight, her presence full of concern, relief, and traces of anxiety.

"Fitzwilliam, you must eat," his father commanded sternly.

A lush, enticing smell intruded, as George rubbed his wrist upon his son's parched mouth. Unbidden, his canines lengthened, extended. His mouth watered. Still he tried to resist the urge. He hated it—hated what made him a monster.

His father's grief faded, submerged by anger and resolve. "Eat. You must," he ordered harshly.

Fitzwilliam could not withstand the twofold temptation—to feed and to please his father. He bit into the proffered vein, suckling at the strong wrist in long, delicious pulls. His lashes fluttered down as warmth entered his bloodstream, following the slow retreat of the deep cold. And then—just as his trembling began to fade—an emotional lashing of horror, fear, and revulsion flooded the nursery in a cold slap, the onslaught nearly pitching him off his father's lap. He opened his eyes, knowing what he would see.

Mother.

Lady Catherine de Bough gazed at the great lump of idiocy currently slurping tea out of her fourth-best china. He was, naturally, absurdly easy to manipulate, which made him somewhat useful. Still, she did not suffer fools gladly, thus had been somewhat annoyed with herself for granting him the living in the first place.

Now, of course, it was obvious. She had learned, over the course of a very long lifetime, to never argue with her instinct urging certain decisions—and hiring the insufferable Mr Collins was such a one. Recently, her usual foggy, shifting images of the future had risen up in crystalline detail; visions flared of Darcy with a dark-haired, impudent *human* wench and she knew at once it meant the end of *everything* important if she allowed the pairing. It had taken some time—and the blood sacrifice of a worthless peasant or two—to strengthen her powers enough to discover the mortal in question. With that discovery, the mystery of her startling patience and generosity with Collins was made clear. She smiled, and the toady vicar beamed.

"Mr Collins, you are well-settled at the parsonage?"

"Oh, yes indeed, your Ladyship. And might I add, your suggestion regarding the rearrangement of the closet shelving was just the thing. All is simply ideal, utterly perfect," he replied eagerly.

"But it is not, Mr Collins. How is a man such as yourself, so completely suited to hearth and home, happy in a bachelor existence?"

He frowned. "Well...um...your Ladyship, I naturally devote myself to my...our flock, to the needs of the parish and of course, to whatever might be of service to your Ladyship. I have not had the time to think of any other duties."

"Be that as it may, it is time for you to take a wife," Lady Catherine ordered briskly. "You have cousins in Hertfordshire, have you not?"

"Oh...why yes, your Ladyship." His voice began to take on a singsong sort of quality as he effortlessly fell under her entrancement.

Really, he was disgustingly easy to direct. Probably it could be done without using her power at all, but success was crucial.

"You will visit your Bennet cousins to take a wife. The second eldest is named Elizabeth. It is she who *must* be wed. Make haste, and do not accept 'no' for an answer. If you return to Hunsford without your bride, you shall die a death of such foul agony you will wish you had never been born." She accompanied her terse words with a blast of her inner force. It left its own peculiar scent in the room, a mix of sulphur and mildew.

Mr Collins hastily departed. He had a letter to write.

Mr Bennet looked askance at the intruders invading his bookroom. His wife met his annoyed gaze with something bordering on triumph. "Mr Bennet, you remember Colonel Forster, do you not? He wishes to speak with you." In an act of tact unusual to her, she swished out of the room.

Mr Bennet waved the colonel into a chair. "Please, sit. What can I do for you today, sir?" He moved to pour himself a splash of port. "Will you join me in a glass?"

The colonel indicated his willingness to share a drink, sipping gratefully. "I have a matter of some import to discuss with you, Mr Bennet. It concerns your daughter, Lydia."

"Has she been making a fool of herself again?" Mr Bennet asked, unsurprised.

"Oh! No, sir. No indeed. I wish to offer for her. In marriage."

Mr Bennet was roused from his usual ennui at last. "Lydia? But... but she is only a girl!"

"She is seventeen years, and I feel I have enough age and experience to compensate for any lack in hers."

Mr Bennet was astonished enough to only gape at his visitor. "You realise her portion is small?" he asked at last.

"I do not care for that. I have a decent living, and expectations of more when I inherit. When I began my military career, I had an older brother. He recently passed on, and as I am a widower, I feel an inclination to remarry. Rest assured, I can provide for her...not in any grand manner but sufficient for us, and she need not follow the drum indefinitely."

"But...but, why Lydia?"

The colonel looked at him with some pique. "Your daughter is a lovely young lady, sir. High spirited, yes—but I like to see spirit in a girl. Says she wants to travel, see a bit of the country. She can do that with me. And when she tires of it, why, we will have a good house and enough that she'll not want. Will you give your blessing?"

Mr Bennet slowly drained his glass, then poured another. He was absolutely flummoxed. The man before him was at least fifteen years Lydia's senior—surely old enough to know better.

"What are Lydia's feelings on the matter?" he brought himself to ask.

"She has agreed to do me the honour, sir."

For some moments longer, Mr Bennet maintained his silence. At last, he conceded there was nothing for it. "If you are sure...I suppose I cannot dissuade you. Not that I am displeased to have her off my hands. I shall leave it to you and my wife to determine when the happy event occurs," he snapped, irritated Lydia was so eager to leave the nest that she would accept a man nearer her father's age than her own. No doubt her senseless mother encouraged the whole thing. Well, he had always known she was brainless, and a fool for a uniform like her mother before her.

It was plainly a dismissal. "Devilish unfeeling fellow," the colonel muttered to himself as he departed.

Jane and Elizabeth returned to Longbourn to find the household in an uproar.

"Married! And to an officer! Colonel of a regiment! Oh, Lydia, I knew you could not be so pretty for nothing!" Mrs Bennet waxed on about the upcoming nuptials, the beauty of the daughter so honoured and the massive preparations already in progress. The two eldest were quickly recruited to assist in everything from meal planning to tatting lace and embroidery to enhance Lydia's wardrobe.

Elizabeth stitched until her fingers blistered. All of Fanny Bennet's girls were accomplished with a needle, but Elizabeth was the most artistic—and thus in highest demand for this all-important work. Besides, Mr Bingley visited most days, and Mrs Bennet insisted Jane be kept free to accept his calls, with Mary or Kitty as chaperon. As for Lydia herself, she and her mother were quite busy with their own numerous calls about the neighbourhood, endless revisions of menus, and of course, frequent visits from the groom-to-be.

The invitation to a ball at Netherfield only increased the chaos. Mrs Bennet chose to look upon the entire event as though Mr Bingley held it to commemorate Lydia's engagement and repeatedly embarrassed Jane with her frank observations of his interest in her eldest daughter, even hinting he might make his own announcement at the party. When Elizabeth began to make over one of her own dresses to wear for it, she was immediately rebuked.

"What do you think you are doing, young lady?" her mother asked in acid tones.

"Mama, this dress does not fit well. I only wish to rework it," Elizabeth quietly explained.

"You have no time for such nonsense! If you *wish* to be helpful, begin on Jane's dress for the ball. You know how important it is for her to look well! Mr Bingley has already claimed the first set. And Kitty has nothing suitable either. There will be officers there! Officers! The colonel is bound to introduce her to several worthy partners. We must be sensible. You are more tree than girl, towering over them all. You cannot have any prospects for the event, so should assist those who still do."

Even a month or two before, Elizabeth would have disclaimed and defied. But after all, what did her mother say that was untrue? She put her dress away.

❧

One fine morning, Elizabeth escaped early to prowl the countryside. It was not that she disliked sewing—it was being shut in, often without even the company of her sisters, that grated. Taking deep breaths of the sweet air, she refused to dwell on her mother's slights or her loneliness. Perhaps she should have taken her sewing basket outside; it was so much easier to be happy in the sunshine.

She wandered, paying little attention to her direction—her only guide the lovely stillness. Her thoughts entered a place needing no company, no intrusions, the beautiful place where day-dreams flourished. Which is probably why it took her some time to realise she was not alone. Her hand rose to her throat in startled surprise.

"Mr Darcy!"

"Miss Elizabeth," he replied ruefully. "Once again, I have forgotten to wear bells."

This reference to another silent approach on another day, weeks before, drew a smile. "I apologise. I was wool-gathering and did not notice you." She looked around to ascertain her whereabouts.

"It is a lovely day, is it not?" he asked.

"Yes. When I wakened this morning, I could not abide staying indoors another moment. Though I fear I will pay for this reprieve when my mother discovers my absence."

"She will be upset you ventured out alone," he surmised sternly. "'Tis a dangerous, unwise practice."

Lizzy rolled her eyes. "She will be upset I ventured out at all. You have likely heard of my youngest sister's upcoming nuptials. Between that and Mr Bingley's planned entertainment, I fear I shall be sewing endlessly."

"You sew?"

"Fancywork, mostly. Though I *could* do a dress easily enough, if Mama would only allow it."

"Why would she not? 'Busy hands, pure heart,' and all that," he offered.

Elizabeth laughed. "You have to understand my mother's thinking. You see, dresses are allotted according to marriageability. Which means Jane and Lydia, as the prettiest, are best gowned. Kitty has first rights to hand-me-downs, and Mary and I compete for scraps."

Darcy stopped walking, staring at her in obvious shock. Elizabeth turned bright red as she recognised, once again, her runaway tongue.

"I did not mean it as it sounds!" She tried to think of a way to undo the words. "You must understand—she has five daughters to settle and our portions are not large. Our estate is entailed to a distant relation we have never met, and she frets about the future night and day while I can offer little to interest the few gentlemen in the neighbourhood. She does her best."

Elizabeth blushed again at the realisation she had taken her family's weaknesses and aired them—to a near stranger—with all the delicacy of a cudgel on eggshells. What was it about this man that loosed her tongue?

To her relief, Mr Darcy simply began walking again. Perhaps the least stupid thing she could do was to walk alongside him and pretend she had never spoken. They walked for some minutes in silence before the sound of his low voice reverberated near her ear.

"Your mother errs, in my opinion," he stated matter-of-factly.

Her cheeks, which had only just recovered from her embarrassment, pinkened again as she recognised his late attempt at polite disagreement. She shook her head negatively. "I am too tall, and obviously too plain-spoken. Do not think I mind it," she said, striving to match his nonchalance. "Lydia has secured a match, of course, but Mama will be uneasy until the ceremony. And I would cheerfully do anything to promote Jane's happiness." She clamped her lips tightly shut, embarrassed at these further revelations.

After several seconds of awkward silence, her companion said, "The view from this aspect is quite fine."

Elizabeth responded gratefully, relieved by his change of subject and his willingness to overlook her clumsy speech. His was not a loquacious personality, so Elizabeth carried the bulk of the conversation by questioning him on Miss Bingley's plans for the ball. He was surprisingly observant for a male, giving her details she was certain her father would not have noticed. She did not mind his silences, although she would have preferred he continue on his way and allow her to finish her walk alone. However, he was a gentleman, and likely could think of no excuse for leaving her.

Longbourn came into view. "I suppose my entertainment for the day is over," she said wistfully. It was somewhat disappointing to have been forced to exchange day-dreams for polite chit chat. But it had not been horrible, despite embarrassing herself a time or two, and she remembered her manners. "Thank you for accompanying me, sir," she said, and, offering a small curtsey, prepared to turn away.

Darcy bowed. "Miss Elizabeth," he began. He stopped, cleared his throat, and then—just when she'd begun to wonder if he'd forgotten what he meant to say—continued. "May I have the first set at next Friday's ball?"

She could only stare, her mouth open in a small 'o' of surprise. His expression was one of distaste, as though he already regretted his offer. But politeness dictated her reply. "I–I would be honoured, sir."

He bowed again. "The honour is mine. Thank you for sharing your walk today." He turned back in the direction he had come.

Elizabeth stared after him until long after he was out of sight.

Five

THE NETHERFIELD BALLROOM—THOUGH LARGE AND RICHLY appointed—was also smoky and crowded, the scent of bodies in close proximity, sweat, tallow, perfumes, and liberally applied pomades assaulting the senses. Elizabeth felt her own nerves stretching as she searched the crowded ballroom for Mr Darcy, certain he regretted his invitation. A gentlemanly gesture, she decided, since she had stupidly sounded complaining or worse—self-pitying—regarding the sewing and the availability of nice clothing. Her cheeks burned to think of her blunders, which were too frequent in his presence to overlook.

Her dress was not new, of course, but she had sewn long into the night each evening after Mama retired, straining her eyes in the candlelight, altering the length, bodice and neckline so it fit better than Jane's castoffs were wont to do. She hoped she looked slightly more stylish and less pitiful, longing to mitigate her words to him. Just in case, however, she had not told anyone of her walk with Mr Darcy, nor the promised dance. If he regretted it so completely as to fail to follow through, she would pretend it forgotten.

When she first saw him, Miss Bingley stood at his elbow, every inch the hostess. *The hostess!* It seemed they both had been stupid; Miss Bingley *must* lead out. The musicians were in place; they would begin playing at any moment. She saw Miss Bingley look up at him expectantly—plainly anticipating opening the ball upon his arm. But at that moment, he caught her eye and, with a murmur to the other female, strode towards her.

The crowd parted to allow him passage. Elizabeth was unsure why the urge to back away was so strong within her. When he reached her, he bowed, but she could not help blurting out her thoughts, as had become her usual trouble when in his presence.

"Mr Darcy—I believe we would distress our hostess if I accept this dance. I fear she would think it unforgivably discourteous."

He glanced over to the entryway, where the Lucases were just arriving. To Elizabeth's surprise, the eldest son, John, strode towards Miss Bingley as if in single-minded pursuit.

"Miss Elizabeth. Shall we?" Darcy asked, his tone bored. The opening notes of the first dance began at that moment, as if he had commanded it.

Elizabeth glanced again towards her hostess and saw John Lucas claiming the dance. *Well, then.* Taking the arm of the man before her, she allowed him to lead her onto the floor. While it was not in her nature to be easily discomfited, she felt she could be forgiven for feeling so now. There was certainly nothing in her previous meetings with him to assume a friendship.

He must begin the conversation, she decided.

Plainly, he was in no hurry to do so. After several minutes, she began to think their silence was to last through the two dances. And so it may have done, except for the interruption of Sir William. Scurrying through the set to reach the other side of the room, he stopped to bow courteously and remark upon Elizabeth, the superiority of the dancing, and—with a good deal of insinuation—his expectations for Jane and Mr Bingley.

When Sir William moved away, Darcy said distractedly, "The interruption has made me forget what we were talking of."

"I do not think we were speaking at all. Sir William could not have interrupted any two people in the room who had less to say for themselves," she replied with some asperity. "However, in our case, perhaps this is wise."

"Where you are concerned, Miss Elizabeth, I have never been wise," he replied.

And that was all he had to say, for the entire two dances. She left off trying to interpret his meaning, for it meant nothing at all, and merely enjoyed the dance for its own sake.

She was always more than he remembered. More beautiful, more graceful, more desirable than any other. He wondered what her mother could possibly be thinking, to miss her perfections. His eyes flickered over her gown, noting it was unlike anything she had yet worn. For one thing, it fit properly. If he looked closely within the stitches of the embroidery, he could see where she had reworked and refitted. And he suspected she had done this to make herself *more* attractive to him. Futilely, he tried to push into her mind to confirm this, to validate his overwhelming possessiveness. It was no use, but he attempted it anyway.

He wanted to bind her to him. Each slight touch of her gloved hand only made it worse. He caught the edge of Caroline's own passions as he danced past her and, shuddering with revulsion, sent out compelling messages to most of the eligible men in the room. Caroline would be inundated with offers for dances...and possibly offers of a more flirtatious sort, as well. Anything to keep her away from *him*. The brief half an hour passed in a blur, as he began contemplating the impossible.

Caroline was having the time of her life; who could have known a simple country ball could produce such delightful results? Naturally, these coarse peasants had never before had the opportunity to mingle with someone of her obvious appeal, in an entertainment so vastly superior to their stupid country affairs. Still, their flattery was much appreciated, especially after Darcy failed to ask for the first set. When she had seen him approach the ill-bred Eliza, she nearly lost her temper. However, she was calm now. Darcy had missed his chance, for her dance card filled immediately, and she was contemplating an assignation in the garden with one of the officers shortly after the supper dance. Darcy had not danced a set with any other, even though Eliza was required to sit out more than one. Gleefully, she noted the only others asking the gawky Bennet girl to dance were doddering ancients.

But why had he asked her at all, and for the first set, no less? The answer came to her at last. *The Secret*. He must have been trying to determine whether Jane revealed anything to her. Of course, she had not...except to her diary. Caroline cursed herself; in her efforts to appease all the males wishing her attention, she had been unforgivably lax with her private schemes. She spotted Colonel Forster stepping out towards the garden—thankfully, alone. Carefully evading the gentleman who was to have been her next partner, Caroline slipped out after the colonel.

"Oh, Colonel! Please...a word?" Caroline used her sweetest 'damsel in distress' voice.

Colonel Forster halted, turning towards his hostess. "Yes, Miss Bingley?"

"I wonder...oh, dear...this is so difficult...perhaps I should not say..." she trailed off in marked confusion, adding a bit of trembling to the performance.

The colonel, always chivalrous, pointed out a convenient bench. "Dear lady, you are distressed. Please, sit."

Caroline decided it was private enough for her purposes. This would not take long.

"I thank you. Yes, I am quite unsettled...and not knowing how I should act, or even *if* I should. It concerns your soon-to-be sister, Miss Eliza. I would go to her father b-but he–he..." she stuttered to a halt.

The good colonel's expression darkened. "I, more than most, am aware of—hmm, the less noble qualities of the Bennet patriarch," he declared. "It is better you should come to me. But I cannot imagine our Miss Elizabeth to be involved in any—"

"Oh—no...you misunderstand me. Miss Elizabeth has done nothing, nothing at all. She is all that is good," Caroline asserted. With satisfaction, she noted the colonel's posture easing.

"Well, then, what is it?" he asked.

"I fear, since Mr Darcy asked her for the first set," she began tentatively.

"Yes, saw that myself. A bit of a surprise, but surely nothing astonishing," the Colonel remarked gruffly.

"No, of course not. It is only, you see, Mr Darcy is betrothed. To a lovely young heiress, Anne de Bourgh, of Rosings Park in Kent. And before you say a word, I know of no rule whereby a man might not ask any woman to dance, engaged or married. 'Tis only...I fear that Sir William—oh, I *ought* not to have mentioned him in particular—let us only say there have been whispers tonight, from those less sensible than Miss Elizabeth, claiming an interest in her behalf, and my concern is Mr Darcy's motives might be misunderstood by the neighbourhood. Because no one knows as yet about the betrothal, which is to be announced very soon." Caroline paused dramatically and added in a whisper, "I should not like Miss Elizabeth to be subjected to gossip. *Such* a dear girl, and my friend."

"Thank you, Miss Bingley, for bringing this to my attention. Miss Elizabeth has a good head on her shoulders even if others enjoy tittle-tattle. I am certain it is of no moment, but I will be sure to mention something if necessary."

"You are welcome, Colonel. If I had not heard *others* speaking of it, you can be sure I would not have said a word. This is such a small community...and if I might ask one favour. Please, do not mention where you heard this. I know it is unlikely you need share this information, but if...if my brother were to find out I was the one who spoiled the surprise of the betrothal to the family, he would be very angry. Might I count on your discretion? Please, sir," she begged prettily.

He bowed gallantly. "Never fear, ma'am. My lips are sealed."

"Thank you, Colonel. I am so relieved and feel a great weight has been lifted. I had best go and find my partner for this dance, as I would hate to disappoint. And might I offer my felicitations on your own grand news!"

By the supper dance, speculation as to the intentions of Fitzwilliam Darcy towards one of Meryton's own daughters, Elizabeth Bennet, was running high. The crowd was fairly evenly divided—half maintaining his request for the first set meant he was smitten, and the other half pointing out he had not asked for another, while the female in question sat out dance after dance. Still, no one could deny that he had not danced with anyone *else* all evening and was caught looking at her more than was strictly necessary.

As for Elizabeth herself, she was so firmly in agreement with the naysayers, she laughed at the mention of the foolish speculation; she alone knew the gentlemanly impulse preceding his invitation. All in all, it had been a disappointing night, with a drought of available partners. She took great comfort in Jane dancing both the first and supper sets with Mr Bingley, at least. All was worthwhile if it hastened her dear sister towards the happiness she desired.

Elizabeth's thoughts were interrupted when Lydia plopped down upon the chair beside her in a most unladylike fashion. "Lud, 'tis scorching hot," she complained, fanning herself vigorously. "My new slippers pinch something awful. I have not had a moment to sit all evening."

"Terrible troubles," Elizabeth murmured dryly.

"Oh, I know it!" she laughed. Whatever one wanted to say about Lydia, she was always ready to laugh. "But you must listen to me, Lizzy. I have heard what everyone is saying, about you and Mr Darcy."

Elizabeth blushed. "There is nothing whatsoever between me and Mr Darcy. He was only polite and has made his disinterest apparent."

"Good. I am glad to hear you are sensible about this," Lydia intoned with the air of a woman much older than her seventeen years. "Because I happen to know, for a *fact*, Mr Darcy is betrothed. To an Anne-de-Someone from someplace in Kent. A wealthy heiress."

Elizabeth had no hopes to disappoint but was annoyed by her sister's assumptions that she did. It made her subsequent words brusque.

"Really, Lydia, he could be engaged to the Princess Augusta Sophia for all I care. But how could you know of such a thing? I truly doubt you are his confidant, which means you listen to foolish gossip. I wish you would outgrow the habit."

Lydia reddened. "I do know, stupid, and I know from an *unimpeachable* confidential source. You are always so patronising, Lizzy, but at least someone wants *me*, while you are only a dried-up, ancient spinster. I only spoke to warn you so you would not make a fool of yourself, as half the world believes you will." With that, she flounced off.

For some minutes Elizabeth made herself sit very, very still, feigning an appreciation of the music. She would not give any onlooker reason to believe her sister had upset her. After a long while, she carefully made her way out of doors, purposely smiling nonchalantly at any she passed.

Darcy's attention was distracted from Elizabeth for several minutes by Bingley's enthusiastic description of Jane's elegance, her refinement, and her enlightening conversation, but most of the night was spent resisting extreme temptation. He had behaved abominably this evening—urging away any man under the age of sixty years with intentions of procuring her hand for a set. If he could not dance with her, neither should they, though he knew his selfishness ruined her evening. The one dance had already caused too much talk while he was so undecided in his pursuit, and though he longed for another, he could not trust himself. It would be simplest to undo the damage simply by asking others to dance—yet he could not bring himself to touch anyone else.

Bingley had just begun a lengthy recital of Jane's dancing abilities, when Darcy's eyes sought out Elizabeth once more—and widened slightly as he noticed her slipping away from the ballroom through an exit leading to the garden.

Abruptly, he excused himself to his friend and deliberately moved in the opposite direction of Elizabeth. He finally let himself out through an east-facing door and quickly made his way to the garden. Tracking her carefully, he caught her scent at last by the garden gate. Devil take it, she would surely not walk home, would she?

Thankfully, she would not. He found her near a copse of trees just off the long drive, her head down, her shoulders slumped. His not over-active conscience awoke with a vengeance, realising how utterly miserable he had made her this night.

"Miss Elizabeth?"

The soft voice startled her. "Mr Darcy! I did not see you. I...I was taking some air." Determinedly, she looked away, hoping he would take the hint and leave.

All Elizabeth wished for was a bit of time; she could admit her sister's words wounded deeply, as they had been meant to do. From past experience, she knew if she were given time to regain her balance, she could laugh at Lydia's taunts. Mr Darcy's attentions, insignificant though they were, had flattered her. Learning her neighbours immediately latched on to the notion of a wedding on such slight evidence was embarrassing. And the idea that most agreed she would foolishly, eagerly jump at such thin bait was almost as humiliating as the fact that she had only danced one other set, with a man old enough to be her grandfather.

Please leave!

"I wish you would come back inside," Mr Darcy said at last. "You will catch a chill."

"I am well."

"It is plain you are not," he scolded. "Something has upset you. But you will be missed if you remain out of doors for long. There will be gossip."

It was the last straw; her eyes flashed as she lost her temper. "Inside, Mr Darcy, is a roomful of people who have nothing better to do than gossip. I am no more than one of the evening's entertainments, because you made it so. I wish you had never asked me to dance. Why did you not escort your betrothed instead of making a mockery of me!"

"My betrothed?" he questioned, his voice significantly colder.

"Everyone knows of her," Elizabeth answered scornfully. "The heiress from Kent...Anne Whomever-She-Is."

"Who informed you of this rumour?" he asked quietly.

Elizabeth shivered at the frigidity in his voice, even wondering at it. For the first time in several days, she remembered she had once thought him sinister. But she would not show fear. "My sister," she replied, equally cool. "She was concerned I might make more of your attentions than I ought."

Turning away from him, she stayed motionless in the darkness. There was only a sliver of moon; she could barely see her hands, but she could feel the bite of her nails as they dug into her palms. His utter silence grated on her too-taut nerves. When she could bear it no longer, she slowly turned back to face him...but he was gone, and she was alone in the night.

The same dream had haunted Elizabeth for years: She strolled through the Hertfordshire countryside in springtime, not minding the chill, warmed by the cheer of the awakening earth, walking in blissful ignorance of the sudden silencing of birds and squirrels and even the hush of wind. Then a soft laugh—heavens, the dream reoccurred so often, one would think she could be *warned* by that laugh, instead of merely curious. But no, she always turned to greet the laughter with an answering smile. The face smiling back was that of an angel, masculine and sensual, framed by too-long, golden hair shimmering in a halo-like nimbus. And then the smile lengthened, widened, and the mouthful of white teeth grew sharp and dangerous, as fangs sprouted from that horrific, appealing countenance. The dream would never permit a scream or escape—she could only bear the pain as those teeth tore into her flesh, with only merciful wakening relieving her agony. The night terrors troubled her all throughout her youth, but mercifully they finally faded. It had been years since the last time she experienced one.

The dreams began again the night of the Netherfield ball, with a vengeance. Elizabeth was unsurprised; somehow, the end of the ball felt like the end of hope.

THE MORNING AFTER THE BALL WOULD BE RENDERED memorable to the residents of Longbourn for the delivery of two letters. Neither missive bore good news.

The first was from Miss Caroline Bingley, addressed to her dear friend, Miss Bennet. As Jane read, her fair skin slowly leached of colour. She excused herself from the table; Elizabeth immediately made to follow, but she stopped her with a gesture.

"Please," she said, her voice only a whisper, "I wish to be alone." She pressed the letter into her sister's hands and hurried upstairs.

"What is it?" Mrs Bennet asked, her voice pitching higher. "What does it say? Is someone ill? Has there been an accident? Mr Bingley? Has something happened?"

Elizabeth read the note; it was brief, mostly full of apologies. But the gist of it was that Mr Bingley's good friend, Mr Darcy, advised him to return to London immediately. Mr Darcy recommended he spend not a moment longer in the neighbourhood, and her dear brother was so excessively dependent upon the great man's sage advice and good will, and so used to following his astute guidance without question, that they would leave at once, and by the time this letter should be delivered, all the household would be on their way to London.

The second letter, coming on the heels of the first, announced the arrival of a cousin—the man who was to inherit Longbourn upon their father's demise. Obviously, he was not a sensible man, his letter a mixture of servility and self-importance. He expounded on the prominence of his patroness, a great lady by the name of Catherine de Bourgh, who had proven her wisdom and acuity by having the sense to appoint him as shepherd of her flock; he apologised for being next in line for the entail with a debasing humility, hinting he should be visiting with the idea of providing atonement.

Mrs Bennet's reaction was immediate and predictable. Mr Darcy was castigated as a villain, a cur, a base deceiver. Mr Collins was a greedy opportunist who would see them living in the hedgerows. She ranted to anyone who would listen, and Elizabeth shuddered to think how awful it would be, had she not Lydia's wedding for a distraction.

Jane responded by lapsing into a quiet grief; no longer did they enjoy pleasant night-time conversations, her laughter a thing of the past. Elizabeth felt none too cheerful herself and could not blame Jane for her anguish.

The evening before Mr Collins's arrival, alone in their room, Jane broke her self-imposed silence. "I believe we made a mistake, Lizzy."

"What mistake would that be?" Elizabeth asked, curious as to what thought finally escaped the brittle shell of reticence surrounding her sister.

"When we determined to marry for love. I can see now. It was the impractical, foolish perspective of young girls. It is no wonder Mama grew so impatient with our ideals. Had we not held out hope for something so unlikely, we might have already been settled into homes of our own. And have children to love with a pure affection we thought to give to our husbands."

Elizabeth had given the same subject much thought over the last several days and answered almost eagerly. "I do not believe we were mistaken, Jane. I think it was a good ideal. But I suppose if God were going to grant such a favour, He might already have done so. Perhaps this whole situation occurred so we would know it is time to press forward. I was actually thinking about Mr Stone."

"Mr Stone? Oh, he must be in his fiftieth year. Who knows

whether children would be a possibility with him? His first marriage ended childless and he is so much older now."

"I know, I know. But he is one of the few who asked me to dance at the last assembly, who might possibly be interested. I heard his sister is ailing and has gone to Cambridge to be with her daughter's family. So, he must need someone now. He is in good health, and he is a respectable, sensible man. I believe he has not remarried because he genuinely cared for his wife, a point in his favour. And he has a sturdy home, a prosperous farm...Mama would not have to worry about caring for me any longer."

She could sense Jane's struggle not to express dismay. Of course, it was easy to feel Jane should not abandon hope, for her sister was a beautiful woman and it was not too late. But how could either of them ignore their circumstances any longer? What was once possibility was now imprudence. She pressed her argument further.

"Think of Mrs Robinson, Jane. She must leave early from every assembly because Mr Robinson *will* say the most foolish things after overindulging at the punch bowl. Yet, if one of the other ladies twits her about it, she defends him most ardently. He is of amiable temperament and a good provider and she will not hear a word against him. I think part of a successful marriage must be to overlook that which is not ideal and centre on the good. Perhaps if Mama were able to..."

Jane took a shaky breath. "It may be a sign to–to put away girlish caprice."

"Yes, that is it exactly. Maybe we could think of it as putting our hair up instead of wearing braids. Or casting off pinafores. And it would have its satisfactions, would it not? To have homes of our own?"

Jane nodded her agreement. "Yes. Yes, of course. Charlotte has been saying so for ever so long. She says we are too proud to recognise what is best."

The girls lay there in the draughty darkness, each contemplating a different future than the ones they had imagined for so long, both saying a silent farewell to happy—if foolish—dreams.

Mr Collins was every bit as insensible as Elizabeth had feared. Mightily fond of the sound of his own voice, he took every opportunity to permit others to admire it as well. This would not have been so awful had he anything rational to say, but he was so obsequious, so empty of wit or interest, it was difficult to do anything in his presence except yearn for his absence. Every mealtime topic was justification for a lecture on vice and folly and Original Sin; a local young sheepherder, killed by some wilderness beast, and the death of Mrs Bennet's favourite rose bush were equal signs of God's displeasure with the citizens of Hertfordshire. Her father baited him mercilessly, but few others enjoyed his wit. Her mother all but accused him of greedily and gleefully taking stock of his future possessions, which only encouraged more compliments on the land, the house, and the daughters of Longbourn.

Especially one specific daughter. Elizabeth very much feared she was his intended means of atonement. Remembering her conversation with Jane, she tried to force her unruly mind's acceptance, though every crumb of her soul rebelled.

She asked him many questions about the rectory, Hunsford, about which he was willing to provide elaborate detail. It did sound like a lovely place, and she clung to her image of it. *A home of my own,* she thought. *Do not look at his thick, moist lips and meaty fingers. Do not imagine him holding my hand in his fleshy, sweaty one. Do not think!*

The day came when her mother took her aside. Elizabeth knew, somehow, what was to come. Perhaps it was in the way her mother's lips were compressed into a firm line, the way she so obviously braced herself for bitter argument, taking no chances that Mr Collins's proposal might meet with refusal. *You are ready now,* Elizabeth reminded herself. *A woman grown.*

"Yes, Mama?"

"Mr Collins is willing to make you an offer," she stated forcefully. "It is unlikely you will ever get a better one."

A sudden, desperate urge to refute this overtook her, but she made herself speak calmly. "What about Mr Stone, Mama? He did ask me to dance at the last assembly. Twice. If Papa were to hint to him, perhaps, that I would be willing..."

Mrs Bennet's eyes widened in astonishment, perhaps softening the harsh lecture she had come prepared to deliver. A disobedient daughter was not to be borne, but the desperation in Elizabeth's words was plain.

"I understand, Lizzy," she said, in a somewhat more conciliatory tone. "I know you will find this difficult to believe, but once I was the prettiest girl in the county. I had suitors. One in particular, an officer...it does not matter now. But your father came calling. He was ten years older than I, a terrible ancient, I thought, possessed of a lovely estate and no great beauty. But my father and mother made my duty clear. And Elizabeth, I have not been unhappy."

Elizabeth would have liked to debate this, as Mama's temperament could not be considered 'cheerful', but she opted for an argument less fraught. "Papa is a great deal less offensive, and more astute than Mr Collins."

"It is not your father who provided what happiness I've had. It is my children and Longbourn. Our home. I ask you, Elizabeth Anne, to do your duty as well. Let me keep my home. Is it so much to ask? I have given up my life for it! If I lose it, my life is over, ruined...wasted."

For long moments they sat together in silence. Elizabeth could not help but notice her mother's hands upon the chair arm, her knuckles white with tension. As if...as if Elizabeth, the daughter for whom she felt the least, held her whole life in her hands. Elizabeth thought of Jane, Mary, and Kitty—of what they would all do without these sheltering walls, of trying to exist as the poor relations of her extended family. So she made herself ask her mother the question which had been burning a thick hole of anxiety into her belly. Her voice was so faint, Mrs Bennet leant forward to hear.

"I am afraid I will not be able to bear what I must do with him to—to have children," she admitted.

Her mother's hand reached to cover hers, in almost unheard-of affection. "It is not awful, Lizzy," she whispered. "The first time hurts a bit, but after...it is over very quickly, a few minutes at most. You can think of something that makes you happy, something taking you outside of yourself. Before you know it, it is finished and he is gone away. Several days of the month, you needn't...you can stretch that time out, he will not know the difference. And while you are with child, and for several months afterward...it is just you and your babies. Those times are so precious. He will almost disappear while you are thus occupied. And then, at last, after one of the children...

he will not remember to come back and will never bother you again."

"What if...what if he does not know he is to...disappear during those times? Mr Collins is neither clever nor prudent."

"Trust me, I can tell. He is not a man of great passions. He will stay away." She was silent for several moments, withdrawing her hand. "But truthfully, Lizzy, you are every bit as clever as he is ignorant. You will manage him, far more successfully than I ever have your father. This I know." It was a compliment, of sorts, though there was bitterness in Mrs Bennet's voice.

Quiet reigned. Elizabeth made herself remember her new resolve; and if this, the first conversation she had managed with her mother in years that did not end in overt criticism, was a sign, perhaps the match was foreordained. Finally, Elizabeth forced herself to speak. "Yes, Mama. Please have Papa give him my answer. Do not oblige me to listen to his proposal or speak to him at all, until I must. And a very quiet wedding, please, with only our family in attendance."

Mrs Bennet nodded, a flash of triumph in her eyes. She stood, smoothing out the non-existent wrinkles in her skirt, as though there were something she wished to add. But at last, all she did was pat her daughter awkwardly on the shoulder, leaving her alone in the parlour. Elizabeth watched her go with dry, burning eyes. *A woman grown.*

Darcy looked at the card presented to him by his butler, feeling all his senses sharpen. Since he had given specific orders not to be disturbed, the moment Robbins entered, he knew it was important.

"Show him in at once," he responded brusquely.

The gentleman who entered was one of Darcy's best field men. An expert in *dissimulo*—illusion, misconception and deception—Augustus Carter was his most relied upon Watcher. The man had not been at all pleased at their desertion of the Netherfield base of operations, making his job—keeping sufficient guardians in the area, unnoticed by mortals—more difficult.

"You have good reason for leaving Hertfordshire, I take it?" Darcy asked.

The other man nodded. "I believe he has fully wakened at last."

Darcy stood, pacing in front of the fire. "Explain."

"A body has been found, a young shepherd. The corpse was desiccated, its heart missing. He left no scent, and I suppose I could be mistaken but—"

"No. We both know you are not." The decision to abandon Netherfield was regrettable; he could have brought whole troops in, unnoticed. But what else could he have done? "What steps have you taken?"

"Increased the patrols. I do not sense him in the district, and if it were me, I would make myself scarce. He knows you are likely watching carefully."

"That would be the reasonable thing to do. Of course, Wickham is not known for his reason. He will leave a body trail wherever he goes, though, and 'tis more difficult in the country to hide when someone goes missing. We will likely be able to track him by the deaths and missing persons in his wake. Have your men branch out but keep at least two of your best in the Hertfordshire area. And you remain as well."

"There is something else."

Darcy regarded him enquiringly.

"A vicar has come to visit one of the local gentry—a cousin or some such. Surname Collins. The fellow is completely human and seems innocuous enough. But he comes from Kent. Boasts to anyone who will listen of his patroness, de Bourgh."

"Are we certain? He truly is a cousin?"

"Oh, yes. I investigated his lineage and he is legitimate. Deuced strange coincidence, though, that connexion."

"Very odd. I find it deeply suspicious that any of de Bourgh's attention, or that of her minions, should appear in an area where there are signs of Wickham."

"Exactly. But it grows more peculiar still."

"Oh?"

"He claims his 'benevolent, charitable patroness' has afforded him this holiday from his pulpit so he might court and marry one of his cousins. Indeed, she has insisted he do so, as soon as it may be arranged. Devilish odd...for one of her sort, taking interest in a vicar's romance? Never mind thinking her charitable!"

A cold chill of intuition snaked down Darcy's spine. "What is the name of the family to whom he is related, Carter?"

"Bennet, sir. They own a smallish estate beyond Meryton. Longbourn, 'tis called."

Elizabeth sat at her breakfast, attending to the task of eating. She never used to find it such a chore, and certainly her mother set a wonderful table at every meal. She stared at the jam tart; it was her favourite, and she understood her mother served them especially to tempt her appetite. Not a bribe *per se*; after all, she had only done the duty owed to her family. But her mother's acknowledgment that the duty was a difficult one, and that her daughter's desire for food had suffered as a result, was important to her. They had connected as one person to another—people who could do things that were hard.

Mr Bennet grunted in that way he had that meant his teacup was empty. She watched her mother fill it without comment. She had a new appreciation of her mother's life and sacrifices. Fanny Bennet would never be an easy woman, but she likely had not ever had it 'easy', entering her marriage without love or even the cleverness Elizabeth always drew upon to find her father's favour. Her joy had been her babies, perhaps leading her to indulge the two youngest daughters, to keep them dependent upon her, and to resent the daughters who most reminded her of the husband she despised. Elizabeth understood better now, but it was still difficult to swallow her food. She made her bites very, very tiny, so she could slide them past the uncooperative lump in her throat.

While Mr Collins droned on as though anyone listened, Elizabeth glanced briefly at her father. He had saved her, briefly—but she almost wished he had not. To her mother's intense dissatisfaction, he refused to give his blessing to the match until they had a period of courtship. On the one hand, she was deeply relieved by the delay. But now, with the odious man courting her in earnest, in some gross rehearsal of how the rest of her life would follow, it was almost too much to bear. The delay to his suit caused him obvious anxiety, and he sniffed around her constantly. To place her hand upon his arm as they walked towards Meryton with her sisters, to pretend an interest in his vapid dialogue, to hear him pay tribute to her modesty, her character, her Christian morals because she refused his attempt to kiss her with his thick, wet lips...she shuddered. The jam tart, of which she had managed to consume precisely two bites, roiled in her belly.

"I...I am not feeling well this morning," she said, pushing her chair back abruptly. "If you will please excuse me. I–I will be in my room." She rushed from the breakfast table, knowing she lied. She was out the door and pushing towards Oakham Mount in hurried strides, desperate for escape, knowing there was none.

THE FEELINGS OF PANIC AND ANXIETY WERE AS uncomfortable as they were unfamiliar. But, as Darcy reflected to himself, they were preferable to their predecessors. Before Carter's report, he suffered equal parts distress and despair—distress that Jane Bennet's inconstancy had wrecked his formerly affable friend, and despair that he had been forced, probably forever, to abandon her sister.

He lectured himself that it was for the best; he could not reveal himself to a female whose memory he could not change. If she took the truth of his nature poorly, he would be forced to drastic measures to ensure the secret went no further. The betrayal was just the push he had needed to do what was right, what was best. Yet, he grieved. He had not loved her, had not allowed the overwhelming, instinctive pull she exerted over him to *become* love. But, even against his formidable will, it had become *something*. For the first time since his intemperate young adulthood, he was tempted to lurk outside gaming hells and alehouses of London's darker neighbourhoods, just to drink the alcohol-laden blood of their denizens. He had been sitting in his study, struggling to resist dark temptation, when Carter appeared.

Darcy set out immediately, of course, and was in Meryton long before dawn. He spent several hours with Carter, thoroughly searching the vicinity where the young lad was killed. His Watcher's instincts were correct; though Carter had not been able to do so,

Darcy scented his enemy immediately. Wickham obviously used the recent rainfall to cover his movements. But where? Had he departed for more populated areas? Or was he yet hidden in the earth? Still—he was feeding, with a bloodlust only partially sated. A badly weakened vampyre would need a great deal more than a young lad to strengthen him for a long journey, but what if he had allies? Assistance from de Bourgh would make all the difference.

Sighing, Darcy glanced at the sun to determine the time. It was a bit early for a morning call, but anxiety rode him strongly. If de Bourgh meddled in the affairs of the Bennet family, there was no time to lose.

He made his way into Meryton, taking a room at the inn so he could wash and change; his valet would be arriving later in the day with his baggage, but if all went as planned, he should be a guest of Longbourn by then. The thought of being in such close quarters with such a *lively* group made him shudder; he could cope with giddiness, but he had experienced the mother's overpowering anxieties and emotional instability at the ball, and she would be difficult for him. And Jane. Egad, if her feelings were anything like Bingley's at the moment, they would be an unceasing dirge ringing in his head.

It was small consolation to predict that Elizabeth's probable feelings of disgust for his own aborted attentions would be blocked; such a spirited girl would not need psychic intonations to convey her displeasure.

He felt the first waves of emotion as he rode up the drive. Devil take it! The manor before him was a cauldron of sentiment, worse than any London ballroom. Steeling himself to bear it—no, to *use* it—he presented himself to the older woman who greeted him at the door. She glanced at his card, then back at him. A wave of hostility firmed her chin. Perfect; even the help despised him. Obviously, their party's abrupt departure from Netherfield had been a topic of discussion—though why anger should be directed at him instead of Bingley was a question he could not answer. Charles was the one who had raised false hopes. The servant left him in a parlour with a nod that obviously meant he should wait.

A few minutes later, he was shown into Mr Bennet's bookroom. He traded gazes with the man observing him so calmly. Elizabeth's father displayed little sentiment, but his annoyance and irritation were definitely present. Darcy dug deeper but could not find anything beyond a shallow perturbation. Evidently Mr Bennet did not share the seething agitation of the rest of the household.

"This is a surprise, Mr Darcy," he offered.

"I imagine it is. I apologise for my unannounced visit. I wonder if I might be permitted a word with a guest under your roof. Mr Collins, I believe his name to be."

"You wish to speak with my esteemed cousin? I would not have thought you acquainted." Darcy felt the other man's amusement, and decided he had no intention of providing Mr Bennet's entertainment.

"Bring him to me." It was a command, accompanied by restrained power, an unspoken demand for obedience. Amusement faded, and Bennet abruptly fetched the parson.

Darcy's first impression of de Bourgh's minion was not favourable, but neither did he sense any particular evil. Perhaps a certain amount of lasciviousness, the symptoms of a man entirely unused to the company of females residing in a houseful of them.

"Why are you here?" he asked bluntly.

"To marry my cousin," Collins answered promptly, responding to the authority of his inquisitor's tone with rather more clarity than was his wont. "I say, have we been introduced?"

"I am an acquaintance of your patroness," Darcy said, more to see the man's response than to explain himself.

Mr Collins immediately burst into joyful soliloquy. Darcy cut off his rambling effusions. "Tell me exactly what Catherine de Bourgh instructed you in regard to the Bennets of Longbourn," he ordered, his hands fisting at his sides against the appeal of violence. Collins was obviously and completely under the spell of de Bourgh's darker influences. Doubtful she had even had to blood-tie him into submission—he was the sort who begged for enslavement.

Still, Catherine *had* exerted some actual power over her minion, for his thick lips clamped shut in denial of his purposes and a mulish stubbornness filtered into the room. Darcy moved in closer, his strong hands clamping over Collins's rounded shoulders. Looking him directly in the eye, he repeated his command.

The words gushed out of Collins with the stink of mildew and sulphur: "You will visit your Bennet cousins to take a wife. The second eldest is named Elizabeth. She is the one who must be wed. Make haste and do not accept 'no' for an answer. If you return to

Hunsford without your bride, you shall die a death of such foul agony you will wish you had never been born."

Darcy's lips compressed to a flat line at this confirmation of his fears. He turned to Elizabeth's father, who had grown marginally more alert in response to his cousin's astonishing revelations.

"Have you given your approval to the match? Is she betrothed to this looby?"

For the first time, he felt dismay in the man's aura. "No. Her mother insists because of the entail, and Elizabeth has agreed, but she is too young to know what she is about, and her mother is a wet hen. I agreed to a courtship, that is all." Bennet shook his head, trying to clear it. Darcy could not allow that.

"Mr Bennet...you feel a sudden, overwhelming urge to nap in your room. When you awaken, you will remember I am to visit you this afternoon. You will make no decisions regarding any of your daughters' futures until after we have spoken. You will feel kindly disposed towards any plans I submit for your consideration. Now go." He watched as the older man stumbled from the room; perhaps he had been a bit too forceful in his suggestion. Predictable, considering the ferocity raging in Darcy's blood like acid.

Shoving the vicar into a nearby chair, he forced himself to plan, not to dwell upon his fury that Elizabeth was to be so much chattel, that she had *agreed* to this travesty of a union. To hear and feel the dullard's expectations of her...

"Agh!" Collins cried. Darcy, realising he had failed to release him, was in danger of crushing the man's clavicle. He stepped back, and Collins shrank into his seat.

Cursing the oaf would not help, and if he injured him, he would only have to waste time putting him back together. He thought back to de Bourgh's implanted directives; fortunately, she could have no premonition of interference, for there were more holes in her commands than there were caves in Devon. They must be carried out, of course; enough malevolent authority had gone into them to make any risk of defiance unacceptable for all the mortals involved. Both Collins and Elizabeth must be wed, and quickly; fortunately, not necessarily to each other.

"Where is Miss Elizabeth now?"

"In her room, ill," the vicar muttered.

"Why am I unsurprised, enduring such a courtship?" Darcy

replied. "Go to bed now and...and sleep until breakfast tomorrow. Give this household a much-deserved respite from your ridiculous presence."

Waiting until he heard Collins's heavy footsteps on the stairs, Darcy expanded his senses, easily locating the other occupants of the house. Mrs Bennet, in the kitchens with someone who must be the cook; Miss Mary, at the pianoforte, with a forlorn Miss Bennet turning pages. Misses Catherine and Lydia were in the parlour with a man...ah, yes, Colonel Forster. He recalled hearing of the betrothal from a mocking Caroline. Of course, he could not sense where Elizabeth might be. At last he located the housekeeper and sent her a compelling urge to join him. Surprisingly, it took more than one nudge. Several minutes passed before he heard her quiet knock.

"Enter," he bit out.

The woman did as he bid.

"Your name?"

"Sarah Hill, sir," she replied, respectful but cold. He was impressed; the two men he had just mesmerised had minds of putty in comparison. It was situations like this which explained why his notions of the aristocracy and social mores were significantly different than his peers. His father had always urged him to take note of character over birth.

"Fetch Miss Elizabeth," he demanded, putting a touch of force into the 'request.'

She looked pained. "I cannot."

His brows rose in disbelief and he nearly shoved her mind into full compliance with brute strength. Something about his expression must have frightened her at last, for she added, "She is not in the house."

"Not in the house? Where is she?"

"I do not know. She ran out the garden door after a breakfast she did not eat. She has not eaten enough in the last three days to keep a mouse alive, before that even. Poor thing hasn't been herself since you warned that nice Mr Bingley off Miss Bennet. Those two sisters are thick as thieves, and you hurt one, you hurt them both. A fine thing you've done," she finished in a huff.

He was impressed again; the servant was forced to betray her mistress, but she managed to tear into him on the same wave of pique.

"*I* warned him off?" he enquired carefully. Bingley had been carefully approached by at least three people after the supper dance, all asking about his friend Darcy's supposed betrothal to a female from Kent. Darcy had not had to say a word. Bingley himself had given the orders for their departure the morning after the ball.

"The Bingley sister told us you made them go. Wrote her a letter," Sarah said grudgingly, looking away from him.

The servant looked at the brute to give him another piece of her mind, only to find herself alone in the bookroom. What had she been saying? She had just come to see if Mr Bennet wanted tea...hadn't she? Well, he was not here now. She shook her head, thinking she would hang laundry out to dry in the brief winter sunshine. Her head needed clearing, and fresh air would be welcome.

Darcy strode across the fields, his anger pulsing. He caught Elizabeth's scent immediately and began climbing. Of course, she had taken the least civilised paths, over terrain easily hiding a predator. Had the girl no sense whatsoever? Evidently not, as she had all but agreed to a wedding with the fool vicar. Just the thought of him *near* her was enough to make him long to kill someone. His temper flared as it had not in decades. What could she have been thinking?

Abruptly, he came to a halt. She sat upon a boulder resting high above the valley floor, barely shaded by scrubby trees. To the east he could see Netherfield; at this height it was merely a small white grouping of neatly arranged boxes. She appeared blind to the scenery, her spine straight as if stiffened with steel, chin up like a good little soldier, jaw clenched. Though he could not read her feelings, any idiot could see her utter misery.

Forcing himself to make a noisy ascent so he would not startle her, he made his way to her perch. To his consternation, despite his racket, she did not notice him until he was appallingly near. It would have been so easy for the wrong person to catch her unawares.

She gave him no greeting, only nodded as though he were a stranger passing through, someone of no interest. He seated himself beside her anyway, pleased to see her look a bit uncertain now he had ignored her disdain. Gradually, however, her expression of mute suffering faded in favour of cleansing anger.

"Good morning, Miss Elizabeth," he said calmly.

"Is it?" she asked. "Well, perhaps it is, for those who can do as they please without regard to the feelings of others. How does it feel to exist in your rarefied world, where one might play fast and loose with the heart of an honourable young woman and then blithely move on to one's next victim?"

His brows rose high at her impertinent words, and she laughed bitterly. "What? Are you astonished at my pique? Should I instead be tempted to sit and merrily converse with the man who has been the means of ruining, perhaps forever, the happiness of a most beloved sister?"

This was not the time, he guessed, to debate Miss Jane Bennet's dubious honour. But he would not take the blame for Caroline's schemes and Bingley's impulsiveness, having warned him over and over to wait until they could be sure about her before paying her attentions that would draw notice.

"I have only just learned the contents of Miss Bingley's letter. I assure you, I said nothing to Bingley regarding leaving the neighbourhood."

She appeared to contemplate this. "Did you approve of his abandonment?"

Ah. Clever woman, to cut to the heart of motive. Regardless, he would not dissemble. He avoided deceit when possible, and would not have approached her again had he not firmly believed her life to be at risk. Whatever truths he could tell her, he would, even if they were painful ones.

"I felt his attentions to your sister were precipitate. I regret deeply that she was hurt by them. But yes, knowing all the circumstances, there was no other possible outcome."

"What circumstances might those be?"

"I am not at liberty to say."

She stood. "Well, then, we are at an impasse. I bid you good day." She marched down the narrow path. He followed.

After several minutes, she turned to look at him. "Will you not leave me be?"

"It is dangerous for a female alone. A young man was attacked and killed not far from here."

"It is broad daylight! I have been walking these woods and fields for years without trouble."

"It is not safe."

He could see she just barely held her emotions in check, her eyes brimming with unshed tears that her dignity demanded privacy to shed. She gave him her back, but her shoulders shook, her entire body jerking with the force of sobs she attempted to contain. And then she stumbled over a tree root, and he abruptly had enough. He would not spare her dignity if it injured her.

"Miss Elizabeth, I must beg you to stop."

"Beg away," she choked out, trying to continue.

He reached out and caught her easily. "No," he said. "You will hurt yourself. There is a boulder just over yonder. We will sit there until you are better able to resume your walk."

She jerked out of his hold but aimed for the boulder. It was a lovely spot, surrounded by oaks—and much more strategic than their former location. He resisted the urge to gather her in close until her distress and anger faded; he guessed she would most likely be unappreciative of any efforts by him to comfort.

Removing his coat, he laid it on the boulder, indicating she should sit. He remained standing, his hands behind his back, peering out, deliberately infusing his vision and hearing for some distance beyond this little refuge. All was quiet, but normally so. If Wickham were in the vicinity, there should be the betraying shrieks of frightened wildlife, or the unnatural silence of woodland creatures holding still in the wake of a dangerous predator.

Darcy returned his attention to Elizabeth, seeing she was once again lost in her own bleak thoughts. It was painful to understand he was a part of her anguish.

"Miss Elizabeth," he said, calling her back to the here and now, "I wonder if you would do me the honour of becoming my wife?"

Her jaw dropped, her mouth gaping in reaction. For the first time, he allowed himself to look his fill, noting the bruised, purple shadows under her eyes, the beginnings of gauntness defining her cheekbones; she had dropped, perhaps, half a stone. Abruptly, he surrendered his anger with her for accepting Collins's proposal; she had already suffered for it.

For some moments she stared at him, opening and closing her mouth as though trying out different words and finding none of them suitable. At last she expelled one. "Why?"

Because I want you more than any female I have ever seen.

Because you are the place my soul rests. Because you were meant to be mine from the first moment I saw you dying.

"All the usual reasons for which a man requires a wife," he said instead.

"To provide heirs, of course," she stated, trying to be sophisticated and ruining it with a deep blush.

"That is the usual reason," he responded calmly. He did not feel at all calm; he found her blush charming and her naivety alluring. The fact he was surrendering all hope of heirs for her lifetime with this proposal made him feel as though he played a starring role in a farce. "I assure you, I can provide a good home, and I will care for your extended family as I would my own."

This mention of her family seemed to drive the shock from her expression, her blush fading to a bleached whiteness. "Even if I were disposed to accept your offer, there are...complications."

"Yes. Mr Collins. I heard. However, your father claims he has not yet consented to the match."

"You spoke with my father?" she squeaked.

"Of course. You did not think I would?"

"I-I suppose...this is all so unexpected. And Jane—oh dear, Jane. I should not even speak with you! How could I tell her I am to marry the dearest friend of the man who so thoroughly disappointed her?"

"Do you think she would rather see you wed to Collins?" he asked curiously and a little coldly.

She gave a small laugh that was somehow sadder than tears. "No, not Jane. She is everything good. I know she has been distressed by the match. But Mama will be difficult. Longbourn is her home. She wants to keep it, more than anything."

Certainly more than she cares for your fate, he thought. With satisfaction, he noted she already expected her mother's response, and was thinking in terms of what the consequences of marriage to him would be.

"Let me cope with your mother. I can be very persuasive."

Her head bent now, the unrestrained locks of her hair falling around her, hiding her from him. "What of your betrothal? To Anne de Bourgh, of Rosings Park, in Kent."

Darcy went down on one knee. "Miss Elizabeth, there has never been another betrothal, simply a foolish rumour. There is only you. I ask you again: will you be my wife?"

To his complete and utter dismay, a single tear traced its way down her cheek—one drop, managing to convey the grief of choking sobs. She turned away.

"Elizabeth...no, do not," he said. Unable to bear it, he took her into his arms, holding her tightly, as though she were a young child. The sympathetic embrace only seemed to grieve her more deeply. He rocked her back and forth, tucking her into his lap, following an instinct he had not known he possessed—to nurture and care for her by any means she would allow.

Her grief became angrier. "I do n-not wish to marry Mr Col-Collins," she cried. "H-have to d-do my du-duty. Be–be...a g-good d-daughter. A good s-sister. Grow up...must...duty," she sobbed, punctuating each word with a fisted emphasis.

He let her beat upon his chest, though his inclination was to stop her—not because she could hurt him, which was impossible, only concerned she would injure her poor hands. Fortunately, she responded to his gentle caresses to her back and shoulders, gradually calming within his embrace. When she was at last fully quiet, he spoke.

"Elizabeth?" he murmured.

She did not answer, and he peered down to see her face. His Elizabeth had fallen fast asleep.

"I will take that as a yes," he said.

Elizabeth came awake slowly, reluctantly. Her dream was so much better than her usual terrors, she was loath to relinquish it. As the fog of sleep lifted, she heard a voice singing, low and deep but achingly beautiful. Seconds later, she realised her pillow was a coat laid upon the ground, and she had what...swooned? Her mind felt thick, sluggish, and unwilling to face the truths waiting on the other side of her eyelids.

Reality would not be denied. Her memory returned as the words of 'Highland Mary' finished on a clear and perfect pitch, a man's mournful promises to remember his poor dead love. She opened her eyes.

Mr Darcy stood, looking off into the distance as though he could see for miles. A brief temptation to close them again nearly overwhelmed her—as much for the sheer pleasure and comfort of listening to him sing as her embarrassment over her tantrum. Sadly, her current feelings of shame meant it had not been a dream. Trying to sit up, however, caused a wave of dizziness and his instant attention.

"You are faint," he observed aloud. "I should have known you would not fall asleep so easily. When was the last time you ate?"

If he were willing to ascribe her juvenile behaviour to illness, she would gladly accept the excuse. "I have had trouble with my appetite of late," she said.

"I am unsurprised. Collins would not enhance anyone's desire for food."

Elizabeth shuddered a little, thinking of the scene the vicar would undoubtedly cause when...*if* she refused to marry him. Her eyes sought out Mr Darcy's, trying to read his expression, but he looked away again. Why had he offered for her?

"You should know, my portion is insignificant and my connexions non-existent. You gain very little with this alliance."

"It is of small import."

"But it is!" she cried. "You know it is. Your offer makes no sense!"

Darcy sat beside her, remaining quiet for some minutes. "You have heard me called 'eccentric'," he said at last. "You have seen I am not comfortable in the company of strangers. I will always prefer the country to *tonnish* pursuits in London. Perhaps it is you who sacrifices."

She scoffed. "Surely you jest. Miss Bingley's descriptions of Pemberley show you have much to offer any wife, even without extensive society."

"I would be honest with you, Miss Elizabeth—or at least, as honest as I can be. I have a...an affliction, for lack of a better word." He seemed to be at a loss for others, but she waited patiently for him to continue.

"You will excuse me if I have trouble explaining, for I have never before done so. Have you ever known, just by the atmosphere in a room, that its occupants had been arguing? You may not have witnessed the row, and all may have rearranged their faces into pleasant expressions, but you can feel the acrimony in the air."

Elizabeth thought of the many times she had sensed her parents' bitterness, as if harsh words still echoed silently between them. She knew when groups of girls, tittering across the room, mocked her unfashionable clothing and dreadful height, even when she did not hear their words. "Yes," she agreed quietly. "I have felt that."

"We all have the ability, I daresay, to know the emotions of others in varying degrees of sensitivity. But with me...'tis more so. I can understand what others are feeling to such a fine point as to know when someone lies or hates or fears or loves. It is intrusive to the point of dishonour. I cannot stop it," he continued in a low voice. "In a roomful of people, I am assaulted with feelings like the blasts of multiple cannon. I can bear it but will never be comfortable in a crowd. This will never change. I will always know which of our friends despise me or are jealous or annoyed. And you, no doubt, already believe me to be a little mad."

"No-o," she drew out the syllable, "but I do not think I will ever agree to play cards with you."

He gave a bark of laughter, squeezing her shoulder briefly in response. She felt the simple gesture down to her toes.

"You, of all people, are safe. In all my years, you are the first person I have ever met whose feelings keep their own counsel. You cannot imagine, Elizabeth, how restful it is for me to simply be here in your presence. Though it would be more useful, at this moment, to know if you wished me gone."

"You talk as though you are an old man," she scolded. "How do you know I am the only one who causes this, um...effect? By your own admission, you avoid society. Your manners are out of practice. Perhaps if you forced yourself out in the world, you would find others equally restful."

"I have been a great deal in company, in any number of countries. It has never happened before."

"Are you certain you know what these feelings mean? They must be subject to misinterpretation."

"Not really. To me, they are nearly as vivid as the spoken word. Even as a young child, I could tell—" He stopped speaking and looked away from her.

Elizabeth wondered, then, what it would be like to understand, without any uncertainty, exactly how one's parents felt at any given moment. It was difficult enough to recognise their feelings when they were angry and upset and you understood why. To be aware of every annoyance, to know every unfair censure would be horrifying. And what of a lover? Feeling infatuation fade, to pinpoint the exact moment your affection became unwelcome or inconvenient. Even if love was strong, no one loves consistently. Recognising the peaks might be exciting, but the valleys would be doubly disheartening.

She cleared her throat. "I imagine it could be a temptation to exploit such a gift. At such times when another's need for privacy became less important than your own curiosity."

He smiled. "I will agree my luck at cards is legendary. But I seldom play unless I must. There is no challenge, and my fortune is adequate without stealing another's." His expression grew serious again. "So, Miss Elizabeth? Will you admit you bring more to this marriage than any other could, or have I frightened you with my madness?"

"Do not call it madness. As you say, we all have an ability to–to empathise, to one extent or another."

"I say it because others would not hesitate to describe me exactly so."

She protested, but there were so many questions tumbling through her head, she barely could choose amongst them. "Why did you leave Netherfield without any word?" she blurted, finally.

He sighed. "I had many reasons, some of them business, some personal. I regret I cannot disclose them all to you now."

"My father shares little with my mother, believing her too dull-witted to understand sensible conversation. I had hoped for a better connexion than the one my parents share."

His jaw clenched. "And you believe marriage to the vicar would provide one?" he asked sharply. "I should have spoken, Miss Elizabeth. I was undecided due to my affliction. But it is a small world. Your cousin was given his living by an acquaintance of mine, Lady Catherine de Bourgh. I heard of his plans to offer for you and decided I could offer you at least as much as he."

"At least," she agreed sardonically. "Does anyone else know of your affliction?"

"Some. The Bingleys, but not Hurst. A few others."

Elizabeth could not help a flare of indignation. "You would trust Miss Bingley? Her letter laying her brother's perfidies upon your shoulders proves her very disloyal, if you ask me."

"Miss Bingley grew up knowing. Our families have been close since before she was born. I vow, she will not betray me in this."

"Hmph. I do not understand why you care to associate with her anyway. Or are some feminine emotions more easily borne than others?"

His brows rose. "Are you jealous, my love?"

His choice of endearment did nothing to mitigate her pique; she knew he teased, but she had her pride. She stood, her chin lifting. "No. But let me be rightly understood—once we are wed, you shall cease *wallowing* in the feelings of other females."

His smile reappeared. "That, my dear, is an easy promise to make."

They were nearly returned to Longbourn when he noticed her slowing steps.

"Does the thought of telling your family of our agreement distress you?"

"Oh, no, not at all," she replied.

He stared. "Please trust me, Elizabeth. All will be well at home."

She looked at him sharply, a blush tingeing her cheeks. "I thought you could not read my thoughts!"

He crooked his half-smile at her. "I cannot." He could, of course, extract the memories of most mortals, but while emotions blasted him, memories stayed in the heads of their owners unless he exerted a good deal of power to retrieve them. "A blind man could tell you grow more anxious the nearer we are to Longbourn."

"I will admit I do not look forward to explaining to my parents, and even less to Mr Collins. He has serious expectations which I have not discouraged," she said at last, determinedly stepping forward along the path again.

"I will deal with everyone," he reassured. "I want you to go directly to your room and stay there for half an hour. I promise you, it is all the time needed to set everything right."

"Oh! Mr Darcy, it is bad enough that you will be exposed to the worst of my mother's nerves, which are not well regulated on the best of days. I insist upon bearing this with you. It would not be right."

He was touched she cared anything for his feelings in this. "Thank you, my dear, but I ask you to trust me. It will be easier. If your mother acts unkindly towards you, it will exacerbate my temper, and I am not an amiable man. My patience will be less tested if you are out of earshot." It was, at least, partly true.

"You have been amiable with me," she pointed out.

But I am falling in love with you, he thought, shocked. Possessiveness, he had convinced himself was acceptable. Desire, he understood. But this! The very rawness of the feeling after decades of ennui was unnerving. He had to force himself to keep walking.

When Elizabeth came downstairs thirty minutes later, all was calm. She had washed, changed her dress, and put her hair up, listening for shrieks and hoping one of her sisters might come upstairs to tell her what was happening. None of them did, but now it appeared as though nothing had happened at all. There was no sign of either parent, no loud wails sounding from her mother's rooms. Her sisters sat quietly in the parlour with Mr Darcy. When she entered the room, he stood immediately. A blush overtook her.

He bowed over her hand as though this was their first meeting of the day. She urged him to sit, taking her place beside him. Jane, thankfully, looked more cheerful than she had in some time, and was just making some awkward remarks about the weather when Mama entered, calling them all to dinner.

Her mother was unusually impassive, hardly looking at Lizzy; her father, on the other hand, practically stared at her, as though she were a puzzle requiring a solution. Mr Collins remained thankfully absent, apparently having retired early. The meal was a long one, and more than once she wished for Mr Darcy's abilities. The only emotion *she* was sure of was her sisters' curiosity.

At the end of the meal, Mr Bennet quietly announced that, henceforth, Lydia was not the only betrothed daughter of Longbourn, and they should all welcome Mr Darcy to the family. Elizabeth bit her lip, trying not to be hurt that her father failed to ask her opinion on the matter. Of course, Papa's estimation of her good sense had seen a definite decline when she agreed to the match with Mr Collins. It was Jane who asked the question everyone wondered: "When will this happy event take place?"

"After Lydia's wedding," Mrs Bennet informed them. "I cannot possibly put together a second celebration until I finish the first."

"Unfortunately, a delay of many weeks will not be possible," Mr Darcy interjected. "I will leave tomorrow to procure a licence and have the settlement papers drawn. We will wed immediately upon my return. I have business affairs necessitating my return to Pemberley, my estate in Derbyshire, as quickly as possible."

Elizabeth stifled an astonished gasp.

Mr and Mrs Bennet each began protests, all of which were quelled immediately by a look from her betrothed. Could that look be learned, she wondered? If so, she would use it on him. His lack of consideration, making the decision without even pretending to consult her was alarming. Still, what were her options? Allow her mother to prevail with Mr Collins?

I am not so foolish as that, she thought.

Mr Darcy alone joined the ladies in the parlour after dinner, his host refusing to leave the comfort of his book room. Within several minutes, a number of small emergencies and weak excuses were offered, until Elizabeth found herself alone with her future husband.

It was a bit embarrassing. "I am sorry," she offered quietly. "They think they are being tactful, giving us a few moments alone, as you are departing so soon."

An expression which might be interpreted as guilt in another man crept over his features. He waved off her apology. "I am happy to have a few minutes with you. We did not discuss our plans. Did I distress you with my haste?"

"Would my distress change your plans?" she asked, with some asperity.

"I regret it cannot," he replied apologetically. "Tell me how I may make it up to you."

"I hardly know you," she said, trying to be sensible. "Your greatest recommendation came from your friendship with a man who broke my sister's heart. And yet, I am not insensible to the honour of your offer. Indeed, my biggest regret is that you will be gone while I face the disappointment of Mr Collins. Anyone who can so successfully persuade Mama would be quite useful during *that* conversation."

He moved to sit beside her on the settee, taking her cold hand in his much larger one. It was a strong, warm hand, conveying more comfort than she expected. "I will talk to Mr Collins myself before I go. You are not to speak to him."

"I cannot allow it, sir. It would even be discourteous for you intercede in this manner. My father and I shall see to it."

He scowled. "My future bride shall never engage in conversation with that man again. Did you think I would leave you here alone while he is still in residence?"

"Have you met this suitor?" she said, noting his voice rising; perhaps he was not quite as indifferent as she had feared. "You mistake the sort of man he is, if you suspect me to be in any danger from his allurements."

"I have met him. Nevertheless, I will not leave you in a distressing situation for which I am at least partially responsible. And you will cast *your* allurements at no one but myself."

She was about to utter a furious protest when she caught a glint in his eye. "Mr Darcy! I did not think you capable of teasing!"

"If we are to marry, it seems like a skill at which I ought to become more proficient," he said, taking both her hands within his much larger ones.

Elizabeth knew a bit of wonder as a curious intimacy filled the room, suddenly deeply aware of her hands caught within his own. She grew bold enough to ask him her most pressing concern. "Mr Darcy, will you tell me—how does my family truly feel?"

He let go of her hands in unconscious protest.

She shook her head. "I know you think I open a Pandora's box. But I have lived inside this box for many years, stumbling around and trying to navigate a safe path. Until I agreed to marry Mr Collins, my mother was a complete mystery to me. My agreement forged an uneasy truce between us, which has now shattered." She swallowed down her sorrow for that.

"Does my sister Jane struggle with anger, as well as her private grief? Is Lydia jealous that I have stolen her glory? Is my father happy with my decision? Can I speak openly of a wedding celebration, or should I pretend nothing is happening and simply send for the vicar upon your return?"

Darcy looked at her with some astonishment. "Your motives are admirable," he said at last. "But it can be difficult knowledge to bear."

"As in the eavesdropper who never hears anything good about himself? I do not expect good. I simply wish to know how bad." Her spine stiffened as she prepared to hear.

He nodded. "Your sister Jane feels considerable relief. I shall not pretend your surprise betrothal has not given her new hope for her own future, though she does her best not to dwell upon it. I hate to disillusion her, but I do not know whether Bingley will ever return to Netherfield."

Elizabeth sighed. "I do not know if she still hopes for Bingley. But we agreed our current situation was a sign from God that we were being foolish to hold out for a more, um, amiable connexion. Do not you dare laugh," she warned.

"I would not dream of doing so," he said, but she could tell he smiled without looking at him.

"Now, while perhaps I do not marry for love, at least no one could call marriage to you a punishment. It must give Jane hope for her own future."

"I am relieved you do not consider me penance," he said dryly.

She giggled, and his expression lightened. "Lydia is indeed envious. But truthfully, Elizabeth, her emotions are shallow and fleeting. She will feel jealousy while your wedding is discussed and be distracted by her own plans within moments."

Elizabeth sighed. "It pains me that her feelings are so superficial. I fear when the excitement of the Colonel's uniform and her changed status wanes, her happiness in marriage will fade with it."

"Very likely," he agreed. She liked that he did not try to cajole her into a more optimistic, less truthful view.

"Catherine is all excitement, and Mary is pleased."

Lizzy nodded. "You have not mentioned my mother."

It was his turn to sigh. "Your mother has many feelings. Outrage. Jealousy. Disappointment. Relief. Perhaps she dislikes Collins and does not care for him as her son, or else truly wants better for you. There is avarice as well. My wealth has not escaped her notice."

"Which of those emotions is predominant?"

"That is the devil of it! Her moods are mercurial and ever-changing. She is exhausting, to put it mildly. I hope you will never suggest she live with us. I will buy her a home in Mayfair first."

"I am sure she can be housed much less expensively. In her mind, naught will compare to Longbourn, regardless."

"If she rides roughshod over your feelings while I am away, remind her the size of her future home depends upon how happy my bride is upon my return," he suggested.

She decided she might as well be honest, although she was wary. "I believe I shall look forward to your return, whatever her behaviour."

"As shall I," he said, his voice husky.

"You...you have not yet told me of my father's feelings." She looked away, preparing herself.

"Lydia's shallowness is his legacy, just as you have inherited his intelligence. Your father feels I am a better match than Collins, whom he considers unutterably stupid. Mostly, he is glad the whole thing will be settled at very little trouble to himself."

"That sounds just like him. He does not...notice much," she said wistfully. But once again he took her hands, and began telling her of Pemberley and its extensive grounds, about the rough natural beauty of the place. It was exciting to consider this part of the adventure. A home of her own had become a symbol of independence.

Jane returned, her eyes meeting Elizabeth's. Neither girl would be early to sleep tonight.

Darcy excused himself quickly. Jane was bursting with excitement and the desire to talk; he could only suppose it meant his bride-to-be was anxious for the same. He brushed a kiss upon Elizabeth's cheek as he exited the room, feeling Jane's surprise at this intimacy. She would be astonished if she knew what he felt, and the kiss was the least of it.

It was difficult to part from Elizabeth but after all, his room was close and his hearing, excellent. He could listen to them all night long, if he wished.

Nine

DARCY HAD NOT EXPECTED BREAKFAST TO BE SERVED SO EARLY in such a small household, but whatever else one might say of Mrs Bennet, she kept a good table and was a punctilious hostess. He helped himself to tea and crusty rolls, awaiting the entrance of Mr Collins.

As expected, he did not have to wait long. Collins did not give the appearance of a man fond of forgoing a meal.

He watched as the vicar loaded his plate from the sideboard, grunted his greetings, then eagerly shovelled food into his mouth. While he ate, Darcy cast his memory back to the night of the Netherfield ball, reviewing the emotional outpourings of the entire assembly in minute detail, especially the unwed females. Were there any whose feelings were suffused with desperation? Who looked upon even the least presentable gentlemen with hope and keen interest?

His excellent memory did not fail him. There were, indeed—a few, as a matter of fact—their anguish a part of what made these events so difficult for him. Delving deeper, he mined his memory for one anxious enough to take risks and strong-willed and practical enough to be happy with the consequences. He could not send a female into danger—but even the Catherine de Bourghs of the world were constrained by the Council to leave humans of good family alone. Of the choices available, only one had a father possessing a knighthood.

He allowed the pastor a few more bites—never let it be said that he was unreasonable. When only crumbs remained and the man headed for second helpings, Darcy arose with him, compelling Collins to follow with a single thought. When they were a safe distance from Longbourn, Darcy—his eyes black with power—twisted de Bourgh's words into an entirely different command.

"Elizabeth will be wed shortly, but not to you. You shall be wed soon, but never to Elizabeth Bennet or any of your Bennet cousins. Make haste with me to be introduced at the house of Sir William Lucas and especially to his daughter Charlotte. Ask for Miss Lucas's hand as soon as she gifts you with her *sincere* smile of encouragement and do not take no for an answer. Wed Miss Charlotte Lucas as quickly as can be arranged and stay with her people for another two months beyond. Do not write to nor speak with your patroness until after you have wed and returned to your home. Bring Miss Charlotte Lucas back to Hunsford as your bride, or you will suffer a death of such foul agony you will wish you had never been born." The aromas of Criollo cacao and ocean-aged ambergris scented the air in sweet, earthy harmony, vines of his intonations entwining around the pungent, fouler tendrils of de Bourgh's power. When he was certain his words had taken root and subsumed the other, he set off for Lucas Lodge, the pudgy vicar eagerly trotting along in his wake.

For the first time in recent memory, Darcy did not choose to ride back to London. Instead, he shared a carriage with the long-suffering Chamberlayne, spending the miles day-dreaming of Elizabeth as though he were a green boy with his first girl. And agonising. He could not deny some of that as well.

He had vowed never to repeat his father's blunders. Yet, here he was, betrothed to a female who did not know who or *what* he was, who could easily be as horrified as his mother had ever been. George Darcy had hidden his nature from his wife for many years, not impregnating her until she was in her thirties. They had been, by all accounts, happy together, his father altering her memories every time he fed from her. A bonded vampyre could only feed from its mate, and his father had most definitely shared a bonded connexion with his mother. The pregnancy ended his father's secret existence—it was impossible to hide a vampyre offspring from its mother without fatal damage to her mind.

Darcy had decided, when he offered for Elizabeth, that he would simply refuse to bond with her. Bonding was not at all common and he supposed his will was enough to prevent it. If he never fed from her, never became one with her, surely no bonded union could take root.

Unfortunately, the process might be more complicated.

He knew few bonded males, and none of whom he was on close enough terms to ask. His certainty that he could contain the process was weakening. Still, it only made sense; if he abstained from full intimacy, their bonding *must* remain incomplete. But could he abstain? And would it matter if he did?

It had stirred him, simply hearing her tell Jane last night that she thought him handsome. It was all he could do to refrain from a farewell kiss. He wanted nearly desperately to have a complete marriage. And as unlikely as its possibility, a child with Elizabeth would be the pinnacle of his existence.

Nevertheless, at some point in the future, once the danger from de Bourgh could be determined and dealt with, he must stage his own death, leaving her enough money to make a new start, a new life. And yet...

Could he let her go? Could he care for her incompletely? Could he even resist the siren call of her blood? For her sake and his own, he dearly hoped he was strong enough.

Entering the Bingley's London home was a lesson in resisting self-indulgence. The thick grief ruling Bingley's heart rolled in waves over and through him, a solemn reminder of what could happen if he let his own feelings determine the future. Promptly shown into Bingley's study, he was appalled at the appearance of his *fidus Achates*.

Bingley's hair was rumpled, his face unshaven; no coat, his cravat hanging loosely, and his person reeking of brandy, the man before him was a wreck such as Darcy had never expected to see in his formerly dapper friend.

"You look the very devil, Bingley."

Bingley gave him a crooked smile. "I would tell you how I feel, but you already know."

"You do have other alternatives, although I am not anxious for you to leave my service, especially at the moment. I am to be wed, you see."

Bingley's brows rose. "You? I will admit, you have managed to surprise me. Who is the...hmm...lucky girl?"

He met his friend's eye. "Miss Elizabeth Bennet."

Darcy may as well have punched him, for the combination of grief, shock, and pain the mention of Elizabeth gave; he felt the other man's hurt on a visceral level. To his credit, though, Bingley merely said, "Indeed."

Darcy's voice softened. "She is in grave danger. De Bourgh sent her vicar to wed her, on pain of death. For some reason Catherine wants the girl within her power. Fortunately, she was careless in how she worded her commands. Miss Elizabeth and the parson must be wed, but not necessarily to each other. I have to admit, simply stopping the ceremony and allowing Collins to go mad trying to fulfil his orders is a temptation. He is *not* a gentleman."

"And you are?" Bingley replied, with just a touch of his old humour.

"Heaven forfend, no," Darcy answered. "But in comparison to de Bourgh, I am a knight errant. I shall wed Miss Elizabeth."

"Because it is such a tremendous sacrifice for you."

"It may be," Darcy said, noting Bingley's rare sarcasm. "As I cannot risk the truth—she continues completely immune to my peculiarities—this may be the most asinine decision I have ever made. I feel as though I am half-bonded to her already, after a simple kiss on the cheek. Living with her will be torture."

A burst of anger shot through him from his friend. "Torture, Darcy? To have the privilege of caring for the woman you love? To be able to see to her safety, protect her, shelter and cherish her? I would give much for that opportunity, myself."

Ah, Charles, but your soul is that of a gentleman, while a beast rules mine. "I stand corrected. Nevertheless, I would ask for your assistance in this one matter. When I can be assured of Miss Elizabeth's permanent safety, let us discuss your replacement."

Bingley's brow furrowed. Loyalty had been bred into him from birth. "Abandoning my responsibilities is never an honourable choice."

"You have never *had* a choice, Charles. Your father had you in the harness, nearly from birth."

Bingley stood. "Never say that, Darcy. I have been proud to offer my services to you, as my father did before me. And I am devilish good at what I do, so do not act as though I am so easily replaceable, or I shall take insult."

Darcy smiled and raised a hand in truce. "I would never dare think it. In fact, I would say you are the best of the Bingleys to ever shelter the Darcy name, and I have known many of them, and found them all good men. It still does not mean you must surrender the reason your heart beats."

"My heart beats for many reasons. I will overcome this, Darcy. I am not yet ready to retire. I have simply been..."

Grieving. Darcy nodded, as if it had been stated aloud. "If it is any comfort, the bond between the Bennet girls is a special one. In the face of Miss Elizabeth's surprising news of her impending wedding to me, Miss Bennet felt no jealousy, no self-pity—only a deep, abiding joy at her sister's good fortune and an intense relief the odious vicar was not to be the bridegroom. I have seldom met a female whose feelings are so full of goodness. I am not at all convinced the test was a fair one. I have no doubt she tried to do what was right."

Bingley nodded his understanding, but the poignancy of his heartache became another presence in the room. "If I had only heard the news of your supposed betrothal through your conversation with Miss Elizabeth, I would wholly agree. But many in the ballroom knew. Perhaps neither of the Bennet sisters can keep a secret, Darcy. Have you considered this?"

"I have. Which is why I plan a white marriage. Still, we do not know all the circumstances. The girls could have been overheard. Caroline was far too smug at our departure for me to dismiss the possibility of treachery. If she overheard them, perhaps she saw her opportunity to act against Miss Bennet. I believe we do not know all of what happened that night."

"Caroline knows her life depends upon her ability to keep a secret, and she does not hate me so much she would entertain that risk. However, it is true that anyone could have overheard. Which is why the ability to maintain the utmost discretion is so vital.

"Perhaps we should revisit the situation once Miss Elizabeth is safe," continued Bingley. "Tell me your plans, and I shall do what I can to assist you with them. I assume I should begin by working out the details of a generous settlement?" he asked. His expression remained serious, but hope crept into the room, banishing the shadows of despair.

"What is so amusing?" Mrs Bennet asked, storming into the sitting room where Jane, Lizzy, and Kitty were laughing and talking. All three recognised her volatile mood.

"Nothing, Mama," Elizabeth said, knowing the first to speak would be the first to draw her fire. She was the usual volunteer.

"That is correct!" Mrs Bennet snapped. "Nothing. Nothing at all amusing about a patched-up wedding, the next thing to an elopement! I hope you do not expect me to waste what little your father allows me on this mockery!"

"Oh, no, Mama," Jane interrupted bravely. "It is the furthest thing from an elopement. Why—"

"Do not tell *me*!" Mrs Bennet practically shrieked. "Patched-up is what it is, announcing to the world: Mr Darcy is ashamed of his bride!" Her eyes narrowed as she turned back to Elizabeth. "Or is he ashamed of *himself*? Were you alone with him, Miss Lizzy? Did you offer yourself to avoid your duty to Mr Collins?"

Elizabeth turned a brilliant red at this cruel and shocking accusation; her mother quickly interpreted her response as guilt.

"I knew it! I knew a man such as him could not be tempted by one of so few charms and so little beauty. How *could* you? Do you esteem so lightly the rules keeping you safe? Would you shame your sisters, your parents? You could have been ruined, publicly—"

"Mama! I did not! I would not!" Elizabeth cried, horrified.

"Mama, please," Jane interpolated at the same moment.

The protests did nothing except turn her mother's attention to another grievance. "And *you*!" she wailed at Jane. "Wasting your beauty on that worthless Bingley! If only you had cast your lures at Mr Darcy! If he was desperate enough to accept Lizzy, for such a beauty as you, he would have been *proud* to host a celebration befitting *royalty*! Oh! None of you care a fig for my poor nerves!" She swept out of the room, leaving Jane and Elizabeth white-faced and pale, and Kitty round-eyed with shock.

❧

Darcy needed to feed, and to feed well; he did not wish to visit those women in London with whom he had once formed arrangements of what (for him) had passed as companionship. It simply felt wrong to Take from any of them now. In fact, he most decisively wished never to see them again.

Instead, he went to a site where he was sure to find the daring—and foolish—seeking adventure: Vauxhall Gardens. One might believe, amongst such crowds and lit by over fifteen thousand brightly coloured lamps, that privacy such as he required would be impossible. One would be wrong.

Wandering the crowded paths, his talent for illusion created the image of a man about town and shortly thereafter, three lovely young ladies—perilously unescorted—giggled at him. Inwardly, he sighed. Although it was safe enough in the well-lit lanes, there was ample cover of darkness for those seeking it, and he could feel the seething undercurrents of the predators always stalking such places. After a single compelling thought, the girls followed him off the path.

He longed to feed; it had been nearly a month, and though he still felt strong, it was unwise to wait. He could smell the blood pounding through the females' arteries, his body answering with all the usual mortal responses to hunger: mouth watering, belly rumbling, everything *except* the normal vampyre response enabling him to satisfy it. His fangs did not extend.

Devil take it. Their scent was amiss. The women stood, waiting in the shadows, endlessly patient in the restful slumber they now experienced within their minds' eye, swaying just a little in their dreams.

He had been trying *not* to think of Elizabeth, certain doing so would feel wrong. Still, possibly he would have difficulty feeding unless he did. Closing his eyes, he called to mind a vision of her as he had seen her last, looking up at him with her beautiful dark eyes. Immediately his fangs extended; he went to the first girl and bent to her throat. Unhappily, he felt his withdrawal—both emotional and physical—as soon as he scented her. In frustration, he actually closed his eyes and pinched his nostrils shut, drawing on his vision of Elizabeth with all the force of his psyche.

It succeeded. Clinging to the image of his betrothed—and refusing to allow any evidence of her absence into his other senses—he fed from each one. As he sealed the puncture wounds at the neck of the third female with a flick of his tongue, he opened his eyes. To each woman, he gave a false memory of being frightened by a rogue—along with a rescue, in his new guise as a grandfatherly sort—and wakened them. Guiding the trio back to safety, he lectured them on the dangers of wandering about unescorted until he was satisfied they would avoid doing so in the future, content he was one step closer to joining Elizabeth.

The elegant townhouse, so carefully furnished in discreet colours and expensive but judicious taste, was much like its owner. The Earl of Matlock was a pillar of the vampyre community, for centuries well known for his wisdom and discretion, as well as his charm. He would have achieved Councillor status much sooner had he been born a vampyre, rather than mortal. Still, the fact he was on the Council at all was a testament to his power. All the other councillors were born to their positions, holding them for centuries—as indeed, Darcy's own father had, and as Darcy had been expected to do.

But Darcy had never had much taste for the politicking and compromise required by government, and despised being the centre of attention. While sitting in Council sessions was not as difficult for him to bear as an assembly of any other persons, Council members' well-practised restraint cloaked emotions thick with layered meanings and discordant, conflicting notions of arrogance and treachery.

He was shown into the library, where Matlock waited behind a large, polished desk; he stood when Darcy entered.

"Fitzwilliam! It is good to see you, young man. What could have lured you away from Pemberley? I was all curiosity to hear you were in London."

"I have no doubt you are already informed of my reasons. Your sources would have apprised you as soon as I applied for a common licence."

The earl waved this away. "Of course, of course. But I wish to know *who* she is, Fitzwilliam. I had begun to believe this day would never come. George would have been so pleased."

Fitzwilliam felt a rare, powerful wave of emotion from Matlock and nodded, feeling their mutual grief for his murdered father.

"Her name is Elizabeth Bennet. Her father owns a small estate in Hertfordshire."

"Human, then. Does she know?"

"No. And I cannot tell her. She is immune to thought revision and all illusion, insofar as far as I can determine. I cannot risk confiding in her, so of course, no children will be forthcoming."

Matlock's lips pursed, and his disappointment leaked into the air. "So why marry her at all?"

"Somehow she has managed to attract the notice of Lady Catherine. I hoped you might make enquiries as to why. Elizabeth has no fortune and little family. Her connexions are closer to trade, though she is the daughter of a gentleman."

"Are you sure marriage is a necessity? I am sure *that female* could be stopped without such, ahem, drastic measures." His distaste for de Bourgh was obvious in every syllable.

"Catherine's curse has made it necessary. I will not have innocents harmed, and she is far too practised in hiding her crimes against humanity. When I am certain Miss Elizabeth is out of danger, I will arrange for her convenient widowhood. I have neglected my estate in the Baltics for some decades."

"This is disturbing, Fitzwilliam. You have several good years left in England. It seems a shame to leave so soon. If you would not make so free in your associations with mortals, you could stay here indefinitely, as most do."

"Regrettably unavoidable. Due to the circumstances, I will not ask you to attend the ceremony. But will you do what you can to unearth Catherine's schemes?"

"Of course! You know I will not rest until I have discovered whatever mischief she foments. Her visions result in her instability, as I have firmly maintained time and again. I do not know how much trouble she must cause before they do something to curtail her. They will not listen."

'They' referred to the Council. Matlock's status as a Turned vampyre sitting as Councillor was a sore point with many, de Bourgh amongst them. His objections to her were equally well known. Still, his network was strong, his House powerful, and his ability to ferret out secrets unmatched. Darcy had no doubt Matlock would do everything possible to assist him.

"I do not like this," Matlock continued. "As many times as I have urged you to marry, please listen when I say you should delay *this* wedding until I have a chance to seek answers. For all you know, you play right into de Bourgh's hands and your Miss Bennet is her tool."

"There will be no delay," Darcy stated unequivocally. "If Catherine has manipulated me into this position, I trust you will see she regrets her interference. As will I."

Matlock smiled, the force of his charm soothing the angst that talk of de Bourgh produced. "I hope I can always deserve your faith in me, Fitzwilliam," he said. "You know I will do all in my power to support you."

Darcy returned his smile, allowing himself to be comforted. He did trust Matlock to do what was necessary, despite the man's disapproval of the haste in which he acted. After all, the seat the earl held on the Council was Fitzwilliam Darcy's own. He could not demonstrate any more faith than that.

Ten

Elizabeth prevented herself from peering out the window. Again. Ever since the express arrived yesterday with the welcome news of Mr Darcy's impending return, she felt restless and on edge. Perhaps she could not help believing, after all, that this was some cruel jest. Even the news of Charlotte Lucas's engagement to Mr Collins could not entirely defeat the sensation she was perched on a precipice of random circumstance, and any stumble would land her on the wrong side. She was not quite sure whether she missed Mr Darcy or whether there was something missing within herself.

Her mother, at least, stayed true to form. She had not relented on her refusal to host a wedding breakfast, continuing to insist Mr Darcy obviously wanted this wedding to be kept as quiet as possible. Charlotte Lucas's eventual inheritance of her home worsened her bitterness and she pestered Mr Bennet several times, in Elizabeth's hearing, to write to Mr Darcy and remind him of Jane's unmarried state, or even of Kitty; he needn't settle for, as she put it, 'fifth best'. In her mind, it was simply wrong for Elizabeth to be rewarded with marriage, having failed to preserve Longbourn for their own.

Mr Bennet—when he bothered listening at all—treated the whole situation as though it were all some strange misunderstanding, and he expected the bridegroom to come to his senses at any moment, or never return at all.

The only concession Mrs Bennet made was to allow Elizabeth to stitch her own clothing instead of working on Lydia's. Elizabeth put her time to good use. What she now wore was formerly Jane's, but after lengthening it with an added flounce, she altered the bodice with inset panels to accommodate her more ample bosom. It was one of the nicer dresses she had ever owned, almost flattering. She smoothed the gown over her hips, trying in vain for calm. He had not written her during their time apart, and the note yesterday was brief in the extreme. Did he already regret whatever impulse led him to propose, as he had plainly regretted the opening set at Netherfield? The sound of approaching hoofbeats warned she was soon to find out.

A slight commotion at the door announced his arrival; Mrs Hill brought him to the parlour where Elizabeth waited with Jane, barely resisting the urge to clutch Jane's hand. As it was, she could hardly bring herself to raise her head in case regret or disappointment awaited her. She looked at Jane instead, only to see her sister's back as she hastily exited.

Her brows knit in consternation, and she met Mr Darcy's eyes at last. "How is it you can clear a room with only a look?"

He smiled, his dimple showing, and her stupid blush returned. "Call it a talent," he said, coming to sit beside her.

She could not help returning the smile. "A useful one, I suppose," she said as she resumed the study of her tightly clenched hands.

A large hand warmed her shoulder. "It is good returning to you, dear. I am happy to see you looking so well."

She peered up at him as if to ascertain whether he was speaking the truth. He was even more magnificent than she remembered, looking more vital somehow, as if he'd grown in stature during his absence. "You look well, too," she murmured.

He leant towards her and she thought he might kiss her, but instead he took her hand in his firm and dry one, his breath coasting upon her cheek. His hand tightened upon hers until suddenly he moved away, standing and facing the window. Briefly, she wondered if the contact did not feel as pleasant to him as it did to her.

"We shall be married tomorrow," he said matter-of-factly. "We will wed in the morning and leave directly thereafter for Pemberley."

"Pemberley?" she squeaked.

He turned back to face her. "I believe I informed you of my need to return to my estate as quickly as possible."

"Yes, but I thought..." she began, but stopped herself. *You thought what? He might take you on a wedding trip? Foolish beyond permission, Lizzy. Mama is correct. He wants no mawkish display.* Scrambling for equanimity, she broached a germinating idea.

"Sir, I wonder—would it be possible for Jane to accompany us? If she were to leave here for a period of time, I believe it would do much to assist her in recovering from her disappointment."

He frowned. "I am sorry, my dear. Bingley will often be our guest. I fear it would be unwise, at least for the present."

Until that moment, Elizabeth had not realised just how much she hoped he would agree—that she would not have to begin her married life alone in a place she knew no one. She stood quickly.

"I need to see to...Mama's dinner plans, Mr Darcy. If you would excuse me for a few minutes, I shall return shortly." She was almost to the door when he halted her, gripping her arm.

"Miss Elizabeth," he said. "Please."

She looked at her feet. "I seem to be in the very unfortunate habit of bursting into tears while you are about," she said quietly. "If you would please excuse me, I will try to preserve the illusion of a female who possesses some sort of dignity."

His hand moved from her arm and she thought he might embrace her—but he only touched her shoulder, turning her back to him. "I have no need for illusions," he whispered, wearing a strange expression of helplessness, as if he did not know what to do with his hands. Guiding her to a chair, he urged her into it, handing her a handkerchief.

Suddenly, she felt utterly ridiculous. Looking up, she said, "I will not cry. I am sorry I threatened to. As Mama often reminds me, I am ridiculously sentimental."

His eyes met hers. "It is not sentimental to love your sister. I would bring her if—"

"I know. We will not speak of it."

"I will dower her," he said quietly.

"No," she said, looking away as she regained composure. "At least, not at present. I fear her feelings are at issue. But perhaps—we have relations in London. My mother's brother and his wife. Jane is always welcome there. If you could talk to Papa? He does seem to listen to you."

"You are sure it would be a good situation for her?"

"My Aunt and Uncle Gardiner are people of whom I need not be ashamed," she said, her chin going up. She understood what he thought of too many others in her family. "I would have invited them to come see us wed except Mama insisted we not host any celebration."

His expression darkened with displeasure. "I am sorry, my dear. We shall take Jane to London with us and see her installed at the Gardiners."

Elizabeth bit her lip. "I would not like to delay you," she made herself protest, though she desperately wished to see Jane removed from Longbourn.

"It will not delay us by much. We shall stay at my home in London the first night and I shall introduce you to the household there, as I should do regardless. We can travel to Pemberley from London. The detour will make little difference."

"Thank you," she said gratefully. "You are too kind. I know you are anxious to return to your estate, but I will be very happy to introduce you to my aunt and uncle. We have always been close."

"I shall be honoured to meet them," he said, withdrawing a flat case from his coat pocket. "I brought you something—a wedding gift."

"Oh! I have nothing for you," she lamented, her cheeks pinkening.

"You have yourself, which is more than enough," he said a little brusquely. "Please, accept this small token of my esteem."

Elizabeth took the box he urged upon her with only slightly trembling fingers. Opening it, she saw it was a lovely golden cross, inlaid with red garnets, obviously old and quite valuable. She lifted it out of its case.

"It was my mother's, a wedding gift from my father. He gave it to me after she died, for my future wife," he said gruffly, when she was silent.

"I thought at first it was much older. 'Tis so beautiful," she almost whispered.

"Perhaps it is too old-fashioned for you. You need not wear it if you do not care for it," he said, reaching for it.

She clutched it to her, refusing to give it up. "Please. It is a gift fit for–for a queen! Will you fasten it? I love it, and you will have no luck repossessing it if you have changed your mind," she said, standing and smiling widely.

Her smile undid him, the most brilliant she had ever bestowed. He placed the heavy gold chain around her neck, clasping it at her nape, wishing he could explain that it was not an imitation of a centuries-old style, but an actual relic. Likewise, he wished he could seal the gift with a kiss, but knew he dared not. He contented himself with the briefest of touches, watching the flesh pebble underneath his hands.

She truly was the most beautiful female he had ever seen. Denying himself a closer connexion hurt with physical pain, but it was imperative he keep his feelings under the strictest regulation.

It had been almost impossible to feed from those women in London because they did not smell or look like Elizabeth. He had no idea whether the bonding had conquered his hearing because they had been tranced too deeply to speak—had he done that on purpose? If his sense of taste altered to accept only her essences, he could not imagine how difficult staying alive would become. But if she owned his sense of touch as well—if he could not feed unless the woman *felt* like her—then he was doomed until the day she died.

Elizabeth saw the moment his mood changed, when the softness in his eyes hardened. Though he did not walk away, he may as well have. His eyes, those changeable eyes, went from green of spring to the leaden grey of stormy skies.

Why? she thought. *He sought me, not the reverse. It is as though the thought of touching me is difficult for him. Why make me his wife?* She remembered his fleeting kiss on her cheek on the day of their betrothal; her skin burned at the spot.

Her mother's words—*'Ridiculous, sentimental girl'*—echoed through her mind.

"Thank you for the gift," she said, forcing a smile. "I shall cherish it. If you will excuse me, I shall send an express to my uncle now." Curtseying, she left him alone; his eyes, now the black of coal, followed her departure.

The roads were good this near Cheapside, and Elizabeth was pleased to see the colour returning to Jane's cheeks. Carriage travel—even in one so well sprung as Mr Darcy's—did not agree with her. She cast a surreptitious glance at her husband. Husband! Astonishing that the word referred to the large, elegant gentleman whose shoulder width appeared to take up the whole of the upholstered bench he sat upon. He stared out the window, seemingly at nothing. He had said very little this entire journey, and at the outset, she felt grateful for Jane's presence. But now she wondered if being so near her sister within the close confines of the carriage was difficult for him. She was accustomed to thinking of Jane as stoic, almost—but to him, no doubt her feelings of disappointment and regret were insidious. Even she could feel them sometimes, usually at night when they both pretended sleep.

Still, she was glad they had this journey together; they had been such good companions to each other for so long. Jane had always been able to distract their mother from the worst of her criticism, especially of Elizabeth. She felt a surge of love and affection for Jane's goodness, and a wave of anger at Mr Bingley for abusing her sister's hopes. *She was too good for him,* Lizzy thought, even as the carriage came to a halt.

Mr Darcy handed Jane down from the vehicle just as her aunt emerged from the house. She flew to Mrs Gardiner as Elizabeth gave her hand to her husband. He leaned down to murmur in her ear, "You are upset. What distresses you, Mrs Darcy?"

The surprise of hearing her new appellation nearly made her forget the question, but then she narrowed her eyes suspiciously. "You cannot—"

"I could see your chin rising and this little wrinkle appear in your forehead," he smiled, touching his index finger to the aforementioned crease.

There was no time to answer him, though, as Jane and Mrs Gardiner joined them. Elizabeth performed the introductions, and they entered the house to find her aunt had laid out a lovely tea for them. While informal, Mrs Gardiner managed to convey a celebratory mood with the variety and quantity of dishes. Shortly thereafter Mr Gardiner returned home early from his warehouses and together they were a surprisingly merry company. Mr Darcy contrived to show her aunt and uncle every civility, and their lengthy visit only ended with promises to return when next they came to London. Although their goodbyes were tearful, Elizabeth noted a marked improvement in Jane's spirits.

❧

Alone with Elizabeth in the carriage, Darcy gazed moodily out the window. He had extended himself with unusual effort to his wife's relations in a bid to win her approval; as things stood, he wished he could determine the success of his efforts with a bit more accuracy. His attempts to gauge her frame of mind since they signed the registry this morning had met with very little success. The journey from Hertfordshire to London with the broken-hearted Jane might have been torturous except that nearly the whole of his attention was fixed upon his wife. He had catalogued her every smile and frown, trying to tally which prevailed. Towards the end of the journey, he had been almost positive she was growing upset, and could not determine whether the pending separation from Jane or the coming night with him was more to blame.

He wanted her. Deeply. Every smile was a fist to his gut, her every touch a prelude to an ache of desire. Elizabeth *expected* to be a wife, and he did not know how to tell her it could not be, or what reasons he might give that would not hurt her. The urge to cherish and adore her was from the deepest and best part of his primal heart.

At least Mr and Mrs Gardiner's fears on her behalf had eased. Now if only he could erase his own.

❧

Elizabeth floated to the surface of wakefulness slowly, trying to recall where she was. Unfamiliar comfort surrounded her; the softness of the sheets felt strange beneath her fingers. Vaguely she remembered her arrival at a grandiose mansion, an attentive maid, lying down on a bed with at least four mattresses. Opening her eyes to candlelight, she finally remembered where she was. *Who* she was. With dismay, she realised she must have slept for hours.

"Elizabeth," a low voice whispered.

She startled, hastily sitting up.

Mr Darcy stood beside the bed. "I am sorry. I did not mean to alarm you. I feared you might sleep the night through without eating your dinner. I have been debating whether to wake you." He pointed to the covered trays on the low table near the fireplace.

She gauged how she might nonchalantly don more clothing, then decided it mattered little. Her undressing gown was perfectly modest, covering her from neck to ankle, her bare toes hardly a siren's lure.

"I apologise for sleeping so long," she said, casting the covers aside and approaching the table. "I only meant to rest for a bit. The bed is exceedingly comfortable." Glancing back at it, she blushed. It doubtlessly figured in his plans for the evening.

"I am glad you were able to rest. Please, come and eat. I was unsure of your preferences, but hopefully something appeals." He determinedly began uncovering dishes and watching as she filled her plate.

Elizabeth caught a fleeting but intense expression upon his face. Suddenly, without needing any of her husband's peculiar gifts, she knew he had been thinking of her in that bed. She had been hungry, but now that particular piece of furniture seemed to cast a very large shadow. Unbidden, her mother's brief education on wedding night duties filled her head. *It only hurts the once*, she reminded herself sternly. But her appetite failed her, and the small bite of roll in her mouth turned to dust.

He noticed, of course. "Elizabeth, please eat. Nothing will happen tonight."

She met his gaze. "You do not, um, wish it?"

"I will always want you," he replied matter-of-factly. "There is no need for hurry. We barely know each other."

"I wish to honour all my obligations."

"Nonetheless, this obligation can wait," he replied firmly.

Elizabeth did not know what to make of his refusal to proceed. It would be better, she believed, to have it over with, but she was not precisely unhappy to put it off. As she ate, she watched him out of the corner of her eye. He did not touch the food, but only observed her.

"Will you not eat?" she asked finally.

"I ate earlier, thank you," he responded, pushing forward a selection of cheeses.

"Truly, I cannot eat another bite, Mr Darcy."

"Please, Elizabeth...I am Fitzwilliam."

Her eyes opened wider. "Fitzwilliam," she repeated softly. Shyly.

Suddenly, he stood before her, his hand out. Before she could think, she took it, allowing him to pull her upright so she was standing before him. Candle and firelight lit the room, but shadows surrounded them, enclosing them together in an intimacy she had never before experienced. His eyes, his beautiful eyes, had darkened again, and she was conscious of the thinness of her gown, the very little separating them. Struck dumb, some primitive instinct insisted she flee, and yet a deeper one promised a much greater reward if she held very, very still. His big hand reached out, touching her cheek, brushing the pads of his fingers across her face in a gesture both tender and affectionate. Grasping her courage, she brought her hand up to touch his where it lay against her cheekbone. Turning her face slightly, eyes closed, she pressed a kiss into his palm.

"Elizabeth," he breathed, her name a hoarse whisper.

She felt a slight drift of air as he spoke and opened her eyes—only to find him gone as though he had never been.

Eleven

The next morning at breakfast, Elizabeth was determined to be cheerful despite her confusion over the previous evening. Evidently, her husband had not made the same resolve. He sat across from her at the table—elegant as a king, newspaper in hand, an untouched cup of tea steaming in front of him—with a cross expression on his handsome face. She looked down at her own dress with some chagrin; someone might take her for an upper servant in such a grand household as his—the signs of a remade gown were obvious to her experienced eyes, and probably to the housekeeper's as well. A little sigh escaped.

"What is the matter, Elizabeth?" Darcy asked, his tone curt.

She bristled. "Nothing at all, sir."

"I asked you to call me by my given name."

"I beg your pardon, *sir*," she replied, matching his tone of annoyance. His eyes flared dangerously, and immediately she regretted her rash impertinence, having known of a few husbands in Meryton who backhanded their wives for less. "I-I mean Fitzwilliam," she stuttered.

To her surprise, he smiled. "No, you did not," he corrected. "I beg pardon. I am not at my best in the mornings. I perceive your distress, but I find having no clues as to the cause is extremely annoying."

She returned his smile, relieved. "Distress is far too strong a word. 'Tis nothing at all. When shall we depart?"

"It *was* something. Please, Elizabeth. *I* shall be distressed if you withhold information affecting your well-being."

"Well-being? No! I hardly dare say it aloud, for when you hear it you will think me silly. I only dislike my dress. There. See? Nothing distressing in the slightest."

Instead of responding, he only looked at her intently, then perused her gown. She felt suddenly self-conscious, chagrined at having brought its shabbiness to his attention. Like many men, he had probably noticed nothing.

"We shall not be leaving today," he said suddenly. "I have remembered some business that should be attended to before we go, as I do not expect to return to town for some months."

"Oh," she said, surprised. He had seemed so anxious to be gone.

"While I tend to my affairs, you will visit the modiste."

"Oh, Mr Dar...Fitzwilliam, no, please. I would not wish you to delay our journey on my account. Please, do not."

"I assure you, the delay is nothing. I truly do have business here. It occurs to me that 'twould be much easier to procure your wardrobe here in town, as the village nearest Pemberley has little in the way of seamstresses to recommend it. We shall order the dresses and have them sent on when they are ready."

Elizabeth studied his countenance, trying to determine whether he told the truth. His expression remained implacable, and she sensed he would not change his mind regardless of further protests on her part.

"I...I thank you then. You are very kind."

He took her hand in his, across the table. "'Tis not kindness. You are my wife. You should be clothed as befits your new status."

She looked at their joined hands. "I can be clothed at any time. We need not delay."

"I want to do this for you, Elizabeth. As for myself, I shall take great pleasure in seeing you beautifully gowned." He squeezed her hand before leaving her to her solitary breakfast.

Elizabeth grew certain the delay was indeed due to his sudden decision to have her wardrobe ordered in London when he joined her on the carriage ride to the dressmaker.

"Your business is complete, then?" she asked smilingly.

He shrugged. "My business is never complete. I indulge myself."

"I believe you indulge me, sir. Or do you worry my country taste might not reflect well on the House of Darcy?" she teased.

His eyes heavy-lidded, he stared at her so intently that she looked away. After some moments, he only said, "I decided I deserve some say in the matter of clothing styles and fabrics."

Head bent, she muttered, "I would not have taken advantage of your generosity."

"I did not believe you would," he replied seriously. "Rather, I am sure you would spend too little."

As he handed her down from the carriage, she said, "Is this usual? For a husband to accompany his wife to the dressmaker?"

He smiled. "Perhaps not his wife."

"His mistress, then?" she asked daringly. She knew next to nothing about high society, but the gossips of Meryton had not left her completely ignorant.

"I would not know," he replied, his voice gentle. "For I have never accompanied either." He bent to whisper in her ear. "There is no one else, Elizabeth."

She blushed, but kept her spine straight. It would be foolish to assume too much. For a man with no other female, he was plainly not overcome by passion for her. Further, while he claimed he could not tell her thoughts, his guesses were painfully accurate.

Despite his assurances, they were greeted with all the fanfare of visiting royalty. She soon realised she could not even glance admiringly at a fabric without her husband ordering her a dress made of it. It would have been flattering had he not overridden her decisions constantly.

Her preferences were simpler, while he had much more extravagant tastes. By the time the fashionable dressmaker presented ball gown plates, Madam Dubois quit pretending to even ask her opinion. Finally, Elizabeth had enough.

"Perhaps I might take my leave, and let you two finish deciding?" she remarked pointedly, interrupting a debate on trims between the pair. Her husband smoothly extracted them from the shop, smiling apologetically at her and offering his arm as they stepped outside. She took it but would not look at him. Elizabeth understood her ignorance in the world of *ton* fashion, and it was his money, which gave him some right to interfere; she only wished he had not made her feel so small in the process.

"Darcy!" a voice called.

They both turned as an elegant, well-dressed man hurried their way. He was pale as though he had not ever seen the sun, and haggard as though he had not slept in years. The introduction surprised her. An earl! The Darcys moved in high circles, indeed.

The two men greeted each other amiably. "I am pleased I found you, Darcy," the earl was saying. "I have been to your home, hoping to meet before you leave town. Will you come to dinner tomorrow evening?"

Darcy frowned. "Mrs Darcy and I were planning to be on our way tomorrow," he replied. "Perhaps, my lord, we could induce you to come to dinner tonight?"

Elizabeth's eyes widened at this conversation. So, she must entertain an earl tonight! She supposed she ought to feel flattered such a one sought out her husband, instead of annoyed that this illustrious fellow would intrude upon her extremely brief 'wedding trip'. A simple overnight stay in London was all the time Mr Darcy could spare for her—which spoke volumes on her importance to him. When the earl agreed to her husband's invitation, she wondered what was wrong with her, that she should resent the honour of this peer's presence at their table to the point of instant dislike. One moment, she had been irked by her husband's high-handed interference in her clothing choices, and now she was bothered by his inattention!

Fickle woman, thy name is Elizabeth, she thought, equal parts chagrin and annoyance.

Several silent minutes later, ensconced in the carriage once more, Mr Darcy spoke. "You need not be concerned, Elizabeth. Mrs Ashford will take the meal in hand. I will inform her myself. No one would expect entertaining of you."

Immediately she was embarrassed; in sulking about this little interruption, she had ignored what ought to have been her duty. And she *knew* she was sulking, which only further irked her. It made her rather too bold. "You mean to frighten me, Mr Darcy, by reminding me of our guest's consequence and my own inexperience? Although the Bennets have never dined with earls, there is a stubbornness about me that never can bear to be frightened at the will of others. My courage rises with every attempt to intimidate."

Her husband's brows drew together, his expression so forbidding she marvelled at her own impertinence—as well as wondering what he might consider appropriate discipline for a disrespectful wife.

"Elizabeth, you cannot think I *mean* for you to be anxious. Nothing could be further from the truth. And I asked you to call me 'Fitzwilliam,'" he reproached.

Perhaps she had not sounded as imperturbable as she had hoped. "I apologise, Fitzwilliam," she said in a slightly more subdued tone.

Darcy moved across the carriage to his wife, taking her hand in his with a shudder of pleasure at the touch. "Do not be sorry, and do not be annoyed with me, darling. The earl has been a family friend for many years. I would not have invited him had he not pressed for a meeting. He is not in the habit of putting himself out, as you might imagine."

"Undoubtedly. I know you are an important man with many duties. Please do not feel you must accommodate my silly disappointment."

"Disappointment?" he asked, feathering a touch across the tinge of pink on her cheeks, wishing with all his heart that he could press a kiss to the rosy surface.

"I thought we would dine alone together this evening," she whispered, as if she confessed a shameful offence.

There were several women of the *ton* who had pursued him specifically in order to wrangle an invitation from the elusive Matlock. Even more who would have tolerated his company solely for the privilege of spending his fortune on wardrobes and jewels. His wife, it seemed, cared naught for either—only wanting his time. His attention. Never had he wished more to close the carriage shades, close out the world—even if only to kiss. He could not; indeed, he could hardly bear her nearness. With a sense of impotent fury, he knew he must put a bit of distance between them—and quickly—or his secrets would be revealed.

"'Tis as well he joins us tonight, else we might have had to host his entire entourage at Pemberley," he said lamely, moving back to his own seat.

"Yes, Fitzwilliam," Elizabeth responded, her tone dutiful. Her eyes were sad, and he raged inwardly at fate's gift of the one female he could never, ever have.

Why the devil was Catherine concerned about a dull, insignificant mouse like Elizabeth Bennet? Matlock asked himself for the fortieth time that evening. He had put himself out to charm her, but the new Mrs Darcy did not possess enough crumbs of personality to respond.

Of course, Catherine had been exceptionally lacking in lucidity when he had hastened to Kent to discover her latest scheme. Though they were nominal enemies on many issues, *she* believed they shared a common goal: the overthrow of House Darcy. Encouraging her to speak was not difficult—the difficulty was in stopping her. Catherine's absurd determination to gain control of Fitzwilliam by manoeuvring him into a marriage with Anne was doomed to failure. Unlike alliances with the ephemeral humans, vampyric marriages could last eons. Who would want to be thus encumbered? Anne had one dowry—an inheritance of political power, which meant nothing to Darcy. Catherine would never have her way in this, but one could not tell her anything. Not, of course, that he tried.

It went beyond matters of survival. House Darcy was formidable, with lands bordering on his own. Catherine, understanding this, believed Matlock would support her every tactical move to overpower them. But here she underestimated him.

Once, long ago, rendering young Fitzwilliam unconscious by trickery, he had Taken the Darcy blood.

The effects were immediate. He was stronger, faster, more powerful. His despised daylight weakness, if not eliminated, was reduced to inconsequence. Drinking from a Darcy regularly, ingesting that brutally strong blood, would permanently improve his already immense powers, allowing him to take a more active part in the government of mortals, increasing his influence in the vampyric one. Alas, the solution was simple—but obtaining it was not. George had been too devilish strong; had he attempted making a blood slave of Fitzwilliam, he would have earned an enemy he could not defeat. And now the lad was stronger than his father had ever been.

Surrendering the idea, however, was unthinkable.

As a Created vampyre, Matlock had risen high in this darker, more violent world, dedicating his life to searching for and finding means to increase the strength and numbers of his House—in such ways as would draw no notice—and then ensuring the loyalty of those he Mastered. Many would call it enough. It was not. Had he been blood-born—with his charisma, ambition, and personal gifts—his line would be as great or greater than the Medicis, the Darcys, the Romanovs, the Drăculeas, the de Bourghs. As things stood, however, no matter his achievements, despite his Council seat, he was considered inferior. It was infuriatingly unacceptable.

After all, the earl had not gone to all the trouble of arranging his best friend's murder, only to lie down and accept disrespect.

For all the strengths of the blood-born, they had monumental weaknesses, manifest in their pride and distrust. There were too few. They were frightened of each other and even of their own lines, wary that the next Born vampyre would be strong enough or cunning enough to displace them. Births were few and far between, mated pairs even fewer.

He had been patient with George, waiting for him to move past his foolish, lovelorn refusal to mate again after Anne's death. Matlock required a wife, and it *must* be a Darcy. George—with his proven ability to procreate—had been his best prospect. If George had a female child, he was bound to approve a betrothal to his dearest friend. With a prescience de Bourgh could never attain, he also nurtured Fitzwilliam, helping the boy overcome his aversion to feeding regularly and acting as his mentor. Strengthening him for Matlock's own, wiser purposes.

The senior Darcy refused to recover his wits. George would never be useful again, unnaturally swearing off females for aught except feeding. When Matlock was certain Fitzwilliam would be agreeable to a connexion should he ever produce a female child, George became expendable. Fitzwilliam's reluctance to carry out his duty to his line—*ergo,* producing offspring—until his father's death made duty clear, meant George was doomed. The murder, truly, was George's own fault, and his son's.

Fortunately, he had nurtured a connexion with George Darcy's greatest weakness, as well as his strength.

Darcy's dislike of the political arena enabled Matlock to charm his seat from him. Now, if only he could charm a daughter out of him as well, the death of his oldest friend would not have been in vain.

The thought of owning a wife with that sort of blood-strength made him salivate. Quickly, he tamped down the rampant emotion, directing all his attention to the delicious dinner, obscuring those feelings before Fitzwilliam could take note of them.

Fortunately for him, his host seemed distracted. Matlock's mind raced ahead of the banal dinner conversation, fixing his attention instead upon his host and hostess. Darcy had proclaimed it to be a white marriage, but Matlock hoped that merely an excuse. Nevertheless, the truth was as plain as the female. How could such a dowdy creature command affection from a male as virile as Fitzwilliam Darcy? By Jove, she was tall as a tree—towering over Matlock's own elegant frame—and only a few inches shorter than Darcy himself. Elizabeth Bennet Darcy could never ignite a man's passion; she was a mouse in the body of a giraffe.

"So, Mrs Darcy," he smiled, putting himself out again. "It was quite the happy surprise to hear of Fitzwilliam's nuptials, but now I meet you, I can see why he was captivated. You hail from Hertfordshire, I hear?"

The mouse nodded, keeping her eyes downcast. "Yes, my lord."

He gamely suppressed annoyance at her brevity, working to draw her out. "Do you play and sing, Mrs Darcy?"

"A little," she murmured.

"Oh! Some time or other I should be happy to hear you. Do you draw?"

"No, not at all."

"Your mother did not take you to town every spring for the benefit of masters? How strange."

"Mrs Darcy's father does not care for London, and with five daughters to bring out, one can hardly blame him for it," Darcy interrupted, looking annoyed.

Matlock immediately retreated from interrogation, revisiting his charm upon Darcy. But he observed the insignificant female with gloating interest. *Five daughters*. Elizabeth Bennet was one of *five daughters*. A lineage prone to daughters was *perfect*. Instead of killing her immediately, he must push them together.

Trapping a lion, with a mouse.

Twelve

Elizabeth felt one emotion when the gentlemen excused themselves for port and cigars or whatever manly thing men did in the privacy of a study. *Relief*. Let Fitzwilliam make excuses for her, if ever they emerged. Regardless of whatever else propriety demanded, she hastened to the sanctuary of her dressing room. Maggie, her conscientious lady's maid, appeared immediately but was sent to bed. Elizabeth could manage by herself and wanted no witnesses if she could not halt the tears burning behind her eyes.

A different earl had appeared at their door than the tired, almost inconsequential peer they encountered on the street near the dressmaker's establishment. The Earl of Matlock was obviously rejuvenated, emanating the power of a man accustomed to obeisance. He had taken one look at her and she practically *felt* his instant dismissal. Though he had been flattering enough, to her, his words sounded as insincere as Lydia's silly flirtations.

And Fitzwilliam! In *his* place was the austere, arrogant gentleman from Netherfield, only looking at her, it seemed, to find fault. Truly though, this was nothing new—each of her tentative efforts to express affection since their wedding had been rejected. Obviously, he regretted his hasty marriage. Gazing at herself in the looking glass, it was easy to understand why.

She had worn her wedding dress again, as it was her nicest gown, but after spending the day amongst fabrics and patterns of the finest quality, she saw plainly the dress was shabby. And her hair! Maggie did her best, but strands escaped regardless, giving her the hoydenish appearance that annoyed her mother so.

It was not, however, simply a matter of wardrobe. All her life, she had towered over those around her. Peering back at her from the glass now was a great gallump of a girl, the very opposite of feminine beauty. She tried hunching her shoulders, studying the effect in the mirror. Did hunching disguise her unwomanly height? Could the dressmaker do something with the fashions to minimise her stature?

Perhaps she could slightly bend her knees, though it would take practice to learn to walk without appearing completely awkward and ridiculous. Not to mention, it was difficult. Still, she should try...

"What are you doing?" Fitzwilliam asked curiously, startling her into a shriek.

"You frightened me!" she said, turning, red-faced, away from the looking glass. "I do not know how you manage to walk about so noiselessly on creaky floors."

"I will be sure to tread heavily," he replied. "What were you doing? Practicing a curtsey?"

Her blush deepened. "Has the earl gone?" she asked, hoping he could be distracted.

"Yes." He frowned briefly before resuming his intense study of her.

Elizabeth felt the weight of his stare. When he pinned her with that particular look, she could not think straight. He was so dazzlingly beautiful.

"I am too tall," she blurted out, his scrutiny rendering her foolish.

His brows drew together. "Why do you think so?"

"I do not 'think' it, I *know*. Most men do not care for the sensation of looking 'up' at their dance partner."

Suddenly he stood before her, so close she could smell the scent of his soap and that special, unusual hint of cacao. His hand cupped her chin, forcing her to look at him. "I do not need to look up to dance with you."

She remembered with sudden clarity what it had felt like to partner with him, not needing to alter her steps to match a shorter stride, nor worry he would not be there to meet her whenever she whirled away. He was the first man she had ever been able to look up to, perhaps in more ways than one. His kindness to her and her sister, his generosity—all were easy to see.

"It was frustrating for Mama," she tried to explain, giving a little laugh to show she did not take herself too seriously. "She wanted me to sit, not stand about like an ostrich, towering over the gentlemen."

"Then hear my voice now, Elizabeth Darcy," he said, his voice serious. "Hear me when I say I find you in all ways extraordinary, including your beauty."

Elizabeth sighed, disbelieving but determined. He had shown himself to be a friend; even if that was all he wished for, honesty would serve their marriage better than flattery. "I know I do not have the experience and upbringing your wife should have," she said. "I recognise I am from the country and know little of the latest styles. I did not mind your advice today at the dressmaker's, I promise. But I did not care for the way you talked over me and discounted my selections. I suppose I was already assured of my own insignificance, well before Lord Matlock arrived. You then proceeded to ignore me for the entire evening. Please forgive me if I do not feel particularly *extraordinary*."

Darcy opened his mouth as if to argue, then closed it again. "I apologise. I was carried away today, imagining you beautifully gowned, selfishly thinking of my own desires. I am afraid you married a beast rather than a gentleman, my love."

"I am sure, with a bit of practice, you can at least assume a veneer of civility," she said, smiling ruefully.

Reaching out, he traced the sensitive skin below her ear. "The veneer is very thin, my wife."

Elizabeth shivered. "I am not afraid of you," she made herself say, only to hear her voice quaver. He did not look precisely gentlemanly at this moment. And his eyes—his eyes were changing, changing colour from their normal green to an impossible storm grey. A trick of the firelight, no doubt.

"I am no Bingley. I am a different sort entirely." His light touch tightened into clenched hands at her shoulders in obvious warning, his expression brooding and dangerous. He suddenly seemed bigger, broader, taller, even menacing. "Elizabeth," he growled threateningly.

He believed she was a weakling; he avoided consummation of their marriage, whatever *that* ultimately entailed, because he thought she would be a feeble, shivering cow. Elizabeth stood her tallest. "I did not marry Bingley," she replied bravely. "You mean to frighten me? You cannot. I am your wife."

Darcy blinked, almost as if wakening, suddenly releasing his grip upon her shoulders. "I apologise, Mrs Darcy. I would never wish to alarm you." He backed away.

"What is the matter?" she asked now with concern. "Something has upset you. You are not yourself."

His voice held notes of forced unconcern. "Matlock brought word of some who are dismayed by my hasty marriage. There may be repercussions I would rather avoid. We must be off early tomorrow, so I will let you rest."

She stopped him with a hand upon his arm. "What do you mean, 'repercussions'? Your family?"

He hesitated. "Not family, no. It is...political in nature."

"I was not aware you were involved in politics."

"There is much about me you do not know."

"I am willing to learn," she returned, unwilling to be put off and pushed aside, as seemed his usual first response.

"All in good time. Go to sleep now."

He dismissed her, and she had no wiles with which to delay him. Unlike Lydia, who was born knowing how to keep gentlemen dancing to her tune, Elizabeth only knew how to say what she thought or keep her silence. The art of flirtation eluded her completely—the differences between her and the other girls in Meryton were vast, as her mother had so often bemoaned.

"I am not tired," she argued, though in truth she was exhausted. "Are you?"

Darcy raked a hand through his overlong hair in frustration. Could she not see he tried to protect her?

No, he thought, she would not see that. The girl who had been up here staring in the mirror, trying to make herself appear shorter, would only see rejection. She had misunderstood his distance tonight, and he had no words to make things better.

Calling upon self-discipline honed by time and massive effort, he forced himself to reach for his wife once more, but with different intent.

He simply held her—enjoying the way she fit him. How could she think of herself as inferior when he was so weak with need for her he could barely function? "I shall call Maggie to help you undress," he told her, but gently this time.

"I sent her to bed for the night," Elizabeth replied. "I can do it myself. With only one maid between five daughters, your wife is very self-sufficient."

He only looked at her, unwilling to explain that Maggie had no difficulty with late nights.

"Ready yourself for bed," he said instead. "I will return shortly." In a few quick strides, he disappeared behind the interconnecting door between their apartments.

When he returned, he found his wife wearing a simple undressing gown, just beginning to let down her hair. He covered her hand with his.

"No," he commanded, plucking at a pin. "I have longed to do this since the first moment I saw you."

Carefully he searched out the pins in her hair, freeing it strand by strand. He picked up the brush, delighting in the thickness of her tresses, having to part it with his fingers in order to get the bristles through it at all. It hung in a thick curtain to her waist, lovely, sensual. He felt her posture ease as he brushed, and the thrill of caring for her in this small, intimate way surged through him.

After Matlock's revelations, he had hastened the man's departure as quickly as possible—desperate to be near his wife and reassure himself of her safety. Her vulnerability brought out the beast in him just as her strength reined it in. The earl was certain Catherine would not be thwarted by his manoeuvres with Collins. She was obsessed with Elizabeth and likely to become worse when Collins returned with a different bride. Matlock felt Elizabeth's life was in danger.

Darcy must bring her to Pemberley, surround her with those he trusted. And it would take forever, with trunks and carriages and servants and lumbering along slowly with his retinue. As it was, he felt as though his bride was caught in an open field during battle—his every protective instinct rushed to the fore. When her hair was shining, he set the brush down. Elizabeth reached for it.

"I must braid it," she said, "or it will be a tangled mess in the morning."

"Leave it." He held out his hand to her.

A brief moment of uncertainty flashed across her features before she accepted. Something burned within him to realise she acceded his rights to far more than her hand with this gesture; it was permission to come to her. As he never could.

He extinguished the candles still burning as she climbed into bed; only the low fire cast its shadows as he undressed.

Clad only in shirt and pantaloons, he slid under the sheets where Elizabeth lay. He gathered her in close, wrapping himself around her protectively. When he had encompassed her almost completely, only then did he feel some relief; anything threatening her would have to go through him first. Flaws he had aplenty, but none of them had to do with his strength, determination, and ruthlessness when defending his own. He *would* protect her.

His wife was still and tense within his arms. Waiting. "Go to sleep, love," he said softly, pressing to her hair a kiss so gentle she would not feel it. It was a long while before her quiescent form and even breathing told him she slept.

He passed the long night by filling his lungs with her exhaled breaths, taking her into himself in the only way he could.

The lengthy ride to Pemberley gave Elizabeth ample time to grow accustomed to Fitzwilliam, but not nearly enough time to understand him. By the second night, she knew she had wed the most considerate husband in England. Possibly, if she would allow it, he would cut her food into small bites and spoon-feed her. As attentive as he was in certain ways, however, in others he ignored her completely. He would cosset and care for her, paying her every attention except the usual ones.

The ones of a wife. His care was kind, and nothing like she had been treated by Mama, and yet, it had the same effect. She felt insignificant somehow, as though she were a child, and her 'husband' played some sort of game. He had never even kissed her lips. She did not know what to do.

Their party more resembled a small army than a family trip to the home estate. He brought a phalanx of footmen, in addition to Maggie and his valet. They overran every inn and coaching yard, lumbering through the countryside at a snail's pace. It seemed plain to her that whatever 'repercussions' concerned him before he left London were ever present. Her own ideas for explanation had grown more fanciful. Currently she leant towards the theory her husband was a spy for the British government. Or, worse still, the French. There was definitely a sinister edge to him.

Although, just possibly, she read more novels than was wise.

"Your brow is furrowing again. What is the matter?" He leant over to touch her forehead.

"Oh...'tis nothing. When shall we arrive at Pemberley, do you think?"

"I hope you are not anxious about our homecoming. It is past time I took a wife, and you will be enthusiastically welcomed."

He felt she needed reassurance that his servants would accept their new mistress? "How large a household is it?"

"It varies," he said, "but generally about fifty at any given time. Many of them are day servants only, residing in and around Lambton, the nearest village."

Elizabeth's jaw dropped. "Fifty?" she squeaked. How in the world was she to manage fifty servants? In her wildest dreams, she never imagined so many. And what kind of a home would require such an army?

"It will be well, Elizabeth," he said soothingly. "Our housekeeper, Mrs Reynolds, is very competent and will assist you in every way. She has had the running of my home for many years."

"Right. Nothing to fret over." Except her husband required an army to travel, whilst the imposing Mrs Reynolds would take her for a giant, badly dressed scullery maid and one must not overlook, of course, that it would soon be no secret that her husband did not share her bed. She began to laugh and could just hear the edge of hysteria behind it.

He moved to sit next to her in the carriage; he was so large, he crowded her. "Please, Elizabeth," he said. "Be calm."

For some reason, this only unleashed anger to add to her fears. "Tell me something truly, Fitzwilliam. Why did you marry me?"

"I explained when I asked for your hand," he replied, caution entering his tone.

"Ah, yes. Because my feelings do not speak to yours," she said bitterly. "Sir, you have made a dreadful error in judgment. You ought to have listened to my mother—she would inform you that I speak all too often. The peace you seek is unlikely to be found with me."

"You appear to take enjoyment in trotting out your mother's foolish opinions. I have made my own evident! For you, I have sacrificed everyth—" He halted mid-word.

"What?" she asked sharply. "What sacrifice do you speak of?"

His jaw firmed. "It does not matter. I misspoke. I beg pardon."

He would say nothing more. As she came to her own conclusions, she went very still. *Well.* He might refuse to speak of it, but she would not allow him to hide from something plainly causing him dismay. "I am not stupid," she said quietly. "A man who has fifty servants does not marry a girl with almost no dowry."

"Such a man has no need of one," Darcy replied, equally calm.

"He does not marry a girl with such close connexions to trade, either," she continued. "He marries the daughter of a duke or the niece of a marquess. If she has a lesser dowry, she must compensate with connexions. In marrying me, you have failed your family, have you not?"

Elizabeth's conclusions were reasonable, he supposed; his own mother had been very proud of her royal ancestry. But even though her beliefs would have the effect of extricating him from a very sticky argument, he would not have her believe herself unworthy—or worse, believe *he* could think it.

"No. My obligations to my family have nothing to do with us. All the people for whom I care are at Pemberley, and I do not fail them by bringing you as their mistress."

Her expression made her doubt plain, of course, and he resorted, rather desperately, to the story he told her in the beginning.

"Nevertheless, we do not know each other well. I will not have you coming to me in gratitude, simply because I am a preferred groom over Mr Collins."

"Gratitude?" she asked. "I thought—"

"You thought I would accept the brave sacrifice of your person," he said coolly, "so you could tender the debt and mark it paid."

Elizabeth frowned. "I do not think of Collins, not ever. I apologise, sir. I should—"

"I am also sick to death of hearing apologies," he hissed, his patience exhausted. He reached for her, his beast needing her and failing to understand why it could not have her, dislodging her hat—just as Elizabeth stiffened and brought her hands to his chest, pushing at him.

He only just stopped himself, burying his face in her hair instead of kissing her, easing his grip into an embrace rather than an assault.

"I am sorry," he choked, utterly dismayed by his lapsed control.

"No...'tis only...we have slowed," she gasped.

Darcy cursed, then had to apologise again. They had indeed reached the last stop before Lambton, pulling into the yard of the White Hart. He could sense the heartbeats of three dozen, at least. Elizabeth scrambled away from him, frantically attempting to repair the damage he caused to her hair, finally shoving the hat back onto her head and stuffing the loose locks into it. She only barely managed to tie the thing before they came to a halt.

"How...how do I look?" she asked nervously.

He was in no condition to face anyone, but made himself look at her. Her eyes wide, several strands of her hair escaped the confines of the crookedly skewed bonnet. She looked like a woman who had been roughly tumbled in a carriage, and the only regret he could muster was that he hadn't been able to finish it. He had to get away. Quickly. The carriage door opened, and he heaved himself out.

"See that Mrs Darcy is given a private room in which to dine and refresh herself. I shall return shortly," he barked, striding away. He did not look back to see Elizabeth's confused embarrassment when he did not hand her down, abandoning her to the servants surrounding them.

❧

Thirty minutes later, her husband still had not joined her. At other inns, he had shared her repast, made conversation, and taken short walks with her to stretch her limbs. Though he disdained her company at the moment, she decided not to forego her little stroll. Leaving behind her nearly untouched meal, she left the room, marched down the stairs, and walked out the inn door.

Immediately, a footman—Andrew, she thought his name—paced himself behind her at a respectable distance. She expected it; Fitzwilliam had informed her that her days of wandering about alone were over. Living in a house of fifty—fifty!—servants, she expected she would soon become accustomed to constantly having people nearby. If she felt a pang of loss for the solitude, she told herself it was more than balanced by knowing she would always have a roof over her head.

Too much roof, she thought before she could stop herself. *Ungrateful chit!* she imagined her mother's scold. She walked faster through the wooded copse, as though she could ever outpace Mama's angry voice.

It is only my uncertainty with Fitzwilliam's moods causing this restlessness. Trying to ascertain what he was thinking, why he behaved as he did was bewildering. One moment, she could swear he felt something for her, if only the normal appreciation of a man for a woman with whom he was allowed certain liberties. The next, he was repulsed. Why, then, had he nearly kissed her in those moments before the carriage arrived at the White Hart? And why had he stopped himself?

Suddenly, the world tilted crazily, and she was unbalanced, falling. Before she could even understand what was happening, she felt herself being lifted bodily. Her scream was cut short by a strong hand slapped over her mouth. Her assailant began to run *impossibly* quickly—but even in the blur, slung over a man's shoulders like a sack of potatoes, she recognised the Darcy footman lying on the forest floor, blood a spreading stain across his powdered wig.

After walking off the worst of his frustration, Darcy returned to the White Hart prepared to offer an apology to his wife. It only took him seconds to realise she was not there—though her scent lingered on the unseasonably warm day.

"Where is Mrs Darcy?" he asked James, one of the corps of loyal footmen escorting their party.

"She is walking, sir. Andrew accompanied her," the young man replied.

Darcy nodded sharply, but knew that until he had Elizabeth in sight, his anxiety would remain unappeased. Following her scent and Andrew's, he strode rapidly towards the wooded path they had taken. Suddenly, he heard a horrifying noise: Elizabeth's scream, extinguished almost before the sound left her throat. The smell of fresh blood permeated his nostrils.

He began to run, more swiftly than ever before, all of his senses fixing upon his wife. At last, her scent became stronger—he was gaining on her abductor. Though obviously it was a vampyre of extraordinary daylight strength, he was not as fast as Darcy—and doubtless somewhat slowed by Elizabeth's struggling weight.

Darcy crested a hill, only increasing his speed up the incline. He was so close he could feel the echoes of her abductor's sudden fear of capture. And then they were directly before him. Abruptly, the creature wheeled, hurling Elizabeth directly at Darcy with all of his considerable strength.

Her scream hardly had time to swell before he caught her in his arms, her eyes huge, and she clapped her own hand over her mouth as if preventing shrieks that tried breaking free.

"Shh," he murmured. "Shh. All will be well, my love." He cradled her gently, sliding his hands across her body, checking for injury. "Oh, love. Oh, my precious love."

The first sobs escaped her control. Darcy held her more tightly, looking in the direction of the escaping vampyre. He was a tiny pinprick on the horizon now, fleeing with all speed. While Darcy longed to go after him, to rip his head from his body and his heart from his chest, the deep shudders of his wife's frame told him she was completely undone. It would likely be a long while before he would be able to bear letting her out of his sight. Suddenly, she pulled away from him, losing the contents of her stomach onto the hard earth.

"You are dead," Darcy vowed quietly. He did not mean the creature who attempted kidnapping his wife; that beast had been doomed since the day of its Turning. But Darcy had seen its creator in its mad eyes and in the familiar scent of its maker, and he swore vengeance. Again.

He carried her. She did not know how long he had been walking—an hour, perhaps?—showing no signs of tiring. It was growing chilly in the late November afternoon, but the sun still shone weakly. Just how far had they run?

She closed her eyes again. Her belly was sore from being pounded relentlessly against her kidnapper's unyielding shoulder. The fastening of her bonnet—one she despised—cut into the sensitive skin of her throat, and the pins anchoring her hair beneath it dug against her skull. She was thirsty and tired and over-full of questions.

"How could we have run so fast?" she asked aloud, her voice scratchy.

Instead of answering, Fitzwilliam pointed to a spot just beyond them. "There is a stream up ahead. You may drink."

Elizabeth wrinkled her nose, distracted for the moment. While desperately thirsty, she also was very aware of the sour smell of her own bile. Fitzwilliam set her down in a shady spot next to a gurgling brook. She watched as he knelt, cupping his own hands in the running water and holding them out to her. It felt intimate and she could not look at him as she sipped from his hands. Leaning back against a tree, she unbuttoned her pelisse, drawing it off and sniffing it. Yes, this was definitely one source of the stink. She wadded up the fabric and threw it as far as she could. Fitzwilliam gave her a look.

"It smells," she said irritably. But she had not been brought up to be wasteful, and rose to fetch it. He stopped her with a touch.

"Leave it," he said. She resumed her seat, and looking up at the sky, almost succeeded in ignoring him.

Suddenly, an urge to be free of everything that seemed an obstacle to peace consumed her. On shaky limbs, she rose and headed for the stream, untying the limp bow at her neck to remove her bonnet. With a flick of her wrist, she sent it sailing into the water and watched as it floated merrily away. Today, she would be wasteful.

She spared him a glance. "It was mostly ruined," she explained. While she was being defiant, she reasoned that her coiffure was more wrecked than the hat and unpinned her heavy braid, releasing the pinch against her scalp. If she could, she thought, she would push her uncommunicative husband into the stream as well. Kneeling at the water's edge, she scooped enough to wash her arms, hands, and face. The droplets clung to her collarbone and beaded upon the wisps of hair escaping her braid.

Her choices were few. She could shriek, as her mother and younger sisters might. Or, like her father or Jane, she could pretend it had not happened. Neither action would lead her to the answers she sought. She was scared, perhaps not of Fitzwilliam, but scared nonetheless. No matter how she looked at her situation, it had surpassed 'odd' some miles back, and headed directly into 'wrong'.

Any other woman, Darcy supposed, would be swooning or hysterical. *His* woman had asked him precisely one question which he had not deigned to answer, and now watched him with speculation in her fine eyes.

Despite the miles they had run, they travelled in a north-northeast direction. He calculated they were by now no more than half an hour's walk from meeting the road. Would she think it strange if their party somehow managed to rendezvous with them there? He could communicate by thought with any in his direct bloodline and had been in contact since the abduction. Knowing his Elizabeth, she would indeed find it odd. He reached out to James, asking him to pretend to 'find' them.

Elizabeth joined him beneath the tree's shade. "Andrew," she said softly, as though it hurt to speak. "He was..."

Darcy covered her hand with his, hating that he was unable to inform her of Andrew's quick recovery. While the footman was taken by surprise by the vampyre who snatched her, the villain had not taken time to completely disable him—vampyres were devilish hard to kill. In fact, Andrew had been in his head apologising for losing Mrs Darcy, his remorse a tangible presence that, more than anything else, told him how near his people were. If only emotions were like their mental speech; he could—and had—told Andrew to stuff it, that his apologies were unnecessary, and to stay out of sight of Mrs Darcy until such time as they could present him as healed. The other vampyre complied immediately—but still, his guilt leaked through to join with Darcy's own, much greater burden.

My fault. He had left his wife alone, with inadequate orders for her protection. *Careless, inconsiderate churl.* She was so fragile; that monster could have snapped her neck without even trying. Thinking of it made him crazed; he wanted to kill something. He wanted to hold on to her and keep her safe within his arms forever.

Elizabeth stared at their joined hands. "Do you know who that man was?"

One of Wickham's misbegotten, he knew. Most likely, the creature would be dead before Darcy could track him. To Elizabeth, he only gave a brief shake of his head. "I have never seen him before."

"Those 'repercussions' you mentioned...was this a part of it?"

His expression grew agonised. "I do not know. But I will learn."

"Are you a spy?"

"What?" he asked incredulously.

"I cannot conceive likely reasons for such an unbelievable act."

He abhorred deceit, hated having to mislead her. "I am a very wealthy man, Elizabeth. I have enemies."

"But why take me? It makes no sense."

He cupped her face in his hands; this part, at least, was no lie. "It makes all the sense in the world. You are everything. *Quod me nutrit me destruit.* What nourishes me also destroys me."

Elizabeth could not understand. One moment, he made the ardent declarations of a man madly in love; the next, he repelled her. But his eyes were changing colours, as they did when he was agitated. And she acknowledged, consciously at last, that the man she had married was peculiar. She had little experience of the world, and almost none with men; he had warned her of his affliction regarding the emotions of others, which was unusual enough. But her abductor had lifted her as if she were nothing and run faster than any horse—and her husband's speed exceeded his. The villain flung her at Fitzwilliam as if he launched her from a trebuchet, from such a distance as to make the wind whistle in her ears; Fitzwilliam caught her as easily as if she were a feather pillow.

She thought of the times he seemed to clear a room or sway others to his thinking with a look. She had seen him do it, yet never truly recognised what was happening. Because it was impossible. But today, she could ignore the impossible no longer.

Fitzwilliam Darcy was not a normal man. There were others—the villain who attempted her abduction shared his peculiarities. However, she recognised one important difference: The abductor was evil. Beyond the obvious, he emanated some sort of malevolence, a wickedness frightening her worse than his strength and speed. And she could not quite say how she understood this, but she gazed into Fitzwilliam's eyes—pitch black now—and she knew he was good. She looked at him and she knew.

But he did not trust her.

All she had were more questions, and a tentative trust in a man who would not return it. She began to tremble.

"I would like to be held," she whispered, in a voice so small she supposed he would not hear.

Immediately, he clutched her to him in an iron grip, so tightly she could hardly breathe. "I will never let you go," he vowed. "I swear, Elizabeth, I will never let you go."

And she did not know if it was a threat, or a promise.

Their carriage charged into the drive of Pemberley as though the shades of the netherworld chased it. Elizabeth, who was by no means a horse-lover, had grown mightily concerned for the poor beasts an hour ago.

"I am afraid for the horses," she muttered.

"We are here," he answered, and she noted they had indeed slowed. They had been riding with the shades down, contributing to the queasy feeling in her stomach. Fitzwilliam gripped her chin. "I am proud of you, Mrs Darcy."

Her hair was wild, her dress ruined. "I look like I was caught in a brawl."

"You are beautiful...brave and beautiful. There are many witnesses to the abuses you endured on this journey. My people will be proud of you as well." He lifted her from his lap. At that moment, the door opened and she watched him gracefully exit the vehicle. Taking his hand, she did the same—but her legs were like jelly, and she would have crumpled had he not supported her weight on his strong arm.

When she had her feet securely under her, she glanced up. It was just dusk, and torches lit the drive. Pemberley itself blazed with light, fifty windows each hosting their own private conflagration. An army of servants, wigged and liveried, lined up along the magnificent stone steps fronting a galleried terrace. If the London house had been awe-inspiring, this was glorious. Her mouth dropped open.

Her husband had failed to warn her she would be living in a castle. Mighty stone walls surrounded its impressive façade. There were no words to describe the mixture of grandeur, elegance, and power of the palace that was to be her home. Four squared turrets guarded each corner of the edifice, rising into the sky. There was no sign of moat or drawbridge, but it was no less imposing for their absence.

He did not introduce her to any but the butler, Morton, and the housekeeper, Mrs Reynolds. "My wife has endured a severely trying day," he explained. "I will show her to her rooms. She will require water for a bath. Her girl's carriage is some ways back, so she will need assistance for tonight."

Mrs Reynolds smiled kindly at Elizabeth, expressing her delight that the Master brought home a bride at last. She was younger than one might expect in such a great house, but Morton was all severe gravity, with silver hair and a ducal appearance.

"I am pleased to meet you," Elizabeth managed.

"We will greet everyone tomorrow, after Mrs Darcy has had a chance to recover." Her husband took her arm and led her past the rows of servants while she worked at staying upright. Each of the twelve steps was an effort. Two footmen threw open the double-doors of the entry, and she found herself in a marbled foyer, twin chandeliers blazing.

"Our rooms are above," Darcy murmured, and she almost laughed. A wide curving, seemingly endless staircase faced her, looking like a mountain at the moment. She had barely tested a shaky leg on the first step, however, when she found herself once again scooped up within her husband's arms.

She gave him a quivering smile. "I believe I can do it myself, if you have but an hour or so."

He only smiled down upon her. "Bath, food, and bed. Tomorrow you may walk all you please."

Gratitude for his thoughtfulness swelled, and she wrapped her arms around his neck and curled her head beneath his chin. "I admit, at this moment, I do not mind," she sighed, too tired to do more than relish his strength.

❧

He entered her rooms after her bath, and Mrs Reynolds dashed away as though her hair was on fire. Fitzwilliam's eyes still reflected streaks of wicked blackness but all he did was pick up the brush and stroke it through her hair. She calmed; Fitzwilliam might be dangerous, but never to her. She was overcome by a sort of affectionate despair, a burgeoning appreciation mixed with all the resentment of being kept ignorant, of being treated as though she were a child. She contemplated snatching the brush away. But, as if reading her mind, he set it down and continued to toy with the strands, circling her scalp in a light massage. It felt too good to forfeit for mere righteous anger, and he continued until a light scratching at the door interrupted.

Servants entered with covered trays. She only recognised her hunger when the delicious smells reached her. Fitzwilliam assisted her in rising, moving her to the settee, serving her from a selection of cold meats and rolls, efficiently filling her plate.

After eating half of what he had given, she set the plate aside.

"You have not eaten nearly enough, Elizabeth."

"I could not possibly swallow another bite."

"Try."

Annoyance bloomed. "You are not my nursemaid, Fitzwilliam. If naught else, I believe I ought to be allowed to decide whether I am hungry or not."

She looked away from him, but he seated himself beside her, touching his hand to her chin so she was forced to look at him. Expecting a lecture, she was surprised when he simply stared.

"What are you doing?"

"This is your expression when you are severely annoyed with me," he said. "I need to learn it."

A startled laugh escaped her. "Oh, I have a feeling you shall be well acquainted with it. Jane would have made a far more agreeable wife."

"She is certainly of a calmer temperament," he agreed. "All smiles, our sister Jane."

Elizabeth's brow puckered. "You need not say it like that. She is such a good person—"

"I never wished to marry Jane."

"Why did you wish to marry me?" she implored. "The *whole* truth, if you please."

The truth! A truth that could never be unsaid. Was he selfish to withhold it, putting off her revulsion for another hour, another minute, another second? He had been reared in pain and conflict, tortured by it. His Elizabeth had suffered differently, but pain was pain; laughing at herself and just a little at others—enough to keep a small flame of youthful hope burning, while her mother taught her to think herself ugly. Her inherent vivaciousness only meant she hid her scars.

Brave still, she tried to be honest with him, telling him her feelings, sharing those wounds, when he stopped long enough to listen. Protecting her physically was not enough; she must be cherished as the gift she surely was. But could he bear to earn her enmity? *Not yet.*

"I know you must be confused," he said instead. "There are reasons why I cannot give the answers you seek, and why I cannot make you my wife fully. But you must know—you *have* to know—it tortures me to abstain. I want for us to be as close as two people can be. I want your scent crushed into my skin, your soul held within mine."

Her eyes widened again, and he could hear the delicate flutter of her racing heart. She opened her lovely mouth and then closed it again. He drew her closer, pulling her arms around him to embrace him more fully. Her mouth was very close to his ear when she whispered, "These reasons...may I ever know them?"

"I very much fear," he answered quietly, "that you will know all too soon."

Fourteen

Richard Fitzwilliam took one look at Darcy and muttered an oath. "What the devil happened to you?" he asked incredulously. The normally immaculate, introverted, bored aristocrat with slightly priggish tendencies had disappeared; in his place was this wild-eyed, dishevelled predator.

Darcy ran his hand through his untidy hair. "No time for Chamberlayne. Has everyone returned?"

"Safe and sound. They found the creature, lacking heart and head. Stinks of Wickham, naturally, but I have trouble believing he acts alone. If he has risen, as you believe, he *must* still be weak. That he was able to renew his deficient excuse for a House bespeaks powerful assistance."

"I drew the same conclusions. His benefactor might be anyone. But with de Bourgh's latest actions..." Darcy murmured.

Richard raised a brow. "It might be her, but do not forget the Romanov warnings of retribution for the loss of their slaves, nor Tsepesh's threats over the dissolution of their little import business."

"Those two know better than to conduct their illicit trades anywhere near my territories. I do not discount *any* of my enemies, but this seems more personal. De Bourgh appears likeliest. Her proven interest in Mrs Darcy preceded this action."

"Ah, yes. I should have offered my congratulations. I admit, I was astonished to receive news of your marriage. I am sorry to have missed your homecoming."

"Your expertise was needed in the search for Elizabeth's abductor," replied Darcy. "Regardless, it is better you meet her today. She was quite undone by the time we reached Pemberley. I fear in my haste to arrive before sunset, I pushed both horses and humans to their limits." He ran his hand through his unkempt hair once again. "The attack on Elizabeth might only be a first offensive. Any of our mortals could be vulnerable, if one of the Houses is making a territorial move and using Wickham to do it. I think we should call in those who are more than a day's ride away. Have them bring their families into the village. Our perimeters are too widespread and coverage too thin."

"You fear another attack?"

Darcy assumed his most professorial aspect as he thought aloud. "Elizabeth was snatched in the bright light of afternoon. As a House we are stronger than others of our race during the day, but as individuals, there are many who are too weak at full light to fight effectively, and almost all must sleep during some daylight hours. At night we are nearly invincible, but the strongest among us cannot be everywhere at once during the day and even we must sleep sometime. Pemberley is too vast. If this is a territorial war, we must summon from our other properties, but I hate to leave those less defended as a consequence. If instead we call in our free agents as reinforcements, word will leak out and draw Council involvement."

Richard nodded. No one who attacked Darcy would expect to remain unscathed. Neither would evidence that Darcy House had the power to raise an army be well received.

"Is it possible he did not know whom he kidnapped? She is human, and few know you wed."

"We know it was a Wickham creature. And perhaps Wickham is in bed with the Romanovs or others, so I will not overlook any possibilities. But de Bourgh has tried to acquire Elizabeth once already, through marriage to one of her people. Now, suddenly, a kidnap. No, I cannot believe in coincidence."

"But a Council member, Darcy? Surely de Bourgh would not risk her seat on the Council by consorting with a known fugitive."

"Somebody did. De Bourgh is my first suspect."

"I will find out what she knows of this. Tonight, I go to Kent."

Darcy cast him a glance. "Be careful, Richard. How you can trust anyone in de Bourgh's House, *especially* her, I will never understand."

Richard laughed. "Life is too uncertain to avoid risk. I find the rewards of communication ample enough to hazard the game. And speaking of games," he said, his eyes narrowed, "when did you last feed? I must say, marriage does not appear to be treating you well."

While Darcy was loath to discuss his personal life, Richard would have to be made aware—especially if his assistance was needed. They had always had different feeding habits, more an indication of their disparate personalities than a disagreement of philosophy. Darcy, exceedingly private by nature, preferred to keep his connexions within his own House platonic, feeding from human females—whose memories he could erase—and only when absolutely necessary. The gregarious, fun-loving Richard was quite the opposite. He too avoided innocents, but no one would ever make the mistake of taking Richard's romantic overtures seriously, while Darcy had been feeling—and avoiding—the hopeful intentions of his bloodline maidens for decades.

"I cannot feed from Elizabeth," he stated quietly.

Richard's brows rose in frank question. "There is much you have neglected to communicate, it seems."

"She is immune to thought erasure and illusion. I cannot ascertain what she feels unless she tells me—though I am improving at reading her facial expressions," he added.

Richard's jaw tightened. "I take it she is supremely unaware she has married a Master vampyre," he said.

Darcy nodded. He did not need to explain to Richard why he hesitated to tell his bride the truth.

"Are you sure she is truly immune? Perhaps it is an anomaly only applying to you."

"She is completely blocked to the London household, Nigel, Harry, James, Thomas, Andrew, Carter, Chamberlayne, Maggie, Mrs Reynolds, and Morton. Even Lord Matlock, whom we met in London, could get nothing. Their gifts are varied, of course, but nothing illusory or invasive has any effect. 'Tis especially frustrating for Maggie and Mrs Reynolds, as neither can anticipate her wishes."

Richard laughed. "That has to be a first for Reynolds. I can only imagine how she felt greeting Pemberley's new mistress without a clue as to her favourite meals. Still, except for Matlock, they are all of Darcy blood, and he is not full-blooded," he said, displaying typical vampyre dismissal of the Turned, though Richard himself was no blood-born. "We must test her resistance against someone very strong and yet wholly unrelated. And you need to feed, Darcy. As soon as possible, I should think."

"I fed less than ten days ago."

"How many miles did you run yesterday, at full speed in broad daylight? Believe me, 'tis obvious you require nourishment."

Darcy turned away. "It has become a bit...complicated."

"If you cannot feed from your wife, Take from Penelope or Mary. They are good girls who care for you, and now you are wed, they will not have expectations."

Darcy made a noise of disbelief. "Elizabeth is human. Why would they look upon her as any kind of hindrance to their hopes? In perhaps fifty short years, if I am lucky enough to get that many, Elizabeth will be gone and—" he stopped short, feeling an arrow of absolute misery at the thought of his wife's ephemeral existence.

"Never mind fifty years. You need to feed *today*."

"I am not sure I can. I seem to be well along the way to becoming fully bonded to Elizabeth. I was only able to feed in London by blocking most of my senses, and 'tis likely become worse since. I was hoping you might be able to help."

"Me? How so?" Richard exclaimed, plainly taken aback by this information.

Darcy turned back to face him. "If you were to render me unconscious, or very nearly so...perhaps the need for sustenance would overcome the visceral instincts of the bonding process."

"Surely you jest. You cannot feed unless I beat you to within an inch of your life? This is madness!"

"You are the only one powerful enough to do it, Richard. Trust me, if my senses are in good working order, feeding from anyone but Elizabeth may be impossible. And I have a strong feeling if I consummate the marriage, even this scheme will prove futile."

"Egads, man! You have spent the last six nights of married life without taking her? Is she so repulsive?"

Darcy's eyes went black. "No," he said shortly, and Richard laughed, plainly pleased with his goading.

"If she is such a treat, Turn her. No fifty-year worries, and she can hardly betray you if she is one of us."

"And risk she does not survive the Change? Not for worlds."

Richard frowned. "I have long wished that you might find happiness, Nephew. Knocking you senseless does not seem like the way to achieve it. When was the last time you slept?"

Darcy shrugged. "Shortly after I fed."

"Then it is essential you do so now. Take your rest, and then we will discuss feeding possibilities."

"I cannot. Elizabeth will wake soon, and I cannot leave her alone on her first day at Pemberley. I must—"

"Darcy!" Richard interrupted fiercely. "You are no good to your Elizabeth if you do not rejuvenate in some fashion. Since I categorically refuse to administer any blows until I am convinced there are no other means, you must at least make an attempt to help yourself. I will stay close today and keep watch. In the evening, after I am sure you are rested, we shall discuss your alternatives."

The stubborn set of Richard's jaw told Darcy that there was no use arguing. He sighed deeply. "I will agree to rest, but I wish to discuss this trip to Kent before you leave."

Richard nodded. "I would not depart before you awaken in any case," he assured. He watched his nephew head for the Pemberley cellars and could not prevent his own sigh. The boy was hiding once again.

Elizabeth woke slowly, stretching luxuriously against the feel of soft linen and warm wool. Even though she knew it to be unlikely, she reached a hand towards the pillow beside her, eyes still shut against reality. He was indeed gone; forcing away her disappointment, she opened her eyes.

The room she had barely noticed in her exhaustion of the previous evening was lovely. She lifted up on one arm; light filtered through warm draperies and gilded the elegant furnishings with soft radiance. As though she had been listening for her mistress's slightest movement, Maggie bustled into the room with a tray.

"What time is it?" she asked, swallowing a gasp when the maid replied that it was after the noon hour.

Elizabeth sipped the hot chocolate, but felt little interest in food. She wanted to dress immediately, anxious to find Fitzwilliam for the promised tour of Pemberley, sparing hardly a glance of disdain for the neat but slightly dingy day dress Maggie laid out. Still, she decided not to protest when the maid spent a little extra time on her hair and asked after Mr Darcy, only to hear he would not return before evening.

"But Colonel Fitzwilliam will be joining you for luncheon in less than an hour," Maggie said, as though this information would wholly compensate for any disappointment.

"Just who is Colonel Fitzwilliam?" she asked, a little embarrassed to admit she had never heard of the man.

To her surprise, the maid's cheeks briefly pinkened. "Oh, Madam, he is the Master's uncle."

Elizabeth frowned. "Perhaps I should wear my better dress," she said.

"Oh, the colonel isn't the type to judge a book by its cover. He won't look down his nose at your clothing," Maggie replied, unintentionally revealing her opinion of Elizabeth's wardrobe. "He is well-known for his charm with the ladies." Maggie's cheeks grew brighter pink.

Nevertheless, Elizabeth was no longer inclined to hurry, and the dress was changed. Finally, head held high, she followed Maggie down the confusing maze of passageways and stairs to the dining room.

Entering, she stopped short in surprise. Instead of the white-haired, severe, retired military man she expected, there was a gentleman in perhaps his fortieth year with a bold stare and rakish appearance. His sideburns slashed across his firm jaw; his hair was over-long, curly, and slightly unkempt, as though he had just come from a long ride on a fast horse. Deep dimples bracketed his mouth, causing Elizabeth to wonder if he smiled more often than his current expression indicated. He was the same height as herself. She struggled to appear poised.

With careless grace, he approached her. "Mrs Darcy, I hope you will forgive the informality if I introduce myself? Richard Fitzwilliam, at your service." He bowed low over her hand with old-fashioned courtesy.

"You must excuse my ignorance of your arrival, sir. I am sure my husband will be sorry he missed greeting you."

The man smiled a bit ruefully. "And I am sure he will not. I reside at Pemberley."

Elizabeth coloured. "Oh...I did not know," she said. "And as soon as I am speaking to Mr Darcy again, I will certainly take him to task for neglecting to tell me."

Richard smiled, a little more appreciatively. "I can see my nephew will need his wits about him to stay ahead of you."

"I would prefer he stay by my side, as staring at the back of his head seems rather dull." Elizabeth managed a small smile and gestured for them to sit. "You will forgive my surprise. When Maggie said Fitzwilliam's uncle joined me for lunch, I envisioned an older man."

He grinned impudently. "You can be excused for thinking it. I am his mother's much younger brother. However, I do have a few years on Fitzwilliam, and never hesitate to remind him of my vast store of experience and, of course, etiquette."

"Ah. Is there a Mrs Fitzwilliam who benefits from your good manners?" she enquired, her eyes dancing.

"Alas, the women bright enough to catch my eye are wise enough to refuse my suit."

Elizabeth laughed. "Maggie informed me of your military career. I should think you need only don your uniform to receive all the attention a man requires."

"Unfortunately, I sold my commission, and so must make do with whatever attention I can garner without the assistance of uniform. The officer's title follows me, but I am no longer active."

This pleasant repartee might have continued for some time but for the entrance of Mrs Reynolds, her serene countenance marred by an anxious frown as she looked from one to the other of them. Elizabeth guessed she had unpleasant news she was not eager to share with her new mistress. She could almost see the colonel's instant alertness, and understood why the appellation stuck, his military bearing and sense of command as much a part of him as his good looks.

"Is something amiss, Mrs Reynolds?" she asked.

The housekeeper glanced at the colonel, waiting for his small nod before replying. "'Tis the Hawkins family sending word. Young Sally has gone missing."

Richard stood at once. "I shall arrange a search party."

"I can help," Elizabeth said.

"I am sorry, Mrs Darcy. I would be most obliged if you would remain inside. Your husband requested I accompany you if you go out, after yesterday's troubling incident. And I am needed to direct the search."

"Oh," she said in a smaller voice. She listened to him give a few orders to Mrs Reynolds and heard his departing footsteps as he strode off in the direction of the stables.

"How old is the girl?" Elizabeth asked before Mrs Reynolds could return to her duties.

"Six years at her last birthday," the housekeeper replied.

"How long has she been missing?"

"Near as we can guess, just over an hour."

Elizabeth gave a little sigh of relief. "Not too long, then. She probably fell asleep and does not hear them calling. It happened to me once, when I was young."

"Very likely. That Sally is a minx, and prone to prowling. But these are troubling times, mistress. Very troubling times." Shaking her head, she left to carry out the colonel's instructions.

With nothing else to occupy her, Elizabeth wandered around the lower floor of the castle, trying to keep her bearings and making note of 'landmarks' so she would not get lost. Off the main entry, passageways branched in different directions, the sheer vastness guaranteeing there was nothing intuitive about the placement of the main rooms. Obviously, however, it was a lavish, exquisite palace—not a draughty, ancient keep—and required every one of those fifty servants to maintain it adequately. There were fires burning in several of the parlours, each ready to be occupied in an instant.

A little awestruck, she admired the view from an enormous plate-glass window cleverly built into the castle wall and facing a lovely prospect of the gardens spilling out from beyond the rise of their hillside perch. From this angle, the beds and tree-lined paths looked rather like a gaily embellished apron, flung out entrancingly to please the eye and invite the viewer to explore. Even in wintertime, without decorative blossoms, the variety and scope were enticing. A set of double doors led to a terrace; from it, the enchanting garden beckoned. Surely, she would be perfectly safe in their own garden? It looked to be securely walled.

Feeling a bit like an escaped prisoner, she scampered out the door and down the steps, ready to explore. There were fountains and foliage, the outermost borders edged by tall, slim trees pointing upwards like giant green flames. She looked up, up, up to the top of the tallest tree, the back of her head nearly touching her shoulder blades, and could not refrain from emitting a shriek of surprise.

Perched up so high she was merely a dot in the treetop was a curly-headed child sitting upon a branch, swinging her legs. The branch was fragile, as delicate as the pixie who sat upon it. The little girl looked down upon her with what appeared to be an impish grin. Elizabeth, terrified, shouted at the girl not to move, to stay still. And then, before she could run for help, the supporting branch broke. Elizabeth screamed, running forward as though it would be possible to catch the little girl.

Miraculously, instead of falling instantly to her death, the child managed to grab hold of another slender branch on the way down. She clung there, literally swinging in the wind. "Hold tight!" Elizabeth called. "I will go for help!"

At that instant, several things happened at once. Whether due to the brittle nature of the branch or her tenuous hold upon it, the little girl dropped like a stone. A 'swoosh' of wind brushed past Elizabeth as something large and black flew by. A blur of motion too quick to see, faster than another scream could pass her lips and suddenly, the dark flying shape coalesced into Fitzwilliam standing beside her, a small girl in his arms.

Elizabeth blinked, trying to clear the black dots of panic, shock and terror from her eyes. Instead of clearing, however, the spots multiplied, joining together to encompass her vision entirely. For the first time in her life, she swooned.

Fifteen

Elizabeth was unsure precisely how long she was insensible; not long, evidently, because she was being carried—again—in her husband's arms. It took her a few moments to piece together her memories, and she kept her eyes closed while she did it. When she recalled what she had seen—what she *knew* she witnessed with her own eyes—it almost sent her over the edge once more.

"Easy, love, easy...all will be well," she heard Fitzwilliam's baritone voice murmur, and realised she trembled within the cradle of his arms.

The softness of mattress and downy pillows replaced the iron strength of masculine arms and chest wall. She felt the unlacing of her boots, the gentle shifting while he turned her to loosen the constriction of her dress and undergarments. When she felt the rush of cool air upon her skin as fabric was pulled free, she finally opened her eyes. Her heart, beating a frantic staccato pulse, slowed as she looked at her husband. This was no black phantom; it was simply Fitzwilliam, his eyes a piercing green-shot grey and concern writ heavily upon his features. He continued to play lady's maid, taking care of her, making her comfortable. He eyed her chemise-covered body as he pulled the sheet over her.

"I do not know where you keep your nightgowns."

"Neither do I," she replied, trying to smile and failing. "I am sure Maggie knows."

"I sent her away. I wish to take care of you myself. I heard you scream, Elizabeth. Devil take it, I heard you scream and I could not reach you quickly enough—" he broke off mid-sentence.

"You saved her. Was it...the Hawkins girl?" she asked, though her throat closed, wanting to swallow the words.

He gave a little nod. He would not meet her eyes.

"That is...good. I am glad. That she is safe."

"Elizabeth...I know how it must have appeared, but—"

"But you have no intention of explaining anything to me."

He looked terribly beleaguered. "It was not what it seemed," he nearly whispered.

What it seemed? Was he saying he had not—literally—flown to that child's rescue? She was so tired of her confusion, the danger everyone except for her seemed to understand, the resentment she could not shake, so tired of questions beating like trapped birdwings inside her head. "I should like to rest now," she replied, closing her eyes. "Alone."

For long moments, Darcy merely stood by her bedside, gazing at his wife. Her hair had tumbled loose once more, defiant against its pins. He wanted to pick them all out, lift her against him, hold her tightly with his hands fisted in it. From his bed in the cellar, the sound of her terrified scream had brought him to immediate consciousness; he had moved with all the speed he possessed. Then, to realise it was the Hawkins child, who weighed more than two stone, with his wife attempting to catch her from that great height! She might have killed Elizabeth! And though the child was vampyre, she was too young to survive such a fall without injury. Not to mention Elizabeth had been alone out there, while some unknown scoundrel possibly lay in wait to take her from him. The beast within him circled, growling, distressed still.

However she justified yesterday's bizarre events, he could not suppose she would easily rationalise today's. Devil take it, no human child could have climbed a tree so high, could they? Even were it possible, there was no way to hide his flight. He would never forget the bewildered expression on her face just before she fainted, staring at him as though he were a terrifying insect.

And now she wished him to leave her alone. Well, that was probably the least of what he could expect. He should count himself fortunate she had not begged to leave Pemberley. Leave him.

Yet.

He could not fix this. Though it was the most difficult thing he had ever done, he forced himself to walk away.

❧

Once her husband departed, Elizabeth sat up, far too overwrought to think of napping. She paced the length of her chamber, insensible to her state of undress. The conclusions she drew were so fantastic, so incredible...but what other possibilities were there?

What else could explain the extraordinary *talents* Fitzwilliam possessed? He could run faster than a horse. He experienced the emotions of others. He could direct people's movements and intentions. He saved lives. And...dear heavens, he could *fly*. Her heart beat faster when she thought of it. There was no other answer. She had married an angel. Well, perhaps not quite an angel, as he possessed flesh as a man. So, a–a saint, then. A man of miracles. Destined for divinity but still operating within a shell of humanity.

What, after all, did she know of such things? He would not speak to her about it, but perhaps God did not permit it. She shivered in reaction to the thought; it seemed blasphemous to think she had spoken to, touched, held! a man who communed with the Almighty.

But what did it mean that he could not read *her* emotions, that *her* mind was closed to him? A cold fear nearly overwhelmed her. How many times had Mama told her she was a wicked, wicked girl?

Of course, a saint must be above the sins of the flesh. Pure. As Fitzwilliam *tried* to be. But she tempted him. Even in her ignorance, she knew he wanted her; he had even told her so. Why had he married her when it would have been far better to put great distance between them? Why did their vows mean nothing?

She had thought he wished for heirs, but recalling their discussion, it seemed to her now that he only agreed with *her* beliefs. Why had he returned to Longbourn after hearing of her proposed betrothal to Mr Collins? Had he rescued her, or was it Mr Collins whom he saved?

She almost laughed. In her pride, she had rejected one of God's servants, only to make another, much greater one suffer. Perhaps, had she been able to submit to marriage with Collins in quick humility, Fitzwilliam would not have been lured from whatever great destiny God had in store for him. Had he angered God by marrying her? Momentous forces were at work here, and she could not understand them. Even her kidnapping yesterday might have been arranged to *save* Fitzwilliam, not to hurt her. Or perhaps both. Wickedness should be destroyed, correct?

With a groan of dismay, she plunked down on the rug before the fire.

To suddenly learn that one was on the side of evil was a very lowering discovery, indeed.

❧

He knew it would not work. The females were lovely, appealing, sweet-natured. Richard had tranced them to absolute silence and stillness. Darcy shut his eyes, plugged his nose, and thought desperately of Elizabeth. But he was still too aware of the differences between these women and the only one he wanted.

"It will not do, Richard. You must stun me and use force. Try not to kill me, but the next thing to it."

"Darcy, you are being ridiculous. Feeding is instinctive. Let yourself go."

For his uncle's sake he tried again. And again, straining so hard, he actually broke a sweat, his body shuddering in great tremblings, attempting to force what should have happened naturally.

"Enough," Richard barked at last. Pacing fiercely around the room as if there were answers to be found in the cellar walls and stone floor, he made an explosive sound of frustration.

"Your wife's experience today has disordered your mind."

Darcy chuckled humourlessly. "Undoubtedly. Next time I ask you to keep watch over her, perhaps you will do so."

"Zooks, Sally is a terror. I could not take a chance she would wander far, not with someone targeting your line."

"Well you failed to look closely enough, as it turns out. Sally might well have broken something falling from that height. Elizabeth was screaming in terror at the sight of it, trying to *catch* the girl, devil take it. From that height, Sally would have killed her. I know she saw me fly. I have no idea what to tell her, or if she will simply begin screaming whenever I come near."

Richard sighed. "Very well. I cannot see another way. I will do it. I hate this."

"So noted," Darcy said, facing him stoically. And then a blast of excruciating pain took him to his knees.

"Again," he muttered. The next hit dropped him to the floor, writhing—but still, sadly aware. "More," he gritted through clenched teeth.

"Devil take you, Darcy. You and your demon-thick skull," Richard growled. He administered another blow; his first one would have killed a human easily, but this last would probably have torn the head off a lesser vampyre.

It did not separate Darcy's head from his neck, but did render him unconscious at last. Richard carefully led the three tranced females to his prone nephew—who was doubly dangerous in this state. Only his instinct to survive *should* be operable. If Richard were not there to direct the situation, Darcy likely would drain the female dry. He brought the wrist of the first near Darcy's mouth, watching with satisfaction as his nephew's incisors lengthened greedily.

To Richard's enormous disappointment, however, as soon as the wrist touched Darcy's lips, his fangs receded.

"No!" he shouted. He tried Prudence with the same results. In desperation, he pinched Darcy's nose shut, shoving another wrist at him. This time he was successful; his nephew's powerful jaws clamped down and he suckled greedily. In fact, he had a devil of a time getting him to release when it was necessary. Finally, Richard remembered to unplug his nose. The moment Darcy scented her, his fangs receded.

He repeated the procedure with the second girl, and when he had taken enough from Mary, let go of Darcy's nose again. Immediately, the boy practically spat her out. Richard was unsuccessful in getting Darcy to Take from the third girl. Nose pinching aside, the ingested blood promoted healing in Darcy's already heightened powers of recovery. He was regaining consciousness.

With a sighed command, Richard ordered the three girls to report to Reynolds, who anticipated them above-stairs. He sat down next to Darcy on the hard floor, waiting for him to awaken. He did not have to wait long. He opened piercingly green eyes to look enquiringly at his uncle.

"Two out of three," Richard said. "And vampyres this time. They will last you longer."

Darcy sat up, cringing a little. "Better than nothing," he said. "I feel rejuvenated already—except for a bit of a headache."

Since that 'headache' would probably fell a bear, Richard did not remark upon it. "Rest here until moonrise," he said. "I will watch over your Elizabeth until then."

Darcy came to full awareness between one heartbeat and the next. He mentally reviewed his condition and found it more than acceptable. The blood and rest had done him a world of good. At least, when he faced Elizabeth, he would not be overwhelmed by his inherent aggression. He would stay in control.

He saw that Mrs Reynolds, bless her caring heart, had put out fresh clothing for him. Chamberlayne would be miffed, but he preferred to do for himself and was grateful. A shave would have to wait.

Anxious to know how Elizabeth fared, he took the stairs two at a time. When he reached the head of the staircase nearest her chambers, Richard awaited him, seated on a padded bench, his legs stretched in front of him; he stood at Darcy's approach.

"She stopped muttering to herself about an hour ago," he said. "Naturally, I seated myself far enough away that I could not hear her actual words. Her breathing indicates she sleeps."

Darcy held a brief, silent conversation with Mrs Reynolds. "She did not eat her lunch. She must be hungry. Did anyone ask if she wished for tea?"

"Maggie tried, but Elizabeth rather insistently requested she be left to herself."

Darcy sighed. This was not a good sign. "Are you for Kent, then?"

"I am off," Richard replied. "Do not be surprised if I bring a guest with me upon my return."

"Richard," Darcy growled warningly.

"We need to know the extent of Elizabeth's immunity," he said calmly. "And I am absolutely impervious to your glacier-like stare, so you may as well accept the inevitable."

"You tell *her*, if she does not behave, I will skin her arse and use it for a hearthrug," Darcy grumbled. "Be careful, Richard. I mean it."

"I always am, dear nephew. I always am." His exit was nothing but a blurred motion too quick for mortal eyes.

Darcy entered his own chambers; somehow it seemed less intrusive to enter Elizabeth's by the connecting door. He was half prepared for her to have bolted it to keep him out, but it opened easily and he passed through her dressing room to her bedroom in quiet anxiety.

Her bed however, was empty; he followed the soft sounds of her breathing to the hearth in her sitting room. And there, he nearly lost his wits.

Elizabeth lay asleep upon the rug before the fire, a blanket from the settee pillowed under her cheek. She wore nothing but the short chemise he had left her in, her long legs lovely in reflected firelight.

What would she do if he awakened her with kisses? He knelt by her side, unable to resist touching the soft, bare skin of her arm.

"Elizabeth, my love," he said tenderly, not wishing to alarm her.

She startled regardless, scrambling up onto her knees and looking around as though she did not recognise her surroundings.

He was afraid to touch her, afraid at any moment she would remember to be horrified by him. He seated himself upon the settee before her, trying to look as unintimidating as possible.

To his chagrin, however, she glanced down at herself, gave a little shriek, and fled the room.

Elizabeth ran, filled with humiliation at her state of undress. Would she never cease to embarrass herself? Oh why, why had she fallen asleep on the rug like some stray dog? She threw open doors, looking for something to wear.

"Elizabeth," her husband's voice called urgently, from far too close behind her.

"Go away," she called, her distress complete. "Please."

Before falling asleep, she had determined a course of action. She would confess her conclusions regarding his sainthood. She would try to learn the proper way to support him in his spiritual endeavours. Perhaps they could study the Bible together; that, at least, sounded comforting and peaceful. She had many religious questions: why did He call servants so obviously inept as Mr Collins into His service? Why had her baby brother not lived beyond three days? What had *she* done to become wicked?

A spike of resentment flared again. Evil ought to be a matter of choice, not predestination.

"Mistress, may I assist you?" Maggie appeared as if from nowhere, and Elizabeth let out a yelp.

"Oh, ah, yes," she said, breathless and flustered. "I am...I need, yes, um, assistance."

❦

While Maggie worked on her hair, Elizabeth gathered her composure and marshalled her questions. But would the girl speak? Her loyalties would plainly be with the angels, but could she help Elizabeth stop her apparent downward spiral?

"I know you cannot answer my questions," she began.

Maggie looked at her warily. "I will answer any I can," she said. "I will not lie to you."

Of course. Angels would not approve of dishonesty.

"Are there written rules? Something to be studied?"

In the looking glass, Elizabeth saw Maggie's puzzled look.

"To what rules do you refer?"

"I assumed you—your people—followed, um, commandments," Elizabeth replied. "And, um, scripture?"

Maggie's expression cleared, and she appeared relieved. "Oh, yes, Mistress," she said. "Master reads his Bible regular, and there's preaching every Sunday. We have service in the chapel here, and another in the village. Mr Marley is rector. He dines here often." She went on at some length, emphasising the Master's good works and various charitable endeavours. As if Elizabeth needed convincing as to her husband's *goodness*. She revealed nothing useful for the less holy.

Elizabeth asked no more questions.

Once she was properly coiffed and dressed, she asked Maggie to deliver a message to her husband that she was ready to speak to him.

Not many minutes later, Maggie returned with a reply—her husband had 'matters of security' to address, and would attend to her when he could, with his apologies.

Hours later, it appeared the time would not be soon. She had a tray in her room, and mentally practised speeches, apologies, and, as the day turned to night and the hour grew late, recriminations. Finally, she rang for Maggie, and had her undo it all. It was very late when she slipped into her bed, and later still before she fell into a troubled sleep.

Darcy had never been further than three feet from her door. When he knew she slumbered at last he moved beside her, keeping watch until the morning light.

Elizabeth's days—and nights—fell into an odd pattern. The whole household shared a decidedly nocturnal schedule. Business was conducted at odd hours of the night, and dinner was never served much before eleven; Elizabeth often was the only one to frequent the breakfast room. Her terrible dreams returned, their cold power interrupting her sleep with silent fear. When Fitzwilliam slept, she did not know; he would not speak to her of much beyond what was polite and impersonal.

She decided it was for the best.

Resenting being considered less than worthy, yet fearing the arguments that might prove it, she pushed all confusion aside in favour of simply watching and listening.

Elizabeth's wardrobe was delivered from London, the number of garments overwhelming. The fabrics were beautiful and sumptuous, the trims rich and expensive. The lingerie was unspeakably fine—chemises of the sheerest linens and silks, petticoats of almost transparent muslin, undressing gowns of exquisite silks and satins.

When she attempted to thank Fitzwilliam, he brushed her gratitude aside. "It was a selfish pleasure," he said brusquely. In most ways, he treated her as a younger sister, or perhaps an elderly aunt. Once in every while, however, she would catch a look upon his face, a certain intensity in his gaze, reminding her that she was still a *temptation*, which managed to be both flattering and distressing.

However angelic her husband, he did not neglect more earthly defences. All of the footmen trained like soldiers, and most every late afternoon and evening, she could find her husband in the ballroom with them, practising swordplay. For some reason, swords were preferred over pistols, and not the stylish short sword one occasionally saw at balls. These were long, ancient-looking metal blades, heavy and gleaming; there were no protective tips, such as fencers used, in a brutal ballet of strikes almost faster than the eye could see. The blood on the ballroom floor made evident a pitiless ferocity, though she never caught sight of a wound. She knew they did not like her there—and they always seemed to know when she was near, however quiet she tried to be. Watching both thrilled and terrified her…but she could not resist viewing the flashing thrust and parry, hearing the tear of fabric and seeing the sweat bead upon his forehead as Fitzwilliam drove his opponent to the very edge of violence. She never saw any get the better of him.

The sun was just setting when Fitzwilliam escorted her to their first church service together in the ancient-looking stone chapel where, no doubt, generations of Darcys had worshipped. No one seemed to think the late hour odd, as they were joined by many of the servants with whom she had become familiar, as well as several families unknown to her. She exchanged smiles with all, hoping the danger would soon pass, and that she would be able to become acquainted with Derbyshire society, visit tenants and come to know their needs. As Fitzwilliam seated her in the Darcy pew, her eyes were drawn to an enormous stained-glass window. The sun's final rays gleamed through its luminous red, blue, and burnt orange, depicting Jesus raising Lazarus from the dead, the whites and greys of the former corpse providing solemn contrast to the brilliance of the other colours.

The young vicar, Mr Marley, gave a thoughtful sermon on the 130th Psalm. Fitzwilliam sang, his voice as pure and clear as she remembered. She stopped singing herself so she could listen to him, surprised when everyone else continued on as though such a voice were a common thing. *Fit for a heavenly chorus*, she thought, and more proof of his piety.

Every Sabbath thereafter, she sought to hear clues within the sermon that might help her understand her new life and new fears and ever-more-distant husband.

God, unfortunately, remained silent.

Did Elizabeth stare at the rector, or was it only polite interest? Her unadulterated attention on Marley was pure torture, his beast pawing the ground and calculating how quickly it could gut the man. He beat back the wave of jealousy, trying to look at Marley impartially. The fellow was a bit of a dry stick, but he was a good man, in the best sense of the word, and no doubt a handsome one. One of Bingley's better finds, really. Was she attracted to that sort of golden-haired choirboy? A growl tried to escape his throat.

His wife was beautiful in dull, cheap, ill-fitting gowns; in the yellow silk she wore tonight, she was exquisite. He must tell Bingley to bring the emeralds when next he came; they would perfectly complement her sparkling eyes. Distracted, he briefly lost his place in the sermon.

The beast grew dominant again. It had been more than a fortnight; he had not fed well enough last time, and Richard had not yet returned from Kent. He needed to get himself back under regulation, but circumstances had not cooperated. He spent hours of each night with Elizabeth, watching over her while she slept, but also with the men patrolling his property, dividing his time so he could resist the temptation to throw himself upon her mercy. He had already seen her horror at the little she knew and had no desire to risk more. He would force himself to rest for two or three hours each morning, then spend afternoons and evenings on business, estate affairs, and training. The last five nights he had explored the furthest limits of Pemberley borders, frantically searching for any sign of disturbance, any hidden intruder. There was nothing to find and no one else assaulted, but his beast refused to calm.

I arrive tonight. She is with me.

"About time," he muttered.

"What was that?"

Darcy looked up sharply. He had grown distracted, and suddenly found himself alone with his wife—something he usually managed to avoid unless she slumbered.

She looked at him with a shy smile that twisted his heart into shreds. He fought the urge to pull her into his arms and simply carry her upstairs.

"I have a meeting tonight," he said instead. "I will be out late."

He could swear her expression showed at least a small sign of disappointment. Did she wish for his company? Or was she so lonely that even *he* would do? He found it mattered little; he would take any small reprieve from her revulsion.

But Anne de Bourgh arrived at any moment, and he would not permit her near Elizabeth before being thoroughly scrutinised. Richard trusted her, or he would not have allowed her on the estate; Darcy had known Anne all his life and had never sensed the malevolence within her that saturated Catherine. As Richard so often reminded him, Anne had no blood connexion to Catherine, and must be judged upon her own merits.

Elizabeth looked up at him then, and the temptation of her—her scent, her lips—was unendurable. So beautiful. So desirable. So fragile. So vulnerable. And Catherine de Bourgh wanted her. He bent over her hand, placing a kiss upon it. "Sleep well, my lo—Elizabeth."

She caught the partial endearment he let slip and frowned.

His expression hardened. He would not apologise for it.

"What is the business you pursue tonight?" she asked, her frown deepening. When he did not answer, she turned away from him and started up the stairs.

"Goodnight, Elizabeth," he called softly. She did not reply.

Elizabeth paced her chambers, unable to calm. Who did her husband meet? Was there peril? The very fact of his mention meant the meeting was important, possibly dangerous. She knew his gifts, of course, which must give him an advantage in any conflict, and surely God was on his side.

Another hour passed before she decided to fetch a few books from the library in the faint hope that reading could distract her from pointless anxiety. Naturally, emerging in such dishabille was a scandalous idea, but the new gowns were difficult to don without assistance and most of her old ones had somehow disappeared. With a shrug of impatience, she chose a modest undressing gown that covered her completely, and then wrapped a shawl over it.

The corridors were dimly lit, so she did not need a candle, but the unusual quiet gave the castle a rather sinister air. She passed several footmen dutifully ignoring her state of undress, but the way they so completely took no notice of her presence made her feel eerily invisible.

Once inside the library, she marvelled, as always, at the massive proportions of the room and the floor-to-ceiling collections of books. Lighting a candelabrum for more light than the two fireplaces provided, she perused a selection of poetry discovered on her last visit. She had narrowed her selection to three volumes when the door opened to admit her husband, the colonel, and the mysterious visitor.

Embarrassed, she looked around at once for a hiding place, but of course it was hopeless. The three of them swung their gazes immediately to the source of the light. Fitzwilliam moved to her with frightening speed. "Elizabeth? Why are you here?"

"So, this is your new wife, Fitzwilliam? You will introduce us?" For the first time, Elizabeth fully viewed their companion.

This was the danger he faced?

She was exquisite. Petite, expertly coiffed, elegant, beautifully garbed—she was everything Elizabeth was not. Her topaz eyes, looking slightly amused, peered up at Fitzwilliam impishly from under thick lashes. Never had Elizabeth felt more awkward, standing before them in her nightwear with braided hair, like one of those humiliating dreams from which one longed to wake.

"Elizabeth, this is Miss Anne de Bourgh. Anne will be visiting with us for a short time. Anne, this is Mrs Darcy."

Astonishment distracted her from embarrassment. "Anne de Bourgh...you are of Rosings Park, in Kent?"

Anne nodded, smiling. "I am. It is a pleasure to meet you, Mrs Darcy."

"The pleasure is mine," Elizabeth answered faintly. "I apologise for my appearance. I only meant to slip out for a moment for a book... I did not think to meet anyone, or I would have..." She stopped herself, realising she babbled. "You will excuse me?" she finished abruptly.

"I will walk you back," Fitzwilliam said.

"No!" Elizabeth protested. "You have business. Colonel, I am so happy you have returned safely. My apologies, again, to all of you." She slipped from her husband's grasp, hurrying out of the room as quickly as she could, her face a fiery red, tears burning behind her eyes. It was excessively mortifying.

Looking at the three of them, she recognised a-a sameness. Not just in their excessive beauty, but in their eyes, in their stance, in their...holiness. They radiated confidence and power, while she shamed herself in an undressing gown.

Disgraced, while meeting the woman whom Fitzwilliam obviously *should* have married.

❧

Darcy started after his wife, but the colonel gripped his arm. He turned back and saw Anne's intense focus, and then her disbelief.

"I cannot hold her," she said quietly.

"Are you sure you tried?" Darcy demanded. "I felt a great deal of compassion coming from you. Perhaps you wished to abet her escape."

She gave him a stern look. "She was embarrassed, and only growing more so. As any female would have been. I take it she was surprised by my arrival? How does she know of Rosings Park?"

Darcy felt chagrin. "I believe she once heard your name paired with mine in a rumour of an alliance."

"Ah," Anne replied knowingly. "*That* rumour. Regardless, I assure you I did try to keep her in place. I could not."

"Tell him, Anne," Richard said, entering the conversation for the first time.

"Tell me what?" Darcy asked, instantly alert.

"Mother is not at her lucid best at the moment," Anne said. "But she is obsessed with the topic of Elizabeth Bennet. I will swear she has no idea, as of yet, that you have made Elizabeth your wife. She still believes her little toad-eating vicar will bring her back as his bride."

Both men stared at her—Darcy, full of distrust as he probed for evidence of dissemblance; Richard, warm and full of promise.

Darcy glanced from one to the other. "If your mother was not responsible for the assault upon Elizabeth, we must discuss a strategy. Who could be responsible for the attempted abduction?"

Richard clapped his nephew on the shoulder. "At the risk of

sounding indifferent, may I suggest we continue this discussion tomorrow?"

"Devil take it, you brought her here to be of use. Let us not waste time."

"He brought me here because he knew you would not take his word on my mother's innocence in the matter," Anne said dryly. "I came because Pemberley is one of the few places I can go to escape her for a time. Nothing else will be accomplished tonight, regardless."

"And how do you know this?" Darcy asked scornfully. "Has your mother shared her skill for predicting the future?"

Anne laughed, a delightful tinkling sound. "No, thankfully. 'Tis only my feminine intuition, telling me most of your attention just marched upstairs with your distressed wife."

Darcy frowned. Devil take it, she was correct. And even though he was fairly certain Elizabeth was more angry than distressed, he would rather feel the sharp side of her tongue than wonder. He took his leave of Richard and Anne with very little courtesy, speeding after Elizabeth so quickly that he caught up to her before she reached the door to her chambers.

"Elizabeth," he said quietly.

She startled. "I wish you would not do that," she said, making him smile.

"I am sorry," he whispered; for just a moment, she leaned into him. Then suddenly she straightened and, pulling away from him, marched into her dressing room. She threw the shawl aside and turned to face him. He studied her face, trying to determine her mood, looking for signs of pique.

"I apologise," she said stiffly.

"For what?" he asked, genuinely curious.

"For appearing in front of your guest in such a state," she said, gesturing to her nightwear.

"It does not matter," he said, waiting for the rest.

"Goodnight, then," she said, presenting her back as she tried to push past him into her bedchamber. He stopped her, gripping her shoulder.

"Are you upset about Anne?"

She did not answer, but her spine—already ramrod straight—stiffened further.

"I told you once, we were never betrothed."

"But you did not see fit to tell me *she* would be our guest."

"I hoped you would not have to meet her."

"Oh? Why is that?"

He frowned. "I-I beg your pardon. 'Tis another thing I cannot explain."

"Perhaps you would answer me this. If you had married Miss de Bourgh, could you have wed her completely? Would *she* have been your wife in all ways?"

He opened his mouth to answer and closed it again. "I never wished to marry her, Elizabeth," he said quietly. "I am not attracted to her in any way. I will not be governed by what is appropriate, correct, or sensible. I would never have been led to the altar for the sake of a more influential family and more suitable connexion." He paused. "I love *you,* Elizabeth," he said, with all the longing of his soul.

From the depths of Elizabeth's pain, anger flared. That he would say this, as if it explained everything, when he explained nothing! When he refused to answer her questions, when he had rejected her at nearly every turn! She had been naïve; there was only one reason a man did not bed his wife. The only sure way to avoid getting her with child was to abstain. Any child of hers must somehow be unacceptable.

"I am not insensible to the compliment of your love," she answered, struggling for control as waves of sorrow and resentment smouldered.

"I hear a 'but'."

Her eyes flashed. "My mother, at least, was honest in her dislike. You claim to love me, while you disdain my intelligence, my trust, even my very touch. To you I am a child, an insignificant female to be dressed prettily, fed, watered, and set aside at your convenience. You married me, you said, because of my marvellous inability to communicate emotions. Did you think it meant I do not have any?"

"I do all in my power to fight your enemies," he growled.

She failed to see what that had to do with his visceral rejection and laughed, the sound without humour. "Ah, yes, my mysterious enemies. The ones you cannot tell me of, who might be more beautiful than one's average goddess."

"I have my reasons, you know I have. I—"

"Fitzwilliam, I do not know why you married me, but it was *not* for love. Perhaps you should ask your God what that even is."

"I know you have been unhappy," he said lowly. "I grieve that I have caused you pain."

Elizabeth took a deep breath. Perhaps he could not feel her emotions, but his were plain. He was a good man—or saint, even—who had no idea how to right what was wrong. She felt scorned and rebuffed—it made her feel helpless. Perhaps he was as powerless in this hurt as she, entrapped by vows he could not break. She did not love him, but she might have. She *could* have. But she had her pride.

"I am done hoping *you* will make things better," she said, her tone quiet but firm. "In my youth, I did not have an ideal, happy home, so I sought my own ideals, my own happiness. I found it in nature, in books, in physical exercise, in pursuing my talents, in my friends, and with my sisters. I will find it again." She drew herself up to her full height, her eyes glittering, her chin high. "I will cease holding you accountable for *my* impossible expectations. But *you* will cease professing a love you *cannot, do not* feel. You do not know *me*, sir!"

Darcy's lips formed a protest; she was wrong! Obstinate, headstrong girl! But the beast within him responded differently. It *relished* her stubborn defiance, finding in her a worthy mate who would allow no man to treat her feelings lightly, *especially* his foolish human side.

Abruptly, his frustration vanished. She was to blame for none of this. He must seek the source of her peril, defeat it, and then cast his fate at his wife's feet. It was where he belonged.

"As you wish, my dear," he agreed sombrely. "As you wish."

Seventeen

Anne de Bourgh remained in residence, but Elizabeth only saw her at the evening meal. Her time was taken up with reading, sewing, exploring Pemberley, long walks on the grounds—trailed by at least three footmen—whenever the weather cooperated, and even when it did not. And she made changes.

She studied the meticulously kept account books, and though she did not have the experience to make real adjustments to an estate so flawlessly supervised, she no longer let her inexperience cow her. She asked questions. She made suggestions. And one afternoon, when Andrew—the footman she judged most amenable—was sword fighting with James in the ballroom, she made a demand.

Plucking a sword hanging from a rack—it was even heavier than she expected—she walked towards the sparring men. Immediately, they lowered their weapons, bowing respectfully.

"I should like to learn to use this, please."

Andrew's eyes went wide, and he was momentarily speechless. "Um. Hmm. Mistress? Surely not?"

"Surely so," she persisted. "You can teach me the rudiments, can you not?"

"Well, um, y-yes, or rather, I–I," he stuttered, before relief washed over his features as his Master appeared.

"Elizabeth," Darcy said, "is aught the matter?"

Her lips firmed. "I wish to learn to fight. With this," she said, gesturing to the sword that even now trembled in her hand. The blasted thing weighed a stone.

"You can barely hold it," he noted.

"All the better I should learn," she insisted. "Andrew can teach me this, instead of trailing me around the gardens."

Andrew blanched.

Darcy eyed her thoughtfully. "Andrew currently sees his life pass before his eyes if he so much as nicks you."

"Oh!" she said. "Why, surely you would not punish him for an accidental—"

"I most certainly would," he interrupted. "However, it will be unnecessary. I will teach you myself."

Almost to her surprise, Fitzwilliam was as good as his word. It became her favourite part of each day, even if he made her begin with a 'nursery' wooden sword, and her dratted skirts were a nuisance to her footwork. He did her the courtesy of taking it seriously, and although she could never hope to match his strength, speed, and power, his praise was as real as his patient appraisal of her errors. And the look in his eyes as she gave the exercises her best efforts warmed her someplace deep inside, her mother's criticisms replaced by her husband's approval.

If sword practice was her favourite time of day, the evening meal —still held very late—was her least. Joining Fitzwilliam, Richard, Anne, and whichever guests had been invited to partake, they seldom had much to say to her nor she to them. Fitzwilliam stayed close by her side—showing her every courtesy, but otherwise quiet and brooding. Strangely, after dinner, men and women did not separate. Elizabeth was no longer astonished when Richard took out his cigar—and Miss de Bourgh did as well. When the port was served, Miss de Bourgh raised her glass.

She found this behaviour unbefitting the angelic, at best, and vulgar at worst. No one else seemed to notice.

How could she like the woman? And *why* should she, when *she* was apparently found wanting in ways Anne de Bourgh was not?

She found no friend, either, in Richard Fitzwilliam, who had grown openly dismissive of her; had he sensed her dislike of his lover?

Her dreams came with each dawn. She would waken upon a stifled scream, certain that the razor-edged teeth in the dream-man's wicked, handsome smile were tearing open her flesh. There was no Jane to huddle against for comfort. Most of the time she could not go back to sleep, hence her early breakfasts. At least Mama was not here to caustically remark upon the dark circles under her eyes.

A few weeks before Christmas, despite there being no plans for a party or ball to celebrate the holiday, she asked for and received enough holly and evergreens to decorate the library. Pemberley maintained a battle-readiness that almost seemed usual now. In her letters to her sisters and relations, she wrote only of the beauty of her home and created pretend Christmas celebrations, telling no one of the stark oddities of her life; some curious protectiveness of Fitzwilliam constrained her.

By the same token, she refused to let Pemberley's current residents see her loneliness. Every night she sailed into dinner as she had marched into a hundred assemblies: head held high, pretending she was serene and confident and full of hope.

One afternoon, when Elizabeth reported to the ballroom for her lesson, she noticed the gauntness of her husband's cheekbones, the unusually pronounced lines bracketing his mouth. Was he losing weight? He had eaten a hearty meal the night before.

"Are you ill?" she asked, instead of reaching for her wooden sword.

Fitzwilliam's gaze seemed to bore into her, his eyes completely black. Shifting closer, he moved behind her, as if he were about to show her a new feint or technique. But instead of positioning her, as he had so many times before, he simply stood quietly, letting her feel him all along her back; then, his breath was hot upon her neck. Unbidden, she remembered the night in London he spent wrapped around her; she had never felt so protected, so comforted, and leaned against him. His arms went about her, holding her tightly, his face nuzzling just below her ear. Her heart raced; her feelings changed from solace to something else.

She tried to turn in his arms, but they were suddenly a prison entrapping her, while a noise emerged sounding suspiciously like a growl.

"Fitzwilliam?" she whispered, not understanding. Abruptly his arms disappeared. She turned, but he was gone, and she was alone in the empty ballroom.

She brooded for the rest of the day before coming to her own decision. This would mark the last day of docile ignorance. Her need for answers had grown greater than her fear of them. But her husband did not appear for dinner. What was worse, no one would tell her where he was or when he might return.

"Why do you care when he eats, or even if he does?" Richard asked insolently.

Immediately she decided she could be as dismissive of good manners as they, quitting the dining room without a word.

For the first time, she entered the connecting door leading to Fitzwilliam's rooms. Feeling bold, she passed through a large sitting area without taking in much beyond upholstered sofas in rich fabrics, a large fireplace, and an oversized painting of Saint Lazarus ripping graveclothes from his body. Shivering, she slipped into the next room —his bedroom.

An enormous wooden bed took pride of place in the centre of the room, each post a fanged dragon fiercely guarding the perimeter, spitting wooden flames forming the top rail. But as splendid as his living quarters might be, they were empty of any clue to his whereabouts.

She next tried Fitzwilliam's study. Andrew stood just beyond its entrance.

"Is my husband in here?" she asked, laying her hand upon the door as if to enter.

"No, ma'am, he is not."

"Colonel Fitzwilliam?"

"No, ma'am. No one, at present."

"Do you know where they have gone?"

For the first time, the young footman appeared momentarily uncomfortable before once again assuming an air of impassiveness. "I believe they may be belowstairs," he said warily.

Elizabeth's brow furrowed. According to Mrs Reynolds, there were only cellars and storerooms below.

"Thank you," she replied. "I suppose I shall have to wait until tomorrow to speak with Mr Darcy, then." She was not mistaken—at her apparent disinterest, the young man looked relieved.

The footmen were all accustomed to her rambling explorations, paying little heed as long as she stayed indoors. After ensuring she was unobserved, she stole down a set of back stairs that Mrs Reynolds had once explained led to the cellars. It was very dark, forcing her to waste time returning for a candle to light her way. In its dim glow, she made her way slowly and carefully. Finally, she heard the echo of voices.

They were in a room at the end of a dark passage; the door was not completely shut, the light from inside the room silhouetting its edges. Curious, she silently crept as close as she dared, extinguishing her candle to avoid the possibility of discovery.

Despite her precautions, she still might have been noticed except that the room's occupants were arguing heatedly. Fitzwilliam, the colonel, Miss de Bourgh, and two other females were there—servants, Penelope and Mary, she thought. The servants stared straight ahead—and directly at her—with nearly identical vacant expressions.

Her husband's back was to her, the set of his shoulders betraying tension or anger. The colonel and Miss de Bourgh were on either side of him, speaking intently in low tones, but she could hear bits and pieces of the conversation.

"You *must*...these females will satisfy...quit being a fool..." drifted out to her from Richard.

And then Miss de Bourgh interrupted him in a voice shriller and more carrying. "By the demon, Darcy, Take me. Mine is purer and stronger than these two tarts and will keep you longer."

Richard murmured something and she laughed.

Elizabeth backed away, hand over her mouth. *Take* her? She might be naïve, but that demand had certain implications she could not possibly misinterpret. Could she? Could Fitzwilliam have lied to her about his connexion with Miss de Bourgh, seating her at his table with his mistress? What did Miss de Bourgh mean, 'purer' and 'stronger'? And she referred to Penelope and Mary as 'tarts'. Were they not truly servants, then? Dear heavens, was *everything* a lie?

For long moments, she stayed frozen where she was, huddled in a corner of the passage. The talking ceased, and she debated running away. But then she heard something sounding very much like Fitzwilliam in pain.

Lunging forward, she abruptly stopped herself mid-movement. She knew almost nothing of what happened between male and female beyond the platonic, and the sounds were...odd. Could she truly bear the answers she sought?

Perhaps Fitzwilliam was no saint, but something else entirely. Her belief in his inherent goodness was already sorely tried by his evasions and his lovely, vulgar houseguest. And now *tarts*? And *taking*? Who *was* he?

In the end, it was the notion of languishing for another endless set of days with only her ignorance as companion that gave her the courage to edge back to the doorway. And what she saw astonished her.

Fitzwilliam lay on the floor; his eyes were closed, and strangely enough, the colonel pinched his nose. Suffocating him? And then Richard said the oddest words to Miss de Bourgh: "Give him your neck."

Miss de Bourgh crouched beside Fitzwilliam. What was she doing? She placed her bared throat near his mouth! Oh, no, no, no, he began suckling her neck! Indignation and fury filled her, and she stuffed her fist into her mouth to prevent an outcry.

Then, her shocked vision readjusted itself to what she truly witnessed. He did not suckle Anne's neck; he *bit*. She could see his throat muscles working beneath the fabric of his cravat; dear heavens, he–he...drank...of her.

Involuntarily, she took a step back, her shoulder hitting the door edge. Fitzwilliam's eyes blinked open, his head snapping towards her...and his mouth! It was the fanged teeth, dripping blood, straight from terrifying dreams, now come to life.

She screamed and screamed and screamed.

Darcy came to full consciousness instantly. Elizabeth—danger! Her screams echoed throughout the stone room as he shoved Anne away, leaping to his feet and searching frantically before discovering his wife's distress was entirely of his own making. With a sinking feeling, he understood all was finished. Elizabeth would never again look at him with anything except horror and revulsion.

"Get her out of here, Richard!" he barked. He turned his back so he would not have to see her disgust, thankful, for once, that he could feel nothing of her emotions.

Richard approached her. She looked at him, terrified. Quite gently, he took her arm and quietly murmured, "You are safe, Mrs

Darcy. Nothing to be frightened of here," while propelling her inexorably out of the room.

❧

What was happening? Blood! Teeth! She barely noticed Richard saying something, his words only buzzing noises through her shock. But even in her terror, Elizabeth caught his wary glance. It reminded her of how her father looked at her mother during her fits of nerves. Seeing it shut her mouth instantly—if she were dying, she would not behave as her mother.

No one has ever harmed me here, she repeated to herself as she climbed the stairs leading away from the dreadful scene. *If murder was their intention, I would already be dead.* Still, when the colonel opened the library door, gesturing for her to take a seat, she took one the farthest distance possible from where he stood.

He poured himself a snifter of brandy and tossed it back, offering her the same. She shook her head no.

"I suppose you wonder what you just witnessed," he began cautiously.

"I know what I witnessed," Elizabeth said quietly. "So...he is a–a demon?"

Richard made a sound of contempt. "This kind of shallow observation is exactly why most of humanity remains impoverished and ignorant. What do you think a demon *is*, Mrs Darcy? Embodied evil? What has that man ever done to you deserving of such judgment? Do you also believe fair-skinned peoples must be the *correct* colour, and those with darker complexions not as *human* as you? That they may be bought and sold with impunity?"

"I find you very offensive, Colonel," she replied, her lips tight with anger at the unfairness of his belligerent accusations. "I believe nothing of the sort."

He lifted a brow. "Oh? But you condemn Fitzwilliam for what he must eat in order to survive. Of course, his own mother did the same. It is only what he expects of you, after all."

"You cannot tell me you find the–the consumption of, ah, blood to be natural?"

"'Tis not so for you. Therefore, your nourishment must be the *correct* sustenance, must it not?"

"My sustenance does not require bloodshed."

He laughed. "Tell that to the cow, pig, lamb, and chicken. They will find your logic most amusing."

She started to argue the humanity of such but thought better of it, coming to the salient point. "Does he hurt others? In order to–to eat?"

"No, Mrs Darcy," he answered calmly, as though he spoke to a child. "He hurts no one unless they threaten his own." He paused, framing his thoughts. "He is of a race called Vampyre, born of a mortal mother and Vampyre father. He must drink blood or he dies—just as you require water and bread. He is smarter, stronger, faster, and truer than any man I have ever met. He also believes you would never accept him, would not have insisted you wed except for his belief in the threat to your life. He loves you and could not leave you to your enemies."

"But why me? I am nobody!"

"Why does he love you? Or why have you earned powerful enemies? My answer is the same in either case: I do not know."

Plainly, he did not think her worthy of his nephew's affections.

"Are you one, then? A...a vam-vampyre?" she asked, not expecting him to admit it.

"I was born of two mortal parents, so I am not as pure as your husband," he said matter-of-factly. "But I have Turned, yes."

It was astonishing. And, oddly, she could not have cared less. Why, she could not say, except he did not display the dreadful, horrifying fangs.

Everything she thought she knew was turned upside down. The urge to escape was overwhelming. "I need to walk," she said. "Let me go walking."

He looked at her for a moment, as if he weighed whether or not she would attempt to run away, and whether or not he cared if she did.

"You will be followed, but not disturbed unless there is a threat," he said at last.

She dashed from the room, not bothering to reply.

The night sky was bitterly dark, the wind whipping through scattered clouds, matching her mood. For a long while, Elizabeth simply moved without thinking, putting one foot in front of the other in the weak light of a lantern. She followed a path, not knowing where it led. It was bitterly cold out, and her clothing was insufficient. She did not care.

Eventually she reached a small rise. Looking around to get her bearings, she saw the imposing castle turrets, gleaming starkly bright amid the harsh moonlit landscape. The castle owned its place, as though it had sprouted from the earth fully formed. It was not precisely welcoming; it was a bit too arrogant, too daunting for that. There was nothing cosy about Pemberley.

Like its Master. He was intimidating as well, and this new facet of his existence was hardly more difficult to accept than her mistaken notions of sainthood and holiness. She had known he was something *other* for a long while. The colonel, while disdaining her fear rather more than she thought reasonable, was not incorrect. He was different; his differences, while astonishing, did not make him evil.

Setting her lantern on a low boulder, she at last let herself simply...brood. How many of the servants and tenants were vampyre? Remembering those wickedly sharp teeth, she shuddered violently.

Her night terrors came to life in those fangs. Fitzwilliam's face was *not* the one in her horror-filled dreams, however. Could she have seen a vampyre, perhaps as a child? Surely she would remember, had such a being attacked her. Would she not?

All men were not good; it stood to reason that variances in honourable behaviour existed amongst the vampyre as well. A vampyre might not necessarily be evil, but she guessed that one who was could do significant damage.

It explained much about feeling more guest than mistress—she was *other* here. What was it the colonel had said? Something about Fitzwilliam's mother rejecting him due to his–his needs. Well, she could certainly understand being unable to earn a mother's love. Was that the reason they were drawn to each other?

Were all vampyre children born with gifts? What would it be like, to have a child so precocious as Sally, who *must* be one? She would add another dozen servants just to keep watch on her.

And most important of all, was this why Fitzwilliam would not risk having a child with her? Did he see something missing within her, think her not strong enough to bear him one? Was there some test, an approval process, before she could try? Had she failed it? Obviously, they kept their existence a secret from other mortals. Did he not trust her?

The colonel had been...Turned, he called it; could she not be Turned as well? Not that she wanted to be, but he might have at least considered it, rather than treat her as a child who would betray him at the first opportunity.

Undoubtedly, Miss de Bourgh was vampyre—probably born vampyre. Fitzwilliam had been feeding from *her*.

Her mood blackened again to match the night.

❧

Darcy stood at the basin in his cellar room when Richard returned. He looked at him questioningly.

"She is calm...or, rather, quiet. She walks within the estate walls."

At Darcy's start of alarm, he added, "With three of our best men trailing her."

"What–what did she say? Or do I want to know?"

"She was shocked, of course. I think, however, she could be forgiven a few hysterics. Essentially, she wished to know whether you were dangerous. I assured her you were mild as a lamb."

Darcy shot him a look, and Richard laughed. "Here's the rub, though. When I confirmed that I, too, am vampyre, she hardly seemed to care. Give her time. Perhaps all is not lost."

"I hardly have a choice. I swear, I would be satisfied if she did not shriek in terror when we meet."

"Come upstairs, Darcy. Anne has an idea regarding the feedings that might be worthwhile. And Carter will arrive soon, with the London reports."

"No. I cannot go up there. Your pity is hard enough to endure—heaven forbid I bear it from everyone. Just let me alone for a time."

Richard looked at him for a long moment. "Very well. I will send down a tray. You took very little from Anne. The meat will help."

Darcy nodded shortly, longing for him to leave. The door shut, and he sighed with relief.

Sitting on the iron bed, he glanced around his 'cell'. When he was a very small child, he discovered the relief to be had in this cellar room, insulated by earth and distance from the rest of the household, a respite from constant battering of emotions in a castle so full of people. Oddly, when he was with Elizabeth, the urge for reprieve faded. She was an oasis of calm; she eased him. Maybe in time, she would not be so horrified. Perhaps...someday...but a vision of his mother's face formed in his mind, and he firmly shut that hope away.

Eighteen

ELIZABETH RETURNED TO THE HOUSE SOMETIME AFTER midnight, going directly to her rooms, speaking to no one. Before she could talk herself out of it, she rang for the maid—who presented herself at once.

"Maggie...are you...do you...?" she asked awkwardly.

"Am I vampyre, ma'am? Yes, ma'am," the girl replied steadily. "I was Turned when I was eighteen years."

"Oh," she said, surprised. Maggie seemed so very...human.

"Do you wish me to continue as your maid, ma'am?"

"Oh...why, I had not—"

In a burst of agitation unusual to her normally calm demeanour, the girl interrupted. "Begging your pardon, ma'am, but I do so want to stay. I've tried so hard, what with your hair being so difficult, not but what it isn't lovely hair, ma'am...and you won't find anyone handier with a needle."

Elizabeth was taken aback. For some reason, a vampyress pleading to be her lady's maid was disconcerting. "Um...why yes, Maggie, of course."

"Oh, thank you, ma'am," the maid cried. "I wish very much to give satisfaction. There are so few positions like this one. We tend to be long-lived, no one is ever pensioned off, and there are so few true ladies to serve. Of them, the good ones keep their maids forever or die so quickly. I—" She stopped speaking.

Elizabeth felt stirrings of alarm. "Should I be worried about the brevity of my existence, Maggie?"

"No, ma'am. It is only to us, 'tis short. As I said, we're long-lived."

"How old are you, may I ask?"

"Yes, ma'am. Not too old. Sixty-three my next birthday."

"Really?" Elizabeth cried, flummoxed. The maid did not look a day over eighteen. There were likely many surprises ahead. But Elizabeth had made some decisions during these last hours of the long, troubling night, and she would not change her mind so easily.

"I must adjust to many things. I hope for your help, with more than my bothersome hair. I need a–a friend, even more than I need a lady's maid. If you are willing?"

"Oh, yes, ma'am. I would be honoured...I do want to see you happy with the Master. I do." She smiled impishly and reached for a brush. "But no one needs a lady's maid more than you."

And they both laughed.

Anne barged into Darcy's cellar retreat without knocking. Immediately he stood, thankful he was still wearing his shirt and trousers, casting about for his banyan.

"Never mind dressing. I need to speak with you."

"I prefer to be clothed when I converse," he replied dryly.

"I have no time for formalities." She thrust a large goblet filled with liquid at him. "Here."

His brow furrowed as he accepted it. "What is this? Old blood? Ugh," he sniffed.

"Not old. I just gave it. Drink."

"'Tis cold," he said with disgust.

"Who cares for that? Do not be so fastidious. You need to eat. You cannot bite. Is starving a better option?"

"When you put it that way," he said sardonically. Tilting the cup to his mouth, he forced himself to drink it all, giving a shudder as he ingested the cooled blood. It lost most of its flavour and texture when thus exposed to air, but hopefully the nutrients remained. For a few moments, he waited; his gut roiled, protested—but it seemed it would stay down. His stomach gradually settled. And then, ever so slowly, he felt strength infusing his veins as the blood finally began to take effect. He looked at Anne.

"I think it will do!" he said, surprised. "Why did I not consider this?"

"Bah. You and Richard work from rule books. 'Tis why you need someone like me," she said, smiling impishly.

Suddenly Darcy laughed. "You are a minx, Anne de Bourgh. And...and a good friend," he said, returning her smile.

The noise of approaching footsteps distracted them both at the same time.

"Elizabeth!" Darcy said, shocked that she would seek him out.

"I hate to interrupt this cosy little tête-à-tête," his wife said coolly, "but I must speak to Mr Darcy. Privately." She glared at them both.

Anne smiled broadly. "You certainly must," she smirked, exiting the room in a wave of black silk and laughter.

Once alone, Elizabeth scrambled for the courage she'd had when speaking to Maggie. The look in her husband's eye was intense, almost dangerous as he studied her...and yet he said nothing. She found herself tongue-tied, not knowing where to begin. It was one thing when the spurt of righteous anger at discovering his *dishabille* in Miss de Bourgh's presence—and hearing his rare laughter—sustained her. Now she merely felt depressed. And a bit embarrassed.

"What was so amusing?" she asked, turning away from him.

"Beg pardon?" he asked, frowning.

"You–you were laughing. With her." She could not help the hurt, hostile note in her voice; she thought of how Miss de Bourgh looked, so sultry and petite and fine, and glanced down at her own gown. It was lovely, but very modest in comparison. It had taken all her courage to come down here and confront him.

Darcy moved closer, with a hesitancy unusual to him. "She discovered something important, something that made me happy. But my dear, she is not you. A friend, that is all."

"A friend whom you allow to see your unclothed person," she said pointedly, even as she blushed at the sight of his bare neck and the visible portion of his chest through the thin shirt. Somehow her embarrassment made her even angrier. "You do not allow me that privilege."

Now he stood directly before her. "Elizabeth," he said, his deep baritone husky. "You must know I did not intend for her to see me like this. In her eagerness to reveal her discovery, I doubt she even noticed." Retreating a bit, he continued, "You wished to...talk?"

Elizabeth knew it time to take back at least a small portion of her dignity. She *would* ask her questions, and he *would* answer, by all the saints. She looked him in the eye.

They were black. For some reason, Elizabeth found this comforting. She had always been aware of his *other*-ness, recognising his differences the first time he looked at her. It had not alarmed her then. Taking a deep breath, she raised her chin. "Yes, I do. Wish to talk, that is. I must know...why our marriage is incomplete."

He appeared surprised by the question. Gently, he stroked her cheek. "If I were to get you with child, Elizabeth, he would be like me."

"Or she," Elizabeth added, and he nodded.

"The baby...could someone else feed him?" she asked tentatively.

A shadow passed over his face; she almost heard his censure aloud.

Her distress poured out. "I do not want to be bitten!" she cried. "I do not care how you...eat...but your teeth.... I do not wish to see or–or feel them. It scares me and I–I will not!" She turned, half-meaning to flee, but his arms locked around her preventing her escape.

"Please, do not leave, Elizabeth," he said. And she was relieved he did not let her go; she did not know whether he meant it at all affectionately—but he had been so distant for so long, and she was so tired of pretending to be brave—his hold comforted her. She turned within his arms, her head lying against his chest and he clasped her more tightly against him. He was real and solid, warm and familiar. Her husband. For a time, she allowed herself to bask in the solace he offered. It took her some moments to realise his trembling.

Could he...could he have been lonely as well? She did not like to think of that, to imagine him distressed in any way. He was so strong, so unique. And no longer a saint. Had *never* been.

"Elizabeth," he sighed, his voice full of...longing? But he let go of her to clasp her face in both his hands. "Yes, dearest. Others could feed any child we create. But vampyre though he be, he would still be a son, or yes, a sweet daughter. He cannot be ignored or shut away or...reviled." His eyes seemed to burn into hers. "He will want his mother to *be* his mother. He will want her to love him regardless of his nature. He will ride ponies and play games and want his mother to notice, to care."

She gazed at him steadily, remembering what the colonel said about Fitzwilliam's own mother. "And be read to," she agreed. "I always loved a bedtime story...or two."

"Yes," he agreed. "I want you so much, Elizabeth. The part of me that longs to lie with you is not concerned with heirs. Vampyres are not especially, ah, prolific. 'Tis unlikely we would be so blessed, but if we were..."

"My mother hated me more often than she loved me," Elizabeth ventured. "I know that pain. I would never consciously inflict it upon any child of mine."

He gathered her close again.

"Does your heart always beat so fast?" she asked, curious, her hand resting upon his chest.

"Since meeting you, it races," he murmured.

"Not always," she said. "You hardly touch me."

"I have wished to do so, more than I can say."

"I have offered, and been rejected," she said, and the familiar resentment reappeared. "Those other females...do they have this privilege?" she asked bitterly.

"What?" he asked, confused.

"Mary and Penelope—the 'tarts', and Miss Anne de Bourgh," she snapped, finally allowing the expression of an anger she could not relinquish. "You...her. You let her—"

"Elizabeth, I was not conscious! There is nothing romantic or intimate between me and Anne—or Mary or Penelope," he added.

She was briefly distracted from her fury. "You have to be unconscious to–to...eat?"

He raised a brow. "A recent difficulty. Tell me, love, that you are not jealous of Anne de Bourgh, or any other."

Elizabeth pushed against him to make more space between them. He allowed a fraction more, but still held her tightly and she gave up her struggle but not her pique. "If *she* were your wife, in your arms, you would welcome *her*...offers. She is a woman, and I am a girl...but you will not give me the chance to become more than that."

"You did not know to whom you offered yourself before. I could not play you falsely."

"Then why marry me at all?"

"Truly, you were in danger, Elizabeth. It was necessary that you marry at once, and I would protect you, always."

She looked up at him, puzzled. "Would–would you have married me if I had not been in danger? If there were no need to protect me?"

"I wanted to, regardless," he said, hedging.

She did not miss the dodge. Pushing him away, she walked to the far side of the cellar. But his voice, when it came, was just behind her, his breath warm upon her neck.

"I do not know. I knew I wanted you, but I would have tried to spare you from this life, from the danger, the violence surrounding me—tried to keep away. But I *cannot* know the answer to your question any longer. The thought of your absence is abhorrent to me."

She whirled. "All these weeks, I have been trying to know you. You, on the other hand, have been trying to hide. 'Tis no wonder I am frustrated."

"Our future is *yours* to decide. What do you want from me, Elizabeth?" he asked, his own frustration apparent.

She sighed. His deceptions had caused her a good deal of pain, self-doubt, and sorrow. Was this what life with him would be like? A constant battle to understand him? They were, for all she knew, different species. "Choices, I suppose," she said. "I do not know the first thing about my husband, or his people. I am a guest in your home, not its mistress. When you asked for my hand, I believed I would be your helpmeet, your–your partner. Instead, I am the most fragile, helpless creature at Pemberley." She looked at him directly. "Why?" she whispered. "Why would you take vows, and yet not trust me with the truth of you? Because I am weak? Inexperienced? Untrustworthy? Do you believe me disloyal? Upon what evidence?"

"No, no," he protested. "Never that. But...Elizabeth—you cannot leave now. I cannot remove the secret of our existence from your mind. You have asked for choices but now have none. You must remain with me for the rest of your life."

"I *vowed* to do so, the day I married you!" she cried.

"You did not know to whom—to *what*—you made that promise! How could you be held to it?"

"I made that vow to Fitzwilliam Darcy. Are you not he?" As she spoke the words, she recognised the truth in them. Her fears were still present, still a part of her, especially when she imagined those dreadful teeth, ferocious and painful. But the fear was a separate thing, apart from her feelings for her husband and her anger at his secrecy. She stared, her eyes catching on his lips...and it was Fitzwilliam's mouth, not the monster's; it was familiar, not frightening. His expression was the opposite of his usual confident air of command.

"I have not explained well." Reaching up, she set her palm upon his jaw. "You wonder at my envy of Miss de Bourgh, when you have never truly kissed me, but–but *feed* from her. And yet, I am unwilling to be your...meal." A tear spilled over, tracking down her cheek. "I do not know what to do."

For a long moment, he stared down at her, watching that tear. And then he took her hand.

"Miss Elizabeth," he said. "May I have the honour of this set?"

Her brow crinkled. "What?"

"You are the most beautiful girl in the Assembly room, the most desirable female at the ball," he continued. "It is entirely possible that I will purposely ruin your evening, impelling any male who thinks to ask you to dance to ask elsewhere, because I am a jealous ape. But a merciful one. When an elderly lecher disrespects you in his thoughts, I only break his ankle, rather than killing him as I wish."

Her mouth opened in a little 'o' of surprise. He held out his hand; she took it.

"Do you waltz?" he asked.

"Oh, no. I have heard it spoken of, but never seen it done," she replied, a little awkwardly.

"Follow my lead," he commanded, showing her the steps.

And...they danced. There was no music, and little candlelight to see by, but Elizabeth did not have to be told his vision was unaffected by the dark. He whirled and twirled her past the shadowy shapes of discarded furniture, around trunks and heaps of indistinguishable debris, until she was breathless and laughing. A few minutes past, she would never have believed it.

"Elizabeth," he said, once they came to a stop at last, "I wish to begin again, if you will allow it. There is a beast within me, who cannot bear to see you even dance with another man, much less wed someone else. Secrecy has been my habit many years in the making, but I shall do my best to open myself to your understanding, if you will be patient."

"I–I will try," she said, her smile fading into resolve. "I am not known for my patience."

"You have been very patient with me, dearest."

❧

Darcy's heart beat hard, and not from the exercise. She had admitted to both fright and jealousy. Did that mean she would welcome his kiss, or be repulsed by it? It was in his nature to take rather than ask permission, but he dared not ruin their tentative peace. He had not touched her mouth to his, afraid to increase the bonding, but now that she knew of his nature, and he had a means of feeding not requiring the act of Taking, what did bonding matter? He would gladly drink tainted, inferior blood for the rest of his life to have the privilege of being near his wife. He could not imagine wanting her more, or needing her less, regardless of the bond.

"I would very much like to kiss you, my love," he whispered lowly. "If you will permit it."

Her perfect mouth opened, then shut, as she studied his. He held the breath he did not need, afraid to move, feeling his life balanced upon her next decision. Slowly, her eyes wide, she nodded.

Carefully, he placed his hands on either side of her cheeks, bending his head to hers. Her lips remained innocently closed as her eyelids drooped, and he knew it was her first kiss. Emotion welled within him as he pressed his lips to hers.

Her mouth remained tightly shut, but he held himself to her, pressing gently, rejoicing in the simple yet intimate contact. And then he felt it, her lips pressing back, returning the pressure he gave. Struggling for control, he forcibly restrained his fangs from descending, gently nudging her lips open. When after a moment they did, triumph filled him, and he deepened the kiss; finally, at long last, part of him entered part of her.

The connexion was electric. He felt something snap into place internally, as though mismatched pieces of his soul had just been joined in perfect harmony. But there was so much more. The kiss became a joyous conduit, as finally, finally her emotions streamed into him, from both head and heart.

The imposed feelings of others, he despised. Elizabeth's, the one person he longed to experience, had been denied him. Until now.

He kissed her frantically, tasting her fears of rejection and of his vampyrism; feeling her frustration, her loneliness, her resentment; absorbing her curiosity, her awe, and her ready, intelligent courage. He felt everything, and more, and felt it all being subsumed by her passion.

Passion for *him*.

Nineteen

Elizabeth awakened in her own bed. But for the first time in weeks, she slept well, no dreams disturbing her night. Maggie moved about quietly; the sunlight peeking through the draperies showed it must be very late in the morning. She rose up on an elbow.

"Good morning, Maggie. Would you order a bath for me?"

"Yes, ma'am. Mr Darcy ordered the water heated, to be ready for you the moment you awakened, so I shall have it here in a trice."

Elizabeth blushed. Still, deciding to push at barriers keeping her isolated and alone, she added, "Hearing you address me as 'ma'am' makes me feel so old."

She caught the smile on Maggie's face before the girl hid it. "You are hardly old. A babe, rather."

"Yesterday I would have challenged you. But sixty-three years! You look so youthful. How fortunate!"

"How *annoying*," Maggie corrected. "I always looked young for my age, and then to be frozen in this childishness. I have dressed very severely so you would think me twenty."

"Do not consider that now. Wear anything you wish! You could be my grandmother...my great-grandmother! How young can one be, to be Turned?"

"I am the youngest I know. Children cannot be Turned...if the mortal is too young, he dies...or too old, for that matter. 'Tis not an easy change."

Elizabeth imagined growing fangs of her own and shivered. "I never did remember to ask Mr Darcy his age," she said, wishing to change the subject. She swung her long legs over the edge of the bed, stretching. "I fear I have slept overlong."

"Mr Darcy gave strict orders you were not to be disturbed. We have been moving about on tip-toe." The maid unsuccessfully tried to restrain another smile.

Elizabeth's blush returned. It was plain the servants believed more happened between herself and her husband than had, in actuality, occurred. She was only just beginning to know him, and his vampyrism was the least of it. He had hidden himself from her, and in keeping his distance, had distanced *her*. When he revealed that her kisses opened her emotions to him, she nearly quit the room! Instead, they talked long into the night, and when the kisses began again, she happily exchanged them. While he was now eager to complete their marriage, sweetly he declared himself more than willing to court her first.

It would be hours until dinner, or even until her swordsmanship lesson, yet she could not wait to see him. She composed a note asking him to join her at his earliest convenience. And giggled at the formal words, for the first time feeling purely confident that he would be willing, nay, anxious to do so.

Richard smirked. "You seem in fine spirits this afternoon."

"Put a damper on it, Richard," Darcy replied, but there was no heat in the rebuke. Indeed, it was very difficult to prevent what he feared was a ridiculous grin.

But Richard's expression suddenly turned serious, and Darcy knew his uncle was determined to air his concerns. "So...do you believe the bonding is fully complete?"

"If it is not, it soon will be," Darcy replied, feeling the wonder of it. Elizabeth burned in his heart; he had loved her before, as much as he was able to love, but now she was his lodestar, her welfare the guiding light by which he would judge every future decision. The connexion he felt with her was true, deep, and indubitably permanent.

"Do you think that is wise?"

"It is essential."

"Why? What is 'essential' about turning control of your life over to a fickle woman?"

"Not fickle, Richard. She is as true a female as was ever born."

"She willingly allows you to feed from her then?"

Darcy's expression turned stony. "'Tis unnecessary. I will continue to ingest as I did last night."

"We do not know how it will work for the long term. Your body could reject it."

"There is no reason to think there will be repercussions."

Richard stalked the room's perimeters. "Devil take it, Fitzwilliam, I wish you had waited. This hellish bonding is one-sided, and no good can come from such inequity."

"Elizabeth has strong feelings for me. She knows what I am and she came to me regardless. She is courageous and open to our differences—not at all like my mother."

"She is mortal—her limitations are many and in keeping with the usual shallow nature of her race."

"Do not, Uncle," Darcy warned. "You were human once."

"And I rejoice that I am no longer," the colonel countered. "If she truly cared for you, she would accept you in all ways. She would nourish you."

"With time, and patience, perhaps she might. But whether or not she ever comes to love me, I love her enough for both of us. I feel happiness. Why would you wish to diminish it?"

Richard gave a very human-sounding sigh. "Bonding afflicts so few vampyric males—and yet both you and your father had to suffer it. It does not seem fair."

A footman's knock interrupted them, delivering a note that brought a smile to Darcy's face. "You are wrong," he replied, uncaring now if he appeared smitten. After all, he was. "I am the most fortunate of men." He strode quickly from the room, leaving the colonel staring after him.

❧

It was gratifying how quickly her husband appeared in the blue parlour where she awaited a reply. "Oh!" she said, her blushes beginning all over again. "Good morning!"

He shut the door behind him and went to her at once. "What did you need, Elizabeth?" he asked, kissing her lightly on the cheek in greeting.

He was always so much bigger, so much more imposing than she remembered; but though her blush burned, she teased, "I thought you might wonder how I feel this morning." And she smiled.

Darcy enfolded her in his arms, kissing her madly. Her hands dove beneath his coat, trying to bring him closer still. "Elizabeth, we should stop," he murmured, in between kisses.

"Why?" she asked breathlessly. "You said you were mine. Have you changed your mind?"

"No-oh," he drawled, obviously struggling, taking her mouth once more. His eyes were black.

"Then you do not feel the same?" she said, smiling slyly.

"Someone could enter," he said, closing his eyes.

"So...tell everyone not to. You can do that, can you not? Just... think it at them?"

He smiled. "Clever girl. *My* vampyres, I can 'think at'. Mortals...I can compel. Usually. Except for one stubborn, beautiful woman who is too desirable for her own good. How did you know?"

"I was remembering the way you managed my father and mother, and how easily you cleared the room of chaperons," she said impishly.

"We have all the time in the world, darling," he assured her, pressing a kiss to the corner of her lovely mouth, and then more deeply. "You are all a man could ever want. I can feel your desires, your passion...and also that you are still being brave."

"No," she said, but she would not meet his eyes.

"I know the truth now," he said, pressing his forehead to hers. "I love being inside your senses. You cannot know how it joys me to say that."

But her many questions about his nature returned. "You...you read my mind?"

His smile faltered. "Most vampyres can manipulate the minds of humans to some degree, in order to compel actions or sleep, scramble the present, and revise recent memories—brief exposures to things most humans would rather forget. My gifts read more deeply, emotional essences, in that I can recognise motivation and predict intentions with a degree of accuracy appearing psychic to the average human. But unless I exert vast power—which I *would not* do—I can only go so far, and no farther. And your feelings are only open when we are together like this." He kissed her again, but she drew back.

"What..." she stopped, then started again. "What of Mr Bingley? Is he...?"

"He is mortal," he said. "His family has served mine for several human generations. He...manages, for lack of a better word, the Darcy interaction between humankind and vampyre. Upon reaching maturity, the blood-born do not age, or rather do it so slowly, a mortal lifetime is not nearly long enough to see it."

"How old are you?" she asked.

"Two-hundred-ten years, my next birthday."

Elizabeth gulped. "I must seem like...like a mere child to you."

He lifted a brow. "That is not at all how you seem, to me."

She felt her cheeks grow hot at his look and sought to return the conversation to her questions. "How do you do it?" she asked. "Do not your neighbours notice your lack of aging? Or are they all vampyre?"

"Not all. I have some talent for illusion, but for the most part it requires a great deal of effort to remain in one place for longer than ten or fifteen years. Charles ensures that any human families who work my lands are discreet and open to differences. The Darcys are known to be eccentric. He employs a vast network of both circumspect mortals and information. He is over-steward of my distant estates, managing their managers, utterly indispensable to me. In addition, he handles little details requiring delicacy. Vampyres are governed by one principle—we must keep our natures from mortals, hiding in plain sight. Bingley and his people listen for rumours or whispers which might indicate our secrets are suspected, alerting me to any who might need...persuasion to forget."

Her eyes widened. "What do you do to them?"

"Nothing so terrible, Elizabeth," his voice a little sad. "I turn their memories into something more acceptable to the human mind. They are unharmed—and believe me, much happier without their former knowledge."

"I should not like to have my memories...adjusted."

"'It would not work in any case. You are impervious to any sort of mind trickery."

"I am?" she asked, her eyes wide.

"You are. Otherwise, you would not remember my words at the moment we met, and I need not have apologised."

Her eyes narrowed. "In that case, 'tis a good thing I am immune to your flummery. I should hate to see you miss an opportunity for improvement of the mind."

"Humility is good for the soul, I suppose."

She laughed, but her expression turned serious. "I am glad you could never make me forget you, Fitzwilliam. I think if you could, there would always be something missing...only I would not know why."

He kissed her again, and she wondered what he felt from her now. Was this love? Every kiss gave him something of herself, but she still knew so little of him!

"So...at dinner? What did you do with your food?"

"What did I do with *what* food?"

"The food you appeared to swallow?"

He smiled. "I swallowed it, milady. Monsieur Philippe would be most disappointed if I did not eat the meals he takes such trouble to prepare."

"But...?"

"I do not have to eat, but I enjoy doing so and it extends the time needed between feedings. Vampyres who regularly ingest human food are far less prone to blood lust."

Elizabeth absorbed this. It made her feel a bit queer—to speak so casually of what she feared most—but curiosity won out. "Is there anything you cannot eat?"

"Yes. On no account am I ever to be served brussels sprouts. Smelly rubbish."

She caught his crooked smile and smacked his arm. "You know that is not what I meant."

"As far as I know, I can eat anything." He drew her to sit beside him on a settee and reached for her again, but she put her hands upon his chest, stopping him.

"There is one thing that is off your menu from this moment onwards."

"What is that?"

"Anne de Bourgh."

He grinned. "As you wish, my lady."

Elizabeth did not appreciate his amusement. "Her easy manner with gentlemen unnerves me. I do not mean to be prudish, but something about her makes me uncomfortable. Perhaps 'tis simply her way of looking at me as though I am childish and insignificant. Should you prefer me to smoke cheroots and drink port with the men? Am I so very different from most of the females of your race?"

"I think you are very different because of the unique way you have of viewing any person or situation. Most mortals would criticise Anne because she does not follow the rules of what is proper for human girls. You, my love, simply assume her rules are different. As they are. Alcohol from the glass or bottle has no more effect on us than water does you, and there is no reason for her to abstain if she cares for the flavour. Smoking is neither promoted nor discouraged amongst either sex, although I, personally, hate the stink of it. I am glad you indulge neither. I personally have noted that amongst mortals, a taste for tobacco seems to adversely affect life span. Your bodies can be unfavourably affected by liquor as well. I would have you stay in good health, Elizabeth."

"I will age regardless. My skin will wrinkle, my teeth will yellow, my hair will thin. And you will remain handsome and young."

"You will always be beautiful to me. The essence of who you are will never fade. I have some skill at healing. You will live as long as any of your race may. It will be my joy and privilege to care for you all the days of your life."

"Is there any way for you to–to make me as you are? Not that I wish to become...I am simply curious," she added hastily.

"I will never, ever attempt the Change upon you, Elizabeth. You have my word." He spoke with a stony resolution she could not doubt. For some unfathomable reason, she was slightly insulted by his vehemence.

"Unless, of course, I should happen to desire such a change," she added challengingly.

"Not even then," he said adamantly.

"Why ever not? Or do you look forward to my much shorter lifespan? You think to tire of me? Or am I simply not good enough to be one of you?"

He stood at once, obviously insulted. "Elizabeth. Do not jest."

"I do not try to be amusing and I do not want to be vampyre. I only wish to understand why you are glad of it." Every word emerged starched and frozen.

His expression softened with her frosty reply, and he knelt at her feet, his strong hands upon her knees in an attitude of supplication. After a few moments, she placed her hands in his.

"Elizabeth, the transition is not an easy one. Many—*most*—die in the attempt, especially females. Have you noticed how few female servants we have?"

"Hmph. I have seen plenty of women about."

"Day servants from the village, yes. But very few who live at Pemberley."

"Obviously, Maggie lived through it! And Mrs Reynolds, unless she was born to it."

"Yes, they were successfully Turned. But for every survivor, I can name you ten who did not. Females are a rarity. I would never risk the loss of you to chance and greed. I will thank God for every day He allows me with you, and I count myself a lucky man if you are blessed with a usual mortal lifespan."

She looked at him strangely.

"What?" he asked, brow raised.

"God," she said slowly. "The services in the chapel. You are nearly immortal. Do you believe in the same God as I?"

"Yes," he said simply. "I have lived a long time and have certain gifts...but I, too, have a Creator. And faith and hope are peaceful things." He laid his head upon their joined hands, and for several minutes she played with the overlong hair at his nape.

"There is so much I do not understand," she whispered softly. "The world is a different place today than it was yesterday. And my place in it is different. I thought to–to visit your tenants, come to know them and assist them. But now..."

"I still have tenants, Elizabeth. Many would welcome your visit. However, I ask you not to go until such time as we have neutralised the threat to your life."

"Are you certain my life is at risk? Could the abduction simply be I was in the wrong place at the wrong time? There have been no other threats, you must admit."

"I would be a fool to take chances. We shall remain vigilant."

"For how long?"

"As long as it takes," he replied sternly. Seeing her concern, his expression softened. "You are so precious to me, Elizabeth. I am so proud of your bravery."

"I do not always feel brave," she admitted. "In fact, these last weeks, as the distance between us grew, running away from my troubles sounded appealing."

He pulled her down to his lap. "I still cannot believe that you ran to me, dearest. Most would..." his words ceased as he drew her into a long kiss.

Elizabeth stopped thinking, only feeling. Every time she pushed a little further, touched a bit more, his response was heady, fascinating, and ardent. Her own touches became more curious, but as he rolled her atop him, other feelings intruded. This was not the dark privacy of a bedroom, but the floor of a much-frequented parlour. And she had practically suggested it as an appropriate setting for intimacy! Remembering her mother's accusations, she suddenly felt ashamed.

"Do not, love," he said, pulling back abruptly. "You are my wife. What we do together is never wrong."

"'Tis not proper," she replied.

"Of course it is," he assured. "Nothing could be more proper than a husband who cares for his wife so much that he cannot wait to share her company."

"I do not require coddling. You can say things as they are, no matter my sentiments."

He rolled them again, so he looked down upon her, taking her face between his hands. "I *want* to coddle you—to take care of you, make you smile," he said huskily. "I wish to feed you sweet fruits from the conservatory, watch the juices of oranges and berries stain your lips. I will have Monsieur Philippe make tarts and cakes for the pleasure of seeing you eat them. I would be your lady's maid, your servant, and dress and disrobe you myself. Your hair would be my particular pleasure...and you would only wear it down, so I could run my fingers through it at will. You would use me as your pillow and your blanket, your hearth and your fire. I want to keep you as close as my own skin, and never let you go."

She shivered, amazed at how much she wanted him to do—to *be*—all those things. And she wondered...was this love?

Twenty

THE PAIN, WHEN IT CAME, WAS EXCRUCIATING...BUT unsurprising. She had been expecting it ever since learning the vicar had married the wrong woman. Sooner or later, someone was bound to mention just *who* married Elizabeth Bennet. Bracing herself, trying to prepare, she bleakly acknowledged the presence of a greater power. She was fortunate, she supposed—it was nearly dawn and she was alone. No witnesses to her weakness.

"Mother," she said.

"Liar!" the voice in her head screamed, and Anne fell to her knees.

Though grovelling would not help, she did it anyway, willing to do or say anything to halt the pain. "He was married when I arrived. I could not stop it! I would have, I would have—" The agony twisted through Anne, cutting off further words.

"Kill the doxy!" Catherine shrieked wildly.

Anne tried again. "Our powers are useless against her, and Darcy protects her. Everyone watches her closely. She is never left alone." At her mother's bitter—and agonising—recriminations, Anne cried, "I have a plan, Mother. Please, listen. I have been thinking of how to undo this since I discovered what happened." The raging attack eased just enough for her to speak.

"Fitzwilliam was not thinking clearly when he married her. I believe he regrets it. He does not feed from her. Who do you suppose he uses instead?"

Abruptly, the pain ceased. "You, Daughter?"

Lightheaded, Anne forced her thoughts to remain regulated. "Yes. I believe that, in time—"

"Time is a commodity you do not have. Bring the girl to me. I will remedy this."

"But—"

"Do not force me to discipline you, Child. I give you three days to act. Do not fail me again."

Catherine departed, and Anne was alone in her head. The dry heaves, however, stayed on for another hour. The link forging mother and daughter was not one of blood. The strength and power of de Bourgh was wrought by and through unholy psychic control of the flesh. Those with whom Catherine forged ties, she owned, and though they were both usually content to pretend otherwise, Catherine had possessed her daughter almost since birth.

It was time, Anne knew, to prove herself truly a de Bourgh.

For the first time in three weeks, Darcy was not in the ballroom for her lesson when the clock struck four. An apologetic James stood in his place.

Elizabeth narrowed her eyes. Fitzwilliam had not spoken to her of any changes, and the night before—between heated embraces—there had been ample opportunity.

"Where is the Master?" she asked.

"In his study, madam," James replied. "He regrets sincerely being unable to make time today for your practice."

She gave him a long look; it was not that she doubted James's abilities, but her daily lesson meant much more than simply improved strength, speed, and tactics. It was a time of affection, of games, of... desire, that sometimes lasted far longer than the allotted hour. At the very least, he ought to have informed her via personal note. Something was wrong.

"If you would please excuse me, James, I must speak with my husband," she said, and went to find him.

He was in his study, standing at the small window, looking over a bleak, snow-encrusted landscape.

Darcy did not turn away from the view, although he had scented her approach well before. There were few places in the castle he could escape that delicious, enticing scent, one that had interrupted his few hours of sleep, screaming for his attention.

"Why do you hide from me?" his wife asked bluntly.

She surprised him again with her directness and insight. He ought to have known she would not be put off by a lame excuse. "I cannot be near you, not now," he said quietly.

"Why not?"

He turned to face her at last. She peered at him with curiosity but not, as far as he could tell, with need. Not with the overwhelming longing that he himself felt at keeping his distance. He could not help his anger at this disparity between their feelings, and his words emerged brusquely.

"'Tis you. You are fertile now."

Her brows knit together in adorable befuddlement, and his brief fury dissipated. "I do not have as much control at the moment, Elizabeth," he said more gently. "You know what I am. I always struggle against the urge to make our marriage complete. And when I do, it will be all I can do to refrain from marking you as mine."

She continued to look confused.

"I will *bite* you," he said.

Her eyes widened.

With sorrow, he smelled her fear. "The urge... the need is twice as potent during those times that your body would more readily accept my seed. When I could get you with child." He moved closer, inexorably drawn, looming over her, dominating, intimidating. His eyes radiated ebony blackness.

For long moments she said nothing. He waited for her to withdraw, perhaps run from him. The beast within prepared to chase, bristling with challenge.

His innocent wife, however, did not understand. "You are so vexed of late," she replied softly. "With enemies surrounding you, it must be difficult to cope with all that you must. I suppose we *should* wait a little bit before we have children. Just time enough for you to ensure we will all be safe." She went to him then, giving him a soft kiss on the cheek before leaving him to his solitary vigil.

Bewildered, he felt its imprint for hours.

❧

Elizabeth held letters. There were two of them—one from Jane and another from Charlotte. It seemed odd to be holding these links from her former life; she felt an almost curious reluctance to read them, as if she would be dragged back into that old world if she did. Chiding herself for the silly hesitation, she opened Jane's first.

Most of it was newsy and written in Jane's usual amiable style, full of her young cousins' antics and the details of enjoyable outings with her aunt and uncle. However, Elizabeth could sense the latent unhappiness woven through her sister's determined optimism. It was especially apparent when she spoke of seeing Caroline while at the theatre. Jane said Miss Bingley had evidently not recognised her in the low lights, as otherwise she was sure she must have acknowledged her greeting. Elizabeth grit her teeth in anger at the obvious cut.

But the gist of Jane's letter was a plea for her to return home for Lydia's wedding. Elizabeth's every feeling rebelled at the thought; after all, neither of her parents had bothered to write a line. They had dismissed her from their lives without, apparently, any more thought than Miss Bingley had given Jane. If not for her dearest sister, she would not even consider the journey.

Setting the letter aside with a sigh, she read the one from Charlotte. And what a strange summation of events did Charlotte provide! They had no sooner arrived at the parsonage, she wrote, than they were summoned to the great house of Rosings. At first, Charlotte wrote, Lady Catherine expected her to be Elizabeth!

I know Mr Collins left Kent with the idea of, perhaps, courting one of his cousins, due to the entail on Longbourn, but he certainly never communicated a marriage to any other! But you cannot imagine, Lizzy, what a fuss she made when she learned the truth of our marriage, and frankly, my husband is fortunate to keep his place (though happily enough, I believe it is not the work of a moment to remove an unwanted vicar). Eccentric is the kindest description I can think for her! Mr Collins is most dismayed, devoting himself to ministering to her and keeping her calm. Such a patient man I married!

And now I must confess, my dear friend: Lady Catherine holds yet another, even stranger misconception, one Mr Collins and I have yet to correct. I was most astonished to learn that her daughter, Miss de Bourgh, is currently in residence with you at Mr Darcy's estate. Lady Catherine is under the impression that Mr Darcy holds Miss de Bourgh in the highest esteem, and she is most certain that a proposal of marriage shall be forthcoming by the end of her visit. I wished to advise her at once of her misunderstanding regarding Mr Darcy's eligibility, but my dear Mr Collins most fervently believes it best to wait until she fully recovers her humours, and that it is not our place to interfere. I admit, having already been exposed to the full force of her displeasure once, I am not anxious to earn it again. I do hope the daughter is an easier companion to you than the mother is to us!

Oh, but the pleasure of having my own household is quite worth any number of disgruntled patronesses, I assure you. My excess of happiness lends me an abundance of fortitude for eccentricities and tantrums. Just knowing I can take comfort in my snug home and lovely garden means everything. Mr Collins quite shares my passion for roses—we have such plans for our garden!

Roses! Charlotte appeared to have no difficulties coping with the marital responsibilities accompanying marriage to the vicar. Elizabeth was relieved that Charlotte weathered her exposure to her patroness with her usual good-humoured practicality, but her news of Lady Catherine's expectations regarding her husband was something of a shock. It appeared Lydia's gossip had not been baseless.

She still had more questions than answers. Of late, Fitzwilliam had been spending more and more time with strangers. Occasionally, he introduced her but more often they remained shadowy creatures of the night. Many mornings he slept, but never with her. He had asked her not to look for him while he took his rest, saying that she would not care for it.

It had been days since their conversation regarding, er, *fertility*, and yet Fitzwilliam had not resumed their swordplay...or their kisses and intimate embraces. How long would her body...*call* him? How was it that Charlotte could bear marriage to the awful Mr Collins with such equanimity, while her own terror kept Fitzwilliam away? Her feelings for him were stronger than ever, but last night, amidst their ever-increasing distance, her dreadful dream resumed. The vision of that fanged mouth, opening wide over her, the horrible pain of it, the ripping of her flesh was as vivid and real as her fear. How could it be? It *must* be the face of a stranger; but perhaps it was not a particular face, but some sort of prescience, a warning? A month ago, she would have laughed at herself for such fanciful thinking, but now anything was possible. And still, even through her terror, she yearned for him. Fitzwilliam's mouth had touched her many times, and never to cause pain.

Sighing, she read Jane's letter through twice more. Her sister was unhappy. Lydia's wedding was only ten days hence. Perhaps the sane choice was to return home for a brief visit while she waited for her body to cease...whatever it did that encouraged *biting*. Even without mystical gifts of any kind, she could see the sadness in his eyes when he explained why he kept away. Guilt and fear warred within her heart; once again, she was lacking.

Her jaw firmed as she reminded herself that she had been willing to go forward despite her fears; it was Fitzwilliam who needed them banished entirely. And, it was true, she did not want to bring children into their lives until the danger passed. She had no doubt her husband could arrange for her safety at Longbourn; in fact, he might be wishing for just such a separation to ease his own pain with distance. An ache of sadness filled her at the thought, but she forced herself to write a note to Fitzwilliam regardless, asking to go home.

"What in the devil is this?"

Elizabeth looked up, astonished, to see her husband as she had never seen him before. He was livid, his eyes wild, his overlong hair flying from his head, giving him the look of a furious pirate. In his hand he clutched her note.

"I...Lydia's wedding..." she murmured somewhat incoherently.

"You cannot be serious! Go to Longbourn?"

He was not quite yelling at her, but Elizabeth did not care for the aggressiveness of his tone. "I am very serious, sir," she said formally.

"Why would you travel to her wedding when they denied *you* even the smallest celebration? Why pay your respects when they do not respect you? Knowing the trip is a dangerous one, why would you be so foolish?"

If Elizabeth's spine could have stiffened further, she would resemble a poker. "Thank you for your opinion of my intelligence. However, my sister Jane begged my attendance and I feel compelled, both by my foolish sensibility and by family obligation, to honour her request if at all possible."

"'Tis not possible," he said implacably.

Elizabeth's temper rose to meet his; had he been gentle in his refusal, she would not have argued, but his ill-mannered rejection put her back up. Still, she would not succumb to tantrums.

"'Tis important, Fitzwilliam," she said seriously. "Jane has not recovered from Mr Bingley's desertion. I must go to her."

Darcy raked his hand through his hair once again, crumpling her brief note in his fist. "Jane is responsible for her own unhappiness. 'Tis not your duty to appease her."

"You are cruel."

"I am honest. Her predicament is of her own making."

"What?" Elizabeth gasped. "How can you possibly say such a thing? You cannot mean it!"

Darcy only looked at her, coldly, she thought, his eyes black now with disapproval. "I do not have time for this. I must go out. I will be back by dawn. You will stay at Pemberley until I say otherwise."

He left her standing alone in the parlour. Discovering him drinking blood from the neck of his houseguest had not chilled her so much as his callous disregard did now.

Anne entered the parlour; Elizabeth had not left it, not since her quarrel with Fitzwilliam. A servant had come to stir the fire, but she had not permitted candles to be lit and sat in near darkness. Anne could see her clearly, though—could see the misery in her gaze. Men were so stupid! Still, she should be thankful for his idiocy. This would likely be her only opportunity.

"Elizabeth," she said softly, infusing as much sympathy as she could manage into her voice.

"Yes?" Elizabeth answered dully.

"I wonder if I might speak with you, offer advice. I have never married, but I have lived near male vampyres all my life. I believe I can help you understand him better."

Elizabeth shrugged.

"I know it does not seem like it, but Fitzwilliam is only behaving as a typical vampyre male."

"That is not comforting. Were you eavesdropping on our conversation?"

"Every vampyre in the house heard his bellowing. You must not ignore his inexcusable conduct."

"I fail to see how I can affect his behaviour, especially since he is gone."

"Hah! A sign he felt himself in danger of losing the argument. But 'tis a battle, not the war. You simply must not allow his last word to *be* the last word. Vampyre males are accustomed to females who stand up to them. Do not be the rug he wipes his boots upon—do not act like a *human*!" She imbued the word 'human' with unutterable contempt.

The comparison had the desired effect, and Elizabeth responded as hoped. "What do you suggest?"

"*I* will take you to Longbourn," Anne offered simply.

Elizabeth's brows drew together.

"We must leave at once," she added. "Richard inspects the borders tonight, so likely neither he nor Darcy will return for some hours. With any luck, no one will notice your absence until tomorrow afternoon."

"But packing...it will take time."

"Leave all to me," Anne said. "Fret not. He will follow you. But he will be far more respectful when you see him next. Dress warmly. Layers."

Elizabeth bit her lower lip, plainly unsure.

"You wish him to think well of you, do you not?"

"Yes," she answered firmly.

"Then meet me at the stables in half an hour, no more. Let no one see you leave, or all our plans are for naught."

❦

Thirty minutes later, Elizabeth made her way towards the stables. She had been in her room, frantically trying to judge which of her clothing was warmest, when she caught sight of her panicked expression in the looking glass. Suddenly, the whole 'plan' seemed ridiculous. Haring off to Longbourn without Fitzwilliam's knowledge in the middle of the night with a female for whom she had no great liking was foolish. Fitzwilliam had been angry and unnecessarily harsh. However, he had already admitted he was having trouble at the moment with control. His behaviour was so unlike his usual self, she would hope for a more reasonable outcome tomorrow. She *would* stand up for herself, but not by fleeing like an errant child. Besides, his remarks about Jane bore further discussion. How could he possibly believe Jane to be in any way responsible for her situation?

Unfortunately, she still had to explain to Anne that she would not avail herself of the generous offer of escape. Elizabeth did not look forward to another confrontation, but it would be boorish to simply fail to show.

The stables were eerily quiet, but Anne emerged from the shadows as soon as Elizabeth neared. "Around back," she whispered.

"I have changed my mind," Elizabeth said, not whispering.

"No," Anne hissed abruptly.

"I am not that angry at my husband, Anne. I am sorry I put you to any trouble. I would rather wait for Fitzwilliam's return and try to speak with him rationally about the situation before availing myself of more desperate options."

"You are being foolish," Anne said angrily. "You are just like every other mortal—too weak, too cowardly to act. He will never respect you. He will grind you into dust."

"I choose to deal with this in my own way," Elizabeth replied, very glad now she had decided to refuse. She did not *like* Anne de

Bourgh. "Once again, my apologies." She turned on her heel, having no intention of standing about arguing in the cold stable yard.

Thus, she never saw the blow coming. She dropped like a stone.

"I am sorry as well," Anne muttered, lifting her easily and carrying her towards the hooded phaeton. "Sorry you had a spine, after all."

Twenty One

Darcy met Richard on a hilltop just north of the foothills closest to Pemberley. "Restless tonight, Darcy? Our sentinels are inadequate?" His uncle smiled knowingly, his massive gelding falling into place beside Darcy's huge stallion.

Darcy did not deign to respond; he knew most of the household had heard his bitter words to Elizabeth. The note she sent him had read only, 'I should like to be taken to Longbourn as soon as you can arrange it, please' and, believing she wanted to leave him, his beast roared its displeasure. Even after coming to understand she only meant Lydia's wedding, and not a permanent separation, it had been wise to put distance between them. A long ride had done much to calm him—that, and the distance between himself and temptation.

"I thought she—" he began, but, suddenly, his entire body tensed. A gaping sense of wrongness pierced his every feeling.

"Darcy? What is it?" his uncle asked, suddenly concerned.

Holding his hand up to quiet Richard, he pummelled into Mrs Reynolds's consciousness, commanding her to look in on Elizabeth in her chambers. Moments later, she delivered the ill news.

"Elizabeth," he gasped. "She is gone!"

As one, he and Richard raced the short distance back to Pemberley. It did not take long to discover the absence of Anne and her phaeton. Darcy's eyes grew black with anger and aggression.

"I will rip her heart from her body," he swore.

"You do not know whether she did this," Richard said in measured tones. "Her mother might have them both. It would behove us to think before we act."

"I will be sure to ask many questions—*then* I will rip her heart from her body," Darcy said, dismounting and handing off the reins to Richard. "If Catherine has Elizabeth, Anne aided her." Forcing calm through his rage, he walked around the stable yard; the smells were fading, but he would be able to scent Elizabeth through a blizzard. In moments he determined their direction.

"I have it," he said, striding back to his mount. "I cannot wait for the others to gather. Are you with me?"

"Always," Richard replied.

The steely thunder of horse hooves echoed off the hillsides for miles around.

Anne glanced once again at the insensible figure slumped beside her. Hopefully she had not permanently injured her, but human skulls were perilously fragile, and Mother wished the captive alive. She could not waste attention considering Elizabeth's state, however; driving her horses hell for leather took all her focus and the burden of Elizabeth would slow her, perhaps fatally. Anne's horses were swift and trained to her will, and she only had to attain the borders of the market town of Buxton, where her mother's people would take charge of the girl and lend Anne protection from Darcy. Hell's fiends, but she hoped they brought an army. Until her mother succeeded in destroying or subjugating Darcy's line, she was a marked vampyre. But she had known, when she encouraged Richard to take her to Pemberley, it would come to this. She had waited a long, long while to prove herself worthy of the powers of de Bourgh.

It was nearly dawn. Unlike Darcy, she would grow weaker at sunrise and fighting multiple combatants alone would be madness. Just a bit farther! She was moments from victory.

They hit a particularly vicious section of road, and even though the phaeton was well sprung it was difficult to remain seated. Elizabeth was nearly thrown, and Anne heaved her back in with a powerful shove, muttering a curse. "What is so exceptional about you? Such a weakling!"

Cold, was Elizabeth's first conscious thought. *Bitter cold.* Gradually, she became aware of other things, and she realised with a great internal sigh that she had been abducted—again. Carefully, she tried to brace herself more securely against her side of the bench without alerting her captor. Her head ached viciously, throbbing with pain at each knock against the side of the hood.

It did not snow, but the air froze her lungs, and, at the speed they travelled, the wind burned her skin.

Fitzwilliam, she thought, with all the longing in her heart. For the first time, she violently wished he had unfettered access to her mind. *Fitzwilliam!*

The horses were too slow.

Darcy now knew where they were headed. Buxton was a thriving high market town, the road well-travelled. Every instinct warned he must get to his wife before they reached it.

He could travel faster without the horse, but it would exhaust his stores of strength, and reason suggested one should not engage in pitched battle if one consumed most of one's resources getting to it. He calculated the time until dawn, Anne's start, and the approximate time of interception, knowing they were close. But then...some innermost primitive sense reached him—a plaintive cry, perhaps, or a wisp of thought. It was from Elizabeth.

She needed him.

There was no power on earth strong enough to keep him from her. He shot away, leaving Richard to grab the reins of his suddenly riderless horse and follow more slowly in his wake.

One moment, Anne barrelled down an empty road, feeling exultant. Not only was she almost to Buxton, but she managed to stay just ahead of morning traffic leading into the town, the road before her clear. The horses were lathered but making excellent time.

The next moment, her passage was blocked by a dark, massive

figure and her horses were slowing—*slowing!*—against her will and fervent commands.

Fitzwilliam Darcy stood casually alongside her blowing, snorting horses, peering at her, considering. Her passenger, apparently unconscious no longer, scrambled down from her perch. Anne made no move to stop her. Her mind worked frantically, thinking how to convince Darcy she took Elizabeth only to protect her.

"Fitzwilliam!" Elizabeth cried, throwing herself into his arms. Carefully, as though inspecting a thoroughbred horse for flaws, he ran his hands over her shoulders, her back, arms, and sides. Her hair had come loose and flowed over the strong hands searching her scalp. Anne knew the second he discovered the swelling lump at the back of his wife's head, the very moment her own death was assured if she stayed another moment.

Elizabeth visibly trembled. "I w-want to go h-home," she said, through chattering teeth. Mortals were so ridiculously frail.

Darcy would not want to leave his female, and Anne had strength not only to run like the wind, but to prevent him from following for a priceless few seconds. Quick as lightning, she threw all her power into a massive leap from the phaeton—one that should have sprung her a half-mile down the road. And yet...she remained. Every muscle, every nerve frozen in place—she could only speak through her clenched jaw.

"I did not know you could hold me this way," she gritted out.

"Neither did I," he said, not taking his eyes—or his hands—off Elizabeth. "It must be the result of how very, very much I wish you to stay completely still." His voice was low and colder than the predawn chill.

At the sounds of an approaching rider, Anne calculated the odds of it being someone who might help her. Richard Fitzwilliam galloped into view, coming to a halt next to his nephew. Surely he would show *some* mercy; had not she been grooming him for decades?

"Shall I kill her now?" Richard asked his nephew indifferently. Elizabeth gasped.

"Return her to Pemberley. Secure her there—and ensure no one but you and I have access to her. This includes access to her mind. Do not feed her."

Darcy gaze returned to her. "I take it your mother has reinforcements at Buxton?"

Anne could not nod, could not even blink. "Yes."

Dipping his head in acknowledgment, he turned back to Richard. "Where is Atlas?"

"I turned the bloody beast loose to make his own way back. He is too mean to be captured."

"True. You will have to ride double, then. I need the phaeton for Elizabeth."

"I will not risk my mount. *She* can walk."

Would Richard treat her this way? After all she had been to him? Perhaps it was an act, for Darcy.

Taking a length of rope from his pommel, he looped it around her throat, twisting it in tight knots at her wrists. It hurt dreadfully, and he smiled coldly. "Silver reinforced," he explained, jerking on it. She stayed frozen and he yanked harder.

"Darcy? You might wish to release her," Richard said. "Achilles has had exercise enough this night without fighting you, too."

Darcy shrugged, but the next moment Anne's joints released. Without a backward glance, Richard spurred his mount forward. As she stumbled along, half-running, half-dragged, she knew there would be no mercy from him.

"I take it silver has a negative effect upon vampyres," Elizabeth said, staring after the pair. "Will not they attract attention?"

"Richard can ensure no one notices," Darcy explained. "Humans are susceptible to illusion, seeing what we wish them to see. Not you, of course." Seeing her shiver, he removed his coat and wrapped her in it. Gently, he scooped her up and set her on the seat of the high-perch phaeton. Leading the horses around to a wide spot in the road, he turned them back towards Pemberley before climbing in beside her. It was all he could do not to clasp her to him, to cling to her tightly. Yet, his guilt choked him. His coldness to her when last they spoke froze his heart, and rage at himself, at Anne, even at Richard, chilled his soul.

"How is your head?"

"Rattled," she replied, and he turned to look at her.

She laughed a little. "This is all so strange. For the past weeks I have been chiding myself for jealousy of Anne, believing my dislike to be churlish and unkind. Now I have a genuine reason to distrust and despise her, and I fear you will kill her."

He carefully drew her hand into his lap—the least of what he wanted, yet all he dared—and held it there. "Elizabeth…for all I want you in my world—'tis a violent one. Only the strongest survive. If I allow you to be kidnapped and make no reprisal, I put my entire House at risk. Please, please forgive me for leaving you vulnerable."

She met his gaze steadily. "When I awoke, I was afraid to move or speak, scared if I did, I would miss an opportunity for escape. But I hoped you would come, prayed you would find me, with all my heart. And you did."

They rounded a curve and the phaeton, though moving slowly, passed Richard and Anne. In the light of the rising sun, with the influence of her silver bindings, Anne could no longer remain upright and was being dragged. Richard gave them a hard nod of acknowledgement.

"Your uncle is very angry," she stated, when they were long past the pair.

"We both are. He brought her to Pemberley. He trusted her, and I trusted his reassurance. Her betrayal sits very ill."

"Are they…were they…*more* to each other?"

"Yes."

"Poor Richard," Elizabeth sighed.

"It was not—" he began, then stopped.

"Like us?" Elizabeth finished for him. "The way we feel?"

He wanted to ask her how, exactly, she felt about him, but—after his spectacular failure of this night—was too wary of her answer. The noise of a dozen men and horses relieved him of the need to speak—the contingent from Pemberley.

James and Andrew spoke for them all as they bowed to Mrs Darcy, expressing gratitude for her safe return. Elizabeth gave them a shaky smile of thanks, and the men departed to seek out any de Bourgh vampyres still in Buxton, leaving only Nigel and Thomas—silent sentinels, shadowy and unobtrusive. For a time, Darcy held his peace, but the acid of regret ate at him until he could not restrain another apology.

"I am so very sorry, Elizabeth. Sorry for how I spoke to you earlier, sorry for my temper and my jealousy, and deeply sorry I left you alone for one minute."

"You could not have known she would do such a thing."

He frowned. "I should never have trusted her...should never have supposed a hundred years of friendship would count for anything with a de Bourgh."

"You had your reasons for believing her trustworthy. Granted, I cannot imagine what they were." She smiled at him.

He could not smile back. "Whatever they were, they were not enough. I am so sorry you were hurt, that you were afraid."

She shook her head. "I always knew you would come. You say you cannot hear me, but you did."

It touched him, this faith she had in him after his miserable failure. And perhaps he *had* heard her call; it was as good an explanation as any. It was not all he wanted from her, but more than he deserved.

"Fitzwilliam?"

"Yes, love?"

"If you were to hold me, could you create an illusion so any who see us would not notice or care?"

"Yes, darling," he replied tenderly, relieved and grateful to be enfolding her in his arms. "This, I can do."

❧

When they reached Pemberley, Darcy carried Elizabeth in, allowing no one else to touch her or assist him. Not even Maggie was permitted entry. No one was to care for her but himself.

Carefully he peeled off cloak and pelisse, unbuttoning the dress and stripping off her stays. He turned her this way and that, unlacing and unbuttoning. "I can have Maggie help me," she said, blushing. It was full daylight.

She has been hurt, terrorised, he reminded himself. Forcefully. Gently he nudged her towards the bed, turning back the bedcovers and watching the silky strands of her hair overflow the pillows.

"I did not braid your hair," he said dispassionately, as though he were only making a casual observation and not burning inside. He picked up a curling lock, twisting it around his finger. "I remember the first time I saw it down. If I had not been lost before, I surely would have been at that moment."

"'Tis always messy. It will never stay confined. I have always envied Jane's hair. So golden, like liquid sunshine."

"Yours is more tempting. More seductive. It puts me in mind of the bedchamber...always escaping its pins."

"We are in a bedchamber now," she said shyly, not meeting his eyes.

"You have been hurt. I will not touch you. Just allow me to watch over you while you sleep."

She did not answer him, only raised up to lift her hands to his chest. He watched, unable to stop her, trying to look only at the fine, fragile bones of her hands—to fix on detail instead of sensation. Those hands moved to the knot of his cravat; it loosened, but his throat remained tight.

"Will you not help me with your boots?" she said, looking up at him with those wide, beautiful eyes that never failed to stir him.

He was powerless against her wishes; his enemies would be full of contempt if they could see him at this moment.

"I will not leave you, Elizabeth. You do not have to offer *anything* in order to entice me to stay."

She bit her lower lip. "It would comfort me."

"I will hold you," he reiterated, trying not to look.

In response, she crawled upon the mattress, laying herself out... lifting the heavy hair off her nape...baring her throat to him.

His groan was a strangled sound; he was over her in seconds.

"Close your eyes," he choked out. His fangs were extended; he could not bear any glimpse of her fear.

It was all too much—delayed reaction to her kidnapping, adrenaline and grief and anxiety and need, all coiled into one huge wanting. He set his lips to hers.

He felt her pain. Her head throbbed with it, making him forget the selfish desires of a moment previous. Without a word he rolled them to their sides, not wanting to put weight upon her. He felt her slight dizziness, even with that small motion, and would have withdrawn immediately...except for the ferocity of her reciprocal need. Anne's betrayal *hurt* her, more than the blow to her head. His strong, soft-hearted wife needed him now, needed him to hold and reassure her. A whisper of fear crept through her desire, and he saw her eyes were still tightly closed, her neck still proffered. She was trying so hard to be brave, to be the wife he needed.

"I will only hold you, nothing more," he said gently but firmly. "My sweet girl," he added, kissing her again, touched by both her offer and the strength of her desire for him. He struggled for self-mastery and found it in the emotional relief she experienced when she realised he would not take her blood.

Oh, how he wished she would Take his, just enough to heal her wound. It grieved him that the fear of it would hurt worse than her injury.

"Am I still...still...?" she struggled for words.

"Fertile?" he smiled patiently. "Possibly. But your body no longer mercilessly demands I ravish you."

"Is that what I was doing?" she asked breathlessly.

"Until your mind and your body unite, the answer is to wait, my beautiful wife," he said, wrapping his arms around her, rejoicing at her reciprocal embrace, her obvious feelings of comfort during his kiss.

"Why did she steal me?"

"I do not know, love. I will find out, though. No one takes you from me. No one touches you. You are mine."

"Yours," she repeated. And then, more strongly, "I will be yours, now. In all ways, I will be your wife. You will not deny me. Kiss me, and find I tell you true."

He began to refuse but paused. Setting his lips to hers, he felt, not simply bravery, not simply desire, and not simply fear...but a soul-deep longing. To be his, and make him hers. To be complete, and to complete him.

"Oh, my dear," he whispered.

He did not ask again whether she was sure, though he wanted to. He did not try to resist, though he was certain he should. She wanted his trust, and evidence of his love, his devotion, and his adoration; he would never add to her pain by failing to show her everything of what was in his heart.

"No one should ever hurt you, least of all me," he said. And though he tried to be gentle, to be careful, he felt how it did.

He would have withdrawn then, except for *her* needs. She wanted all of him—the intensity of his passion, the strength of his muscular form, the warmth of his ardour. Not just possessed but possessor; he was hers every bit as much as she was his.

"Mine," they both cried together, a single voice, as the two became one.

❧

Much later, still intimately connected, he could feel the beginnings of her megrim making itself known once again in place of fading bliss. Along with pain in her head—and now other places—he could sense her fatigue, her desire to close her eyes and let her troubles fade as well.

"You own me, Elizabeth," he murmured, rejoicing to feel her pleasure in his words. His heart overflowed. "I love you, dearest. I love you so much," he said, feeling as he uttered it how poorly he expressed what was in his heart. But her response was...uncertainty. A lack of confidence in—not him, not exactly that. It was, he suddenly recognised, a disbelief in her own worthiness to be loved. He knew it, because he struggled with the same feelings himself.

"Shh..." he said, stroking her sweaty skin. "I will keep telling you until you believe me. Go to sleep, sweet love."

"What would happen if I bit you?" she asked sleepily, surprising him.

He thought about how to answer her. "My blood has healing properties to humans," he said hopefully. "A few drops and your head would pain you no longer."

Still joined, he could feel her revulsion of the idea. He was sorry he mentioned it—it felt a great deal like a personal rejection.

"'Tis too strange a thought, I fear," she said. "I will be well...I just need to sleep."

He nodded, tucking her head into his chest and holding her tightly—but he relinquished his connexion with her. Some of her emotions, he could admit, were painful to know.

"You must feed, Darcy," Richard said. It had become a familiar scold over the last three weeks. Worse, Richard was right. Darcy knew he must, but it felt like such a profound betrayal of his bond with Elizabeth, he had been delaying.

"You look positively haggard. Flying to your wife's rescue depleted your reserves and you have made no effort to replenish them. You barely sleep. What is more, you study Elizabeth as though you are the fox and she, a particularly well-filled henhouse. I am surprised she has not grown uncomfortable."

He had not noticed any discomfort, and with the number of hours he spent with her, it would be impossible to miss. *'Tis because she trusts you,* his conscience reminded. *Implicitly.*

"Very well, Richard. Ask Mrs Reynolds whether she would be willing to donate."

"Anne's blood is stronger."

Darcy's countenance became stony. "No," he said with finality.

Richard shrugged. "Unfortunate. I would not mind tearing her throat open to retrieve it for you. Tell me again why she yet lives?"

"Catherine will want her back. I want Catherine. She hides behind her allies, but she cannot stay hidden forever."

"It would be kinder if we killed her. Catherine is not known for her tolerance of failure," he said indifferently.

"Happily, I am not interested in kindness," Darcy replied.

Agnes Reynolds was more than willing to feed her dear Master. She joined them in the study, where Richard made a clean incision, and the artery flowed generously from her wrist into the waiting goblet. Darcy's mouth watered at the sight, his fangs extending effortlessly. He was so famished he snatched the goblet before it neared full.

This time, the feeling of revulsion was much stronger. His incisors retracted before the cup ever reached his lips. He forced himself to swallow it all, remembering Anne's blood took time to settle.

Instead, he grew more and more nauseated.

"Devil take it, Darcy, you are white as a ghost!" Richard exclaimed.

His ears rang, his belly roiling. In an instant, Mrs Reynolds produced a basin from heaven only knew where, holding it to him in the nick of time. He vomited every bit of what he had consumed, violently retching with the dry heaves long after he emptied his gullet. It left him needier than ever.

At that moment, someone knocked at the study door.

"'Tis Elizabeth," Darcy gasped. "Do not let her see me this way."

Richard strode to the door, his large form blocking any view within. "Have you seen my husband?" Darcy heard her ask.

"He is occupied at the moment," Richard said. "I shall send him to you the moment he is free."

Her reply was laced with suspicion. She might not be bonded in precisely the same manner as Darcy, but she instinctively responded to his distress. "Something is not right. Let me enter," she begged.

"That would not be wise," Richard closed the door in her face and ignored her subsequent pounding.

"Smooth," Darcy muttered. "You could have invented a decent excuse."

"What is *her* excuse for refusing to feed you?"

"Stifle it, Richard."

When Darcy vomited Anne's blood, Richard's anger and disappointment were huge. It had taken him days to convince Darcy to try it, all because of some ridiculous promise the fool made to his self-absorbed wife.

"I want your word," Darcy was saying, his voice noticeably weak. "Swear you will take care of Elizabeth all the days of her life—no shortening it to bring me back. Swear you will do all in your power to ensure her happiness."

"An excellent point, Darcy," Richard responded slyly. "The woman attracts enemies like bees to honey. If you go to ground, who will protect her?"

"Take her to the Baltic estate. Surrounded by water and far more defensible than Pemberley."

"Take her yourself," Richard barked. "Darcy, *ask* her at least."

"I swore to her I would never do that," he said adamantly. "I will not break my promise."

"What about your wedding vows? Surely disappearing from her life was not part of those."

"She did not wed this part of me," he insisted. "She never agreed to share this burden."

"You must ask her! Give *her* the choice."

"Elizabeth is very good at doing her duty. She would agree if it sickened her. I will not turn what we have into revulsion."

"Am I to tell her that you would rather die than ask anything of her?"

"I am not so easy to kill, as you well know. When the bond is broken, I will be able to feed again from others, as Father proved."

"But until then, you will retreat to the earth, all *but* dead."

"I am not happy about it. There is no other way. I trust you to care for her and the others of my House, for my sake. I know you would not expect me to relive the worst parts of my past, at Elizabeth's hand."

"And how am I to explain your desertion to your bride?"

"I will...write to her. Soon. I dare not see her again—'twould not be safe. And then you will arrange for her to hear of my death. Protect her, please."

"I thought *you* were determined to protect her from her enemies. 'Twas why you married her in the first place."

It was not the only reason, Darcy could admit now. But Richard cared nothing for love, only wishing to see him fed no matter the cost to Elizabeth. "Anne admitted that Catherine has been plotting against Elizabeth, all to ruin me. Tell Catherine that as long as Elizabeth is in good health and free, Anne's life will be spared. The moment that changes, Anne is dead." Darcy glowered at his uncle. "Anne will only be returned if Elizabeth dies of natural causes after a long life. If she makes any move against us in the interim, both their lives are forfeit. She is not stupid. She wants her daughter back. Fifty-odd years is nothing, a far better bargain than she would ever expect after such an attack on a Darcy."

Richard stalked from the room in disgust.

❧

By the close of the fourth day of Fitzwilliam's absence, Elizabeth no longer believed any of the flimsy excuses proffered by Maggie and Mrs Reynolds. Richard Fitzwilliam was outright hostile—as though *she* were responsible for Fitzwilliam's baffling departure! Her own search of the castle revealed nothing, but of course, Pemberley was huge and unlikely to give up her secrets. Elizabeth, however, inexplicably felt he was still nearby. Finally, out of ideas, she determined to force the issue.

Elizabeth winced at the bloody mess on the ballroom floor. The colonel was there, soundly defeating poor Nigel; he made no effort to pull his strokes, neither of them bothering to disguise their wounds. She shrieked when Nigel sank to the floor, Richard's blade lodged in his chest—earning her an eye roll from the colonel. But Nigel yanked the blade out of his body himself, limping towards the door, using the blood-spattered sword as support.

A servant brought out a fresh blade for the colonel and Andrew entered. Elizabeth realised she would be ignored indefinitely.

"Colonel? A word, please?"

"If you insist," he said insolently, barely glancing at her.

"Where is my husband?"

"Busy," he answered shortly. "Leave it alone."

"You have answered a question I did not ask," she replied, determined. "I did not ask if he had time to speak with me, nor do I care for your personal opinion regarding my interest. Is Fitzwilliam still at Pemberley?"

For a long moment, she thought he would not answer, but at last he did.

"Yes."

"Is he in the house?"

"Yes."

She strode away from him purposefully.

"Where do you think you are going?" he called after her.

"To find my husband," she gritted out.

"You will not find him if he does not wish it."

She whirled. "I will find him if I have to disassemble this place stone by stone. I will hire every soul who lives in this country to tear the place apart. I will take pickaxes to the walls, dig up the gardens, and burn anything left."

"I could lock you up, you know," he said, his eyes amused.

"I would not put it past you," she snarled. Snatching up a sword in both hands, she lunged at him as though levelling an overhead strike. Richard parried, but at the last moment, Elizabeth sidestepped and dropped her attack to his foreleg, slicing into his femur. She winced, but quickly yanked the weapon free. Assuming a threatening stance, she pointed the sword right at him. This man kept her from her husband—she would *make* him bring her to Fitzwilliam, else die trying.

"Not a bad feint," he grunted.

"Take me to him," she demanded. "Or one of us dies. Now!"

"Does Fitzwilliam know you are so bloodthirsty?" he taunted.

"Does he know you are a clodpate?" she hissed. "Take me to him now, or I shall stick you like the pig you are!"

He set down his weapon, lifting his hands in the air. "I surrender," he said in mock fear. "Follow me."

She followed him belowstairs into the cellars, noting he showed no sign of a limp from the wound she'd inflicted. Richard walked unerringly through the dim interior, past myriad rooms she had already searched. Finally, he tilted out a torch sconce. The entire wall rolled away, leaving a black cavernous opening. Richard grabbed the torch, lighting it without a flame.

"After you, milady," he said, still mocking.

"No, thank you," she answered evenly, determined not to show fear, following him down, down, down. The light of the torch exposed rough-hewn walls; sounds of scurrying preceded them, and every now and again she felt the silky-sleek whisper of a spider's web against her cheek, making her shudder. She tried to take comfort in the sword she still held, but no doubt he was very capable of disarming her. Perhaps he only brought her down here to lock her up, as he had threatened. It was not as though anyone would search, with Fitzwilliam gone.

He stopped before a thick, heavy door. "He is in there," Richard said slowly. He faced her, his expression serious in the flickering torchlight. "It could be dangerous for you to enter. He has not eaten in too long, and he is...leaving life behind."

"What?" Elizabeth gasped. "Why? Why will you not feed him?"

"Why do you care? His eating habits disgust and repel you. You instructed him to keep this part of his life out of yours. So he will, though it slays him."

"I never wanted him hurt and you know it! Why will no one tell me anything?" Her eyes were full of unshed tears of frustration.

"He is a fully bonded male vampyre. That means he can only feed from one person—his female. If she will not feed him, he cannot eat. If he cannot eat, his body ceases to function. Once you die, the bond is broken naturally. Or," he said, one eyebrow raised, "I can kill you and destroy the bond by that means."

"I know which you would prefer. Why do you fail to mention a third choice—that I feed him, you beef-witted coxcomb?" she snapped.

"There is that option. How careless of me to forget."

"I am going in." She dropped the sword to struggle with the heavy door. He put his arm across it, blocking her.

"He has not eaten in overlong, Mrs Darcy. He may bleed you dry."

She knocked his arm out of the way. "Well then—that will solve all your problems, will it not?" With all her might, she tugged at the door until she wrenched it open. Slipping inside, she pulled it closed behind her and threw the bar, sealing herself in. Despite her brave words, she did not wish to give herself the option of fleeing.

The agony is over quickly, she reminded herself. *Fitzwilliam's life is more important than pain.*

"'Lizabeth?" Fitzwilliam's voice, his and yet not his, sounded at the same time a sudden burst of candlelight glowed from the corner, relieving the pitch black. "You...must...leave."

"I—I have come to...to..." She could not find words.

"Go!" he ordered harshly.

His seeming ire ignited her own. "According to your uncle, you have decided to disappear off the face of the earth rather than take my blood. How could you, Fitzwilliam? I do not think my mother, at her worst, ever struck such a blow!"

The next instant, he was behind her, his arms surrounding her in an unbreakable grip. His head bent to her neck, nuzzling. She shivered with fear.

"Too far gone, love," he growled, "No words. Will kill Richard... cannot release you."

He held her, pinned, unable to move; his voice was lower, deeper, hardly recognisable...he made a noise almost inhuman, a sort of growling. *This is Fitzwilliam,* she told herself, but when she found herself, suddenly, lying on a cot, his big body poised above her, she nearly fainted with dread. "Whatever you do...will you do it quickly?" she implored.

He looked at her as if utterly uncomprehending. A sound came from him, but not words she could recognise. Her mind scrambled, her thoughts racing, as she struggled to contain the panic. Fitzwilliam seemed frozen, as if he, too, fought in some way.

Her fright grew to fever pitch.

❧

It was all Darcy could do not to plunge into her neck at once. Ah, angels and demons, she was *here* and smelled so alluring, so scintillating, so perfect...and she was *here.* The beast, far more in control than he, could smell fear coming off her in waves. Unfortunately, the predator within him only took her terror as evidence of its superiority, of his ability to have her. *Now.* The delicious scent of her blood called like the most enchanting siren's song, meat to a starving man.

She spoke again, and he could hardly follow her words—his own were gone. With all the effort he was capable of exerting, he struggled to push the beast back, make sense of what she said. *God, give me strength,* he prayed.

Darcy looked down upon his wife, her eyes shut tight and her hands white knuckled as she clenched the bedclothes. Moments before he had been lying in her exact position, fighting against the impulse to rip the door off its hinges and seek her out. Instead, she had delivered herself up to him. He wished he could tell her what this Taking meant to him, what *she* meant to him—but only one word was left of English, and he did not think she would care for it any longer. *Mine. Mine. Mine.*

But both man and beast loved her—if they could not comfort, neither could they harm.

His fangs were fully extended, of course, his mouth watering. He felt as he had when he took her virginity, the same excitement laced with trepidation—but he had known how to ease her then, how to replace her fears with pleasure. He could not make her want him now, perhaps never again...but it would not be, he warned the beast, for lack of trying.

"Do you–have a...a stick or a strap...s–something for me to bite down on?" she asked.

Utter confusion suffused Darcy's countenance as he comprehended her request. "No, no, no," he groaned. He could not explain, he had no words...but he could show her. Show her she was too important, too precious, too rare a gift to ever mistreat or abuse. Even his primitive self knew how to worship.

He lightly scraped his fangs over her throat, only a slight, teasing pressure—but she was too frightened, and he felt her body stiffen underneath him. Still, she did not flinch. Courage she had, his long-legged beauty. Courage despite her terror.

He suckled first, bringing the vein nearer to the surface, shuddering with want and need. When he could feel the lifeforce thrumming potently beneath his tongue, her blood calling to him in sensual excitement...at last, at last, he let himself Take.

Elizabeth's taste was beyond any sweetness, filled with smoke and fire, her emotions purer in this form than from any lovemaking they had ever shared. Her initial fear rapidly transformed into a glut of ecstasy and fulfilment, pleasure and acceptance, until he had to once again force control. His physical strength, even at his weakest, was so much greater than hers, he could easily harm her. With powers reviving, his strength returning, his continued Taking would result in bloodlust if he surrendered solely to sensation.

Never hurt what is mine. Never.

Darcy wrenched his fangs free, laving his tongue across the tiny punctures to seal them as if treasuring the last small taste of her.

Immediately, she yanked his head back to her, clutching him to her throat in frustrated desire. "More," she cried, trying to bring him back to drink again. "Please, more!"

He halted her remonstrations with deep kisses, increasing the power of their intimacy. His control was restored completely, the smallest intake of Elizabeth's blood superior to feeding from any three vampyre. She was his perfect match, his other half. With his fangs' retraction, he delighted in plundering her mouth as he had been unable to do in far too long. Too quickly, though, she pulled her mouth away.

"I want you to Take more," she begged.

"Elizabeth, love, 'tis the effect of the bite," he tried to soothe—though he found her responsiveness beyond pleasing. For most, the bite was pleasant and desirable—and forged a natural intimacy usually leading to mating. But apparently in Elizabeth, his venom was a source of unmatched power. "In a few moments the craving will ease." His own cravings would take a good while longer, control or no, his eyes black with unfulfilled appetite and leashed desire.

She shook her head, not meeting his eyes. "'Tis not...that is not why..."

"Love?" he asked, at the sight of the lone tear trickling down her cheek. He stopped it with his tongue, licking its salty flavour before it could drop off her chin. "Tell me."

Finally looking at him directly, she said, "I was scared for no good reason. I let foolish, childish fears *hurt* you, weaken you. For many years I have had dreams—of being bitten by some sort of vampyre-like male, and...in my mind, it hurt so dreadfully. When I saw you biting Anne, it reminded me of him. I believed the dreams, instead of asking you, trusting you would never, ever harm me. I want to give all you need, and more."

"Oh, my love...my precious, brave girl," he said thickly, his throat tight. He had hoped—indeed, it had *seemed* she had no memory of her terrible encounter with Wickham. Unfortunately, her memories had evidently been buried—and her exposure to him, no doubt, awakened them more fully. He would have to explain to her...but later. At the moment he had no words except for the love overflowing his soul.

"I have Taken all I need, my darling," he crooned. "Next time I will go much more slowly...we will take hours. Drinking you, loving you...oh, dearest Elizabeth."

"Why did not you Take from me before?" she asked. "If you had,

I would have learned sooner my fears were groundless. You must have known it would not hurt me—and yet, you were going to let yourself..."

"A man who felt less, might. I could not—*ever*—force you to do anything breeding resentment and fear."

"You foolish man." She held up her hands to cup his face. "Never again. If you ever again shut me out, I shall..." but words retreated as she moved her mouth to his.

Though the beast within was under his control, it was hardly tame. He could not resist expressing his feelings as only a man violently in love can be supposed to do.

Darcy lay awake for hours, watching his wife sleep. It was difficult to tell if her pale skin was *too* pale. He knew he had Taken too much. But, even now, remembering how she offered herself to him in every way, he could hardly have Taken less. She chose that moment to burrow closer to him—was she chilled, or did the terrible dream yet haunt her? Mixed in with his anxiety were feelings wholly unfamiliar to him, emotions dredged from somewhere unknown in his soul...stirring hopeful fancies such as eager young boys dreamt, the innocent thrills of furtively passed love notes and quick, stolen kisses. He wondered if they were *her* feelings, echoing within him even now.

Somehow, he doubted it. How ironic was it that she, the most precious to him in all the world, was the one mortal whose dreams he could not enter, whose memories were closed? Instead, he watched over her as she slept, ready to comfort her if her dreams grew harsh.

Physically, he was wholly renewed. If not for the fear his strength was stolen at her expense, he would say he was better than he had ever been. Had Elizabeth slept too long? Surely she should eat now? He reached his thoughts towards Mrs Reynolds, caught *her* anxiety and immediately felt guilty. They would all be wondering whether he had murdered her, would they not? And Richard! Bringing her here and literally abandoning her! After he had begged him to protect her, care for her. Bitterly, he realised his uncle could not be trusted, at least not with Elizabeth's safety.

❧

"Mm..." his wife murmured, without opening her eyes. "Do I smell buns?"

"I asked Mrs Reynolds to bring your favourites," he smiled, relieved and grateful she seemed well. He watched his wife as she stretched, nearly drooling like a green boy at the sight.

She turned those wide, lovely eyes upon him, the room's dimness unable to hide the new knowledge in them. Perhaps he could...*No*, he commanded himself harshly. "I have an undressing gown here," he said gruffly, "and clothing to replace what I...destroyed."

Elizabeth only smiled at him, much to his chagrin. She reached over to the nearby tray for one of the warm buttered buns; the expression on her face as she consumed it had him overheated in moments.

He lifted a glass filled with the juice of freshly squeezed oranges from his own conservatory, holding it out to her. "Here, darling," he said. "You need to replace the liquids I took."

She did not take the glass from him but scooted onto his lap—nearly causing him to spill it, in his surprise. "Replacing my blood with fruit juice?" she smiled curiously, snuggling into him. He did not know which astonished him the most—her candour or her easy affection.

"Believe me, this will help you," he said, tilting the glass to her lips.

Rolling her eyes, she took the glass from him, swallowed a large measure and set it down again. "There. Can we do it again now?"

"What?" he nearly swallowed his tongue.

She shook her long hair away from her neck, baring it to him.

"I cannot, love, 'tis too soon," he said, annoyed when his voice came out as more of a groan.

"Why not?" The sulky note in her voice made him laugh, restoring his good humour.

"Eat your breakfast, dearest, and I shall give you a short lesson in surviving a vampyre husband," he said, handing the juice to her once again.

As he rewarded every bite and sip she consumed with kisses, she soon lost her displeasure. "If I eat lots of sweets before you drink from me, will I give you a bellyache?" she asked impishly.

"I ache for you always, whatever you eat," he said, kissing her on the nose, trying to tempt her with a piece of bacon, frowning when she turned her face away.

"I am overfull now," she said. "I could not possibly eat another bite." She snuggled into his arms, and he chose the one subject guaranteed to cool his ardour.

"Tell me about your dreams, love." He felt her tense, and carefully drew her closer still, smoothing his hands across her stiff spine.

"They were foolish. I have too much imagination, as my mother often chided."

"Tell me."

She sighed deeply. "In the dream, I am walking alone in the wooded area above Longbourn. Suddenly, directly in front of me, I see a man. I always think he is beautiful." She paused her narration and looked at him. "Why cannot I learn from experience? I have had this dream for years, and 'tis always exactly the same. Why do I gawk at his prettiness instead of fleeing? Or better still, why not think, 'Oh, this is the beginning of that awful dream', and wake myself up?"

Her dismay was so real, he was overcome with the desire to comfort; he tilted her lips up to meet his and spent several moments thoroughly kissing her. "Enough of this," he growled at last. "Keep talking."

"There is not much more to it. He says, 'You cannot see me, you will not run from me,' which I think is odd, and then he clutches my arm. I begin a protest and abruptly his face changes—his teeth have grown out...just as yours do when you Take," she said quietly. "Still, I am more concerned about his hold upon my arm than his teeth, and I try to jerk myself away. And then...and then...he lowers his face to here," she pointed to her chest, "and he...he...hurts me." Her eyes filled with tears. "I do not know why a dream should be so affecting," she choked. "I suppose it is because I have never told anyone of it before."

"Oh, Elizabeth," he said quietly, his voice filled with sorrow—because he knew exactly what had happened to her. Silently, he reiterated his vow to expunge George Wickham from the earth.

"So, he bites into me, ripping me open," she said, trying to speak quickly and get to the end. "The pain is overwhelming and vicious, and I scream and then waken. But," she continued, "I do not know why I was so scared of you. After all, I saw you drink from Anne and you did not tear her to do it. I am so sorry I compared you. It was just the teeth, I suppose. How foolish. If the dream villain's defining physical feature had been red hair, should I be afraid of all red-headed men?" She shook her head.

Darcy stared at her in open-mouthed astonishment. His wife was truly the most amazing creature he had ever met. As if red-headed men, a common enough sight, compared to a being with blood-sucking fangs! He pulled her up to his mouth, kissing her desperately. If she were any other woman in the world, her experience would have rendered her terrified of his entire race. Only his Elizabeth, with her unique ability to see others as individuals, could find fault only with her own understanding. And then he was laughing, laughing while kissing her and she began laughing as well.

Chuckling still, he kissed into her wild joy. *Joy*—this was it: the strange, indescribable feeling first experienced this night—a soul-deep happiness such as he had never known.

"Does what I eat change the flavour of my blood?" she asked.

He struggled to bring his mind back to more practical matters. "If you were to drink enough liquor, I could become, briefly, inebriated on the strength of your drunkenness. I hope you will not, as I do not care for the loss of control that accompanies such excess."

"I do not care for it either," she said with a grimace. "I just remembered something...about our last disagreement. I fear Miss de Bourgh knocked it completely out of my head. You said Mr Bingley's abandonment was a situation of Jane's own making. How you could possibly reach such a conclusion?"

"I do not wish to criticise your sister, Elizabeth."

"Please, speak freely. I simply cannot fathom how Jane could deserve such censure."

Despite her assurances, she removed herself from his lap and donned her undressing gown. Obviously, his wife was no longer in the mood for cuddling.

He resolved to explain the situation as quickly as possible so they could move past it. "As you can well imagine, whomever Charles marries must be the soul of discretion. He had to test this—and before you judge him harshly for deceit, please, think of Hurst."

"Hurst? His sister's husband? What has he to do with anything?" she asked, confused.

"I suppose you could not help but notice his constant state of apparent inebriation?"

"What do you mean, 'apparent'?"

"It was proven, before Louisa's engagement was announced, that Hurst is a sorry gossip with little discretion, completely inappropriate for someone whose family secrets could revive the practice of witch hunts and demonic executions. Charles disapproved of the match and would not agree, but Louisa would not give it up. She swore she would be happy with him, that she would keep him, and herself with him, away from the family. His estate is in the country and Charles is not the most formidable of guardians. To make a long story short, they were finally allowed to marry. At first it went well—but in time Louisa learned she had tied herself for life to one who has no hobbies or interests except frivolity and gossip. Every time he overspends himself or grows bored, he insists upon inflicting himself upon the Bingley homes, thus forcing us to keep his brains scrambled so he will notice nothing. Jane is an intelligent woman, and her husband's dealings with me are far more involved than mine with the Hursts. Should I be forced to keep her mind prisoner? Or could she be happy with a husband who is only an occasional visitor in her life?"

"I understand what you are saying, except that the thrust of your argument is that Jane could not be trusted with the truth. I completely disagree."

"I will give you that her reasons for betraying Charles's confidence were generous ones. Her loyalty was to you, not Charles. I can appreciate that. I told him his choice of deceptions was a poor one and that another trial should be arranged. If he was not deeply involved in investigations for me at the moment, I am sure he would be trying to manage it."

"I still do not understand. What is it that Jane supposedly confided in me?"

He looked at her enquiringly. "Regarding my fictional engagement to Anne, remember?"

Elizabeth appeared taken aback. "But Fitzwilliam...Jane did not tell me that rumour. Lydia did. And do not even think of saying Jane would have divulged *anything* she knew to be confidential to Lydia. I would sooner believe pigs could fly to the moon. Mr Bingley put Jane in a terrible position with his awful deceit, and I am sure she must have suffered for it. But she did not say a word to me."

His brow rose. "This makes no sense. How would Miss Lydia hear such a thing?"

"Who can say? But I will tell you this: Charlotte—Mrs Collins—informed me of the same rumour in her recent letter. And she was apprised of it by none other than Lady Catherine!"

"Devil take it," Darcy swore. "Catherine. I cannot see...but I have underestimated her interest in my life, once again. I am sorry, my love."

"Then you will tell Mr Bingley that Jane had nothing to do with any indiscretion?" she asked hopefully.

"I will do what I ought to have done in the first place," he said, frowning. "I will ask her. I will know whether she lies."

"Jane does not lie. She does not know how. Deceit is simply not in her nature."

He looked at her regretfully. "My dear, Charles's life is *filled* with deceit. He hides things, situations, and people for his living—he hides my existence, in a manner of speaking. His easy, open countenance disguises more secrets than you could ever imagine. How could Jane deal with it?"

Elizabeth would not be dissuaded. "I do not know—but surely it is up to them? She is miserable, Fitzwilliam. Her heart was broken. You must go to her at once, and then to Mr Bingley."

"I will, Elizabeth—as soon as any threats to you are mitigated."

"No!" she cried so loudly he startled. "You do not know how long that will take, and she might accept the proposal of the first prospect who offers. You remember the resolution she and I made to each other? That resolution convinced me to entertain an offer from Mr Collins! *Mr Collins!* 'Tis unthinkable that she might someday learn the love of her life was lost to her, not through any fault of her own, but because we allowed her to languish in despair for years while you...met with people!"

He heard the utter contempt in her tone and suppressed a smile. "Alas, I have gone from dangerous demon to plodding bureaucrat in one short day," he sighed gustily.

She narrowed her eyes. "You mock me."

"Only a bit," he admitted, pulling her back into his arms.

Her body stayed tense in his embrace for several moments before softening. "Nevertheless, Fitzwilliam, we cannot let Jane remain unhappy endlessly. There must be someone you can send, some way you can fix this sooner."

"Bingley is due to visit soon. I suppose we could invite your sister to come as well?" he suggested, which notion pleased her tremendously. Most of his attention, however, was on the confession he had yet to make. "I remember the first time I ever saw you," he said quietly.

"I remember that too," she smirked, obviously thinking of his discourtesy at the Meryton assembly.

"No, love...you do not. You were just a girl, only twelve or thirteen years. And you were dying."

"What?" she cried, pulling away, trying to see his face. "Do you jest?"

"I do not, dearest," he said gravely. "Let me tell you."

He told her the whole of it—the attack she suffered at the hands of his enemy. "I nearly left you there to die," he admitted sorrowfully. "George Wickham...I thought there was nothing on earth I wanted more than to stake his heart with silver and present his severed head to the Council. But one glance at you...and I knew I had to save you, or at least try. It was simply too *wrong* to do anything else."

He eased his fingers through her hair, a gesture of comfort. "I truly thought you had forgotten, darling. After I healed your physical wounds, you remained unconscious—which was perfectly normal, considering your terrible injuries. I brought you to some neighbours and mesmerised them into believing they found you fallen from a tree."

"Oh!" she said to that revelation. "The great tree-falling incident. I do remember *that*—not that I have any memory of falling out of a tree. I did have a great headache, made worse by the number of lectures my mother administered. The odd thing is, I *did* enjoy tree climbing, though it was my own guilty secret. For better or worse, you succeeded in curbing an unladylike occupation. I assumed it was divine retribution."

"It was not. But if you take up the hobby again, please tell me first. I would prefer to be present, in case I must catch you."

She laughed, just a little, but her brow furrowed.

"Who is this Wickham? Why did he attack me? Why did his bite hurt so terribly?"

"I believe, to him, you were simply...food. He did not bother to ease his Taking. He is a villain, a scoundrel, a thief, a murderer, an abomination. He is my half-brother. And he killed our father."

"What?" Her shock was plain. "Why?"

He sighed, hating the story he now revealed. "His mother was my father's...mistress, for lack of a better word. Shortly before Father met my mother, he impregnated her—but once he met Mother, he would see no other. He financially supported George and his mother, even made George his heir. But there is no question he abandoned Mrs Wickham almost completely to raise her child alone. I did not arrive for another ten years."

"Did your father change his will in your favour?" she asked, plainly struggling to understand such a monstrous crime.

"Not for another century. When Mrs Wickham died shortly after George's eighteenth birthday, Father tried to take his place in George's life, bringing him to Pemberley. It was George's own dissipation, his entire lack of scruple or principle, his vicious propensities that led to his dispossession. He claims the murder was a fair fight over his inheritance portion. I am sure there was nothing fair about it. My father was so much stronger...I am sure he was tricked. But Wickham timed it well, and there were none who could disprove his story. He has an unsurpassed gift for deceit, I maintain, because he always believes his own lies. Fortunately for Wickham, Matlock found him before I could, and brought him before the Council. He prosecuted him for murder of a Council member, which should have meant an immediate death sentence. Unfortunately, I have enemies on the Council as well as friends like Matlock. Wickham was sentenced to one hundred years of starvation, in silver—a painful, humiliating punishment, though not nearly a strong enough penalty for his crime. He served less than half of it when he managed to escape, though, which makes him fair game. I hunted him, meaning to exterminate him, and I almost had him, until he hurt you."

"I am so sorry," she said softly, her regret apparent.

"You have nothing to apologise for, Elizabeth."

She gave a tiny shrug. "I wish it had not been me who prevented you from deserved vengeance."

He grinned at her. "I actually feel exceptionally proud of my discernment, at this particular moment."

She smiled. "How did you heal me? It sounds as though the wound was...grievous."

"I forced my blood into you, Elizabeth. As I told you, it has healing properties. You were so close to death, I was unsure it would be enough."

"Thank you," she said, bringing her lips to his and conveying her feelings of gratitude, affection, and desire.

"It was completely selfish," he said, humbled by her acceptance. "I have only gained by it."

"Hmm," she murmured. "I believe I have gained more," she whispered, kissing his ear...his jaw...his mouth. A lengthy mutual sharing of pleasure followed, and it was difficult to say who benefited most.

Twenty Four

"YOU MUST ACT!" CATHERINE STOOD BEFORE THE EARL, shrieking her demand. He responded by taking a pinch of snuff, an affectation sure to annoy. He had no interest in soothing her, certainly.

"I fail to see why, or how I should do so."

"He has my daughter!" she hissed. "Chained in a silver dungeon!"

"You attempted to abduct his wife," the earl drawled. "He had his case against Anne brought before the Council, and by and large he has their support. You overstepped, Catherine. Do not cry to me of your failures. You are fortunate Darcy has not yet dragged you into his claim."

"Pah! I do not worry about his piddling justice. I should think you would show more of an interest. We are *supposed* to be allies!"

"*Had* we been working *together*, I would have advised against your foolhardy plan. It was doomed to failure."

"As if yours was so much the better?"

Matlock scrutinised her expression. She could not know for certain he bore responsibility for the first attempt, the mock abduction; she probably only guessed, although it was possible she had pried the truth from Wickham. "Darcy has many enemies, my lady. I will not take credit for their failures, just as you are welcome to yours. But I, at least, learn from the mistakes of others. It was obvious from his personal rescue of the girl that he cares far more for Mrs Darcy than was originally suspected. Only a fool would try to whisk her away from Pemberley while he was still in residence."

This reference to Darcy's strong feelings for the chit had the expected effect. Catherine exploded in tantrums, ranting while Matlock idly contemplated the ways he could rid the world of her presence once he no longer found her useful. He had been thrilled at the success of his early plot, wherein Darcy chased after the girl as though she were the Teumessian fox and performed a great, heroic rescue. The Master of Pemberley obsessed over his new wife.

If Darcy got a child on Elizabeth, Matlock's own plans would be one step closer to fulfilment. He was furious at Catherine's bumbling attempt to abduct the Mouse—as he privately named Mrs Darcy—and was pleased she had been so quickly foiled. *Stupid trull.*

"We cannot allow it!" Catherine droned on, as if he were paying attention rather than imagining her staked in silver-bladed misery. "We must act immediately, lest he successfully Turn her! Their marriage would last eons!"

She had captured his notice at last. "What do you mean, lest he Turn her?"

"You never *listen*! My vision showed him in an act of Creation… with *her*. How can he marry Anne if he possesses a vampyre wife? I refuse to wait centuries for…"

Catherine raged on, spouting more of her gibberish. Matlock analysed his own sense of alarm; it was completely unacceptable for Darcy to turn the Mouse—or at least, not before they produced at least one daughter. Of course, many of Catherine's so-called visions were merely products of her delusional mind. Darcy married the girl to protect her from danger, and nothing was more dangerous than attempting to Turn a human female. As long as she was cosy and safe at Pemberley, the boy would do no such thing. However, Catherine believed her own rot. Just as she had sent Darcy straight into a marriage she abhorred, if she was not stopped, the foolish termagant was perfectly capable of twisting fate towards the very worst outcome.

"This vision of Darcy Turning his wife," he interrupted. "How far ahead do you see it? Have you even tried to discover whether she lives through the Ordeal? Perhaps you viewed her death, as is likely."

"I am the vessel. I do not *choose* what I see," she spat. "I could not tell if she survives, but I say we prevent him from making the attempt! Surely it was for this reason I was given the warning, you addlepated malt-worm!"

"Careful, Catherine. Your pique has rendered you unwise," he uttered in such cold tones, she was temporarily silenced. It was a mistake to deliberately provoke him, and even she knew it. "Go back to Rosings, woman. You have tried and failed. Allow me to manage the situation henceforth."

With a curse, she left him. For several moments, Matlock allowed the blessed quiet to calm his ruffled temper.

He was certain—absolutely certain—Darcy would not attempt something so hazardous, risking the death of his mortal. Darcy was fastidious, careful and prudent. If given enough time, the marriage would bear fruit. But he did not trust Catherine, who had as much access to Wickham as he did, nor had he missed her malevolent glare as she departed.

Darcy indulged in his new favourite pastime: doting upon his wife. Reading poetry together in the cosy warmth of the library, braving the inclement Derbyshire weather for walks on the grounds closest to the house while she teased him, and—because his tongue was not nearly so sharp as hers—retaliating physically. He had chased her through the maze yesterday, holding back so she would think she eluded him, as if her giggles and scent could not lead him to her as easily as if there were no shrubbery at all. When at last he captured her, he had done nothing except kiss her for the longest time.

He loved kissing her. Utterly satiated and extremely well fed for perhaps the first time in his life, he had discovered the incredible pleasure of kissing. He could spend hours indulging in the activity, taking his time, exploring the softness of her chin and cheeks and brow. The taste of her ear, the slope of her nose, the tickle of her lashes—these must be mapped thoroughly. Her neck, with its tantalising pulse, lured him endlessly. By the time he would finally take her mouth, the feelings he discovered were rich with joy and passion.

"You promised, you know you did," she said as he teased the skin of her neck with his teeth.

"Elizabeth," he said gently, "I cannot Take from you every day. I do not need it, and 'tis not healthy for you. Not even just a little...and you are a bit pale, sweetheart."

"Who could be anything but pale in this dratted Derbyshire weather? You have not Taken from me in days." She drew him closer, trying to pull him to where she wanted him.

"*Three* days...and I bit you only last night. I shall do *that* as much as you wish." He was happy to give her the pleasure-inducing venom without draining any of her life force, but he could not continue Taking and Taking and Taking.

"Not that kind of bite...the other," she said.

"I do not need to, Elizabeth," he said. "I am strong now. I told you, once per month—perhaps even less, with you—is ample unless there is some unusually great expenditure of energy."

She smiled slyly. "You have had many...expenditures of late."

"Dearest," he warned, hiding his smile.

She reached for his face, held it in her hands. "No. Do not call it Taking any longer. It is Giving. I give you life. You give me wholeness."

He allowed his forehead to press against hers. She humbled him utterly. He slid his mouth down over her cheek, down her jawline, to that precious pulse point. Fangs extended, he Took—or gave—and so did she.

"Oh my dear!" he sighed, taking her mouth, carefully measuring her feelings for weakness, but feeling nothing except a sweetly exquisite happiness. He buried his face in the mass of her hair, escaped from its confines once again.

"Every time I am alone with you for any length of time, my coiffure suffers," she said, sighing happily nevertheless. "'Tis the bane of Maggie's existence. I fear I am a sore trial to her."

"On the contrary—Maggie is devoted to you. Her eagerness to please you and care for you precedes her entrance to your apartments, and thankfully so—she is so stealthy that otherwise even I might be taken unawares."

"Really?" Elizabeth asked, almost shyly.

His wife was unused to admiration. "You inspire excellence in those around you. Everyone is keen to earn your smiles and approbation. The footmen compete to open your doors, guard you on your walks, and be defeated by your sword. Perhaps it is because your smiles are so generously bestowed. You ought to be stingier with them."

She laughed, a delightful gurgle that thrilled him. "They are, to a man, the worst teachers, pretending to be taken in by my feints no matter how clumsily executed. If you ceased to practise with me, I would never gain any skill." After a few moments, her brow furrowed.

"What is it, love? Tell me what concerns you," he whispered.

"I want you to promise me something," she said seriously.

"What?" he asked, a feeling of foreboding creeping up his spine.

"I do want to try and have a child, Fitzwilliam. But whether or not we are successful...I want you to Turn me. Before...before I am old and unlikely to survive."

He moved away from her abruptly, unable to bear her distress whenever they had this conversation. No matter the number of times he explained the danger, she would not be dissuaded. He tried a different approach.

"You know I need an heir," he said. "We will try for as many years as we possibly can."

"What will you do if I cannot produce one?" she said. "You said yourself that births are much rarer for Vampyre. You will let me die for such slim hopes?"

"'Tis my duty to continue to try as long as possible for progeny," he said pedantically, hardening his heart against the hurt in her voice.

"I would do it for you, if it were within my power to keep you with me forever," she said sadly.

He pulled her back into his arms. "Why will you not rail at me and accuse me of faithlessness," he growled, "instead of growing ever more sorrowful until I am ready to move the planets from their alignment to please you?"

"Could you do that?" she asked curiously.

He tilted her face up so that he might kiss her again. What would he do without her, he wondered, when her brief life was done? The physical bond might break but his life would be over. To remind himself as well as warn her, he reiterated the dangers more explicitly. "Elizabeth...the Ordeal of Creation is a foul process. I would have to drain, rapidly, every drop of blood from your body. I exercise power to prevent your organs from taking the natural course, from dying too quickly. I haven't enough venom to make that pleasant—'tis *not* like feeding. It begins to be painful before half finished, and rapidly degenerates to agonising. Many die from this torment alone, it is so great."

"You forget...I have felt it. I know what I ask—I am not ignorant."

"So you have. But what follows makes the bloodletting seem painless. I force my blood into your body and if your heart accepts it, it will begin to beat, to compel the new blood through it. Along the way, the blood changes things internally. It is excruciatingly painful. During the Changing, most die, their mortal organs unable to withstand the terrible pressure to become something else. It is an awful death, your gut collapsing, your insides reforming—while the Vampyre blood attempts to heal and yet only prolongs the agony."

Instead of reacting to the horror he described, his wife only asked, "Why did I not Turn when I was a girl, I wonder? When Wickham hurt me."

He shook his head. "You had not yet reached womanhood. Children cannot be Turned. And even so, you had not died yet—my blood healed your heart before your mind failed." He stroked her hair, remembering forcing the blood into her and the inexplicable, irresistible urge to compel her to *live*.

"If I had been grown, would you have Turned me?" she asked softly.

He realised he probably would have. Of course, it was much easier to Turn someone whom you did not love. "If I had, assuming you lived, you would not have thanked me," he said sternly. "The pain of Changing is only the first. Afterward, there is the pain of Thirst. It is a horrific torture. If not for the Shield, I believe there would *never* be a successful Turning."

"What is the Shield?"

"The Shield protects the newly Turned who survive transition. They are, literally, impossible to kill for a brief period of time, which varies according to the strength of the individual and the vampyre blood used for Change. It might be a few days or a few weeks." It also prevented the newly Turned from suicide; to the newly created, death was often a highly desirable outcome.

"But these are not lengthy sacrifices, Fitzwilliam. I would pay the price gladly."

"I know you would, my love. But the fact remains that most are not given any opportunity to pay it. Most die, and die horribly. We simply cannot risk it. We will celebrate every day of the life you have been given, and when you go, I will find a way to join you in death as quickly as I can."

She gasped and began to protest, but he cut her off. "I will not kill myself. But there are dangerous occupations for vampyres as well as humans. I will seek an honourable death, pursuing the evil abounding in this world."

"What of your duty? Your responsibility to create and then raise an heir, a subject about which you have preached most diligently? That charge does not dissolve with my death."

He hated the pain in her voice, the despair he could feel as clearly as if he were still connected to her. "We are doing our best on that score as it is," he said, trying to cheer her. "And we will hopefully be successful. A child would be a part of us both, and a vampyre child is likely to live on for many generations. For him or her, I would live as long as I am needed." As his father had, he remembered, after his mother died in a carriage accident while he was not nearby to heal her. His father had pressed forward through the sadness of his bonded mate's loss, for his son's sake.

For a long while they held each other, the only sounds the crackling of the fire.

"Fitzwilliam?" her voice came to him softly.

He pressed a kiss upon her head. "Yes, my love."

"I was hoping children would not come until the danger passes. It seems, however, in this world, the danger is never past."

"Too true," he said sadly.

Her voice grew stronger. "The next time I am fertile...will you try very, very conscientiously to give us a babe?"

He felt a piercing sensation, almost akin to pain, somewhere in the vicinity of his heart. It took several moments for him to control his emotion enough to speak. "It would be an honour, my dearest, loveliest Elizabeth."

Lydia Forster was lonely. She would never admit it in her letters home, all of which extolled the virtues of Brighton, the fine and sociable circles suiting her so well. And there were parties, many of them, which she dearly loved.

Marriage, however, was not quite what she imagined (not that she had given it much thought). There had been vague ideas of unlimited allowances, cosseting, and most of all, discarding all notions of authority. Untrue, on all counts. The colonel was not unkind, even occasionally useful. But though they had only been married a few short weeks, the heavy hand of authority was becoming familiar. The colonel expected a certain standard of behaviour. He was indulgent in the matter of hair ribbons, but completely rigid when it came to entertaining officers. The few wives nearby were dull creatures, besides which, Lydia was seldom interested in advancing friendship with other females. All told, she once had far more freedom as a daughter of the Bennets of Longbourn than she experienced now in the heart of Brighton's more vigorous society.

"Mrs Forster?"

Lydia turned at the unfamiliar voice—and startled. The man before her, resplendent in an officer's redcoat, was simply the loveliest she had ever seen.

"Who are you? How did you get in my room? La, I cannot believe you got past the drag—"

"Hush."

Lydia stilled at once, staring into his fathomless eyes.

"You will come with me now."

She immediately rose, her mouth gaping just a bit, hurrying to his side.

Well, well, Wickham thought. He might not have even needed to compel her to achieve cooperation. Lydia Forster was astonishingly easy.

Twenty Five

"You cannot avoid speaking to me forever, you know," Richard said. "I would prefer you try to tear my heart out than persist in this snit."

Darcy's eyes narrowed and he nearly launched himself at his uncle. Then he remembered he was ignoring him and returned to his dinner.

Elizabeth looked from one to the other. "It is not as though I gave him much choice, you know," she muttered—but of course, Darcy heard her, lifting a brow.

"I threatened him," she said, a bit louder. "With a sword."

"Threatened, nothing. She ran me through!"

"Oh, stop whingeing. 'Tis not like it was a silver blade," she snapped back.

Darcy looked from one to the other, perplexed. "You...stabbed him, Elizabeth?"

She shrugged. "Only in the femur. He would not tell me where you were."

"She used a trick," Richard said peevishly. "She cheated."

For the first time in days, Darcy spoke to his uncle. "Fighting fair is the best way to be killed in a sword fight, as you well know. I do not, for one moment, believe you were in mortal danger. On the other hand, had I been any further out of my mind, *she* could have been."

It was Richard's turn to shrug. "I knew you would not harm her."

"You cannot have known that. I certainly did not."

"You were hardly out of your mind yet. Not even as enraged as your father the first time Anne tried to kill you, and yet he did not lay a finger on her. Devilish bonding madness—should have dropped *her* out a window," he muttered.

Elizabeth gasped, her eyes widening. "Why would you allow her to come here, if she had already attempted murder—"

Richard looked at her, taking in her outrage and comprehending her misunderstanding. "Not Anne de Bourgh. My sister, Anne Darcy. His mum. Mortal, you know—the only species deserving of life...according to *them*." His bitterness was obvious.

"Richard," Darcy chided calmly, as if this were merely a repetition of an old argument.

As Elizabeth's eyes grew even wider, Morton entered.

"Excuse me, Mr Darcy—Lord Matlock arrives. His coach just passed the northern sentinels."

"What the devil is Matlock doing here?" Richard wondered aloud.

Darcy pushed back from the table. "Have Mrs Reynolds prepare his usual room, Morton. I will go and meet him. You will excuse me, my dear?" he asked Elizabeth.

"Of course," she replied. Both she and Richard watched him go.

For several minutes they continued at the meal, neither eating much, both consumed with their own thoughts. Finally, Elizabeth broke the silence.

"I do hope the earl has good news."

Richard laughed sardonically. "What, you think Catherine has confessed her guilt and turned herself over to the Council for discipline? Surely you are not so naïve. I doubt he would have ventured into the wilds of Derbyshire to relay anything good."

"You are such an uplifting person, Colonel," Elizabeth said sweetly. "A little ray of sunshine."

He only shrugged. "I believe I will join my nephew in the welcoming party," he said, rising. "Forgive my discourtesy at leaving you to dine alone."

Elizabeth stared at the remains of dinner for a few minutes, recalling her meeting with Matlock in London. Remembered the way he seemed almost to look through her, how insignificant she felt in his presence. As she had absolutely no interest in greeting him, she retired to her rooms—though in this household, it was far too early for rest.

Once Maggie retreated, with hair brushed and nightclothes donned, Elizabeth decided to write to Jane and extend the invitation to come north. It was a difficult letter to write, as she actually had no idea what the practical Jane might make of the existence of...*others*. On the plus side, Fitzwilliam reassured that he could erase any unwanted memories from her sister's mind, should it not go well. On the negative side, if that *were* the case, there was no possible chance of happiness with Mr Bingley—and Elizabeth very much feared Jane's affections were fixed. Not only that, if all went poorly, how could she ever receive her sister again? So much rested upon Jane's ability to accept the incomprehensible.

She did not mention Mr Bingley, only her longing for a sister's company and apologies for failing to join her at Lydia's wedding. She told Jane a carriage would be sent for her, should she agree to come, and her hopes there would be no delay in replying. She made two copies, for she did not know whether Jane was still at Longbourn or whether she had managed to return to London after the wedding.

And then she fretted and paced and wondered why Matlock had come.

❧

Fitzwilliam peered at his dear friend with some concern. Matlock was never free with his emotions, but the urgency leaking from him was too specific to miss. "This is a surprise, my lord. May I offer you a brandy?"

Matlock shook his head. "Not unless you have a lush somewhere about, drunk on it," he replied.

Darcy smiled thinly. "Tell me what you have learned."

Matlock sighed, leaning back in his chair and stretching his feet out towards the library's fine fire. "Devilish unpleasant weather in Derbyshire," he said. "Marriage must agree with you, Fitzwilliam. You appear in fine fettle. I hate disturbing you and your charming wife, but I have heard rumours from a most reliable source. Mrs Darcy's sisters may be at risk. Supposedly as potential hostages to trade for Anne's release."

Darcy frowned. "But they are mortal! Living in mortal communities! If she takes this battle into the human arena, how does she expect to keep the Council out of it? They shall take everything she has and then curse her with a fascination for human excrement, just for amusement. She is mad!"

"As I have been saying for years."

"Yes, but she has always protected her power base. Even her original move against Elizabeth was a subtle one," Darcy asserted, "and her subsequent attempts have never involved the human population."

"I have done a bit of research. There are two sisters still at home, one in London, and one recently moved to Brighton. If she were careful, she could take two of them without causing much disruption, because of the distance between them. And if she did not take them both at once, and was clever enough...it could look like a strange, awful coincidence. I—"

"What is strange and awful now?" Richard asked, entering boldly and taking up the thread of the conversation.

Richard swore after hearing Matlock's explanation. "Tell her we will exchange Anne in return for a blood promise of the Bennet family's safety," he said.

Darcy looked at his uncle in surprise, and then expressed his agreement with the suggestion. But Matlock remained negative.

"I do not think it will do. You are well aware of her fixation with the idea that her daughter would mate with you. I can only think your marriage to the human has somehow further unhinged her. I managed to meet with her—to confront her and remind her that all she need do is wait for the human's death. She—"

"I would thank you, my lord, to avoid cavalierly referring to my wife's demise," Darcy said coldly.

In response, he received a short waft of puzzled emotion before the earl's face revealed his chagrin. "I apologise, Fitzwilliam. That was coarsely put—I did not mean to be unfeeling." He cleared his throat. "Ah...what I meant to say is, Catherine is completely irrational now. I do not believe her goals, at present, will be met by a simple exchange of hostages. I am afraid her ire is no longer directed solely at Mrs Darcy, but the entire Darcy line. And she rather recklessly wondered aloud as to whether Mr Bingley would be long in your service."

Equal expressions of alarm passed between Richard and Darcy. "Surely," the colonel said, "she would not dare. Perhaps there are only a few who would notice the absence of Bingley, but they are an important few. He maintains extremely close connexions within the human British government."

"Perhaps not," the earl sighed. "It may have been mere bluster. But I dared not risk keeping the conversation to myself. I offer my services to you, if you can think of any way in which I might be of use."

Darcy carried on a brief, silent conversation with the colonel, then turned to Matlock. "I may take advantage of that offer." His countenance was dark and brooding, and the room filled with the emotions of the two other men in it—Matlock's unfailing concern, and Richard's longing to be *doing* something. Yet both held themselves still, awaiting his word. In the fireplace, a log caught and an explosion of sparks issued in a loud pop.

Darcy seemed to recollect himself then, straightening. "I apologise, sir, for keeping you standing about in your dirt. Your room has been prepared, and there is hot water if you wish it. Ask Chamberlayne for anything you lack. Shall he bring you a meal?"

The earl stood. "No need," he smiled. "I ate along the way."

Darcy was more disheartened than he liked to admit. What was Catherine's game? He could hardly believe she would take such risks, doing something so likely to bring the full condemnation of the Council upon her. Their cardinal rule, their most sacred law, was to escape the notice of humankind. Vampyres were stronger and harder to kill—but they were vastly outnumbered. They were also secretive and sly by nature, and alliances or close friendships were the exception rather than the rule. Some strengths transferred through the blood, and most vampyres were leery about giving aught beyond their own lines any advantage they possessed. Most did not have any interest, either, in building up the vampyre population—reluctant to give rise to a potential new enemy or see any of their peers, or even their own progeny, allowed a surfeit of power. His own House was large enough to be considered a great risk—but even so, was insufficient to battle all the crowned heads of Europe.

He strode into Elizabeth's chambers, hardly knowing what he would tell her. He was a little surprised to see her abed so long before dawn, as she had been keeping his hours. She reclined against several pillows, a book upon her lap—but her attention was obviously elsewhere, her gaze distant, not even noticing his entrance. He took a moment to drink her in.

It settled him, somehow. She was safe, in his home, her blood in his body and her heart in his care. She had never verbally confessed her love—such declarations, perhaps, would never come easily to her—but he could sense the depth of her feelings whenever they were connected in any way. If he longed to hear the words, he could live without them.

Something made her look up just then, and her smile upon seeing him was a gift. Almost as quickly, however, a furrow reappeared on her brow. "What did the earl want?" she asked.

Sighing, he seated himself at the edge of her bed before relaying the news. It never occurred to him to disguise or soften it, much as he wished to protect her.

"I fear our family and friends are at risk," he said, explaining the news Matlock carried.

"Oh, Fitzwilliam," she said, utterly dismayed. For several moments she was silent, thinking. "Is he sure Jane is in London? I would not have believed my mother so happy to release her after Lydia's wedding. How recent was his information?"

Darcy admitted he did not know.

She looked into his eyes, her own expression intent and earnest. "What do you propose we do?"

"The colonel has already gone to fetch Bingley and put out the word to our people in London. He will bring him here. I will send a man to Brighton for Lydia, and see after your other sisters myself... after Matlock agrees to stay at Pemberley watching over you."

"Matlock should go with you. I am safe here." He was somewhat surprised by the mulish set to her mouth as she protested.

"I will take men with me, Elizabeth—but I cannot leave you without the strongest protection possible. In fact, I would go so far as to say that unless he agrees to stay, I cannot go."

"I do not care for him, Fitzwilliam," she admitted reluctantly. "There is something about him I find unpleasant."

Darcy tilted his head, staring at her with surprise. "Truly? I have known him all my life, and never have I met *any* who dislike him. Even those who are jealous, greedy or otherwise disapprove of him on principle cannot dislike him. Only my reluctance to leave you unprotected conquers my jealousy of leaving you with such a paragon."

"His charm eludes me," she said. "Perhaps mortals are more immune to his appeal."

"On the contrary, the opposite has been my experience. He is well known for his charisma in any interaction with the human community."

"I cannot even like the thought of my sisters alone with him. I do not care for him at all."

Darcy could only shake his head, feeling insulted on Matlock's behalf. "I can assure you they would be completely safe with him. However, daylight has never been a Matlock strength. I could accomplish the whole business much more quickly, and I feel time is of the essence."

"Please, Fitzwilliam...allow me to accompany you. I know you can protect me far better than he ever could."

He looked at her for a moment, brushing the soft skin of her cheek with his long fingers. "I agree I can...but, darling, it will slow me considerably if I bring you along. Do you wish to take that risk?"

She huffed a little, distressed breath. "No, I suppose not. But I beg you, take the earl with you. Perhaps he would be useful in the rescue."

"Allow me the luxury of knowing you are well-protected. James will travel with me and I shall send word to my man in Hertfordshire to watch over Longbourn while I seek out the Gardiners and determine Jane's whereabouts for certain." He stood. "I shall prepare to be off then, as soon as I speak with Lord Matlock."

She rose up as well, crawling off the bed and facing him. "You will feed before leaving."

He shook his head. "Darling, I am not planning a month's absence. I will hopefully be no more than a week."

"If you love me, you will allow me to give this to you. I need to know you are at your peak, with every bit of strength possible."

"I have never been healthier, love. You are my manna from heaven. And there is no time."

"It would take you seconds and it would comfort me. You need not...do anything else. Just this—only this. 'Tis all I ask."

Darcy longed to be off, but it would probably take far less time to take a quick nip than to argue with her about it. And they were about to be parted—it was hardly a great favour.

He drew her close to him, drawing the satin of her hair away from her pale, lovely throat. He felt her shiver, saw her eyes drift shut, her head tilting back allowing full access. He kissed her skin, suckling gently, not wishing to rouse any yearnings without satisfying; but as he could not mesmerise her, his venom was the only way to prevent pain. Piercing her skin, he took a delicate sip—and instantly, experienced her anguish.

He had not realised, in the stoicism with which she accepted his imminent departure, just how desperately she despised the separation. In the confident way she assumed he would protect her loved ones, he had not detected her grief and terror. In the easy manner she offered her blood without any further demands, he had not been able to tell how she longed and feared for him.

But now, he knew it all. Gently he withdrew from his bite so he could speak.

"Elizabeth," he said, careful to keep his voice steady, "you must know this—I will ensure the safety of your sisters, and then I shall return."

"I know that," she said, pressing her lips to his, and he felt her confidence and faith in him as well as all the rest.

He paused his kiss, tipping her face up. "I *will* come back to you," he said. For long moments he simply looked at his wife, memorising her every feature. She met his gaze, wordlessly conveying the depth of her feelings in another kiss.

"Go now," she said into his lips, and he felt the courage it took to say the words, and what it cost her.

He did not make her say them again. With a last longing glance, he slipped from the room.

Twenty Six

Elizabeth woke to see the late afternoon sun streaming in through the window. Maggie bustled in, as usual able to determine her mistress's state of wakefulness from afar, setting a tray of hot chocolate, juice of oranges, fresh fruit, and steaming buns on the bedside table. Even though she did not feel much like eating, Elizabeth knew it would distress Maggie if she refused. Besides, Fitzwilliam had made it clear she must eat and drink heartily to compensate for his Taking, and she meant to be fully restored by his return.

A wave of apprehension nearly overwhelmed her, thinking of Fitzwilliam's absence and the presence of the earl. Promptly, she chided herself for maudlin thoughts. She would deal with her cowardice—beginning with Lord Matlock. She glanced over at the dress Maggie had laid out for her to wear.

"Not that garment, Maggie," she said. "I will wear the grey."

"The grey?" Maggie replied, her tone not disguising her dismay. "I'm not sure..."

"The grey," Elizabeth reiterated firmly. She did not care to explain why she wished to wear one of her oldest dresses, the only one besides her wedding dress dating from her Longbourn days and just barely rescued from the rag bag. She was not quite sure she *could* explain it. But all her new apparel was of the latest style—meaning, showing a great deal more of her figure than her conservative country attire. The grey covered her from neck to wrist, and for some reason she knew her mind would be easier. She wanted all the armour available.

Jane Bennet was nervous; she had never travelled this far alone. Her previous trips to her London relations had been made with others traveling from Meryton or in a conveyance hired by her uncle. And, of course, her previous trips had been made with the full knowledge and permission of her parents and the Gardiners.

She was running away. More or less.

Her mother, always difficult, was now completely impossible. She had never before understood what Elizabeth had been required to bear—unable to fathom how hurtful it would be to have nearly every word from her mother's mouth be critical and disapproving. Jane felt she would scream without stopping if she had to endure one more harangue on allowing Mr Bingley to slip away. The worst part was the self-doubt accompanying her mother's reproaches that she was too fat, too dull, too insipid, too meek. Perhaps Jane *had* been tentative in her expressions. For all her reputed beauty, she had *never* successfully held the attentions of a gentleman. Of course, before Mr Bingley, she had never particularly wished to.

Her mother made it plain that Jane would do her duty and do it soon, and she would not leave Longbourn until she was wed to the first likely gentleman in the neighbourhood, no matter how elderly or unappealing. Jane could not bear it. At present, with her heart so bruised, she could not think what else to do but leave a letter of explanation for her parents and flee.

Certain her fellow passengers looked at her askance, she felt all the mortification of her lack of companion. Even Lydia had never behaved in this hurly-burly fashion.

Yet despite the stench of too many unwashed bodies in too small a space and the nausea accompanying the rock and roil of the heavy vehicle, Jane was not sorry. She was finished with sorrow. Perhaps Uncle Gardiner would keep her until she could obtain a position as a companion. A fresh start, her own choices; it was not too much to ask, surely?

Darcy's journey was not much more pleasant than Jane's, though he had no troubles with crowding or illness. Even while he urged his mount to strenuous efforts, speedily carrying him ever further from Pemberley, he suffered Elizabeth's absence like a dull ache in his bones.

They stopped only when necessary for the sake of his horseflesh, relying on specially trained beasts stabled between Derbyshire and London for just such emergencies. They did not sleep, riding day and night and day again, reaching his London home in record time. Once there, Darcy paused only long enough to wash off the dirt and change his clothing so he could call upon the Gardiners.

But the Gardiners were unable to be of use, not having seen Jane since the occasion of Mrs Forster's nuptials.

Thus, Darcy was soon mounted once again, taking the road to Hertfordshire. He was two-thirds of the way there when he passed the post coach lumbering down the road in the opposite direction. But he had finally come within range of successful mental communication with Carter, his man in the Hertfordshire area, and in his distraction, did not spare it a glance.

Elizabeth knew her answers to the earl's polite inquiries were monosyllabic; she could barely tolerate being in the same room with him, her feelings much worse now than their previous meetings in London. What was this charm her husband assured her Matlock possessed? When she looked into his eyes—which was as seldom as possible—she saw only a coldness, fathoms deep. His conversation was all civility, but she believed his true sentiments to be the opposite.

He deemed her a country bumpkin, unworthy of blacking Fitzwilliam Darcy's boots. This she could accept; after all, she was accustomed to dealing with contempt, and she tolerated the colonel's prejudices without difficulty. There was something else about him, though—to look into his eyes made her stomach recoil, so she kept her eyes on her lap. His voice had the same effect as a noxious odour, so she could not encourage any conversation. In short, she was utterly repelled by him, almost embarrassed by the lengths to which she would go to avoid him.

Remembering her similar—although not as intense—feelings of dislike for Miss de Bourgh, she decided her response must be some consequence of her experience with Wickham. Of course, none of the Darcy vampyres caused such sentiment...but that was probably different. In some manner, they all shared her husband's blood. They would of course feel more like family.

The castle seemed oppressive this evening; Nigel informed her Matlock was out with the night patrols, but his aura seemed to cloak all of Pemberley. After she dismissed Maggie for the night, she tried reading, but words on a page held little interest. It took hours for her to fall asleep, and once she did, her dreams were awful. In them, she was alternately chased by Wickham or dashing after her elusive husband. She awakened with a start, her heart racing, her thoughts confused.

It was still dark, the darkest hour of the night, the hour when everything seems most hopeless. What had wakened her? Sweat was drying on her back, the covers twisted around her legs, evidence of the disquiet of her dreams.

Lighting a candle, she bent to the hearth, thinking perhaps she should try again to read, knowing sleep would elude her. At that moment, a thump startled her into straightening. It had come from the nearest window.

Pemberley's windows had glass, of course, but some, as this one, had iron bars over them; she felt perfectly safe from intruders. Heart pounding, she walked to the wood-framed window, unbolting it; it swung inwards. Pinned by a wicked dagger precisely to the frame's centre was a piece of parchment. The blade pierced the letters of her name, scrawled in black ink across the sheet, and she stuffed a fist into her mouth to stop herself from crying out. Setting the candle in a holder, with trembling hands she reached for the knife's handle. There was a chain or necklace of some sort hanging from it, and she looped it around her wrist. It took a great deal of strength to finally pull the knife from the frame. Trying not to envision that blade splitting her open instead of the paper, she quickly bolted the window.

'Tis there to frighten me. I shall not be affected by dramatics, she told herself.

The note was brief, the handwriting bold.

Elizabeth Bennet,
If you care to see your sister alive, present yourself for exchange now, in the Churchyard at Kympton.

Tell no one or she dies before sunrise.

In lieu of signature, there was a bloody print of a small finger.

Elizabeth stared at the note in horror, her eyes resting upon that rusty-coloured fingerprint. With trembling hands, she held the necklace up to the flame. Golden, heart-shaped, a locket. Lydia had received it on her twelfth birthday and seldom was without it. Brash, silly Lydia. A monster had her baby sister.

Had Fitzwilliam been home, he would have defeated her enemies. He could have saved her sister. But Matlock was in charge now, and he had no love for her, would do her no favours. He would have little pity for her sister, an insignificant human sibling who stumbled in the way of his objectives. Darcy's footmen had been instructed to follow Matlock's orders. She had no one to rely upon now except herself.

"What do you mean, gone? How can she be gone? Jane would never do such a thing!" Mrs Bennet declared shrilly.

"All I know is, I went to her room to...um, borrow one of her ribbons and they were all gone. As well as her brush set and all those lovely silks she acquired when everyone thought she would catch Mr Bingley," Kitty explained, still miffed at Jane's unfair procurement of fine lingerie. "Her chest is nearly empty, and I am sure some of her day dresses are missing as well."

At this, Mrs Bennet rose without a word and stalked into Jane's chamber. The bed was neatly made, but in a wild gesture, she threw the counterpane back as if she expected to find her missing daughter beneath it. In her distress, she did not notice the small piece of stationery she dislodged as it caught a current of air and flew beneath the bed.

"Oh!" she cried. "That selfish, unthinking girl! So cruel to her dear mama. I am frightened out of my wits, and have such tremblings, such flutterings all over me, such spasms in my side and pains in my head! Hill! My salts!"

Mrs Bennet's demands echoed throughout Longbourn. Mary and Kitty were both required at their mother's bedside while Mr Bennet tried to discover what had become of Jane. He thought it inconceivable for her to have departed without leaving any word, and finally bestirred himself to make some discreet inquiries in Meryton. He did not trust anyone else in his household could do so without creating scandal.

It was just before the village outskirts that he came upon Lizzy's husband, much to his astonishment. "Mr Darcy! This is indeed a surprise!" he called, and then, seeing the stern expression on his son-in-law's face, asked, "Lizzy! Is she well? Or do you bring me news of Jane?"

"Elizabeth is well," Darcy answered, dismounting. "Why do you enquire about Jane?"

Mr Bennet's eyes narrowed in suspicion. "Is that not why you have come? Has Elizabeth cooked up some scheme to take Jane away from us? I must demand you bring me to her! For a daughter to leave her family like a thief in the night...'twas not well done, sir!"

"Jane is gone?" Darcy asked, examining Mr Bennet's response, feeling only the other man's misgivings and real alarm.

"This morning," Mr Bennet slowly replied. "You know nothing of this?"

"No," Darcy replied, "but rest assured, I will discover all. Leave this in my hands and do nothing else. My man, a Mr Carter, will make contact with you soon. And I will write." Without further ado, he remounted and turned his horse back towards London, leaving a bewildered Mr Bennet staring after him.

Jenkinson, clothed in funereal black, kept watch over Pemberley. He saw the guards patrolling the grounds; they did not see him. It was his particular talent to lie in wait, unnoticed, like a spider waits for prey.

It had been an hour since he left his little calling card. He took it as a good sign that no alarm had been raised; the windows were still dark. He had only remained crouched upon the castle wall long enough to see her pry the knife from the window frame, but he was certain no one, especially a female, would leave such a missive unread until morning. His instructions were direct: She must come now. He almost bristled with impatience, but quelled it. He could cloak his intentions, his presence, from all but the very strongest of vampyres. Fortunately, the *very* strongest were nowhere near his prey at this particular moment.

At last, he spotted her. She was clothed in a dark dress; she carried no candle and moved slowly, one hand before her to feel for obstacles. *Mortals,* he thought, scoffing internally at their poor eyesight. Twice, he had to draw off Darcy guardsmen with noises designed to detour them in an opposite direction, but at last she approached the stables. Because of the horses' natural aversion to vampyres, only humans tended them here, and he made sure those now dreamt happy dreams. Emerging from the darkness, he made his voice as subservient—and quiet—as possible.

"Mistress! May I 'elp ye?"

She startled, not having noticed him until he spoke. "Oh! Y-yes. I need a horse saddled. And a groom to accompany me...to Kympton. At once." He heard her struggle to put a measure of authority into her voice and could have laughed her feeble efforts. *His* mistress had more authority in her little toe than this female possessed in her entire body.

"I could take ye ter Kympton, mistress," he replied easily. "'Taint far. But we'd 'ave to wake up the stable lads to git yer 'orse saddled. The beasties don't care fer me none, 'twould set 'em screamin'."

"No! That is...it is not too far to walk?"

"Not 'ardly. P'raps two miles or a bit less. Ye ken to light a candle fer the Master, do ye?"

"Um...yes. You can...see the way?"

Jenkinson grunted. "'Tis bright as day ter me."

"Who are you, if I might ask?" There was something about him she did not like, but she was so full of dread, she could not like much at the moment.

"A Darcy man, mistress. Called me in from London. Ralph Jennings, at yer service."

"Oh...yes, of course. Yes, I would like very much for you to lead me safely there. And I do not want others to notice I left to–to pray."

He felt almost giddy. *This was too easy. No possible way for*

Darcy to intervene, he thought smugly. By the time any discovered Mrs Darcy's absence, it would be far too late.

Elizabeth felt fortunate for the guard's willingness to accompany her, being respectful enough to obey her command not to alert others to her absence. Anyone else would stop her, leaving Lydia to die. But she was afraid, and more so with every step she took farther from Pemberley.

"How much farther to Kympton?" she asked, after several minutes of silence.

Jennings muttered something that may or may not have been a reply to her question. At least the moon had risen, so she did not stumble. At each crossroads, he pointed a direction, so she had no fear of becoming lost.

At last she saw, shining in the moonlight, a small stone church. It looked neat and picturesque and an unlikely setting for anything nefarious. "Is this the place?" she asked, turning back to Jennings.

Her heart leapt to her throat. He was gone, disappeared into the night. She was alone.

Fitzwilliam! she thought, her courage dissipating. *Please come home. Please appear out of nowhere, as you always have, and hurry in to save me, as you always do. Save my sister, too. You are so much better at rescue than I.*

Tears glistened on her cheeks, escaping against her will.

But he was not here. There was no one else.

It has to be me.

With great effort, she pushed down her terror, swiping at her tears impatiently. Tears never helped.

The silent churchyard echoed as she stumbled on a rock in the pathway, landing in the dirt. For some moments she crouched where she fell, her bruised knees reminding her of how stupid this venture was. The garnet cross Fitzwilliam had given her before their wedding swung from its heavy chain, and she clutched it, praying for courage that had departed with Jennings.

A sudden fear that her journey had taken too long seized her; was it lighter now, the grey of dawn replacing bitter darkness? How was the exchange to take place?

Carefully, she made her way to the low iron gate, feeling for the latch and cringing at the loud betraying creak when she finally managed to open it.

It matters not, she told herself. Stealth was not her object.

She had only the slimmest hope the kidnappers would honour the exchange; she was not truly as stupid as this foolhardy adventure indicated.

But she had counted the cost, and it was only her own skin. This de Bourgh vampyre had been trying to gain control of her for months! Fitzwilliam had done everything in his power to prevent it, but now the danger spread to others too weak and helpless to fight back. Whomever her enemies, they would not provoke their Council foolishly—she *had* to believe that once they had her, they would leave everyone else alone. And if—*when*—she died, Fitzwilliam would be free from the chain of her blood. He would see to vengeance, and her loved ones would be safe. Closing her eyes for a moment, she offered a brief prayer that no one else would be hurt on her account.

It was all she could do.

She thrust the door open.

Inside the gloomy chapel a single taper burned, casting dim shadows. Elizabeth walked up the aisle towards its meagre, cold light. It was not until she drew quite near the lectern that she saw a smallish pale bundle huddled at its base. No, not a bundle...a person...Lydia! Thank heaven.

Elizabeth ran the few remaining steps to her sister. "Lydia? Lydia, are you well?" she cried, wrapping a supporting arm around her, trying to lift her and see her face at the same time. "Lydia, please, talk to me!"

"She will not wake for some time, I am afraid," a voice behind her said calmly.

Elizabeth stiffened but did not turn. "What did you do to her?" she asked, her voice full of anger and pain.

"Heavens, nothing at all, child," the voice replied. "Hardly touched her. Far too many humans looking for her. Wife of a military officer—makes for all kinds of complications and we prefer to keep things quiet. She will have a devil of a time explaining this little sojourn to her husband, though." He chuckled, as if his mayhem was a fine joke. "Just told her to sleep for a spell. All's right and tight."

"There will be those who look for me as well."

"Yes, well, no humans, I daresay. But I suppose we had best take our leave, regardless. I am sure your would-be rescuers will take care of returning your sister to her loved ones." His voice was openly mocking. And strangely familiar.

Elizabeth put her hand to Lydia's mouth, waiting until she felt the small exhale. It seemed her sister was, indeed, simply sleeping. And he was right—Matlock would discover where she had gone and marshal his troops to retrieve her. She had left the note and knife on her bed, where hopefully Maggie would find them soon. Could she possibly delay the villain long enough for rescue?

As though he read her thoughts, she was suddenly roughly yanked from her sister's form. Lydia tumbled back onto the hard floor. Elizabeth struggled, but his grip encircled her like an iron prison; he held her with one arm effortlessly, while with his other hand he pinched her nose shut and covered her mouth.

She could not breathe. Her limbs flailed, trying to kick him but her strength was no match for his. Soon she began to see spots before her eyes, the room spinning dizzily.

"Much feistier than the sister," her abductor said approvingly. She fought harder, but it was futile. As she slowly lost her grip on consciousness, he drew her more securely against him, allowing her head to fall back against his arm. If only she were stronger, it would have been a mistake. Gathering her remaining resolve, she gouged her nails at his eye. Laughing, his eye bleeding, he only drew his other fist back. Just before the blow landed, she glimpsed the face of her captor. His awful, handsome visage was the last thing she saw before he knocked away the last of her awareness.

It was horribly familiar; she had seen it in her dreams for years and years.

Twenty Seven

In the peace and quiet of Darcy's study, Charles Bingley's thoughts returned to their usual resting place—somewhere in Hertfordshire. He greeted the news of Darcy's return to town with pleasure, glad to escape Caroline's constant complaints and his own disconsolate thoughts. But when Richard proceeded to inform him of de Bourgh's nefarious designs upon Mrs Darcy's family, he was beside himself with anxiety over the fate of Elizabeth's sisters.

One sister, in particular.

"Excuse me, sir," Darcy's London butler addressed Mr Bingley.

He was so lost in cares—and memories—he had failed to mark the man's entrance.

"I apologise, Robbins—I was wool-gathering and did not notice you. What is it?"

"A messenger arrived bearing a note from Mrs Darcy's relations residing in Cheapside. When I informed him the master was not at home, he explained that Mr Darcy enquired about Miss Bennet earlier, and there is new information as to her whereabouts. As Mr Darcy has now departed London—" He broke off mid-sentence, confident his dilemma was understood. All of Mr Darcy's servants, both human and otherwise, were used to relying upon Mr Bingley, who only awaited daylight before departing for Pemberley.

Charles's heart began beating harder the second Robbins mentioned 'Miss Bennet'.

"Thank you, Robbins. Leave it with me." He reached for the envelope, surprised his hand did not tremble with eagerness, barely managing to wait until the butler closed the door behind him before ripping open the seal.

The moonlit road to Derbyshire was silent except for the pounding of hooves. Darcy had changed his horse but an hour past, and already his fresh mount was lathered. The moment he discovered Jane was likely a victim of abduction, he rode hell-for-leather to Pemberley, leaving word for James and Richard to see to the situation in London. The weapon his enemies held was too powerful—he knew Elizabeth would do *anything* to ensure Jane's safety. Devil take it, she would probably risk herself even for her irascible, selfish parents; he ought never to have left her behind. Even though Matlock and his own men were guarding her, he could not prevent a terrible feeling he ran too late, just a bit behind the machinations of his foes.

Stealing humans—especially gentry of any sort—was unthinkable for any who submitted to Council authority. Wickham, who had nothing left to lose, *must* be at the heart of this matter, no matter who directed him.

Wickham! Such evil! His only gift was depraved corruption; those he Turned never lived much past their Shielded phase. For most, it meant mere months; others might live for up to a year. But during their short lifespans they were strong. Incredibly so. All inherited the Darcy gift of tolerance to the sun. And every last one had no mind of its own, responding only to its Master's will.

Darcy, too obsessed with information gathering, realised he had responded too quickly to Matlock's news. Bent on playing knight in shining armour for Elizabeth, he had instead left her vulnerable. And if de Bourgh partnered with Wickham, it meant he was not only fully empowered but had formidable protection against discovery by the Council!

If only his father had permitted him to destroy George long ago! But then, George had always been clever and charming. As his half-sibling, Darcy was immune to his magnetism, but most were not. His father, both guilt-stricken for earlier neglect and eager to believe in his goodness, resisted the truth until his brother's ugliest deeds came to light in ways his father could not deny. George Darcy disinherited him before the Council, excommunicated him from House Darcy, and destroyed his procreative powers. Still, their father refused to take that final step—and concede that his son, flesh of his flesh, was a thing of irreconcilable evil.

And now Wickham was no longer constrained but encouraged.

The moon shone brightly, reflecting against a low stone wall edging the roadway. Darcy was just calculating the distance to the next posting station when he felt a sudden eerie sensation of loss and pain, as though someone fisted his heart with a malevolent grip and brutally squeezed.

Elizabeth!

Someone had ripped her from his protection and power—he knew it with every fibre of his being. Immediately he levitated into full flight, a lethal shadow against the night sky—leaving behind a bewildered, riderless horse on the empty road.

Elizabeth returned to consciousness slowly, surrounded by darkness. A stone floor, cold and hard beneath her, pillowed her head; she shivered as its wintry stones seeped into her bones. For a time, she huddled there, trying to wrap her pelisse tighter about her shoulders. Something soft skittered near her skirts, igniting her will—if not her strength—to stand. Her first efforts were failures. She stumbled twice before regaining her equilibrium, gritting her teeth against waves of nausea. Drunkenly she lurched forward, arms outstretched, finding a slimy wall upon which to lean. Her head throbbed with every beat of her heart.

Willing herself to take small, even breaths, knowing she must keep her wits, her first goal became determining the size of her prison. She blundered around the perimeters blindly, finding that as time passed, she grew warmer and slightly less shaky.

It was not a large room; there were no windows—or else they were higher up than she could reach—and it was empty except for a rough bench bolted into one wall. The dampness slicking the walls made her think it might be a cellar. She stepped up onto the bench and immediately bumped her aching head on the low ceiling, further reinforcing the idea. The door was solid, without a latch on her side.

She bent to peer beneath it without success and a creature, probably a rat, dashed across her foot; involuntarily she screamed.

Keep moving, keep moving, she chanted.

The face haunting her dreams was now brought to life: George Wickham, her husband had explained. His own brother. Why had he taken her? Was Lydia rescued? Would stink and filth, hunger and indignity be her only future? Back and forth she paced, from wall to wall, the darkness caging her with relentless despair. Finally, exhausted and sick, she huddled onto the bench, pillowed her head on her hands, and turned all her thoughts to Fitzwilliam. At least in her dreams, she was warm, safe, and beloved.

Bingley's palms sweated; this was an extraordinary condition. He had been trained from birth to expect the unexpected, to manipulate people and situations, and to lie through his teeth. The current state of affairs was hardly unusual, even though he was more vested emotionally in the outcome.

A neat maidservant answered the door of the tidily kept house in Cheapside. He peered around curiously as she left him in the foyer; the address might not be exalted but the home was large and tastefully appointed. They did not keep their own cattle, obviously, but in London that was hardly a necessity. His observations were interrupted by the return of the servant. "Mr Gardiner will see you in the study, if you'll follow me, sir," she said.

He entered a room kept comfortably warm, and a man stood to greet him. One could tell by the laugh-lines surrounding his eyes and his otherwise genial appearance that he was normally of good humour and calm nature. However, those eyes were now narrowed with suspicion, hard lines bracketing his mouth. "Mr Bingley," he said quietly, not extending his hand. "Please have a seat."

Bingley sat. He could read censure in Mr Gardiner's countenance and debated possible explanations for his presence which might lessen the man's hostility. But the fact was, this was Jane's family; Bingley must still protect those he was sworn to safeguard, but he would use as little deception as he possibly could.

"I am sure you wonder at my effrontery in presenting myself," he began.

"Your very acknowledgement that it *is* effrontery should have been reason enough to discourage this visit," Mr Gardiner answered tightly.

"I realise you have no reason to welcome me, sir," Bingley continued. "Indeed, I nearly left this duty to Mr Darcy's uncle, simply because I feared your dislike for my person might lead you to disregard the importance of my message." It probably would have been wiser to send Richard, who would have mesmerised them all into instantaneous submission. Convenient as that might be, he knew the Gardiners could be left with a constant, vague uneasiness until such time as they were reunited with Jane—and depending upon how strong-willed they were—possibly night terrors and even melancholy. Besides, the thought of Richard compelling his Jane was a violation he could not abide unless it was absolutely necessary for her safety. As it was, he had inflicted enough damage upon her in the short period of their acquaintance. He would attempt a more open approach first.

"What is this important message, then?"

Without further hesitation, Bingley explained. "Mr Darcy is a powerful man. He has, in the past, been the object of attempts by unscrupulous persons to manipulate him for their own nefarious purposes. They have never been successful. Recently, however, an attempt was made to reach him by a threat to his wife. This, too, was fortunately unsuccessful," he said quickly, seeing the alarmed expression in Gardiner's eyes. "Mr Darcy is very serious about the protection of his loved ones."

Mr Gardiner opened his mouth as if to speak, then shut it again. Finally he asked, "Why are you here, Mr Bingley?"

He took a deep breath. "We have received information that Mrs Darcy's sisters are a likely future target of these enemies," he said. "And the most likely of all is Miss Bennet. Mr Darcy has men watching your home and Longbourn, as well as agents on the way to Brighton to see to Mrs Forster. However, Mrs Darcy has requested that Miss Bennet be allowed to journey to Pemberley, to take up residence until such time as her safety might be assured." He held up one hand. "Please know that we believe she would be safe here with the precautions we have in place. This action is purely for Mrs Darcy's peace of mind."

"And if I refuse?" Mr Gardiner asked, his lips thinning.

"Perhaps Miss Bennet could be allowed to make that decision?" Bingley replied carefully.

For a long moment, neither spoke.

"In what is Mr Darcy involved, that he should have drawn the attention of such blackguards?" Mr Gardiner spat in frustration and worry.

"I am afraid I must leave many of your questions unanswered. But one thing you should understand—Mr Darcy is one of the most honourable, upright individuals I have ever known. He has done nothing to deserve the enmity he faces—except perhaps having been born into a position of wealth and power, with talents and gifts that others equally wealthy and almost as powerful, envy."

"Says you," Mr Gardiner snapped.

"I assure you," said Bingley calmly, "that a good part of the reason I was unable to offer an official courtship to Miss Bennet is the situation in which I find myself, respecting my duties to Mr Darcy. I reluctantly believed it best to distance myself in order to protect her. However, as fate would have it, she is at risk regardless."

"If you could not finish it, why did you ever start?" Mr Gardiner asked, aggravated. "To raise her hopes, only to crush them. She has suffered, though I daresay I shouldn't tell *you* that. And now, she asks me to find her a *position* as a *companion*. A companion!" He raked his hand through his thinning hair.

"Mr Gardiner, I apologise for my actions. I have been miserable as well, though I know *I* deserve to be as Miss Bennet does not. I should not have, but I dreamt I could have something special with your niece. I will be honest. I still dream it. But I swear to you now, the invitation to come to Pemberley was extended by Mrs Darcy, and if there is any chance whatsoever my presence in Miss Bennet's life would be a detriment to her happiness, I will remove myself. My intentions are strictly honourable."

The older man leaned back in his chair, surveying the ceiling as though there were answers to be found in the plaster. With a heavy sigh, he looked back at Bingley. "I want you to swear to me that Jane will not be hurt, whatever happens," he said, "but I suspect that is something you cannot promise. However, her situation here is tenuous at best. I cannot, in good conscience, send her into service as she wishes. I can offer her shelter here, but I know it will not be long until my sister goads my brother Bennet into fetching her back to

Longbourn. She is of age, and if I were certain she would defy her father and resist returning, I would keep her with me and let you be devilled, despite your assurances of this invitation from Lizzy. But Jane is too tender-hearted to openly flout her father's authority—as he so seldom exerts himself—and I fear she will be an easy mark for his pleas. At least her mother would be unable to influence her prospects from Derbyshire. Perhaps Mr Darcy will be able to work out a different future for her than the one I foresee if she remains behind."

Bingley recognised the slights to his honour, but though his pride was offended he did not allow it to show in his respectful answer. "I understand, sir. I can only repeat my assurances that she will be protected. I wish speed was not of the essence, but we must be on the road at daybreak and cannot delay beyond. I will send a carriage, if I may."

"Unless, of course, my niece refuses to go. I will not force her from my home."

Bingley nodded, a shadow crossing over his face. He, too, hoped that force would be unnecessary.

❧

George Wickham chuckled to himself. Life had definitely improved in the last month. Of course, after spending ten years beneath the soil of Hertfordshire, and fifty years bound in silver before that, any change was bound to be for the better.

He had been astonished to learn his half-brother had married—and utterly shocked when he recognised the delicious scent of the 'loathsome' bride Lady Catherine demanded he fetch. How ironic and appropriate that the female who enabled his escape from Darcy would also enable his revenge! He glanced up to the portrait of his beauteous mother, his most treasured possession—the one thing he insisted Matlock send to him immediately. She seemed to be looking down upon him approvingly, and he smiled.

❧

Matlock cantered through the night, keeping a tight rein on his mount—for the beast did not much like its rider and required a firm hand—searching, feverishly, for Mrs Darcy. He parted from all the other searchers fanning out from the Kympton chapel, heading first for Wickham's hideaway—only to find that the bird had flown. Catherine must have arranged a new sanctuary. Fortunately, upon heading back towards Kympton, he picked up a very slight hint of George's scent trail.

If—*when*—he found them, Wickham no doubt believed he would hand over Darcy, and it was imperative he continue to believe it. Matlock must trace the Mouse immediately, and force Wickham to surrender custody of her to him. It would not be easy to do so without rousing his suspicions. Neither could he allow any of his other searchers to come upon the captive and risk exposing his dealings with the outlaw, and thus he continuously destroyed Wickham's scent as he found it. Being both desperate to find her quickly and unable to summon the assistance he needed in order to do so put him in a devilish bad place, and he would gladly slit Catherine's throat and pull her heart up through it when he saw her again.

Dawn neared and he had lost the scent again. Regardless, he must rest soon. Cursing a blue streak, he was startled by the sudden appearance of Fitzwilliam Darcy directly before him.

"Great Saints!" he cried aloud, before he could prevent the exclamation.

"*Where is she?*" Darcy roared.

Matlock's horse reared in fright—and frankly, Matlock could not blame it. Darcy was enraged, his eyes glowing red, fury leaking from every pore. Always large, he now looked bigger, stronger, and more frightening than any monster. His fangs flashed, as menacingly thick as a jungle cat's. Barely keeping his seat, Matlock struggled past his own fear.

"Darcy, dash it, calm yourself. I need my mount if I am to continue searching in daylight."

The *thing* that now was Darcy apparently had difficulty with speech. His words emerged in a prolonged baritone growl, raising the hair on Matlock's nape.

"*Why...? Should have...protected!*"

"And I would have, had you warned me that she was likely to sneak out of her room in open defiance of those guarding her! Somehow de Bourgh managed to deliver a letter directly to her, threatening her sister's life if Mrs Darcy did not come to Kympton in the night. She did not *tell* me, Darcy. I had so many out patrolling, I am certain she was not compelled. One of us surely would have felt it. Her maid found the letter on her bed, along with a necklace I surmise belongs to the sister. She snuck out without saying a bloody word! I would have taken care of her *and* the sister, had she only come to me!" The frustration, fury, and fear he felt rolled off him in waves. These emotions were genuine, so far as they went.

Darcy's glowing eyes narrowed. "*Sister?*"

"She was found at Kympton, just as the letter claimed. Mrs Darcy obviously exchanged herself for the girl. But we have thirty searching, and—"

Just like that, he spoke to thin air. *Botheration!*

George Wickham was ridiculously bloodthirsty, desiring his brother's death above all things, and with enough of those devilish creatures of his, it might be possible. On the other hand, Matlock had never in his life seen such molten rage as in Darcy's power-red eyes; if Darcy were the victor, Wickham would be crisped to a cinder. Neither outcome was acceptable. He needed them both. Something almost like panic rose within his breast.

Forcibly he calmed himself, inhaling deeply, opening his senses. His sensory skills were extremely sharp, and yet he could smell no trace of either the Mouse or Wickham. Darcy had only come this way because he had, no doubt, caught Matlock's own scent on the slight breeze. Matlock would, simply, return to the beginning of the trail, and find what he'd missed. No one was a better tracker than he, Darcy included.

Then he would rescue George *and* Fitzwilliam, and even the Mouse. And he would slaughter Catherine at his earliest opportunity. He vowed it.

Twenty Eight

George was hungry again; he had always needed to eat more often than his peers, which of course made his years of starved imprisonment by the Council even more excruciatingly unfair. They fed him, but only enough to ensure he was conscious of his every agony. Yet another reason to hate Darcy; Matlock informed him of every effort Darcy expended in securing that imprisonment.

His belly growled. What he wanted, of course, was a taste of that sweet little sampler in his cellar. However, he knew she would be far more amusing for him to work with after remaining in blackness for a day or two. He certainly planned to drink her—but he would enjoy her flavour much more with Darcy looking on, helpless to do anything except watch her scream. *Delicious*!

One of his Made entered the snug parlour. "What?" he snapped.

As expected, the thing did not answer; speech was unusual for any of his line.

"Darcy? Someone spotted him?"

The creature's head bobbed in agreement, pleasing George. He would reward it...later. For now, his nemesis approached, and George rubbed his hands together giddily. This hideaway was perfect—only one way in, with a ring of his creatures surrounding in every direction. No possible way could he fight them all, and when they succeeded in capturing him, he had a solid silver chair, a gift from Lady Catherine, in which to chain him. *Delightful!*

The sounds of fighting began an hour later; nothing so puny as what humans termed a 'mill,' this was the shuddering of uprooted trees shattering like matchsticks, boulders hurling, and ground shaking in earthquake-like tremors. The contest persevered until the rosy light of early evening...but as the explosions lessened, the battle winding down, George heard none of the sounds he anticipated—the grunts, groans, and indiscernible babbling of his creatures as they dragged forth his brother's body. He should have allowed them to slaughter him, but he had so wanted that great pleasure for himself.

Well, then. Time for a new plan.

At the sudden blaze of light, Elizabeth startled awake. From her cellar gaol, she had heard a brutal storm raging throughout the day and hoped it could help, somehow, provide cover for Fitzwilliam or keep her enemies away. Apparently, any reprieve was past.

Face what you came to face, she warned herself. *Lydia is safe. 'Tis all that matters now.*

"Elizabeth," he crooned, and it was the sickeningly sweet voice from her dreams. "You will come with me now."

Every fibre of her being urged refusal, but could it be this vampyre believed he *could* command her? If, perhaps, she pretended obedience, might there be an opportunity for escape? She could not risk betraying what might be her only advantage. On shaky limbs, she stood and walked to him. To her chagrin, he clasped her arm tightly in an iron grip once she was near. *Stupid*, she chided herself. Probably not every vampyre possessed the skill to compel.

"Come, Pretty," he murmured. "I have a surprise for you. Behold, the bridegroom cometh."

Elizabeth's step unconsciously slowed at his words, but her captor never paused for a moment and she stumbled. He did not appear to notice, only dragging her up the stairs as though she were a sack of meal. She was of no consequence to this pitiless monster, no more than a tool to be used and discarded—or worse—once he finished. If Fitzwilliam was, indeed, nearby, then she was nothing more than a lure to his doom.

Fitzwilliam! she thought. *Danger! Leave!*

Urgently, desperately, she attempted to communicate with him in her mind, sending him those warnings with all her heart and inwardly lamenting her deviant immunity from his normal abilities. As if she had spoken aloud, Wickham suddenly stopped and stared at her. "I cannot sense anything from you. You might as well be a corpse with a beating heart." He gazed at her intently; she noticed his eyes did not glow, as Fitzwilliam's did at the expenditure of power, but rather turned an ugly shade of flat, muddy yellow. Did he try to see inside her mind? At last he shrugged, giving up and pulling her forward once again.

"I take it this is why he did not know you were still alive, lo those many years ago," he chuckled, pressing a cold kiss to her neck, making her shudder. "I did not pay much attention at the time—too famished, don't you know. This must be your attraction for the all-knowing, all-feeling Darcy. Only he would appreciate a mute."

They reached the front door, and he abruptly dragged her through it. To her horror, she felt the cold, sharp point of a dagger at her throat. "Darcy!" he yelled, in a voice so loud it echoed off the surrounding canyon. "Come, or I kill her this moment." He pricked her skin with the knife point.

For several moments, all was quiet. Elizabeth took in their surroundings. She could see no evidence of the storm she had believed raging, no fresh snow or mud. They were high in the mountains and it was very cold, almost nightfall. She shivered against the blade at her neck, willing her husband to stay out of sight.

The dagger point pierced her throat once more; she could feel it there, burrowing in. It did not precisely hurt yet, it was so sharp, but she could feel blood trickling down her neck and into her bodice.

Fitzwilliam appeared before them, not ten yards away. Elizabeth gasped in shock.

Blood slowly dripped from dozens of wounds, his face slashed, torn flesh dangling. As he limped closer, she saw with horror that one of his hands was a bloody stump. Why did he not heal? He had told her he healed quickly, that he was all but immortal!

With every step Fitzwilliam took, Wickham retreated an equal distance. It seemed he had an obvious destination in mind as he yanked her back over the threshold. She tried to capture Fitzwilliam's attention, but he did not take his eyes off the dagger at her throat. Now that they were indoors where candles were burning, she could see his eyes glowing an eerie scarlet red she had never before seen. She forced her voice to emerge from the dryness of her throat.

"No! Leave here!" she managed, before the blade dug further into her flesh.

Fitzwilliam growled, an inhuman sound, but Wickham did not pause. In a flash, he pulled her into a windowless room, bare of anything except a single chair.

"Sit!" her captor demanded, as though Darcy were a dog.

Darcy looked at the chair and back at Elizabeth, repeating that low growl. Elizabeth felt the knife burrow viciously deeper and could not prevent her cry at the sting of the blade penetrating her flesh, though she stopped herself at once. Too late. Fitzwilliam threw himself into the chair.

The effect of this rather ordinary-looking piece of furniture was immediate. It was Darcy's turn to groan in agony, his reddened eyes rolling to the back of his head. Abruptly, Wickham dropped Elizabeth to the floor, reaching for the chains bolted to the chair. In moves too quick for her to follow, he had her husband shackled chest, arms, and feet. With a look of intense satisfaction, his blade emerged once again; he held it directly over Darcy's heart.

"No," Elizabeth screamed, running towards them.

Wickham turned away from his gloating to offhandedly smack her away, knocking her into the room's opposite corner as if she were a gnat. She hit the wall headfirst, seeing stars. "Stay! Do not move!" Wickham commanded her, returning his attention to his bound victim.

Darcy let out a growl of pain and frustration, straining against his bonds.

Wickham laughed. "Ah, sensitive where Mrs Darcy is concerned, are we?" he grinned maliciously and stalked back to the corner where Elizabeth lay, only half-conscious. Gripping her by the collar of her pelisse, he dragged her up against him.

Darcy stilled in sudden alertness.

"I see I have your attention, Brother," he smirked. He turned Elizabeth to face him as she struggled feebly. Slowly his tongue emerged from reddened lips; he licked up the blood dribbling onto her throat, obviously enjoying Darcy's tortured growls.

"I believe I have need of a new Creature," he said casually. "I shall Turn her now—or try to. It will be unfortunate if she dies in the attempt. Or would you *prefer* her death, my brother? An interesting conundrum, would you not agree?" His lips skated over the soft skin of Elizabeth's throat.

Elizabeth suddenly turned into a madwoman, clawing at Wickham's face, kicking and scratching. Unfortunately, it was a short battle. No match for his strength, he merely backhanded her into the wall once more.

"Spirited little thing, ain't she?" Wickham smiled. "I know exactly the use I shall have for her, once Turned," he purred. The bleeding claw marks striping his face were already healing, as Elizabeth did not have the capability to hurt him in any real sense. "Perhaps, though, I will not wait. It makes the experience that much more satisfying." Darcy fought so hard against his bindings they groaned in distress.

"My, my! I do believe, Darcy, had you not spent the day playing with my creatures, you might have been able to break those silver chains. Would not have thought it possible without seeing it for myself. Now, I will not delay your pleasure in watching me Turn her."

He strode over to Elizabeth's inert body, hauling her up and slapping her across the face until she opened her eyes, flinching away.

At that moment, something else captured Wickham's attention and he let her drop to the floor again. She moaned in pain. "Hush," he barked holding up one finger. For long moments, he listened intently before turning back to Darcy.

"Someone approaches," he said contemplatively. "They are at least a mile away yet, but this canyon echoes. Since you have devastated my ranks, I shall have to greet whomever it is myself. But never fear, Brother. I shall continue right where I left off." He knelt to where Elizabeth had fallen. "And you, my pretty—do *not* move from this spot. No matter who calls you or what Darcy asks, you are to stay here. Do you understand?" He stared at her with his murky yellow eyes.

Elizabeth slowly nodded. Her hair had come unbound in the struggle; blood dribbled down the wounds at her neck and forehead. "Little wild one," he mocked, pinching her cheek. He jumped to his feet briskly. "I shall return shortly," he said, bowing mockingly to them both as he left the room. They heard the key grate in the lock and his footsteps move away.

Elizabeth ran to her husband but before she could speak, Darcy violently shook his head to warn her that Wickham's hearing was acute. She put her mouth directly against his ear, whispering softly. "Drink from me."

Once again he shook his head, this time in refusal. In a voice so low it was more growl than words, he said, "You. Hurt."

"I am not," she whispered. "Just a bump or two. I have hurt myself worse falling out of trees." She smiled weakly. "You are injured, Fitzwilliam. You do not heal."

"Silver," he shrugged, indicating the chair and his bindings.

"That cannot be the only reason. You were not healing before he bound you. Please, Take from me! Fitzwilliam...he will make me a vampyre. I shall live through it, my love, I promise you. I will take his strength and then use it to destroy him." Her voice wavered. "Fitzwilliam? What is it?"

Two tears, blood-red tears, fell from his eyes.

Darcy was still too much the beast to explain, unable to warn her of the horror in the things Wickham created. Having destroyed at least a dozen of the creatures today, he had seen a measure of peace fall over each of them when they understood their lives were at an end. And what he threatened before—during—the Turning... Wickham would hurt her in a thousand ways before he finally let her die. He would never allow her soul to survive.

"'Lizbeth," he ground out.

She looked him full in the eye, not flinching from the wildness, the brutality of his wrecked appearance. "Yes," she murmured.

"Trust...me?"

"Yes," she said again. In an easy movement, she pulled her hair away from her neck, and laid her throat to his mouth. Then she wrapped her arms around his neck and waited.

His fangs elongated at once; still, he hesitated.

"Love you," he growled.

"Yes," she whispered. "Love you too."

Darcy's heart broke in that moment, to have her say it now—when he was most likely about to kill her—the words he yearned to hear for so long. That she would tell him while he stank of death and violence, his choices and future gone dark...he wanted to howl his pain and frustration. But the beast in him surged forward, instinctively acting when the man could not. His incisors plunged into her neck. He had little venom to soothe her, to make this better; but though she flinched, she did not pull away. In fact, he felt her press closer to him, wordlessly urging him to take more and more.

His strength began to return incrementally as he feasted on her blood, although the silver prevented him from recovering fully. He felt the point at which he should stop, felt her arms loosen as her consciousness receded. He felt the cold sweat breaking upon on her forehead when the pain began in earnest, and then dried itself in feverish heat as he sucked the hydration from her body. Still, even though he knew how much he must be hurting her, she stayed with him in spirit for as long as possible. Gradually, as he grew glutted in strength and power, even the silver was unable to prevent him from experiencing overwhelming vigour as he seized every drop of his bond-mate's blood. Mercifully, her heart stuttered to a halt, her breath cut unnaturally short as she experienced the beginnings of human death.

He could not allow it. Before his missing hand could fully regenerate, he wrenched his wrist from the blood-slicked silver, breaking the limb in several places but ultimately tearing one arm free of its silver manacle. There was nothing on earth, no metal strong enough to keep his most primitive self from trying to save Elizabeth. His hand's healing was rapid now that silver did not inhibit the arm, the breaks quickly mending and the hand reforming. He did not notice the pain of bone regrowth and nerve regeneration. He saw nothing except his dying wife.

Using his one free arm, he supported her pale, lifeless form so she was clutched to his breast. Only then did he release her vein, her head lolling. Around her neck, Elizabeth still wore the garnet cross given her as a wedding gift; he did not consider the irony of using his mother's necklace, manoeuvring his weak new hand until he reached it, using the chain to pull it to him.

"Forever in me. Take me into you," he growled. Gripping one end tightly, he gouged it into his neck at the artery; blood began spurting, and he tilted to direct it into Elizabeth's mouth. He alternated between using his free hand to work her throat and jaw, forcing her to swallow his blood, and re-gouging his neck every time the wound began to heal. It was awkward, trying to keep her wedged against his chest and working one-handed to force the blood into her. Some spilled uselessly down her front; he only worked harder, using his power to coerce more down her throat.

Even with what was lost, it was not long until his charged blood began to do its job, compelling Elizabeth's body to swallow on its own. To begin to crave. And shortly after that—and far more harshly than usual, since he had hardly any venom to offer during the process—the unearthly pain commenced.

He let her drink more than what should have been required, hoping it gave her some sort of advantage—but in truth, there was no way to tell. While she drank, at least there was distraction from the pain and fulfilment of the vicious thirst. Once he had given all he could, there was no escaping the agony; worse, he could only clutch her to his bound chest, keeping guard over her and watching with fiery eyes for his enemy's return. He must—*would*—protect her, even one-handed, if only she would live until Shielded.

Her every anguished moan slew him. Occasionally she would take a rasping breath as she fought against her own lungs while her humanity took a different shape and form. Again and again she seized in his hold, her body contracting with violent attrition. Darcy wanted to whisper love words, telling her she could now be with him forever, but his beast, still in control, had no such vocabulary. He swore at her instead, vicious threats if she dared leave him, calling her name over and over, summoning her back. He had no real sense of time. The world shrank to this one small, low-ceilinged room. Only Elizabeth's infrequent screams of agony told him that she yet lived. The candle burned lower now. Wickham did not return, and Darcy could not guess why.

His rage grew as her torture intensified. The trickle of humanity left inside him reminded that even death was a better alternative than subjugation to Wickham's terrible degradation and horror. He tried to comfort himself with hope that she might actually survive.

But then, her body began convulsing; he could barely hold onto her. Seizure after seizure gripped her, ripping through her in painful waves. He felt her essence slipping out of reach. His beast-fury flared beyond control of any mental boundaries. With a crack as loud as cannon fire, the silver chair split in twain.

Matlock needed George, needed his creatures to keep his own House in order and properly subjugated. But they died far too quickly, needing constant resupply. Yet, one wrong word from Wickham to Darcy, and Matlock was dead. Matlock understood Darcy's abilities, but George resisted the truth of his half-brother's strength. George mistook a retiring nature for cowardice and an overdeveloped sense of honour for weakness. Matlock had concluded long ago that Darcy was far more powerful than even the two of them together; the fact he discovered his brother's hideaway first was only further proof. However, the stink of Wickham's creatures was overpowering; if George had managed to murder Fitzwilliam, he would slay him.

"Who have you killed now?" Matlock asked, with some trepidation. "The place is drenched in blood."

"No one as yet," Wickham shrugged sullenly. "'Twas Darcy, who laid waste to a dozen of my poor creatures. But I have him now, bound in silver. I have decided to let him watch his wife be Turned. She will make a lovely addition to my line."

Darcy killed that many? Alone? Incredible. Matlock *must* stage a rescue, repairing his standing with the man. "I am impressed you were able to bind him," he said coldly. "But Catherine's plan was flawed, as usual. Too many persons of power are uneasy. You should not have used free mortals."

"I needed one for bait."

"I counselled you to wait upon your revenge, and you agreed."

"I did not believe Catherine acted without your consent. I never thought she would defy you," Wickham said slyly.

"When last we talked, I warned you to take no action on *any* of Catherine's lunatic plans without discussing them with me beforehand."

"I was bored. You never let me have any fun."

"Well, your fun is finished," Matlock said. "You cannot kill Darcy today. Too many of his line have discovered your direction," he lied. "I have only delayed them. You must flee. This victory must await another day."

George turned white with anger. "No! I have waited too long as it is. You forget your promises, my lord."

"It is your own fault for toying with him instead of taking care of business. If you failed to remove his heart and head while you had him at your mercy, you were a fool. Your opportunity is lost. Escape now and you will live to see tomorrow."

"For my mother's sake, he must suffer. His punishment cannot be swift."

"Your mother was his father's sin, not his."

"He is his father's son. I have sworn to execute him, just as I vowed to exterminate the man who sired me and then burned my living seed from my body."

George could blather endlessly on this subject, and Matlock had no choice but to allow it. It would take time to persuade George to surrender his advantage and his prizes. It did not help that Catherine had led him to believe he would go unpunished for his crimes.

"Are you daft?" Matlock asked incredulously. "If the Council learns you murdered Darcy, they will have every House in the world calling for your death. I will no longer be able to hide you. Catherine used you. She hoped you would kill Mrs Darcy and Darcy would kill you, clearing the whole mess for her. Have you forgotten her obsession with marrying him to her daughter?"

It took nearly thirty minutes of such arguments before Wickham agreed to leave. "I want her, though...Darcy's woman. Let me Turn her and I will go."

"She is human, you wretch. Another human murder is just what you do *not* need."

Wickham waved this reasoning aside. "She is naught but a human who belongs to Darcy. She left the protection of the human world and has no claims on vampyre justice."

"Do you not comprehend your position?" Matlock hissed. "You murdered a *Darcy*, and the only reason you lived to tell the tale is my support and manoeuvrings. I called in every favour I was owed to save your wretched corpse, and I have not accumulated enough good will to earn you another reprieve so soon. Human or not, she is Darcy's legal *wife* and her death will bring the outrage of the entire world upon you. *Patience*, George. Go to my seat. Stay at Matlock, in comfort. I will hide you and we will make plans—better plans than Catherine's feeble schemes which leave you vulnerable."

"Very well," George agreed petulantly. "I will leave. But I will Take from his wife first. 'Tis the least of what he deserves and what I am owed."

"Certainly," Matlock agreed, looking at his pocket watch. "But hurry. If you are not far away in thirty minutes, Darcy's men will catch you with your breeches down."

"Do not fret," George replied, laughing. "I will not treat her to my finest performance." He had just turned back towards the cottage when a sound split the air like a lightning strike, echoing across the surrounding mountains, sizzling their ears and raising every sense to high alert, halting them both in their tracks.

"What the devil was that?" Matlock breathed.

Wickham grabbed Matlock's wrist in a death grip, his expression panicked. "I believe it was the sound of silver shattering. Darcy...he may be free."

Matlock stiffened. If Wickham were caught now, all his plans would fracture like George's silver. "Be gone. To Matlock. Put as much distance as possible between us." He shook off George's still-clutching fingers. "Go!"

George ran, blurring into the shadows of the night.

Coward, Matlock thought, amused now, pacing down the road towards the cottage, ready to play the hero.

Twenty Nine

"Darcy!" Matlock yelled, rushing into the little house. Following Darcy's scent, he dashed into the room where the couple were gaoled, breaking through the door as though it were made of paper.

In the blink of an eye, he found himself stretched flat on his back and pinned by the throat. In all his life he had never seen Darcy in such a state—worse, even, than when he saw him last. Dried blood caked his clothing, his eyes glowed an evil red, his thick fangs extended, ready to tear flesh, as he growled. Growled!

"Darcy!" he gasped. "Great gads, man, what happened to you?"

For some moments, Darcy did not answer, just stayed crouched over him as though he were a rabid predator. At last, he eased up a bit and Matlock was able to push away.

"You...smell...of him," Darcy snarled.

"If by 'him' you mean Wickham, I should reek of him, as we fought only moments ago," Matlock replied. "I nearly had him, too, but the slippery devil escaped. I had to choose between chasing him and rescuing you and your wife. He boasted he had you bound in silver!" He pointed to the shattered silver chair. "How the devil did you manage to break out of this? I would not believe it if I had not seen it with my own eyes." He kept up his chatter, edging around the room to see what Darcy protected so determinedly.

"Dear heavens," he said quietly. "This *is* something."

Darcy returned to the far corner of the room, lifting the body of a female off a bloodstained rug and back into his arms as though she weighed nothing. That body was shivering, convulsing, seizing into spasms strong enough to break bones.

"Darcy...she..." he hesitated, then cautiously approached—being careful to make no sudden moves. Finally, he crouched beside them.

"Fitzwilliam," Matlock began gently, "she suffers deeply. It is doubtful you do her any favours by prolonging this." He reached out towards the tormented female, only to have Darcy's hand clamped around his wrist within a half-second.

Darcy rumbled low in his throat.

Matlock sighed. "I will not touch her. Free my arm." With a last vicious growl, Darcy reluctantly obeyed.

"I do not know how far away our men are. These mountains interfere with mind contact," Matlock said. "We must return her to Pemberley. I shall commandeer some sort of transport. I am sure I can convince someone along the road to donate their vehicle to our cause."

Perhaps she will die quickly. One can always hope, he thought. Matlock simply radiated hope.

Darcy felt it and his hostility towards Matlock eased. He nodded impatiently. "Hur-ry."

Matlock rode his mount hard. Running would have been faster, but he was too furious; he needed time to cool. It was not overlong, however, before he came upon a hired carriage travelling across the mountain road. Its passenger was 'convinced' to swap modes of transport, and the coachman was advised of his change of route via the same method. Two hours later, Darcy, Matlock, and the dying Mouse were on the road to Pemberley.

❧

"Just over this rise we shall catch our first sight of Pemberley," Mr Bingley said, speaking to Jane for the first time in hours. They had been up at dawn on this, their third day of travel on this strange, silent trip. Mr Fitzwilliam chose to ride alongside, and though she heard him request Mr Bingley join him, he always chose to remain with her. She found Mr Fitzwilliam to be an alarming individual—almost fearsome. And Mr Bingley was no longer the charming, easy gentleman from Netherfield, but quiet and serious, maintaining a silence she would not break. Nevertheless, she found herself grateful for his quiet companionship as they approached her sister's new home.

She peered through the trees, her breath catching as she spied her first glimpses of a majestic castle, a lovely, gleaming jewel in the morning sunlight. The road wound in upward spirals to the castle perch; on the opposite peak, she could see another carriage travelling towards the same destination. She gauged its progress whenever she caught sight of it through the trees, idly wondering which of them would reach Pemberley first.

Abruptly, her carriage lurched forward; she heard the crack of the coachman's whip and had to clutch the seat edge in order to avoid being thrown into Mr Bingley's lap.

"What is it? What is happening?" she asked, but Mr Bingley could only shake his head. They practically flew around the curving road. When they reached the final straight stretch, Jane could see through the window that the other carriage raced just as quickly from the other side. As they pulled up in front of the drive, Mr Bingley reached across to touch Jane's wrist.

"Miss Bennet, if you would please wait here for just one moment," he said. Jane stared at his gloved hand, and he carefully removed it. "I shall return for you shortly," he said, opening the door and closing it gently behind him.

Jane heard the sound of Mr Darcy's voice; she had no intention of disobeying Mr Bingley's instructions to wait, but—curious and a bit nauseated from their mad dash—she cracked open the door for more air and to take a peek. The sight before her eyes was chilling.

Mr Darcy—looking as though he'd been in a carriage accident—extricated the body of a woman from the other vehicle. Mr Bingley and Mr Fitzwilliam both attempted to assist him and were waved brusquely away. Another man, who would probably be considered quite handsome if he were not so deathly pale, leaned against the carriage wall, impassively observing the scene. And the woman... bloodied, injured, lying still and white as death in Mr Darcy's arms was, without a doubt, Elizabeth.

"Lizzy! Lizzy!" she cried, struggling gracelessly to exit the carriage, tripping on her skirts. She would probably have fallen except Mr Bingley was immediately by her side, preventing her from reaching her sister.

As she watched, Lizzy began to flail as though she struggled to get away, convulsing in some sort of apoplexy. Once again, Jane attempted to break free of Mr Bingley's grasp in an effort to go to Elizabeth's side—but he would not allow it.

"You must not, Miss Bennet," he said quietly. "You cannot help her now. Darcy will see to her."

"What is wrong...oh dear heavens, what happened to her?"

Mr Darcy looked at her, seemingly only realising her presence for the first time. She had never seen a man so handsome nor so grief-ravaged. A drop of blood tracked down his cheek, looking startlingly like a tear. Then he gathered up his wife and raced through the inner portcullis, never granting her a word of acknowledgment.

It took her some moments to recognise Mr Bingley spoke to her.

"Let us go inside, Miss Bennet," he said. "Mrs Reynolds will show you to your rooms. You can rest..."

"How can I?" she interrupted incredulously. "How could you think I would possibly do anything except stay by my sister's side? If she is ill, she will need me!"

Suddenly, Mr Fitzwilliam stood before her. "You must go to your chambers, Miss Bennet," he said, staring into her eyes. "You will rest and take tea and most of all, you will not be anxious for your sister," he added.

Still, it took several more suggestions before Jane could be coaxed from her panic—the bond between the two sisters proved incredibly strong. By the time Mrs Reynolds led her away at last, Mr Bingley looked nearly as pale as Jane.

❧

"Come, Bingley. Darcy will have something fortifying for you in his study," the colonel said, drawing him indoors.

"I fear your suggestions will not last long," Bingley replied, allowing himself to be persuaded. "Jane... Miss Bennet is so disturbed by Mrs Darcy's condition, she cannot accept the solace you offer."

"Ignorance is often a cold comfort," Richard shrugged. "I knew bringing her here was a mistake. Perhaps it would be for the best if she develops a horror of all things Darcy."

His companion stiffened. "That is not the outcome, of course, I hope for personally," Bingley said quietly.

For a long while, neither spoke. The only sound was the fire crackling in the hearth; Bingley had a glass of Darcy's brandy he did not drink, and Richard only stared out the window into the gathering gloom, obviously receiving mental communication from the other inhabitants. Bingley finally opened a book, but hardly made a pretence of turning the pages.

"These Bennet women are difficult," the colonel said at last, the direction of his thoughts as obvious as his annoyance with their subject matter. He ran his hand through his hair. "There is something wrong with them! Pig-headed! Pure trouble." He snorted. "I should say, *most* of the Bennet women are stubborn—not all. The youngest sister is here and is so easily influenced that even young Vernon has no difficulty in assuming control of her whole consciousness. Vernon!" he said in disgust.

Bingley was not inclined to agree with Richard's opinions, but his need for information was greater than his desire to argue. "Pig-headed? Pot, meet kettle," he said dryly. "What has been happening here? You said Darcy had no intention of attempting to Turn his wife, and yet he did! Why is Miss Lydia...ah, pardon, Mrs Forster here?"

Richard sighed and provided Bingley as much explanation as he could.

"Wickham! Egad." Bingley shook his head. "Where do you keep Mrs Forster?"

"She is being held in one of the guest chambers. I suppose someone will need to return her to Bath or Brighton or wherever the devil she belongs." He groaned in annoyance. "And she is married to an army colonel—burying this will not be easy."

Bingley sighed. "If he is a sensible man, he would do nothing to announce her disappearance. He would likely have only a discreet few searching, at least for a few more days. I would try telling him she was homesick. No doubt he will write to Longbourn, so we must have his missive intercepted and respond appropriately at once. Even if he is suspicious, he will realise 'tis ruin if any find out otherwise—so play on his protective instincts and his reputation, his honour. It will suffice. He will *want* to believe you."

"You are better at this sort of thing than I am, Bingley. I should make you do it."

"We both know you have, ultimately, the superior technique."

Richard shook his head. "Never underestimate your own gifts. I suppose I must go. I cannot do so, though, until I know Mrs Darcy's fate. If anything happens, I greatly fear Darcy will not recover. Devil-dashed bondings eviscerate the surviving spouse."

"My grandfather told me old Mr Darcy recovered from the loss of his wife, Anne—at least, to a great extent. He never knew him when Mrs Darcy was alive, of course, but thought he seemed content enough."

"Perhaps. But it seems to me that Fitzwilliam shared more with his Elizabeth in a few short months of marriage than did George and Anne after nearly twenty years. Mark me, there will be the devil to pay." Richard shook his head in disgust.

"I suppose Darcy would say he'd rather have a few weeks of true happiness than twenty years of mediocrity," Bingley countered.

"Don't be such a milksop. Obviously he wants forever or he would not have attempted a Turning. That has always been his problem—he wants too much. Cares too much."

Bingley took a sip of his drink. "You know, Richard, for a former soldier you are not much of a risk taker."

"I can take risks. But I choose my battles wisely."

"Wisely? Sometimes you have no choice if you want the prize. What is so prudent about settling for—"

They both abruptly stopped speaking, their conversation interrupted by the sound of a feminine scream echoing through the marbled corridors. And then they both ran.

❧

Darcy carried his wife's inert body to their chambers, searching her features for any sign she would awaken. Her latest seizure and erratically beating heart were the only evidences of life. Struggling against despair, he gently laid Elizabeth on the soft mattresses of the four-poster. Carefully he undressed her, cleansing her of blood, sweat and evidence of her ordeal before clothing her in a clean nightdress. Caring for her so intimately had the effect of reclaiming at least a portion of his humanity from the beast ruling him. He felt some of the primitive wildness receding, even as grief and fear remained. Tenderly he combed her hair back from her face; it was a tangled mess, far too difficult for him to deal with alone, so he disregarded it—smiling grimly as he thought of what Elizabeth would say if she could see it now.

"Come back to me, Elizabeth," he gritted out. He could at least try to speak the words in his heart. "Do not make me live without you. I need you, love, more than lifeblood. You *are* my life." He did not know all he said to her; he begged and pleaded, soothed and cajoled. He talked until his voice rasped and strained, trying to connect with a part of her that might still respond. He feared if he left her alone for one moment with her fight, she might take death's easier pathway to peace.

"Your favourite sister is here," he said. "But you cannot talk to her like this, love. She wants to see you, to see your new home, but you need to wake to show her. Come back to Jane. Come back to me!"

She lay silent and still, unresponsive.

Night was falling; soon, it would be twenty-four hours since the Turning. Other than Maggie, he had never Turned a female—and he had only Turned Maggie because of his rage at the violent circumstances of her death. But none of his many Turnings had required more than twelve hours before becoming wholly Shielded, before awakening...or dying fully.

"Oh, Elizabeth," he cried, burying his face in her neck, trying to breathe in her scent and will her to live.

In that moment, her eyes opened...and not, for once, to roll back into her head, marking the onset of another fit. "Mr Darcy?" she questioned, peering at him with some consternation. "I feel very strange."

His head shot up, his eyes widening. "Elizabeth! Elizabeth...you have come back! Oh, Elizabeth," he gasped, gathering her close in ecstatic relief. He did not notice, at first, that she was trying to pull away until she shoved at him rather forcefully.

"Elizabeth?" he said uncertainly. "Are you in pain? Do you—"

"This is very odd, Mr Darcy," she interrupted, looking at her surroundings blankly, then down at her nightgown. "I am sure I should not be receiving you here...though where I am seems to have escaped me at the moment. Have I been ill? If you would excuse me, I..." she trailed off, and he could see her eying the open neck of his shirt with a sudden, visceral awareness.

Two small, sharp white fangs emerged. "Oh, Elizabeth," he murmured, leaning in more closely.

She was on him between one heartbeat and the next, her teeth tearing into his neck with no finesse whatsoever. Instinct provided what her mind had not yet grasped, and she drew his blood into her mouth in rapid, greedy gulps. He held her to him as a mother might a newborn babe. A primeval, desire-mixed joy filled him as he nourished her with his own body. Gradually, she stopped drinking; then, her fangs receded, and she slowly drew away.

She looked up at him curiously. "I am not sure why I did that," she said, but neither did her actions appear to trouble her. She scooted off his lap, putting a more proper distance between them. "How long have I been ill? Where am I?" she asked, glancing around the room with mild interest.

"Not long. Elizabeth, you are at Pemberley. 'Tis your home."

Her eyes traced the high ceiling with its exquisite mouldings and artistically painted ceiling. "Nice," was her only comment.

Because he could not help it, he reached out to touch her cheek. She allowed it but did not otherwise respond. In fact, she lay back down on her pillow, giving every indication she meant to go back to sleep. He sighed deeply. She was Shielded now, while her mind and body accommodated the Change. Vampyres were always difficult to destroy, but any possible weaknesses would disappear during this brief Shielding period. For this little time, his wife was truly invincible. However, mentally she would be disengaged from reality as she adapted to a new one.

He did not care that she was not yet herself. She was alive and she was safe. Apparently, she was also his forever—just as soon as she remembered she was married to him. He grinned and leaned over to kiss her forehead. She did not react.

He moved a little away, scooting back against the headboard, perfectly prepared to watch over her for as long as necessary.

After a few minutes she opened her eyes. "Do you notice anything unusual about me?" she asked calmly. "I mean, excepting the fact I just drank your blood."

He smiled, taking her hand. "No. Not a thing."

"I do not breathe."

"You can if you wish to," he replied. "In fact, it is very good for you to occasionally fill your lungs with air. You simply do not *need* to."

She appeared to contemplate this. "I suppose that might be useful. I cannot think how, at the moment."

"It comes in handy while swimming under water."

"Oh, yes, so it would. But I cannot swim," she said, her brows furrowed. "I have always wished to learn though. I think. I am very muzzy-headed at the moment."

"I will teach you," Darcy said. "We have a pond that is perfect for it in the summer. Not that the cold would affect you adversely, 'tis simply more comfortable to swim in warmer water. Your body will adapt to whatever temperature it has to in order to survive, but warm will always feel better than cold."

Whatever Elizabeth might have replied was lost when the bedchamber door swung open. Jane stood there, her cheeks flushed, her expression panicked.

"Lizzy!" she cried. "I planned to come to you, to help you...and somehow...I must have fallen asleep! I have been searching! Oh, dearest," she exclaimed, running to the bedside and catching up Elizabeth's hand. "You looked so very ill when we arrived." Noting her sister's improved colouring and countenance, she added, "But I must say, you look a great deal better now."

Elizabeth regarded Jane calmly, peering at their joined hands. Then, almost faster than the eye could follow, she snatched up Jane's wrist and bit down with an expression of blissful enjoyment, as if she were a child with a sugary treat.

Jane screamed and screamed and screamed.

Thirty

By the time Bingley rushed into Mrs Darcy's bedchamber, there was not much to see. He pushed past Richard, whose speed had allowed him to arrive moments earlier, to find Jane holding her wrist against the front of her gown. Blood seeped down the fabric, the expression on her face one of shock, horror, and pain. Darcy held his wife protectively on the opposite side of the room; Elizabeth frowned, looking both annoyed and confused, but not fighting her husband's hold. It was easy to guess what had happened.

He approached Jane at once, but she backed away from him.

"Miss Bennet," Bingley said, speaking gently, carefully, but with uncommon authority. "Please, come with me. Your wound must be tended. All will be well, but we must leave. Now."

He blocked her retreat but did not attempt physical contact. Her eyes were wild, looking from one to the other of them, fear stamped upon her lovely features. Bingley merely crowded her in the direction of the door. To avoid touching him, she had no choice but to move in the path he manoeuvred her. When she exited the room at last, the colonel followed them out, shutting the door behind him. Jane stared at them both.

The colonel met her gaze with contempt. "As I said, Bingley. Nothing but trouble, both of them." Jane flinched.

"Miss Bennet, please. Come downstairs," Bingley said in that same even tone. He had some experience with this, of course. While he ought to have turned her over to the colonel for a thorough memory revision, he could not bear the thought of Richard's harshness intimidating her further. Mrs Reynolds rounded the corner just as Jane ventured forward, and she startled.

"Mrs Reynolds, Miss Bennet has been injured. Will you bring bandages and warm water to the library?"

The housekeeper nodded. "Yes, sir. At once." She sped away.

More slowly, Bingley made his way towards the library. He was relieved when Jane followed him, and Richard did not.

When they entered the great room, he saw Mrs Reynolds had already left the requested supplies, along with a jar of some sort of healing unguent. He gestured Jane to the sofa nearest the fire, which had been built up to a fine blaze casting extra warmth into the library's vast interior. He pulled up a chair to sit in front of her, picking up the cloth and dipping it into the basin provided. He reached for her wrist; for a moment, it appeared she would refuse.

"Please, allow me to cleanse it," he said, and she gave up her resistance.

It was still bleeding, just a little. And evidently it was painful as well, judging by the way she winced as he worked. New vampyres seldom used much finesse. Hopefully, the ointment Mrs Reynolds provided would prevent scarring. Once he had it firmly bandaged, however, he did not relinquish her arm. Jane stared into the flames, avoiding his gaze. She was shocked, frightened, and so stunningly beautiful, he ached.

"What happened to my sister?" she whispered, still not looking at him.

He weighed what he knew against what he felt. He had made a mistake before, not trusting his instincts. He should have gone to her, given her a chance to explain. Darcy had briefly explained Elizabeth's revelation regarding Mrs Forster, and lived with bitter regret. Bingley was confident his employer and friend trusted his judgment enough to support whatever decision he now made. A life of secrets, of deceit and lies. Was his love enough of an exchange?

"Your sister has...changed," he began weakly.

"An understatement," Jane replied wryly, surprising him.

"Yes. She is not well at the moment. But she will get better. Better than she has ever been in her life. Stronger. Healthier."

"I do not understand."

"Jane...I must confess I fell in love with you within hours of our meeting. I have been miserable without you. But I had to leave you because of all this." He gently stroked her wrist over the bandage before continuing.

"Fitzwilliam Darcy is...different. My life, and the lives of my father and my father's father have been spent protecting him, keeping others from discovering who and what he is. He is of a race that must drink blood in order to survive. He is the best of men, honourable and decent. He is not evil."

He knew he did not express himself well. How could he ever expect her to understand?

"My sister...she bit me. She hurt me."

At least she had not utterly rejected his words in horror. "She did not know. She has only just been Turned, and is not yet herself. But this part of the Change only lasts a short while."

Jane shook her head. "I do not understand any of this. I can hardly comprehend what you are telling me, it is so fantastic, a waking dream." Her gaze caught his, and she looked at him keenly. "Why, if you are charged with the protection of such...such things, did you toy with my feelings? If you had no intention of—"

"I had every intention," he interrupted. "But I erred. It is a tradition in our family, to–to test the discretion of any who might be considered a potential spouse. I told you a secret, Jane, but I lied. It was a lie, as you discovered, all that nonsense about Darcy and Anne de Bourgh."

"I never—" she began, as horrified understanding struck.

"I know, I know. *Now*, I know. In some strange, awful coincidence, someone else told the same lie at the same time. But I thought..." Silence fell as Jane attempted to come to terms with all she had discovered this evening.

"I wish he had not done this to her," she said at last, a tear trickling down her cheek. "Lizzy was perfect as she was."

Bingley did not know whether to be relieved or discouraged that she returned to the subject of her sister's Change. "Her life was in danger," he explained. "Whatever my deceit in the past, my motives for bringing you to Pemberley were truthful. I sought you out because of the danger you are in—a danger caused simply because she loves you. In Darcy's world, there are plenty of villains, though he is not one. Somehow, she managed to draw the notice of some dangerous, powerful…others. The reason he gave me for marrying your sister in the first place was to protect her from those others, though he has held a *tendre* for her since first they met. He left her here at Pemberley when he learned the plot against her extended to threaten her sisters…and me. In his absence, she was abducted by those enemies."

Jane gasped.

"I do not know all the details. Darcy went to her rescue and was captured himself. The rogue who held them is capable of great horrors. Darcy must have been desperate to even attempt the Turning. It is not always a successful process."

Jane gripped his arm. "Perhaps it was not successful in her case either. She seems…"

"No, no," Bingley reassured. "She is not mad, only confused. And, you see, during this period of–of confusion, she is quite infallible. Nothing and no one can hurt her. She could walk through a burning building or face the guillotine and bullets. *She* is safe…but perhaps others near her are not quite so, at present. She suffers from a terrible thirst for…"

"For blood." Jane shuddered.

"Yes. But it will not always be this way. I mean, she will always need it to survive, but only once every few weeks, and Darcy will meet her needs himself. For now, he will look after her and ensure she does nothing else she might regret when she returns to herself."

Jane looked at him in sudden dismay. "Are you…are you…?"

"No, Jane. I am as you are." He took her cold hand in his. "I realise this is difficult to take in. But I ask you to consider carefully what you want. I can have Richard erase your every memory of this. You can return to blissful ignorance, and—once the danger is past—to your family in London. Please remember, everything is unchanged in your life from what it was yesterday and last month and last year. The only difference is now you know more truth. Your sister…*hers* is the life that is uprooted and torn asunder. She faces a whole new world, with different hopes, expectations, and challenges. The only thing you have to decide is this: how close to her do you wish to be? She cannot go back. Only you can go forward, with whatever intimacy you care to share with the Darcys."

"I do not want to become…to–to…"

"That is not what I meant," Bingley interrupted. "I could never make you what they are even if you wished it. I wish to offer you my heart, dearest. But this is who I am, this is what I do: I care for the Darcys. I protect them from dangerous prejudice and mob violence. I hold their secrets safe and ease their way in a world of men who would *never* understand. I swear to you, I will always watch over your sister on your behalf, whatever your choice in this. However, as my wife, my partner, you could join me in my duties. Our children will be raised to know and protect their secrets, and our children's children will do the same. Because Mr and Mrs Darcy will likely outlive us by many centuries, God willing."

He pressed a kiss to the hand he held and returned it to her lap. "Mrs Reynolds is waiting to help you to your room, and she will see you have everything possible to aid your comfort. Take tonight to think on what I have said. I shall seek you out in the morning to hear your answer. Until then, I shall see that you are undisturbed. Whatever your decision, you are safe here, I promise. Trust that much, at least."

Bingley stood, gave her a bow, and left her to her scattered thoughts.

❧

A gentle voice called his name. "She needs to feed again, sir."

Mrs Reynolds met his gaze with sympathy.

"I know," he replied.

"Maggie and I have given all we can for the nonce."

Elizabeth would do better with blood from the strongest on the estate. Darcy knew he did not have enough in him to provide it, and it was killing him. He had nearly allowed her to drain him as it was. A glance in the mirror told him his eyes were black, his cheeks hollow, his skin pale. The beast within was beginning to rule and his judgment was likely affected. His wife lay asleep, restlessly twisting within the bedclothes.

"Bring Richard," he growled. "And Matlock as well."

"Richard probably has enough to satisfy."

"Believe me," he said, "we shall need Matlock."

It was not long before both men were at Elizabeth's bedside. Richard looked at his nephew hovering protectively over his wife, and unknowingly repeated Mrs Reynolds' sentiment. "I am sure I can do this alone, Darcy. I fed this morning. I have Penelope waiting for me, after. I know this is difficult for you."

Matlock only raised a brow, watching Darcy warily.

"I did not ask Matlock here for feeding purposes," Darcy replied. "He is here to prevent me from killing you while you do it." His eyes glowed suddenly red.

Richard nodded, sighing. Elizabeth's eyes opened but she was unseeing, locked in her haze of blood-need, her fangs fully extended. Darcy instinctively reached for her.

"Hold him, Matlock. Whatever you do, do not let go," Richard ordered.

He extended his wrist to Elizabeth, and almost faster than the eye could see, she was on it. He glanced over at Darcy. Matlock gripped him tightly; plainly, it took all his strength to hang on to him, even though Darcy was in a weakened condition, his eyes glittering scarlet orbs, focused only on Elizabeth's mouth at Richard's wrist.

"Hurry," Matlock grunted, his biceps straining.

"This vein is too devilish small to Take faster."

"Then give her your neck."

"Certainly. Excellent idea. Let us save time and simply dig my grave first?"

"I am not going to be able to hold him back much longer."

With a curse, he forced Elizabeth to release his wrist. She sank back onto the bed with a moan of displeasure. Instantly Matlock released his hold on Darcy, who lunged for his wife. Richard stopped him.

"Darcy!" he barked, his hands clamping in a grip of steel on Darcy's shoulders. He heaved him around to face him. "Darcy, she needs to eat. I need to feed her. You need to get hold of yourself."

Darcy dropped his head into his hands, obviously trying to make sense of the words.

"Can you understand me?" Richard said, more quietly.

Darcy nodded.

"You need to feed, too."

"Shielding protects her skin. Until she understands, allows," he growled, "cannot."

Richard grimaced. "Devil take it, she's ruined you," he said, shaking his head.

"No," Darcy said. "I must...I need to—" he broke off, plainly unable to articulate his feelings while the beast ruled. He shoved Richard aside and climbed up on the bed with his wife. Leaning against the headboard, he gathered her into his arms so his body cradled hers. She turned to look up at him, her eyes full of confusion. She had Taken enough from Richard, evidently, to rejuvenate her, but the intense mental armour of Shielding kept reality at bay. She stared at his neck, wanting.

"Mr Darcy?" she questioned. "What is wrong with me?" It was the most lucid thing she had uttered in hours. She closed her eyes once more, her head falling back against his shoulder. "Thirsty," she muttered.

"It will be well," he managed, wrapping his arms more tightly around her. "Richard...give to her."

Warily regarding his nephew, Richard approached the bed and extended his wrist.

Darcy could not prevent the growl forming deep inside his throat, but he forced his eyes away from the proffered arm. Instead, he breathed in her scent, and when she latched on, attended to the sound of her swallows of nourishment, at the way her heartbeat strengthened as she drank. The knowledge that it was not his blood, the frustrated fury of the beast stabbed at his consciousness in painful awareness...but he beat the agony and the humiliation back with all the will and love he had in him.

It seemed to take forever. His own heart rate accelerated wildly as he fought madness. It was a physical pain splitting his soul, and it was all he could do not to cry out in rage and shame.

At last his uncle's voice penetrated. "'Tis finished, Darcy."

Blinking, Darcy met Richard's gaze. Pity poured off his uncle, causing him to fear something had gone amiss with the feeding, and his eyes shot to Elizabeth. But no, she was perfect; her restlessness appeased—at least for the moment—and her skin pink and healthy-looking. Darcy shook his head; Richard was a fool to pity him for what was only a temporary setback. He had Elizabeth and would keep her forever. His heart swelled with love as he cradled her, quelling any primitive frustration.

"I hope her Shielding does not last much longer," Matlock said.

Darcy turned to him, having forgotten he was in the room. Unlike Richard, Matlock radiated a complete absence of emotion, unusual in the normally warm and compassionate earl. Elizabeth turned to Matlock at the same moment as Darcy.

Like a shot she was out of his arms, knocking the startled Matlock to the floor. Her fingers extended as if they were claws as she dug them into the cavity of his chest with the obvious and brutal intent to rip his heart from his body.

Matlock reacted instinctively, throwing her off him with such force, her body embedded in the wall. Had she still been human, it would have killed her. As it was, she tore herself from the plaster and launched herself at him once more. Darcy grabbed her. Her strength was no match for his, but he was amazed even so at the exertion it required to hold her back. She let out a feral scream of frustration.

"Out!" Darcy yelled. "Everyone out!"

For several moments after Matlock and the colonel hastily departed, Elizabeth tried to break free of his hold. Then, abruptly, she stopped struggling; Darcy continued to hold her firmly but turned her in his arms so that she faced him.

"What is wrong with me?" she asked again.

"You only need to rest, sweetheart," he said gently. "All will be well."

Her hair was full of plaster dust and he loosened his grasp, using one hand to brush it back from her face. He touched her scalp and felt a good-sized bump from her impact with the wall. It would heal quickly but might cause her pain for the next several moments. His beast within growled, infuriated at this injury to his mate; it was just as well that Matlock was out of sight.

She reached up to his throat and he wondered if she was going to attempt to kill him, too. But she only touched the pulse point at his neck, almost wonderingly. "You taste better," she said, "than that other man."

For the first time in several hours, he smiled.

Thirty One

Elizabeth tried to think, though it was almost impossibly difficult. She could appreciate the beauty of the furnishings surrounding her without any idea where she was, mists of confusion scattering her thoughts like feathers in the wind. Mr Darcy was beside her day and night—but if she tried to determine why Mr Bingley's handsome houseguest should be her constant companion, a thick fog descended. And the craving...who could think with this maddening thirst?

The evil man visited once more, but she managed to frighten him off. Or he escaped. She was not sure.

Everybody made a fuss about it. Could they not see he was vile? Did they not notice the rot-infested pustules covering him? Everyone else was kind, though not as kind as Jane. Dear, sweet Jane...where had she gone? She had seen Mr Bingley—she was certain he looked in on her more than once. Perhaps she was at Netherfield, after all.

She no longer found it odd that she thirsted for blood—all she cared about was getting more of it, becoming a connoisseur, of sorts. The females were less filling, but she tolerated their blood when she could not get anything better, like the grumpy man's.

"Elizabeth," said Mr Darcy. He spoke to her again, in his very pleasant, deep voice. His blood tasted the most delicious of all, rich and salty-sweet...but he was stingy with it.

"Elizabeth, can you hear me?"

She opened her eyes. It was easier to keep them closed; fewer questions occurred to her then, any of which would invoke the numbing bewilderment. But she opened them now to find Mr Darcy looking down upon her; for the first time, she thought he did not look...himself. He was gaunt almost, his cheekbones much sharper in his face. His hair was still silky-looking though, if grown longer than ever. She reached up to see whether it felt as soft as it appeared. It did.

He smiled at her when she did that. Did he like this, when she touched him? It was not a proper touch, she knew that...but the reasons why were lost.

"Do you remember Charles's visit?" he asked.

"Charles?"

A shadow crossed over his face. "Mr Bingley? He came in to see you yesterday, but you fell asleep while he spoke."

"Oh. I think I remember. You would not let me drink him. He smelled nice."

His brow furrowed. "He had news. Your sister, Jane, has agreed to marry him."

"Jane? Marrying Mr Bingley?"

"Yes, love. Jane will marry him. Richard will procure the license, and Mr Marley will marry them from Pemberley."

Elizabeth closed her eyes again. She wanted to ask who Richard and Mr Marley were, but somehow knew it would not make sense. Was she mad? The fog tried to descend, and she clung to what she understood.

"Jane...marrying? She is...happy?" It was hard to even elucidate this much.

"Yes, I believe so." Mr Darcy closed his eyes for a moment, appearing as though he, too, struggled to find words. Perhaps he was affected by the madness, as well.

For the first time in ever so long, a shot of fear pierced the fog and bewilderment surrounding her. "Jane...Jane...here?"

"Yes, love. As soon as you feel yourself, we shall bring her in to see you."

"Mr Darcy..." she panicked, trying desperately to hold onto the thought. *Jane...Jane...* "Must...protect Jane," she managed.

"She is safe, Elizabeth."

"The man...the rotting man...where?" She bit her lip, trying to maintain her place in the conversation, grappling for control of the fog.

Darcy sighed. "Do you mean Lord Matlock? He is gone back to London today. You will not have to see him for a long time."

At this news, something within Elizabeth eased. Seconds later, she forgot all about it.

Matlock departed Pemberley, his fury a scalding, acid stew. It was all he could do to control it while Darcy was present; he probably had not, really, but doubted Darcy expected him to be pleased. Tossing him—the *Earl of Matlock*—out on his ear. Forcing *him* to leave Pemberley without even a by-your-leave. All for that rabid mouse he married! *Booted*, before finding opportunity to kill her when her Shielding wore off! She had always been inferior, a mute trull—and no longer a mouse, but a mad dog.

Then there was her extremely suspicious behaviour, attacking the moment her attention fixed upon him. It was impossible she sensed his duplicity, but it gave him another reason to despise her. All his efforts to guard Darcy's interests aside, there were kings in *his* blood! She should *worship* him!

Matlock allowed his fury to boil over. Until he rid the world of the odious long-meg, his plans were stymied. His procreative schemes for Darcy had been ruined the moment she was Turned. And if she was suspicious of him, he might never be allowed closer to her. Darcy was so ludicrously overprotective.

As soon as his carriage rounded the first bend, within the coverage offered by the tree-lined drive, he was out of it. His coach continued on without him, his minions trained to notice nothing of his comings and goings. He slipped into the woods, stealing along a path George Darcy had shown him long ago.

Hardly a quarter-hour passed before he managed to slip back into Pemberley. At this hour, when the sun was just setting, there were none as strong as he, save Darcy, who was safely hovering over his travesty of a wife; no one detected his entrance. Of course, it did not hurt that he himself had arranged the duty roster for this night. The strongest of the guard were patrolling the property perimeters, and of course, Richard was now away dealing with Wickham's mess in Brighton.

Matlock headed directly for the cellars. Fitzwilliam had no idea Matlock knew of many of these entrances and exits and well-hidden tunnels in these underground passages; if the boy understood how careless George Darcy had been immediately after Anne Darcy died, he might have cause for concern. But he had not *had* to understand. His father's best friend had taken care of *everything*.

His anger peaked once again. *He*, who had held both Darcy men while they bathed his shoulder in weak, pitiful tears—*this* was how he was repaid? *Intolerable!*

Vernon guarded the cleverly concealed entrance to the tunnel he sought, the young vampyre plainly bored witless. Matlock created a noise of just the right timbre, echoing further down the passage. As expected, the jinglebrain ran to investigate. It was a moment's work to open the complicated mechanism barring the entrance; shortly thereafter, the wall slid silently away, closing again behind him.

With unerring accuracy, he found his way to the silver gaol. The excruciating metal created its own strength-sapping call; opening it would be the most difficult part of this little visit. Fortunately, its workings were similar in nature to the entryway lock, and it took but several minutes to open. Swinging the door wide, he glanced inside.

The female lay on the silver-plated floor, as there was no bench, no reprieve from exposure. She twisted restlessly, feebly attempting to escape the burning sensations. It could have been worse, he supposed. They could have left her naked to smoulder against it, shaving her head—'twas what *he* would have done.

Weak.

At last she noticed the draught from the tunnel and raised her head. "Who is it?" she hissed.

Fading into the passageway, he melted back into the shadowy darkness, not revealing himself.

Cautiously she exited her prison, scrabbling like a rat, stumbling and falling in her frailty. Once she escaped the silver cell, she fell back against the tunnel wall, gasping as though she required breath.

Of course, she could not fully recover without feeding, but every moment beyond the silver prison helped. Staring into the inky darkness, her eyes narrowed—probably sensing his presence, or at least *a* presence. But his illusory talents were exceptional, and in her present weakness, she had no chance of recognition.

It did not take her many moments to gain enough strength to make good her escape, though she obviously did not know her way. When she reached the tunnel head—and the obvious dead-end—she gritted her teeth in frustration. Before she could cry out, though, he pressed a certain stone. The wall slid open.

Vernon, returned to his post, swung around in surprise.

It was all the opportunity she needed. In less than the blink of an eye, she was on him like a rat to a carcass. Though imprisonment and lack of nourishment weakened her, it also lent her predatory force. She overpowered the much younger vampyre immediately, paralysing him with her power.

Matlock knew this was his cue to expunge his scent and depart—this little act was simply revenge against Catherine for ruining all his plans. Yet he could not stop watching, witnessing her grow stronger as the younger man faded. The moment she had sufficient potency, her powerful hand clawed into Vernon's chest cavity, his struggle growing fiercer as he grasped, rather too late, that his life was almost over. What had he thought, that she would feed from him and leave? With almost a surgeon's stroke, she tore out his heart, crushing it between her fingers, fixing a glut of power with intense precision upon his neck as his arms flapped feebly, his tendons stretching and bubbling beneath his skin.

Matlock left before she finished; it was past time for him to go. Still, he had enjoyed the show. Anne de Bourgh was, indeed, her mother's daughter. It was almost a shame, departing without providing the knowledge she would require in order to save herself. Almost.

Darcy brushed a cool cloth over Elizabeth's forehead. Richard had fed her one last time before leaving for Brighton; that duty could no longer be put off without risking permanent damage to Lydia's reputation. Surely this Ordeal could not last too much longer. She twisted restlessly in the bedcovers, her fangs lengthening in her dreams of drinking.

Suddenly, his head snapped up. A coldness entered him like an icy shadow, bringing the spectre of death. It was one of his own. Immediately, he reached out with his senses to each of his people. His line. His House. His family.

Vernon. Vernon was gone, his life force snuffed out. Darcy jumped up, mentally shouting for James and Andrew.

Master? came their dual thoughts.

Vernon has been killed, he told them. *What was his assignment this night?*

And when they told him, he knew Anne de Bourgh was his prisoner no longer.

"All to me!" he roared, both mentally and aloud, his fury touching the furthest reaches of Pemberley's vast grounds.

It was enough to bring Mrs Reynolds and the rest of the household running. It was enough to wake Elizabeth from her troubled sleep, though she remained confused.

It took only moments to gather the vampyres of the household along with his cadre. Because Darcy could not speak to his wife mentally, he communicated verbally—and with difficulty, as the beast reared up, his eyes glowing brilliant green to black to flaming red.

"We are under attack," he said. "Vernon is dead. I know not how, but Anne de Bourgh has escaped. I do not know what assistance she might have, only that she is loose. If she is wise, she flees far and fast; I do not know if she is wise. James, stay here with my wife. Andrew, take all non-combatants, including Bingley, Miss Bennet, and Mrs Forster, to the north tower."

Maggie stepped forward. "I would stay with my mistress, sir."

"She is Shielded from any harm," Darcy said. "Otherwise I would not leave her. James is for my peace of mind only."

"She is confused, and I can keep her calm," Maggie said. "Let me stay. Please."

Darcy nodded, wishing fervently he had not sent Matlock and Richard away. "Very well. Everyone else is needed to search. All those who can ride, must. No one is to go out alone. Stay in twos or threes. I will begin with the cellars and go through to the turrets. Nigel and Thomas will direct the search of the grounds, beginning in the nearest gardens."

He was gone so quickly that it took the others a few moments to regroup, some following him below and the rest of them presenting themselves to his two lieutenants. And the hunt began.

Anne did not dare move a muscle or so much as blink. All of her powers were currently in use masking her own scent, while tracking the scents of all within this castle. She was very accomplished, of course, in *camoufler*, in blending into the shadows, but she was also her mother's finest—and only—pupil. Coated with the blood of the Darcy vampyre, she manipulated the part of him that was Darcy-scent into her marrow. Darcy could not scent her, and had *finally* departed the castle to join the search out of doors because, for the moment at least, she was Darcy-blooded, smelling only of himself. The effect would not last long before decomposing; it would, perhaps, be prudent to leave Pemberley at once. But that was expected. She would not be predictable, not Anne of de Bourgh.

Unexpected, however, was Elizabeth Bennet Darcy's pathetic single guard —James, she thought—and the little maid. *So much for Darcy's protectiveness*, she smirked. James was strong, but *she* was the future of House de Bourgh.

She found another Darcy lieutenant guarding a silly group of humans in the northern turret, and the remaining vampyres were mere servants, their gifts focused on chores and meals. Plainly, Darcy believed she'd fled.

After locking her away from all contact with her line, torturing her in silver, starving her—after she had fed *him* from her own vein—after preparing for *years* to be his true bride, Darcy believed she would allow these insults to pass? Well, more fool he. Would her mother run? How could Anne possibly expect to remain heir to her mother's power if she showed cowardice now? Killing his pitiful human wife was the least of what her pride demanded; she would return to Catherine in triumph, not shame.

At last, Maggie had the happy opportunity to brush out her mistress's hair. It was a tangled mess, and putting it right caused some grief—Mrs Darcy hissed at her, initially. But gradually she soothed her into accepting the calming strokes, the snarls gone, her tresses gleaming, shining against her pillows. Braiding would be ideal, but it looked so pretty in all its varied hues; she wanted the Master to see how lovely his wife was, instinctively understanding Mrs Darcy to be the only hope for calming him when he returned from this awful night's work.

Maggie fed her from her wrist, ignoring her mistress's grimaces and watching her as she peered at James reflectively, as though debating his flavouring. "'Tis all we have now, Mistress," Maggie said evenly, turning her attention away from the guard. "You've fed from the Master and now you're spoiled. Not everyone tastes as he, eh?"

"As if you'd know," James huffed. "Unless you've been very discreet."

"Hush, now," Maggie said firmly. "Mrs Darcy knows I'm teasing." She watched James with some concern. He was not at all composed, grieving over Vernon, no doubt, and longing to be out stalking his prey—stopping his pacing only long enough to look out the window, his sharp eyes piercing the night.

"You should calm," Maggie said. "You're vexing Mrs Darcy."

He glanced at Mrs Darcy, currently lying in peaceful repose upon the four-poster, and rolled his eyes. "I think she copes well enough."

"Perhaps. But tying yourself into knots—"

A sudden noise halted her words and they both froze. It was the soft sound of a woman's laughter, easily recognisable.

"It sounds as if it comes from the maze," Maggie whispered.

James held up his hand for silence, then shook his head. "No," he said softly. "She is bouncing the sound of it to the garden, but she is inside the castle. I cannot tell where exactly, but possibly near the North Tower."

At once they tried for a mental connexion with their friends and fellows in the turret, but heard only the sound of Anne de Bourgh's mirth. They exchanged looks of dismay.

"You must go to them at once," Maggie said.

James's expression was serious as he glanced at his mistress. "She will be safe, but you will not. Come, wake her, we will all go."

Maggie shook her head. "She is too confused and would only slow you. I will stay with her. She grows frightened when she does not understand what is happening, and that evil de Bourgh does not want *my* head."

James nodded. "I shall return quickly," he said, slipping quickly and silently from the room.

He had only been gone for moments when the door swung open;

a wild blur shot through the chamber. Maggie found herself held immobile, unable to so much as squeak, even her capacity to communicate via thought paralysed as an intruder charged at Mrs Darcy.

❧

In a lightning reflex, Elizabeth threw herself off the bed and directly at the interloper. Her eyes glowed eerily and her fangs extended.

"What is this?" Anne cried as she clawed at her attacker in surprise. "You, a vampyre?"

But Elizabeth, acting purely on instinct, had no vocabulary; she made directly for Anne's heart.

And here Anne made a fatal mistake; she made no attempt to defend herself and throw off her opponent, which might perhaps have met with success—for though Elizabeth was impervious to mental attack, she was young and inexperienced, and Anne much older and quicker. Rather, Anne chose an offensive manoeuvre—not understanding Elizabeth was Shielded. For all her strength, Anne could not so much as pierce the skin over her breast, while Elizabeth had already managed to penetrate Anne's chest and clutch the beating organ in her fist.

Anne screamed, shoving the total weight of her formidable psychic powers at Elizabeth's head, enough to cleave it from her neck—enough to cleave an *elephant's* head from its neck! She expected it, waited for it, *needed* it, her best aggressive, lethal manoeuvre that had never failed against a weaker foe.

Nothing happened. Meanwhile, even so fearsome a heart as a de Bourgh's had its limits. With an unearthly scream, Elizabeth tore it from its owner's chest.

It beat within her hand for a half-second before she crushed it. Immediately, Maggie was free to move, shouting mentally for James to return at once.

He was unneeded. Elizabeth neither hesitated nor showed mercy. Anne's head was removed from its moorings, a feat of brutish strength and horrible instinct. When James arrived seconds later, Andrew close upon his heels, there was naught for them to do except call for help clearing up the mess.

Elizabeth dropped the head she still held and stood staring uncomprehendingly at the carnage and her own bloody hands. The more incomprehensible the situation to human sensibilities, the greater the effects of Shielding. She swayed on her feet, and Maggie was there at once.

"Come, Mrs Darcy. We'll take you to the Master's chambers and clean you up. I expect Mrs Reynolds will have your room restored in a jiffy," she said, taking Elizabeth's unresisting arm.

"The Master is on his way home," Andrew added, peering at the blood-spattered walls. "Saints alive, how'd she manage to kill that one? Devilish powerful, the de Bourgh creature. There wasn't much left of Vernon, t'all."

Maggie shook her head. "I do not know. The mistress attacked her before I even understood the danger. It was uncanny. I knew she could not be killed because of her Shielding, but I never knew of any Shielding that could inspire such a defence. Most remarkable." Still astonished, she led Elizabeth from the room.

Andrew smiled cheerfully. "Better a de Bourgh than a Darcy. I don't suppose the Master will much care, as long as his bride din't break a fingernail while milling. Never seen a man quite so horn-mad over a female." He was still chuckling as he left the room a few minutes later, whistling as he searched for a sack for the illustrious remains.

Thirty Two

Elizabeth opened her eyes to see Mr Darcy returned. Her hands hurt; in fact, she was sore everywhere. Why? She looked to him for answers, and then forgot the question.

His eyes were red, which was odd. It was twilight, she somehow knew, though the drapes were drawn and only the fireplace flames dimly lit the room. Perhaps his eyes reflected the red within the hearth's blaze. His presence in this bed with her was improper, too. Also, peculiarly, he wore only shirt and trousers, so she could see the skin of his throat. She could not contemplate these matters, lest she invite the descending fog. Instead, she reached up to touch the new sharpness to his cheekbones. He held very still, almost quivering beneath her touch.

His lips were soft. His face was harsh, his brow and nose giving him an almost hawk-like appearance, but his mouth was an anomaly. She traced its edges with her fingertip. Impulsively, she touched the surface of his teeth.

"Some of your teeth are...strange," she murmured. "Sharp." His incisors looked as though they were lengthening. *Decidedly* odd. She placed her index finger on one.

He moaned.

Her eyes flew to his, which were now closed. Perhaps he had a toothache. "Does it hurt?" she asked.

"No," he muttered.

Curious, she touched the other one. He made another noise, perhaps more growl. Touching the pointed tip, it pierced her skin, a drop of blood bubbling. Instantly, his tongue shot out and he began suckling her finger. It was not...unpleasant.

She knew better than to examine her actions or his. Better to go with the feelings, not try to fight them. The only way to find out what he experienced was to duplicate his movements. With her other hand, she found his where it clutched the bedclothing so tightly, it shredded beneath his fingers. She pulled his hand up to her mouth.

He understood what she wanted better than she did. Gently he put a finger forward and lightly rubbed one of her incisors.

It felt exquisite, a strangely familiar tension. She had experienced these alluring feelings before, she knew suddenly. *Mr Darcy* had made her feel this way before. And she understood, instinctively, that it was good, that together they would help ease the plaguing pain of the thirst.

She suckled his finger as he had done to her, but it only made her restless. The sensations he evoked by stroking her teeth faded as soon as he stopped.

"Again," she demanded.

Instead of appeasing her, he removed his hand from her mouth. "I must go, Elizabeth. But I cannot leave you." His tone was harsh, accusing, unlike his usual gentle manner of speech.

Her eyes narrowed, dropping to the expanse of skin revealed by his open shirt.

There. His pulse beat, working at his throat edge. Her thirst was great, but for the first time she realised her preference for Mr Darcy was unrelated to his delicious taste. With primitive intuition, she knew drinking from him satisfied her, in a way all the others could not. She lunged but was not quick enough. He blocked her access, infuriating her.

If he would not give her his neck, she would find other places upon his person that would work as well. He was lean but strong; smooth skin covered rippling muscles that clenched and firmed beneath her gaze.

If she had been more aware, she would have noticed his eyes still burned a vivid scarlet. As her hand reached out to touch him, the intense heat he radiated should have scorched her. But she paid no attention to these visual, sensual cues that Darcy's beast was taking control.

"I am strong," she said, impressed when she tore his shirt as easily as if it were paper. His newly revealed chest showed her that his body was not quite like her own. Neither did it seem utterly foreign or unexpected. *I know this already,* she realised. *It belongs to me.* He was formed for her pleasure, her benefit.

"Mine," she said. "Take."

❧

Mine, Mine, Mine. Her proclamation was a chant inside Darcy's head, battling in his brain. Would she allow it? But it did not matter; the beast had been given its freedom, and it was hers.

He pinned her to the mattress, his strength so vast, he had no idea whether or not she was struggling against him. The beast simply did not care, taking her mouth and her feelings into itself.

Those feelings were chaotic, confused, excited, jumbled, an all-consuming thirst burning like acid in her head. She was nearly crazed.

The beast cared for none of that. It latched onto her willingness and anticipation. The beast was hungry, needed desperately to feed... and so it Took her into itself, gave of itself, in every possible way.

❧

Her cries woke Darcy to himself, catching himself mid-swallow. Her blood had grown stronger than the finest brandy, more potent than the wickedest home brew. Saints, how much had he taken? Had he injured her? But no. He could feel the life force of her emotions...less confused now. Calmer. He had drunk enough to revive his more civilised self.

"Elizabeth?" he asked. It felt so perfect, to be within her, invading —he could not tell if he was asking permission or begging pardon.

Her eyes opened. "Fitzwilliam?" She touched his cheek. "What has happened to you, my dearest? You need to feed, do you not?" She tipped her throat back, offering.

"Elizabeth," he said again. "You are back. You have come back to me."

She smiled, not questioning their intimacy. "Was I gone?" she said, pressing his head down to meet her pulse once more. He Took.

He could feel her confidence, her desire, and her need to care for him through their connexion.

"Bite me," he implored, withdrawing.

"I want to Take from you," she murmured, breathless and excited. "I do not want to hurt you."

"You will not. You cannot, my dearest love," he said. "It is good."

She bit then, and he experienced the utterly exquisite pleasure throughout his entire being, fully blooded and more robust than he had ever been. He felt the shuddering exchange as she pulled on his vein; long before he felt she had Taken enough, she withdrew.

"Take more," he urged.

"I must not take too much," she replied. "'Tis enough."

Drawing back, he looked down, still feeling, through their connexion, the plaguing thirst. Her restraint in the face of such pain was unexpected. Most newly Turned humans had to learn to withdraw; their natural impulses, if uncontrolled, were to bleed the host dry.

"Take a little more," he whispered tenderly.

"I should not...what if I cannot stop? You taste so good," she nearly groaned.

"If you take too much, I can always take some back," he said, licking the pulse point on her neck before meeting her eyes once more.

"How can we do this?" she asked. "If we keep exchanging the same...blood...one would think it would grow weak."

"Would it?" he asked. "I only know that one sip from your body is more invigorating than nourishment from a hundred others. Even more now than before your change. There is something about you," he said, "that revitalises me. That fulfils, fortifies. You are exactly everything I need, perfect in every way. Let me become so for you."

Through their renewed intimacy, he could feel her Ordeal was incomplete; her feelings were marbled with confusion and bewilderment. But he also sensed pleasure, attraction and affection. And she knew him, at least.

"Do you remember everything now, Elizabeth?" he asked, his voice husky.

She waited several moments before replying. "I am trying," she whispered. "Answers are...almost within reach."

"What do you remember...about me?" he questioned.

Her brow furrowed as she strained for more, her eyes widening. "You insulted me!" she accused.

A sudden grin lit his face. "You *would* remember that," he said wryly.

But she did not notice, murmuring, "With my body, I thee worship...you married me!" she cried, surprised.

"Do you suppose we could be together like this, had I not?" he asked, still smiling.

"I suppose I have been allowing great...liberties," she replied, smiling back. But the smile quickly disappeared, her head twisting from side to side, as Darcy felt her shocked responses. Memories crashed in upon her, one after another like a row of falling dominoes. "Kympton...monster! Wickham! *Lydia!*" she gasped.

"She is well. But I swear, if you ever do anything as monumentally foolish as delivering yourself to my enemies again, I promise to lock you in the cellar and never let you out. Devil take it, Elizabeth," he broke off, his eyes glowing in anger and pain.

"She was in danger! My fault. I had to—"

"I would have taken care of it."

"You were not here! I had no time to wait!"

"I left you with one of the most powerful vampyres in England! You have managed to insult Matlock in every possible way."

Her brow furrowed. "Matlock. There was something...wrong. Bad. I cannot..." she shook her head, plainly unable to elucidate what disturbed her.

Darcy winced as she suddenly gripped his arm with extraordinary strength.

"I am sorry," she cried out, her feelings of remorse overwhelming him.

"What is it, love?"

"I...I made a mistake. I bit Jane. I—"

He hushed her. "Love, love, it was an accident. She understands you did not mean to hurt her."

"So sorry," she murmured.

And then he felt her burst of wild astonishment.

"Blood! Am I? A *vampyre*?"

"Yes, my love," he said. "You are Turned, and you are mine as I am yours, for as long as we both shall live...which is now, God willing, centuries instead of the few short years we once had." He waited, kissing her until he was sure she passed into acceptance. Memory recovery from the Shielding period was notoriously erratic, some remembering almost nothing, some recalling a few moments explicitly and others not at all. He continued to prolong their connexion, not wanting her to be alone while troubled.

Thus, he felt her sudden, stabbing sense of sheer horror and revulsion.

Plainly, she had just remembered killing Anne de Bourgh.

She slept for five days, waking only to feed. Darcy could not tell if this was an extension of her Ordeal, or if coping with de Bourgh's death and her own change had driven her under the covers. Hunger fully sated, he had no excuse to delve into her deeper feelings, and she seemed too fatigued to offer.

But late one afternoon, as he entered their apartments, she was sitting up. "You are awake," Darcy said, surprised. It was usual for new vampyres to sleep all day—and most older ones, as well. Even a Darcy-turned vampyre needed time—sometimes years—to adjust to the sun. As it was yet two hours before sunset, he had reason for his astonishment. Richard had not wakened during daylight hours for his first year. And not only was she awake, but she had not torn into his throat in a hunger panic; though she still had the thirst cravings of a new vampyre, she exercised the control of a seasoned one.

"Yes," she said, avoiding her husband's gaze.

Deftly he manoeuvred her into his lap and held her to his throat. She pulled back, for the first time refusing to feed.

"No. I want to wait."

"There is no need for you to do so."

"There is every need," she answered quietly.

"Elizabeth, I understand your wish for control. Believe me, I do. The best way to achieve it is to meet the requirements of your body. As long as you are well-fed, you will not be a danger to yourself or others."

"And what if it is not possible? What if you are not nearby? I know I must feed, but I also must not become a ravening monster if I cannot. Let me push myself, learn to extend my limits just a little."

"If you want to learn something, let me teach you how to bite correctly."

A shocked expression flitted across her face. "I have not been…? Oh, no!"

He chuckled. "Sweetheart, does a new-born babe feed himself? Here, open," he said, tapping her chin.

Obediently she did so; her fangs were already slightly extended. Carefully, he stroked one into lengthening fully. She shivered in response.

"You have a gland, here," he said, caressing a point directly above the incisor, "that contains your venom. You will want to release that into your bite as you pierce the skin, mitigating the pain of puncture."

"How?"

"Your body already knows how. You need only to be aware of it. Take my vein, and as you do so, imagine the venom essence entering my skin with your bite." Obligingly, he stretched his neck before her mouth. He could feel her quivering, fighting against her need to consume him greedily.

"Was I…have I been hurting you?" she questioned, instead of doing as asked.

"No," he declared stoutly, for what was the simple discomfort of broken skin against the tremendous pleasure of feeding her?

"I hurt Jane, I remember," she said. "She…she screamed and has not been to see me since. And Maggie and—"

"Elizabeth! How were you to know?" he interrupted. "Would you blame a baby who bit your breast while nursing?"

An arrested expression crossed her face. "If I have a baby now, will it take blood or milk from me?"

He grew utterly still. When he spoke, his words were gentle. "Love…remember? You cannot have children now."

"You said it was rare, not impossible! Which was true even before I was Turned!"

"Darling…the only story I have ever heard of a vampyre pregnancy supposedly occurred over a thousand years ago."

"I am barren, now?" she asked in a small voice.

"No," he disagreed. "That word means desolate and alone. You are warm, alive, and full of promise. We have each other and our people. We are blessed, Elizabeth."

Her head shook. "No, no. You need an heir. You...you must take another, as Abraham did Hagar." She was trembling, rambling. "Go far from me to do it, though, I must not see—no, you must feed. Lock me up, so I do not kill her. I cannot trust—"

"Stop," he interrupted. "You are in shock, or you would not say such things. I will have no other. I need no child."

"'Tis not true! You have your people to think of! What would they do without a Master?"

He was silent a moment, because this was a sore point. A Masterless clan was vulnerable, subject to exploitation from stronger Houses. Meanwhile, he had taken too long to answer, and Elizabeth struggled to break free.

"Hold still, love," he said, subduing her easily. "You and I together will find a solution for our family, one not involving betraying our vows. I would not, even if I could. And I cannot." He took her hand. "I am only for you. No other. Please," he begged.

At last she ceased struggling, but he felt her distress in her panting, unnecessary breaths. "Please," he said again. "Let me give to you."

With a slight moan of despair, she bit him—but even in her anguish, she did not forget his little lesson. Though she did not time her venom perfectly to alleviate the sting of entry, shortly thereafter it was coursing through his veins. And it was superb, luscious, intoxicating him beyond thought. As soon as she released his vein, he dove for her mouth.

Forgetting, in his yearning, that to share her now was to share her grief as well as her desire.

It was all there waiting for him. Emotions harsh and sorrowful enough to bring his pleasure to a crashing halt.

He could not fix this, could change nothing. It was awful as well to know that even if he could, he probably would not. Despite her grief and mourning for the children she would not bear, despite all the power and lives at his command, he was not strong enough to wish another fate for her than the one that both cursed her and bound her to him.

She felt it, of course—felt his diminished desire. "I need you," was all she said.

He gazed down at her sad eyes and bent to gently touch her lips. Trying to express his tenderness and love, he licked delicately; when she opened her mouth, he tangled his tongue with hers, giving substance to their connexion. The sorrow she tried desperately to contain washed over him in waves....yet she attempted to pull it back. To keep it from him. To protect him. His love for her overwhelmed him then, making space for desire amidst the despair.

"You cannot keep me out of this," he said. "We will mourn together. You are mine, and I am yours, always."

And then he felt it—her rush of desire, as she fixed upon the exciting prospect of a marriage without mortal limits. Elizabeth smiled up at him. "There is that," she said.

"I–I do not know myself."

She spoke from within the circle of his arms, into the dark, quiet contentment of the aftermath of passion.

"No, not completely, I suppose. And yet, you are still *you*. The essence of you, what makes you Elizabeth, is still here," he said, placing his large hand over her heart.

"Does that mean I was always...a murderess?"

"No!" he said harshly. "You are not."

"Anne's blood is on my hands, Fitzwilliam. My memory of my actions is unfortunately clear. I shall never forget."

"Had she attacked me in the same manner, would you despise me for defending myself?"

"No...no," she protested. "But you—you are a warrior. It is your honour and duty to deal with those who would harm you or your family."

"And why cannot you be a warrior as well? It has always been within you. Every time your mother's rage needed a target, you stepped forward to take the brunt of it. Jane has told me of your bravery."

"There was no bloodshed in our family squabbles!"

"There were wounds, regardless. And scars preventing you from seeing your courage for what it is. My race is a bloodthirsty one. We would live endlessly, except for our plots and schemes and internal wars. We do not fear illness and the weaknesses of mortals, and yet death stalks us relentlessly. What I need in my female is not softness and frailty—I need one who can defend herself and those around her. I needed you to do exactly what you did, Elizabeth. Do you think Anne would have stopped at killing you? What was to prevent her from attacking Maggie next?"

Elizabeth opened her mouth, then closed it again. At last she said, "Had I *decided* to–to defend Maggie, or even myself, I could excuse it. But I did not. I saw her and before I knew who she was or what she was trying to do, she had to die."

"Which was just. I would have killed her myself."

"But I evidently made the same decision with Matlock. My instinct is murderous. It was only luck that with Anne..."

"Young vampyres make mistakes. It happens. No one is perfect or expects you to be."

"And if my mistakes take an innocent life? How do I live with myself?" she whispered.

He did not try to answer, for she would not care for his opinion. He was ruthless enough to count the cost. Even Matlock, a true friend...well, he would certainly protect the man with all his might, but there was no choice, truly. Matlock was strong, old, and responsible for his own life.

"I love you," he said instead. "I love you beyond reason. I need you, Elizabeth. You are my heart."

"It is difficult to argue against love," she whispered. "But help me by protecting those I might hurt." She took his lips again.

Darcy felt the gradual easing of her fears. "I know you. All will be well. Give it time. We have all the time in the world."

WHEN LADY CATHERINE DE BOURGH FELT ANNE'S ESSENCE blink out of existence, she did not scream. She did not cry. She did not shriek. Her people would have been far happier if she had. She stated one word: "Silence." After that, the first vampyre who made the slightest noise, she executed.

After a week of tiptoeing around—and three more executions, one due to an ill-timed sneeze—the strongest vampyres of her House were called to her table. They were served a beautiful meal of several courses, all consumed in utter stillness as the vampyres' nervousness grew, all of them chewing as slowly as possible, fearing a noisy gulp might mean death—and a belch, death with torture first. Finally, Jenkinson accidentally dropped his fork. All heads swivelled in his direction, waiting.

Lady Catherine turned her head slowly towards him. "Tell me," she said coldly, "what you have been able to learn regarding my daughter's death."

Of course, everyone knew. The Council had released an official statement, citing law, precedence, and Darcy's claims of self-defence. But no one relied upon official statements. The de Bourgh vampyres traced every rumour, every bit of gossip they could glean. They had a fairly certain picture of what happened, and though it was surprising such a young vampyre had been able to execute the mistress's daughter, none felt her fate was particularly unjustified. Most, in fact, were astonished Darcy hadn't killed her long before; after a second attack upon his wife, her life was forfeit regardless.

Of course, it wouldn't do to voice that opinion.

Jenkinson's nerves made his speech rather more East End than usual.

"A laidy clever as Miss de Bourgh...Darcy weren't able ta keep 'er down. Nobody's figgered as 'ow she managed ter squeak free, she were that gifted," he said glibly. "One might 'spect as 'ow she'd flee, an only save 'erself. But nawt she—'er bein' a de Bourgh an' all, she 'ad to show em they done wrong, 'oldin' 'er captive. So Miss de Bourgh goes an' challenges em, fair an' square-like, an' all the bloody Darcy vampyres set upon 'er, still weak from torture an' starvin'... well, fin'ly even she couldn't last."

He arranged his features into a look of intense mourning. "It were Mrs Darcy, may she rot in silver ferever, what took 'er poor brave 'eart and 'ead, killin' 'er."

The silence following his declaration was fraught with unease. Everyone awaited Lady Catherine's response.

"Indeed," was all she said, but everyone present felt a slight lessening of tension.

After a few moments, she requested another vampyre, Greaves, tell what he knew about the new Mrs Darcy. He, too, was prepared—as the vampyre world was agog with curiosity regarding her. He was careful as Jenkinson had been with his verbal sketch, repeating rumours that the Darcy wench was a mute, portraying her as incompetent, stupid, and unfairly violent. "It is said," he repeated carefully, "that Darcy guards her personally now, so afraid he is of your revenge."

Once again, all awaited her response. This time, she smiled.

A collective sigh of relief went around the table.

"Darcy does well to fear," she said at last. "Naturally, I shall not let her live. My plans are in place. Send for my vicar at once."

"I am ready," Jane said.

"Ready?" Bingley enquired.

"Well...not exactly ready. But my relations and yours will be here within the week, and 'tis probably best to–to be more comfortable by then."

"Ah. To see your sister, you mean."

"Yes."

"Do you envision it will be an uncomfortable meeting? You do not show any discomfort with Mrs Reynolds or any of the household who are Other."

"*They* are not Elizabeth. I do not expect you to understand, but we were so close. If she is too changed, I will not be able to disguise my response. She has always been perceptive and will see it before I can grow accustomed to the differences. I will, I am sure. But I would not have her feelings hurt because I am too timid to accept her easily."

"All will be well."

"How can you be so sure?"

Bingley smiled warmly. "Because you have already accepted that she *has* feelings, and that, like the Elizabeth of old, she is perceptive. You acknowledge the ways in which she is likely the same. I am not anxious for you at all."

Jane looked at him, concern in her eyes. "I hope you are correct, sir. So much."

❧

"I am not ready. Maybe we should wait until tomorrow night?"

"All will be well, Elizabeth. You have never looked lovelier." He meant it. Maggie had outdone herself, and his wife looked so beautiful in her scarlet gown that almost all he could think about was removing it.

"Maybe I should not wear this dress. 'Tis a bit...extravagant for a family meal."

His eyes glowed as he looked at her. There was nothing particularly immodest about the dress, but its rich colour emphasised the pale purity of her skin, the dark silk of her hair. He went to her, lightly tracing her exposed collarbones with his gloved fingers.

"You look majestic. I can hardly keep my hands to myself. I want her to see that you are *more* now, not less."

"I do want to look my best but—"

"But nothing. You are perfect, Elizabeth." He bent to kiss her, with careful restraint, drinking in her fears. "Close your eyes," he said, and when she obeyed, he fastened a clasp around her neck.

She touched her throat in surprise. "What is this?" she asked.

He turned her around so that she was facing her dressing table mirror. "Open."

Elizabeth gasped. In its reflection, she saw the heavy weight circling her throat was an exquisite diamond and ruby necklace. Two large emerald-cut diamonds surrounded the centre teardrop ruby pendant, each dangling two prism diamonds, all set in gold filigree. "Oh, my," she breathed.

"These were part of my grandmother's bride price," he said. "I have never seen anything more beautiful." He did not look at the jewels.

Her hand fluttered at her throat. "They are fit for a queen. I suppose I must live up to them," she said, trying to smile. "I will try to be braver. Thank you."

"They are barely worthy of you," he averred, offering her his arm in escort downstairs, watching her gloved fingers play with the sparkling diamonds. Even though he could not read her emotions, her nerves were obvious. One would think she was meeting a hostile enemy rather than her dearest sister. Knowing Elizabeth, unfriendly foes would be easier for her.

They entered one of the downstairs parlours where Jane and Charles waited. Jane was dressed in her nicest gown as well, though it was not nearly the quality of Elizabeth's finery. Evidently both girls felt the need for armour.

❧

"Hello, Jane," Elizabeth said. "I hope your accommodations have been pleasant?"

"Oh, very," Jane hastened to answer. "Your home is just beautiful, Liz— er...Elizabeth."

Concern crossed Elizabeth's expression. "I am still Lizzy, Jane," she said softly.

"Not in that dress," Jane replied matter-of-factly.

Both Mr Bingley and Darcy relaxed a little when Elizabeth giggled. "Fine feathers, I know." Her expression sobered. "Jane, can you forgive me? I am so sorry I hurt you, and I can assure you it will never happen again—"

"Do not say it. Charles explained you did not...I am very glad Mr Darcy saved you, Elizabeth," Jane said earnestly. "I would much rather you be safe and alive, even if you are..." she trailed off, unable to verbalise her thoughts.

"I know it is a lot to take in," Elizabeth said, approaching her sister carefully. "But I think, truly, I am still Lizzy."

Jane reached out for Elizabeth's hands and gently clasped them. "Seeing you now, I know you probably never were simply 'Lizzy'," she replied. "I was so afraid to see you again, to see you changed. And now you are the *you* that you always should have been—so beautiful, I almost cannot look at you. I-I am so proud to be your sister."

Elizabeth wished she could cry, so great was her excess of emotion. However, since vampyre tears tended to fall in shades of pink or red—and since she wished neither to frighten Jane nor ruin the silk of her dress—she fought for control. When Mr Bingley cheerfully reminded the girls that they would blue devil Monsieur Philippe if they were late to dinner, she laughed and allowed him to escort her to the dining room, her husband offering his arm to Jane.

Over dinner, they discussed wedding plans. The talk turned to their invited guests.

"We shall try to keep more usual hours, but Jane, I can barely function in the mornings. Fitzwilliam is only just able to awaken me before the noon hour. We will have to say a life of luxury has made me indolent."

"Do not worry. I am sure Aunt Gardiner and Mama will both assume the very best of reasons for a daily indisposition." Jane smiled at her sister.

Elizabeth paled, and Darcy looked at his wife with concern. Even Charles sobered, but Jane was paying no attention to subtleties. "Do Caroline and Louisa know the truth about Lizzy?" she asked Charles.

"I have not told them, but I expect they will know quickly. The differences are plain," he replied.

"Of course. It is so obvious," Jane worried aloud. "Do you think our family will notice any...oddities? Mama is not at all discreet, and would likely divulge clues that others, more wise, might discern."

"I think not, Jane," Darcy said at last. "We have had many human guests here before. The household knows all the protocols and can maintain appearances."

"Oh, I did not mean to imply any lack of discretion or training on the part of your, um, people." Jane flushed, embarrassed.

Elizabeth smiled reassuringly. "Do not worry. Fitzwilliam knows Mama and can cope with her. She will be dining out on her stay at Pemberley for the next year. Papa will take one look at the library and we shan't see him again. We will hope Colonel Forster and Uncle Gardiner can keep each other entertained. I wish it were not so cold. In finer weather, Pemberley has sport aplenty."

Mr Bingley waved a hand, unconcerned. "We shall have billiards and cards. Richard will engage Colonel Forster in discussions of military exploits, and every Londoner has an opinion about the French. Time will pass quickly. Mrs Reynolds runs a tight establishment. If there are any irregularities, there are plenty available to ensure none remember them."

Charlotte Collins sat placidly by the fire in her snug little parlour, her knitting basket beside her. Her hands were busy, and she was engaged in her favourite mental pastime—creating lists of things that needed doing in the next week—when her husband entered.

Her brows rose in surprise. She and Mr Collins had a routine from which they never deviated, and his invasion of her private parlour broke that tacit pact. Looking up, she immediately stood.

"Mr Collins—you are positively whey-faced! Come, sit down. Can I bring you tea?"

"No, no," he moaned. "My brandy, please. Oh, quickly!"

Charlotte hurried to his study and found the decanter her husband normally denied possessing. She splashed a bit in a glass and offered it to him, waiting until his colour appeared a bit restored to ask more questions. He kept darting glances around the room, as though he expected to be accosted at any moment.

"Please, Mr Collins...what has upset you?"

"M-my Lady," he started.

"Lady Catherine?" she asked, and he winced.

"She–she was very angry," he almost whispered.

"Of course, she is not herself," Charlotte agreed. "Her daughter's death is a sore trial, indeed. A curricle accident, and her reputed to be such top-sawyer. A terrible shock."

Mr Collins grabbed her wrist. "With *me*," he hissed. "Angry with me! Blames *me*!"

"Oh, surely not, my dear. You have misunderstood."

He did not release her, squeezing tight enough she was sure she would have bruises tomorrow. "I did not misunderstand," he argued, his voice high with fear and distress. "She orders us to pack. To leave."

"What?"

He dropped her wrist to run a hand through his thinning hair, and Charlotte moved out of reach as he drank the last swallow of brandy. "She claims Miss de Bourgh's accident was Cousin Elizabeth's fault. That she would not have any relation of hers near and will not rest until I suffer for it."

"This appointment is yours, and the Church, not her ladyship, must remove you."

"You did not hear her. She cares naught for any authority but her own."

Charlotte's brows rose at this apt description of his patroness, never thinking to hear him be so blunt. "I am sure when she calms—" she began.

"If we are not away by Friday, she will burn down the vicarage, she claims."

"What?"

"She was...mad. Terrifying." He lifted the glass to his lips, then dropped it when he discovered it was empty. It hit the rug and rolled under the settee. "Terrifying," he repeated.

For some moments, the only sound was of flames crackling in the fireplace. Charlotte contemplated possible courses of action. At last she said, "She is irrational in her grief. I am sure she will change her mind, but we must not provoke her. We shall go to Meryton for a nice, long visit."

"We cannot," he said.

"Of course we can. I will send an express to Papa at once."

"She said we must not," he said weakly.

"Well! She forces us out of our home! What does she care where we go, as long as we are gone?" Even as she spoke, however, she knew the woman was indeed capable of having an opinion about where they might take shelter.

"She threatened to see Lucas Lodge burned to the ground if we find refuge there. Said she would see us lose everything of value, just as she has."

"This is mad! It is criminal...surely she—" Even the pragmatic, level-headed Charlotte found herself flummoxed by their unreasonable patroness. Yet, she had seen enough of her to know she was capable of extreme opinions and outrageous behaviours. Sadly, the wealthy Lady Catherine was probably invulnerable to the consequences of committing any number of crimes. Her disposition was uncertain at best; in her rage and grief, she might truly cause mayhem. Perhaps it would be best to do as ordered, pacifying her until the worst of her rage faded.

Mr Collins continued to whimper, moaning to himself. "What shall I do?" he whined, over and over, working himself up into a case of the vapours.

"Mr Collins, you must calm yourself!" she said at last, using all of her considerable self-control to keep her tone even.

"Calm! Calm, you say? When my life has been uprooted, my home torn from me, every succour denied me?" With each statement of loss, his voice rose higher and louder, becoming increasingly hysterical.

Charlotte was finally obliged to administer a sharp slap in order to stop the tantrum. He stared at her in surprise and outrage, but at least he shut his mouth so she could think. For long moments she sorted through and discarded options. None of her siblings were in a position to take in her and her husband. Both Mr Collins's parents were deceased, and he had no family besides the Bennets. She was unsure of whether Lady Catherine's strictures included them, but the thought of turning to Mrs Bennet for aid and succour was daunting, even to her. It would be far better to seek protection from someone more able and willing to give it.

At last she gave a deep sigh. "There is only one choice. I shall write to Mrs Darcy tonight."

"Elizabeth! You look beautiful! Marriage so obviously agrees with you!" Margaret Gardiner enthused. "Does she not look wonderful, darling?"

"Wonderful," Edward Gardiner agreed. "Never better, my dear." He enveloped his niece in a warm embrace.

"I am so happy you are here at last," Elizabeth welcomed. "We were beginning to be anxious."

"Horse threw a shoe, and we could not get a new animal. Had to wait for the blacksmith," Richard said. But he exchanged a look with Darcy and Elizabeth suddenly realised he had delayed their arrival at Pemberley until he was certain she would be awake. Had that been her husband's idea, or his? It seemed far too...considerate for Richard.

"I am glad it was nothing more serious," she said. "You remember Mr Bingley, of course?" Charles and Jane stepped forward, Jane receiving the same warmth as Elizabeth. While Mr and Mrs Gardiner did not, perhaps, show quite the same enthusiasm in greeting Charles, they were cordial, plainly seeing Jane's cheerful serenity. Mrs Gardiner chatted amiably with Fitzwilliam about her early childhood memories of nearby Lambton, and Elizabeth reflected that at least she had some relations of whom she need not be ashamed.

As the evening wore on, she grew ever more appreciative. Mr Gardiner smoothly deflected his sister's embarrassing, slighting remarks, while Mrs Gardiner—supported by Colonel Forster—exerted herself to curb the worst of Kitty and Lydia's exuberance.

Caroline Bingley's behaviour, however, put even Mrs Bennet to shame. Upon discovering Elizabeth's Turning the day previous, she had immediately offered up her womb as a convenient receptacle for the Darcy heir. The whole scheme was repugnant in every sense—but she plainly had not given up hope.

At the beginning of the evening she pretended great amity towards Elizabeth, as though they were the dearest of friends. But as the sultry looks Caroline aimed at Darcy grew bolder, Elizabeth's revulsion grew more intense—to the point she nearly growled, her inner beast poised for attack. Her only option was to ignore the woman entirely, administering such obvious cuts that the entire company noticed. Caroline grew openly spiteful as the evening dragged.

Elizabeth could hardly wait for the card tables to be put away and the night's entertainments finished. Caroline would hereafter be related by marriage, but never again would she be allowed at Pemberley, even for Jane and Charles's sake.

Perhaps, she thought, she should ask Fitzwilliam to nudge their guests' thoughts in the direction of their pillows. What she wanted most was to wrap her arms around her husband and let him distract her from her cares. And perhaps to feed again. He had fed her once today already, though, and she was determined not to behave like an infant vampyre. But she could imagine it, could almost feel his blood filling her mouth, rich as heavy cream and sweet as foamy, hot chocolate. She clamped her mouth shut against the involuntary response of lengthened fangs, hoping no one noticed. Idly she wondered whether there was any of the beef stew left in the pantry. Or even a slab of meat, anything to divert her from her yearning for more blood. *When will the mad cravings end?*

"Look at her, Louisa, staring at Mr Darcy like a mooncalf," Caroline said, nudging her sister. She spoke in a low tone, though she knew the vampyres would hear, probably hoping Darcy would be embarrassed by Elizabeth's 'childishness'. Unfortunately, it was another of those moments when all conversations paused infinitesimally, permitting her to be overheard by everyone.

Darcy glowered, his eyes sharpening to glittering onyx. Charles began a reprimand, but Lydia, surprisingly, spoke first.

"Oh! Miss Bingley, I daresay you, being a single lady, would not understand the joys of happy matrimony, and what might pass in a look between a wife and her husband. I had no idea of the particular advantages of being married until I wed my dear Colonel, though I always thought it would be very good fun if I was."

Jane's eyes widened. Elizabeth looked expressively at Lydia; but she, who never noticed anything of which she chose to be insensible, gaily continued, "Why, you told my dear Colonel of Mr Darcy's affections for some female in Kent! You ought not to possess such decided opinions of romance until you experience the happy state yourself!"

Caroline ought to have been alarmed at this revelation, but as ever, gave no thought to her past deeds except as they gave her pleasure. Indeed, she had quite convinced herself that she heard the rumour of Mr Darcy and Miss de Bourgh's attachment with the rest of the crowd at the Netherfield ball, and denied the accusation vehemently.

"Mrs Forster, I am sure I *never* believed such a thing. I scotched such rumours as soon as they reached my ears!"

Lydia did not enjoy this refutation of her word, nor was she polite enough to allow it to pass. "Why, 'twas you who told us in the first place, and we believed you at the time! Is it not so, Colonel?"

Colonel Forster found himself in the unenviable position of having to declare one of the ladies mistaken. However, mere civility would not keep him from his duty to his wife.

"Miss Bingley, now, you did tell me of Mr Darcy and his impending connexion to the gel in Kent. I have a keen memory for detail. Military demands it of me!" Misinterpreting the look on her face as embarrassment instead of rage, he hastened to add, "We all know you had Miss Eliz—er, Mrs Darcy's best interests at heart when you took me aside. Did not want to see her hurt by loose tongues." He smiled benignly.

"Caroline!" Charles stood, his face white with fury.

"Charles...I did not...you cannot b–believe..." Caroline stuttered. One could almost see her mind working as she tried to think of a means to swing the tide of favour in her direction.

"Darcy, would you accompany Caroline and me to your study?" Charles asked, not looking at his sister. To the rest of the party, he said, "We have a small matter to discuss, if you will all excuse us briefly."

Most of the company looked slightly confused. Jane and Elizabeth, however, exchanged glances.

"I believe this concerns me, as well," Jane said, standing. Charles nodded, and they followed Darcy out of the room.

Elizabeth felt her husband's power, and realised as Caroline moved jerkily, lagging behind, that she was forcibly compelled to obey the summons, resisting with her puny strength. Richard impassively watched her go, but Elizabeth could not manage his aloofness. Fury welled up within her like a fire raging. What she could bear was one thing...but the pain Caroline caused Jane!

Suddenly, Richard stood before her, a restraining hand upon her shoulder. "Mrs Darcy," he said, in low, commanding tones.

She blinked. "Yes?"

He looked pointedly at her hands. She followed his gaze, noting she had shredded the fabric of her chair, the stuffing bleeding from it.

"Oh," she said, trying to smooth the ragged edges back, a fairly useless endeavour. Had her family noticed her destroying the furniture?

Richard turned around to face the group. "Nothing to see here," he said, meeting everyone's eyes in turn. They all returned to their former conversations, and Elizabeth clenched her hands in her lap and pasted a smile on her face.

"Now that was odd!" Mrs Bennet said. "Why would anyone care about that old rumour now? I will have to ask Miss Bingley what it was all about."

"Mary, perhaps you would play for us? I have not had the pleasure of hearing you in some time," Mrs Gardiner requested. Elizabeth watched as her guests allowed themselves to be distracted, doing her best to calm the violence burning within her heart. Louisa Hurst alone remained immobile, her eyes fixed upon the passage leading to Darcy's study.

"I cannot believe you —"

"Stifle it, Caroline," Charles ordered coldly. "I do not want to hear one word from you. If you speak again, I shall ask Darcy to seal your foolish mouth for the next ten years."

Jane shuddered, looking askance at Darcy, plainly wondering if it were possible. Evidently Caroline believed him, for she subsided, sinking down upon the settee, her head bowed.

"Darcy, I have to know the truth of Caroline's behaviour the night of the ball we held at Netherfield. Even before that, probably," he said harshly.

"You realise what might happen if we look so deeply?"

For a moment Charles appeared to hesitate...but he glanced at Jane, and his jaw firmed. "Please," he said. From the settee, Caroline uttered a small gasp.

Darcy deliberated for several minutes, but, finally, called for Richard. Doing this would require both of them.

Richard and Darcy towered over Caroline, casting her into shadow, and she cringed as both steeled themselves. Most vampyres could manipulate the minds of humans in order to compel actions or sleep, scramble the present, and revise memories; Darcy's much greater gifts made it easy for him to recognise motivation and predict intentions. It took vast power, however, to go deeper and *extract* memories. And then, of course, they could never fit back inside the mortal's head once freed. The resulting hollows sometimes caused damage to the remaining ones—a lifetime of megrims and memory problems could result. Darcy set a heavy hand on her head, feeling her flinch under its weight.

Mining for memories was similar to attending a bad play: constant action onstage and yet little worth watching. If the person was interesting and intelligent, there would be moments of wit and insight. But even the cleverest spent a goodly portion of time considering what they might eat for dinner and other tiresome, mundane affairs. Both men felt nothing but dread at the idea of entering Caroline's brainbox.

With good reason. Her most recent memories were—unsurprisingly—full of fear and frantic bids at self-preservation, casting about for ways to put a positive light on her every action while desperately trying *not* to remember the ways in which she was most culpable. Darcy fed innocuous memories to Richard in order to clear them out of his way. There were thousands of reflections upon hats, reticules, sleeves, patterns, and, nauseatingly, his own buckskin-clad thighs.

Zounds, could the woman be any shallower? Even Louisa was only worthwhile as an audience for her gossip. Caroline's head gave whole new meaning to the phrase 'small-minded'.

The more she attempted suppressing guilty memories, the larger they loomed. He 'heard' her confess to Colonel Forster of Darcy's supposed secret alliance with Anne de Bourgh; going back further, he uncovered her abuse of Jane's privacy in order to learn of it. Caroline had, beyond question, betrayed her brother. He stepped back, utterly repulsed.

Caroline held her head in her hands, moaning a little. Neither he nor Richard felt any pity.

"She read Miss Bennet's diary," he announced. "Once she stole the secret, she told Colonel Forster, feeling quite sure he would not keep a confidence affecting the welfare of his sister-to-be."

Jane's jaw dropped.

"Jane," Charles said. "I am so very sorry."

"Unfortunately, apologies will not change matters," Darcy continued. "Caroline has demonstrated a treacherous nature, unbalanced by any family loyalty. She cannot be trusted."

No one missed Caroline's already pale skin leeching of all remaining colour at his words.

"She is no longer a Bingley," Charles pronounced. "I will witness."

"Jane!" Caroline cried, finding her tongue. "My dearest sister... you *will* be my sister. I will do anything to make this right! Anything, anything!" she sobbed pitifully.

Darcy made a noise, and her cries abruptly ceased. "Are you sure, Charles?" he asked gently. He did not question Caroline's fate, which been sealed as soon as he discovered her betrayal. He would not, however, force Charles to watch.

Charles nodded. He turned to his betrothed. "I am responsible for her, and I feel it necessary to take permanent action, dearest."

"Will you kill her?" Jane asked, and Darcy felt her fear.

"I will not, though it might be kinder," Darcy replied. "I will remove every memory that could endanger us if she were to reveal it or betray us. There are many, dating from her early youth. It will change her irreparably. She will not be...as she is now."

Darcy watched as Jane pondered his words. He knew she struggled to comprehend this new world, their ruthlessness and their punishments. She was too good, he thought. She wished everyone happy and would see no one hurt. She would protest, and Charles might lose her.

Jane looked at Caroline. "You nearly ruined my life," she said quietly. "And, perhaps, your brother's, and the only thing you are truly sorry for is being caught out."

Darcy nodded, surprised Jane could see so clearly. "True. There is complete absence of remorse."

Jane took a deep breath. "If you would betray your own brother, how can you be trusted with Elizabeth? Your contempt for her is no secret. I would not give you a dog's life to protect, much less that of my dearest sister." She looked directly into Darcy's eyes. "Do what you must, Brother." Charles took her hand in his, kissing it.

Touched by her faith in him, Darcy turned back to Caroline. His eyes, fully black, narrowed on his object, and he placed his hands upon her head once again. What he did now was even more difficult —he did not want her to lose her ability to care for herself and thus make her more of a burden for her family. It required a delicate touch, sifting carefully, so he did not damage what she needed to maintain reason. Richard helped, his hand on Darcy's shoulder, lending his power, allowing his nephew to pass him all the memories having to do with vampyrism, the family history and businesses. Finally, they both stepped back.

Darcy looked around. Charles was sitting on the settee opposite the one where Caroline was slumped, Jane asleep upon his shoulder.

"I suppose that took longer than it seemed," Richard said.

"A few hours," Charles agreed quietly.

"I will bid you goodnight, then," Richard said, bowing slightly. Before departing, he gripped Charles's shoulder. *The height of sentimentality for Richard*, Darcy thought.

"It is much easier to kill than to force someone to forget so much," Darcy said, sighing. "But she will be able to eat, drink, talk, and walk. She should remember everyone close to her, and she might be able to learn again. I tried to leave the harmless memories alone, but there was probably damage..." he trailed off.

"If I had taken a firmer hand," Charles said softly.

"That would have been your parents' responsibility. By the time she became yours, she was set in her self-centred ways. I am to blame too. I have never cared enough to get involved. I ignored her."

"It is not your way. You feel things too profoundly to interfere frivolously, and you are too much the gentleman to play God with the mortals surrounding you."

"I played God—or the devil—tonight, I fear," Darcy said grimly. "I could not find much good within her, and I could not leave her with the ability to cause pain. Blame me if you must blame anyone."

"I am not much for blaming anyone but Caroline," Charles replied, and bent to waken Jane, who startled but quickly recovered.

"It is finished?"

"Yes," he replied. They both looked at Caroline's slumped figure.

"She will probably feel the headache for a few days," Darcy said. "We will put it about that she has a high fever. She will not be the first person who was changed by illness."

"If she is not recovered by Sunday—" Jane began.

"We shall be married regardless. We will not delay." Charles voice was firm.

For a moment or two, they were all silent. And then Jane rose and went to Caroline.

"Caroline...Caroline," she called softly.

"Wha...what? Oh...I feel so strange," she peered up at Jane. "You look very familiar. Forgive me, I cannot quite recall?"

"I am Jane Bennet. Your brother Charles's betrothed."

"Charles?" She looked around, finally fixing upon him. "Charlie? You are to be married?"

Darcy had not heard him called by his childhood nickname since Caroline was a little girl, and it briefly surprised him. She turned back to Jane. "I do not feel well. I am sorry...I cannot quite remember your name?"

"No matter, Caroline. Let us get you to bed. You will recover soon." She held out her hands. Caroline stared blankly for a moment, and then, realising, took them, allowing Jane to help her up.

"I feel so...out of sorts," Caroline whimpered, clasping Jane's hand.

"I know, dear. All will be well." Responding to Jane's calm, comforting tone, Caroline allowed herself to be led from the room.

"You are nice. I like you. What is your name?" Caroline was saying as they left.

The men watched them go. "Now there is a gracious woman," Darcy remarked. "Jane is exceptional. You are a lucky man, Charles."

Charles smiled for the first time in hours. "This is true." He turned to his friend. "I thank you for all you have done, and continue to do, for me and mine," he said soberly.

They shook hands and separated—Charles to find his bed, and Darcy to find his wife. He had need of her this night.

❧

"I somehow knew I would find you here," Darcy said as he neared her in the gardens.

Elizabeth smiled; she had felt his approach long before she saw it—his power a luminescence darkly, invisibly glowing—and responded to it like a compass pointing north. Pointing to him.

"I like the way colours appear at night," she said. "In the daylight, everything is so leeched of colour. The light overwhelms and whitewashes. But the garden at night...there are such subtleties visible only in the dark."

He drew up behind her, wrapping his arms around her as she leant back against him. "Wait until the roses bloom," he said. "Or until anything does. There is not much to see as yet, except in the conservatory."

"I know it will be dazzling. Darkly dazzling in the moonlight," she smiled. "Like you."

"My wife is the dazzler," he answered, nuzzling her neck. His hand wandered up to delve into her hair, plucking pins so it came tumbling down.

"The servants can always tell where we have been. They need only follow the trail of hairpins."

"If you simply wore your hair down, we could quit buying the bloody things."

"That would certainly provide my mother with more commentary."

"Tell me again why I have not thrown her in a carriage bound for Longbourn? Or better still, a ship bound for America?"

"Because, my love, I wanted Jane to have the wedding of her dreams. Now, perhaps, you will tell me what Caroline did to try and prevent it? If you say Jane confided in her, I shall refuse to believe it." Her tone was reasonable, but the bush beside her was nothing but slivers now.

Darcy drew her away from the shrubbery, chuckling a little. "Of course she did not. However, she did write of it in her journal. Caroline simply read it."

"She read Jane's diary?" Elizabeth gasped.

He nodded, brushing his cheek against her hair.

"Do you know," she said at last, "I thought Caroline mean-spirited and self-serving...but still a lady, in the simplest sense of the word."

"Apparently not."

"What will you do?"

"'Tis already done. The Caroline you knew is gone," he said harshly. "I have removed all of her memories regarding the Vampyre world. Since she has known of us from the nursery, the loss was great. It damaged her."

She reached up to stroke his cheek. "I am sorry," she said. "It must have been difficult."

"No, not terribly," he replied. "She hurt you and your sister, not to mention Charles. Deeply and without remorse. She used your youngest sister and her husband as her tools. After blithely doing her best to destroy several lives, she simply forgot about it. She ought to have been shuddering in fear of discovery when she learned all her victims would be in one place. Her thoughts were too full of seduction schemes to fit in repentance, or even alibis."

She kept her hand on his clenched jaw. "You have known her many years, have you not?" she asked gently.

For long moments they were silent.

"I am remembering how sweet she appeared in her christening finery, and her father's joy as he held her," he said quietly.

Elizabeth put her arms around him, and he folded his about her. They stood together in the darkness for a long, long while.

Thirty Five

"This just arrived, Mrs Darcy. The messenger awaits a reply."

"Thank you, Morton," Elizabeth replied, taking the missive from him. As Morton bowed out of the room she examined it curiously, recognising her friend Charlotte's hand. Why would Charlotte send her a letter by special messenger?

As she read it, her eyes widened.

"What is it, my love?" Darcy asked. She handed him the letter. They were in their private parlour, nearly ready to join their company. The late afternoon sun slanted into the window, and Elizabeth narrowed her eyes against it. It was past the time she usually joined her family, but she had been lost in the pleasure of loving her husband.

"It makes no sense. Surely she does not imagine punishing Collins would be any sort of penalty to us?" Darcy looked up from the letter and frowned.

"She may know of my friendship with Charlotte?"

"But Catherine would also know Longbourn will someday go to Mr Collins. Taking away the vicarage is only a short-term punishment, no matter the sting."

"I like to think my father will live for some time," Elizabeth said wryly. "If they are not allowed to go to Lucas Lodge, they are truly without recourse. Charlotte has no other family in any position to take them in, and apparently neither does Mr Collins. They are homeless."

"Not at all. There is only one likely place for them to go—and they are on their way."

"We can hardly refuse to take them in. After all, it is my fault Mr Collins has lost his place."

"I beg to differ—Catherine is the author of all schemes leading to her daughter's death, including Anne's hubris in failing to escape. I have other homes, and one of them will do well enough for the Collinses." Darcy scowled. "This stinks of treachery."

"They are only a day or so behind their messenger. Perhaps they should come here, if only so you can determine exactly what Catherine plans? Would not you be able to tell if she had compelled one of them to commit some nefarious deed?"

"I do not want anything from her within a mile of you."

"You could speak to them first…examine them, whatever, however you need," Elizabeth said, some urgency in her voice. "After all, you must admit I am no longer so easily destroyed, and especially by a human. I am on my guard. And if there is no deceit, I would love to see Charlotte."

Darcy turned his back to her, staring out the window blindly, his brow furrowed. "I do not like it," he said at last.

She went to him, wrapping her arms about his waist. "I know," she said. "It does not have to be a long visit. And then you could send them wherever you like."

He huffed a little. "You know I can deny you nothing."

"And I, you," she replied, leaning closer. They were very late joining their guests.

The Collinses arrived the following day. Darcy and Richard met their carriage before it rolled onto Pemberley soil. Both spoke with—and examined the minds of—not only Mr and Mrs Collins, but also the maid accompanying them, the coachman, and even the horses. Nothing seemed amiss; no one acted upon any will but their own, and while Darcy could easily read the ugly spectacle Catherine had created from Collins's memories, he could not find any subsequent mischief. They were permitted to drive on.

"So very kind of Mr Darcy and his uncle to greet us!" Charlotte enthused when the carriage was once again underway. "I am excited to see Elizabeth again, despite our troubles. Who knows? Perhaps the Darcys will have need of a vicar. Oh! Look at it, dear! You can see the turrets in the distance!"

Charlotte was completely distracted by the splendour of Pemberley and did not see her husband blink slowly at the sight of the castle. She did not see his eyes change from their usual watery blue to Jenkinson's rougher shade of mildew-grey. Even if she had, Charlotte was far too practical to ever recognise a stranger's eyes staring from her husband's flaccid features.

"You did not need to attend me," Elizabeth said to Jane as they strolled in the frigid air of the Pemberley gardens. "It is too cold for you."

"Yes, I did," Jane replied. "The only thing worse than Mama's taste is her advice. I am sorry I insisted we invite them, Lizzy. When I think of how offended I was when I realised how much Mr Darcy did not want our parents here, I feel stupid! He was entirely justified."

Elizabeth sighed. "I do not expect her to change."

"Why will she not, Lizzy?" Jane replied. "She will soon have three of her daughters married, all in very eligible matches. She *chooses* misery."

"It has become a habit, I expect. I know her life has not always been easy, but she cannot part with her anger."

"I suppose she is not evil, just disagreeable and thoughtless. And she will find herself alone in the end, because none of us can tolerate her," Jane said sadly.

"We must retrieve Mary and Kitty, but to have them in our lives seems unwise. I cannot trust Kitty to be discreet, and while Mary is circumspect, she is so very...traditional."

"Perhaps we could have Mr Darcy and Charles speak with Uncle Gardiner. They could arrange for allowances and living expenses, and Mr Darcy could compel Mama to permit it."

Elizabeth nodded. "I am sure he would do it if I asked. Yes, an excellent solution, if Uncle Gardiner agrees."

"I believe he and Aunt Gardiner are anxious for our sisters' sakes and would like to do more. He might not even accept monetary recompense."

"Now that, I *would* insist upon. They have four children of their own, and we can well afford it."

"True. I shall speak to Charles tonight, if we have a private moment."

Elizabeth eyed her sister thoughtfully. "Just think, Jane...after tomorrow, you will not have to rely upon a few stolen moments of privacy. You will be his wife."

Jane blushed, looking at her feet. "Yes," she agreed softly.

"I have wanted to ask you if you have any questions. I would not make you uncomfortable for the world, but please disregard *anything* Mama might have said about marital duty. Her experience is not...applicable."

Jane looked at her beseechingly. "I spoke with Aunt Gardiner. She was much more positive than Mama, of course, but even she did not tell me anything practical. I feel so stupid, Lizzy."

Elizabeth thought carefully about what she could say. She decided it best to be blunt, and if Jane ran screaming, she could beg Fitzwilliam to scramble her memory of the conversation.

However, Jane listened attentively and asked enough questions for Elizabeth to be certain she understood the business. "The most important thing is to trust Charles. He is a good man and he loves you and would never ask you to do something wrong or bad." Jane's answering smile was reassuring.

By unspoken decision, they headed back—it would be dark soon, and she had neglected her guests long enough. They were both surprised, however, to round the corner of some tall hedges and nearly run into Mr Collins. Both sisters gasped, looking at each other and blushing to think he might have overheard their conversation.

"Oh! My dear cousins! I..." he looked around him with obvious confusion. "Why...I did not mean to...where can Mrs Collins be?"

If he had been eavesdropping, he covered it well. "I am sure she is indoors—all the ladies were in the gold parlour not long ago," Elizabeth said, observing his blue lips. "Why did you leave the house without your coat?"

"I am not sure...the others were playing billiards...such a wasteful activity...I went in search of the library...I saw you and my dear cousin Jane from the window and thought to join you...I did not suppose it would be so chilly." He looked so befuddled it made Elizabeth sorry for him.

"We were just returning to the ladies. You may escort us in," she said cordially.

"In...yes," he said vaguely.

Elizabeth's brow furrowed in consternation. Directly after the wedding, she would have Fitzwilliam take another look inside Mr Collins's head. He did not seem altogether right.

❧

"You may congratulate me on my genius at any time," Catherine gloated.

Matlock was silent for a moment longer, and not to compose a scathing retort. He was awed. Truly, deeply, awed.

The vampyre, Jenkinson, lay huddled in a bed. Where his eyes had once been, there were only empty sockets. His ears were missing. Every time the missing body parts tried to regenerate, Catherine dug them out or cut them off again.

"I give him my blood, which is so robust, he heals too quickly—the only drawback," she remarked, sticking a silver knife perilously close to his heart, undoubtedly doing damage. She shimmied it around while the man moaned. "There...that will weaken him long enough for me to have my dinner." She strode briskly from the room.

Matlock followed. "I commend you, Catherine. I am impressed." He had spent the last several minutes listening to a *very* private conversation between Mrs Darcy and her sister, all relayed in Jenkinson's East End accents.

"Jenkinson may be lacking eyes and ears now, but they are still intact," she said. "Those organs' essences are now contained within the body of my former vicar. Jenkinson can report the conversations 'he' sees and overhears, and if one of the Darcys approaches, he need only blink to bow out of the vicar again. Best of all, Collins cannot recall a thing of what occurs while Jenkinson is in command of those senses—and Darcy should not be able to sense him in the bare half-second it takes for Jenkinson to withdraw."

"Very creative. Brilliant, even...to a point. You have a spy in their midst, but what good will it do? I doubt Darcy will keep the vicar close enough, for long enough, to learn anything of significance. And your Mr Collins is hardly much of a weapon," he said, his voice laced with contempt at the thought of the pudgy vicar.

"I am confident he will keep him long enough. One of my dear friends in Russia who owed me a favour delivered today. Come and see."

He followed her down to a cellar, bare except for an iron cage. At first, Matlock thought it contained a dog, but then he saw its legs were short and the head broad and rounded like a bear. It had thick, dark, oily fur with a bushy tail, and smelled abominably. As he approached the cage, it growled menacingly and revealed a mouthful of sharp silver-tipped fangs. *Interesting.*

"What is it?"

"*Rosomakha*, my friend calls it," she said, her eyes glittering. "It is the fiercest of creatures. This one argued with an enormous black bear over a kill. The bear lost. Ripped its heart right out of its chest." She laughed.

"Ferocious," he agreed. "Though I fail to see what good it will do."

"This animal will obey me, making short work of all I set it upon—the heart first, then the head," she boasted. "I must be within a reasonable distance to maintain control, but I need not ever set foot on Darcy land. I shall arrange the attack for morning, when any Darcy guards are at their most sluggish. Of course, I shall not be at my best either, but I shall not need to be at fighting strength. All I require of Collins is that he open a door or two for the beast."

"Darcy will kill it before it nears striking distance."

"*It* will kill the female before he knows what happened," she returned contemptuously. "Once it knows its prey, it is unstoppable—tenacious, and impervious to mental assault. In the time Darcy wastes attempting to kill it by usual means, Elizabeth Bennet will be slaughtered."

"Darcy will know someone allowed it in. He will rip minds apart to find the traitor. Your vicar will not survive."

She shrugged. "What do I care? As soon as Jenkinson tells me the trull is dead, I will bolt. I shall allow Jenkinson to regenerate and the vicar will die once the connexion is broken, regardless. By the time Darcy discovers my scent, I will be safely away in a lair I have planned specifically for this occasion." Her delighted, high-pitched giggle filled the air.

Matlock smiled. Mad she might be, but her plan could successfully end the life of the odious Mrs Darcy. Perhaps when Darcy was widowed, he would even help him discover Catherine; she had grown entirely too dangerous. Of course, Catherine must reveal the location of her lair to him first. But he had no doubt he would charm it out of her. No doubts at all.

❧

Elizabeth was not ready to waken. The vampyre sleep was, for her, luxurious oblivion. No enhanced senses to tame, no strength to repress, no burning, acid thirst. She did not dream. Therefore, the sensation of lips at her ear was not the product of sleeping fancies, but reality intruding. She rolled onto her belly.

"Elizabeth," a husky whisper broke into her consciousness.

She resisted. "Want to sleep," she grudged.

His low chuckle worked against her defences, but she continued to resist wakefulness.

He let it go on until she opened her eyes, glaring at him in frustrated longing. "Good morning, sweetheart," he smiled, and bent to kiss her. One moment they enjoyed a blissfully passionate interlude, the next moment it crossed to a place beyond urgency. She dove for his neck.

Darcy only stretched, making her access easier. He loved this, loved her passion, her thirst, loved to satisfy all her needs at once. But as she drank, he did not feel her thirst lessening—and then it spiked with shocking power. Through their connexion, he could feel her feelings growing maddened, the warmth and love that nourished him as much as her blood, fading. *Bloodlust.* Her body was locked into a feeding frenzy that would continue until she drained him.

Flipping her over onto her back, he tried to extricate her fangs from his neck; she only growled and clutched more tightly, digging deeply, oblivious to his shredded his neck and pain. Worse, since she rapidly glutted herself, he was growing dizzy.

There was no help for it. She could not kill him, but when she came to herself she would not understand how to revive him. If he were unconscious, he could not protect her; besides which, the thought of exposing her to Richard's criticism was distasteful. With considerable effort, he jerked her from his neck.

She fought him wildly, frantically trying to latch onto whatever flesh she could, willing to tear him apart to reach his blood. He restrained her, doing his best not to hurt her but requiring great strength in order to prevent her from breaking his hold. It was quite some time before the bloodlust faded into a black sleep.

When he was certain she was down, he could not stifle his concern. While not unprecedented in young vampyres, usually it affected the underfed; he had believed he *pampered* her, cosseting her with frequent—daily or even twice-daily—feedings, keeping her healthy and strong. Could something be wrong? She looked so vulnerable now, so still and lifeless.

For an hour or more, he lay beside her, watching over her. When her eyes opened at last, she seemed disoriented.

"Fitzwilliam? What—"

Then she saw his neck, which was healing more slowly due to the amount of blood she had taken.

"Oh my heavens," she cried. "Oh, Fitzwilliam...oh, no, no," she moaned, reaching out to touch the pink slashes of healing flesh at his throat.

"All is well, love. 'Tis nothing."

A tear traced down her cheek. "I am so very sorry," she said.

"You are not to apologise," he ordered. "You could not help it. I need you to answer a question for me, Elizabeth. Answer me truthfully. Have you been thirsting?"

Elizabeth turned away from him. "Yes," she admitted. "I am thirsty all the time. An hour after I have Taken, I am parched. I–I hid it from you, avoided your kiss except when feeding, trying to overcome it, but obviously, I have failed."

"Sweet love," he admonished tenderly, "you are never to hide anything from me. It is my fault for underestimating its strength—I have felt it from you, but did not realise you suffered so much, so often. Your body is *telling* you what it needs. Hiding those needs is dangerous. I do not begrudge you anything, you must know that."

"I want to be strong. No one else needs as much as I do. Your blood is powerful. Its effects would satisfy any others of your House for weeks. Richard said yesterday that he wished you to go with him to search some mines for Wickham and asked me how often I must drink from you. When I confessed I fed daily, his contempt was obvious. I try—"

"I would not leave you to search, regardless. I do not care how much you take, nor how often. I care even less for Richard's opinions. How many times must I say it, Elizabeth? Why will you not trust me?"

"I do," she said quietly. "I am sorry for failing you."

He sighed. "Do not apologise. Just promise me, love, that you will tell me of your needs and be honest when I ask you."

She nodded. "Please, Fitzwilliam...will you Take from me now? You do not seem to be healing quickly."

The last thing he wished was to Take while she suffered thirst, but it was more vital than ever that he stay in top form. He bent to her throat, and despite his desire to give, was nearly overwhelmed by the pleasure of Taking. His hands coasted over her back, feeling the strength of her shoulders, the softness of her curves, and his hands wanted her. His eyes raked over the skin at her neck, her firm jaw, the strands of hair curling at his cheek, and his eyes wanted her. Her scent filled his nostrils and he wanted to breathe her in. Nevertheless, he did not need more intimacy to know her deep distress. With a kiss, he sealed the punctures closed.

Her fingers moved to his neck, the flesh now unscathed, all evidence of her attack vanished. "You see," he murmured. "Gone. You are not to fret about a little scratch."

"I am so sorry," she said again.

"You will let me feed you now," he insisted.

"I am well," she replied. "No thirst. I promise."

"Good. We shall keep it that way. You do not have to take much. Only what I took from you."

Elizabeth sighed. She took his wrist to her mouth, but he pulled it away.

"No, not like that."

"Then it will not happen."

"Elizabeth, you can see I am well. There is no reason to—"

"This is not about you," she interrupted harshly. "I will feed this way until I trust myself again."

Jaw clenched, he gave her back his wrist. There was no time to argue, but he *would* change her mind. He shoved his fear of her odd behaviour into the back of his mind.

CAROLINE DECLARED HERSELF WELL ENOUGH TO ATTEND THE wedding. "I love weddings," she cried. "I love Charlie. I love Jane. She is so pretty." The astonishment on Louisa's face kept Elizabeth from bursting into sentimental tears herself.

Lit torches edged the lengthy red rock path between the estate's chapel and the castle proper; most of the party opted to walk back afterwards on the firelit pathway, though Mr and Mrs Bennet—immune to the romance of it—took the carriage provided. Elizabeth was especially grateful for the night air. Mr Marley had indulged in a lengthy sermon before attending to the vows, and before it finished, she thirsted again.

It felt like defeat. She had glutted on Fitzwilliam's blood only three hours before. Now, her predatory senses alerted her to every heartbeat. Elizabeth forced herself to hold her aunt's arm lightly, a deliberate measure to avoid mesmerising her acceptance of an unholy bite. She chatted about a friend in Lambton, blissfully unaware, while Elizabeth's mouth watered, her fangs lengthening. Everyone else had drifted ahead of them—*did I do it on purpose*, Elizabeth wondered? Separate her from those who might assist, create a more vulnerable quarry? *Oh, no, no*, she thought, as a wave of hunger shuddered through her.

"Let us walk faster, Aunt," she urged. "'Tis...awfully cold."

"It is chilly, but since I indulged in fur trims, I truly don't feel it,"

Mrs Gardiner happily nattered on. "And these torches are lovely! So truly romantic."

"You should be walking with Uncle." Elizabeth quickened her pace, barely resisting the urge to drag her aunt along even faster.

"Your uncle prefers discussing fishing with Mr Darcy. Slow down, Lizzy—oh, dear, I believe I have managed to acquire a pebble in my slipper."

She bent low to remove it, clutching her niece's arm to support her weight. A wave of overpowering thirst clawed at Elizabeth's gut; she almost bit her own wrist in order to appease her instinctive reaction. Desperate, she seized one of the rocks on the path and shoved it into her mouth, clamping her teeth down on it. To her surprise, the strength of her teeth and the force of her jaws were enough to shatter it in her mouth; what was even more shocking, she found it particularly delicious. With its mineral taste coating her tongue, the overpowering urge to bite receded along with her panic. She finally remembered what she ought to have done minutes ago.

"I wish Fitzwilliam would return to escort us," she said. Though she did not speak much above her usual tone, she knew he would hear her if he paid attention at all.

Her aunt, oblivious to Elizabeth's actions, shook out her slipper and slid it back on her foot. In the time that took, Elizabeth pocketed a few more of the red rocks, sucking on the remnants of one as if it were a peppermint candy.

"All fixed," Mrs Gardiner said, smiling. "Shall we continue?"

Darcy emerged suddenly out of the darkness. "Ah, here you are at last," he said genially. "Most of the party has already reached the house, so I returned to find you lovely ladies."

"Oh, Mr Darcy, you startled me," said Mrs Gardiner. "Elizabeth scarcely wished for you, and here you are!"

"Are you well, my love?" Darcy asked his wife, coming to her side.

She took his arm. "Now, I am."

Matlock stared with distaste as Jenkinson's blood pooled on the squabs of his lovely barouche. "He is ruining my upholstery," he complained.

"Put some blankets underneath him," Catherine shrugged. "It was not my idea to take your vehicle."

But I needed an excuse to remain with you, he thought. *I have not yet learned where your safe haven might be.* Aloud, he said, "Your carriage is hardly suitable for such a long journey, my dove. Mine is much more comfortable."

"I rarely travel further than London. Mine is built for speed."

"Exactly. A journey of four days requires rather more—" he began, when Jenkinson began muttering. It took a few moments before they realised he quoted a marriage ceremony. They listened as Jane Bennet and Charles Bingley were joined in holy matrimony.

Catherine's lip curled in distaste. "Those Bennet chits do well at manoeuvring themselves into the paths of rich men. I would like nothing better than to kill them all."

"All the rich men, or the Bennet girls?" he mocked.

"I am happy you find this amusing," she replied coldly.

"Oh, I do. Nothing could be more entertaining than imagining Darcy's wife torn to shreds. But for my concern regarding the consequences you might face for arranging it, I would be the happiest man on earth."

"I told you—he shall never find proof. Have more faith," she snapped.

"He found George quickly enough without even a scent trail. He is unbelievably quick, knows the area well, and murderous instinct guides him truer than any northern star. Why should I not be anxious?"

"Shall he find me while I am surrounded by silver?"

"My dear, if you are surrounded by silver, how will you avoid incapacitation?"

Catherine smiled serenely. "I shall not be directly affected. I have a hideaway in the Peak District, within a lead mine bounded by silver mines. Lead is difficult enough to track through. The presence of silver makes it impossible. I have equipped it for my comfort so I shall be safe for as long as needed!"

"You must feed eventually."

"The miners will provide adequate sustenance. And I need not remain for years. 'Tis too large an area to monitor indefinitely, as he is bound to concede. I shall rely upon my allies within the Council to restrain him against his lack of proof," she said pointedly.

"Of course, my clever dove. You know you may rely upon me." *Rely upon me to find the site of your mine*, he chuckled inwardly.

❧

Darcy stared out the window of his chamber, peering over the expanse of garden it overlooked. Winter's morning light did not flatter it, but soon, spring with all its beauties would come; he longed to show Elizabeth the gardens in full bloom. *Elizabeth.* He took in a breath he did not need in order to release a sigh.

There were few physicians of his race—and they did not treat vampyres, but rather the fragile humans surrounding them. Vampyres did not take ill; when wounded, they either regenerated or died. Their only natural enemy was other vampyres.

Yet, something was definitely amiss with Elizabeth. If she failed to take blood every two to three hours, the danger of bloodlust threatened. It was not overly strange that eating meat helped her condition, but the red stones? They even tried different rocks, but only the red ones 'tasted right'. It was beyond odd, but he had a supply of them washed and placed in bowls throughout the castle. Discreet inquiries had unearthed nothing except that her symptoms were unheard of in the vampyre community. The blood thirst was so strong, it wakened her during the day, so she could not sleep it away.

He did not mind feeding her frequently—in fact, it gave him pleasure to do so. But she knew as well as he did that her inability to go longer between meals was unorthodox at best, ominous at worst.

Pulling a stone from his pocket, he examined it closely. Other than its rusty colouring, it was very ordinary. Carefully, he put it in his mouth and sucked on it as he had watched Elizabeth do. She assured him its taste was appetising; to him, it tasted...like a rock. He spit it back out into his hand, sighing again.

To the relief of the entire household, most of their guests had departed. He had yielded to Elizabeth's appeal that he 'encourage' some sense in Lydia, placing a strong suggestion that she be mindful of every caring and decent action by her husband, and that she consider his affection before impulsively responding to every circumstance. Heaven only knew how long it would last, but such inclinations *could* become habitual. He could admit the Forsters appeared happy together as they took their leave. Sadly, Elizabeth had not permitted him to plant a suggestion within her parents regarding a sudden and overwhelming urge to visit America.

Jane and Bingley had departed on their wedding trip; owing to security concerns they would only go as far as Darcy House in London, but they would at least be able to enjoy many of town's entertainments. They had taken a cheerful Caroline with them, but she would reside at Charles's house, as before. He gave a half-smile, imagining the happy surprise awaiting the Bingley servants.

Richard accompanied the Gardiners and Bennets back to their respective homes, Mary and Kitty staying on with their aunt and uncle in London. The Forsters, the Bennets, the Bingleys and the Gardiners would all be watched round-the-clock by his men. Hence, he had fewer at Pemberley than usual, but those here were especially diligent. He expected Richard's return at any moment—he would not dally.

There was still the problem of the Collinses. Mr Collins yet wandered the house at night, and though he was carefully watched, did nothing worse than drink brandy. The vicar's feelings were full of indignation, as well as a good deal of resentment. None of it seemed directed at Elizabeth, however, and looking inside his mind again and again, Darcy found nothing more than the frustration of a man who had lost his job and most of his dignity with it. Mrs Collins was growing concerned, however. He could feel anxiety pouring off her—she was far too practical to ignore their essentially insecure situation. She desperately hoped for Darcy to find her husband another place, while knowing Collins's behaviour did not merit such a favour.

Which, of course, it did not. He had always required much of those he installed as spiritual shepherds to his people, and Mr Collins demonstrated almost none of those finer qualities he insisted upon. He was not a particularly bad man; he simply was not a particularly good one. His wife was the best thing about him, and he regretted he could not simply appoint *her* to a post. Unfortunately, human sensibilities would not stand for it.

Until Darcy could work out an acceptable solution, he was stuck with them. At least Elizabeth enjoyed Charlotte's company, though there remained the concern of her thirst rising in one of its unexpected waves and putting her friend in harm's way. Thus far, the rocks prevented her from attacking anyone. She kept them with her at all times and dosed herself with them like medicine. It was all too bizarre, and he sighed again.

"Fitzwilliam?" Elizabeth said, her voice husky and fatigued as she rose up on her elbow.

He turned to face her. "Are you hungry, my love?"

She winced. "Yes. I am sorry, I—"

"Shh, shh," he soothed. He lay down beside her at once, moving aside the neck of his shirt. Pushing her up to his exposed skin, he felt the tension in her upper body and knew she struggled not to attack.

"Here you go, love," he said, but she pushed away and grabbed his wrist instead.

He sighed again. She bit expertly now, her venom giving him a pleasurable rush of sensation. But she did not trust herself with bites to any of the larger veins, and her restraint pained him. Though he could and did heal quickly, causing him the slightest injury disturbed her deeply.

"Elizabeth, love," he said softly, bringing his wrist up so that she had to come closer in order to stay joined. Her venom traced its way through his body, which reacted to the pleasure in its usual fashion. "I should let you go back to sleep...but I do not want to."

He wanted to bite, pulsating with a need that had nothing to do with hunger. He latched onto her neck, and her blood filled his mouth. It tasted richer, even better than usual somehow, the creamiest, sweetest blood in existence. After only a swallow, he was filled. He quit drinking but maintained their connexion through his bite; she returned his feelings in full measure and even more so, showing him limitless passion, until they were both complete and sated. After decades of staying in complete control, he surrendered it all to her.

A strangely peaceful mood enveloped him, the full opposite of his earlier state of anxiety. How could anything be wrong when they could do this together? He had felt her, been one with her, given himself to her, shared her joy. She was his everything. Nothing would hurt her; he would never allow it. He had felt the burn of her thirst, but he also felt how great her will to control it.

Her eyes closed, her body relaxing into slumber before he reluctantly surrendered the connexion. He pressed a gentle kiss to one cheek, then to the other, finally leaning to kiss her belly before pillowing his head on this slight cushion of softness. And in this serene quiet, with Elizabeth still as death in sleep, he heard a sound like the whispered flutter of hummingbird wings. It took a few moments for him to first, recognise the unfamiliar sound, and next, understand from whence it came.

And then came hours of listening, doubt and incredulity battling hope and wonder, before he could truly begin to believe what his every instinct shouted. It was a heartbeat. Not hers. A tiny, swiftly beating vampyre heart.

"Can you hear it?" he asked quietly.

Agnes Reynolds straightened at last. She nodded, her expression full of both pleasure and astonishment. "I don't understand it, sir. 'Tis impossible—but there is no doubt. Hopefully there is no danger in it for her. She is stronger than human females."

"It seems to me it is faster than the heartbeat of mortal infants," he said, having never paid attention to such details.

"Yes, much faster. Everything about a vampyre birth happens more quickly. I do not think we can risk calling Dr Morris from Lambton. We sent Carter to London with his wife for Sally's birth. Mr Bingley arranged for assistance there and can undoubtedly do so again."

"Mrs Darcy cannot go to London. 'Tis not safe."

"Why would I want to go to London?" Elizabeth said, raising up on her elbows and looking from Mrs Reynolds to her husband with sleepy curiosity.

The housekeeper exited and Darcy approached the bed. Seating himself upon the mattress edge, he regarded her tenderly.

"You must eat," he said, pulling her onto his lap, up to his throat.

"Fortunately, I can eat in Derbyshire. I need not go to London for that," she said wryly. However, a wave of hunger shuddered through her, and she captured his wrist.

"No, Elizabeth. Not that way. I will not let you lose control. We will be careful." She started to argue, but evidently something about his tone commanded her in a way that brooked no opposition as he urged her to his neck.

When she was sated, she carefully sealed the punctures at his throat. As she licked them shut, he bent to kiss her—sweetly, softly.

"Do you need to feed?" she asked.

He smiled. "I did so a few hours ago. Do you not recall?"

"I recall everything about this morning," she said. "I also recall there is talk of sending me to London."

"To be precise, we were discussing *not* sending you there."

She frowned. "Do not tease. I know what this is about."

"You do?"

"Yes. How could I not? I must feed a hundred times more often than anyone else. I lose control if I do not. I eat rocks, for heaven's sake. I am broken, and you must try to find someone to fix me."

"You are perfect. Not broken at all," he said, nuzzling her neck.

"Fitzwilliam, you need not spare me. Have you a theory? Do you know of a cure?"

"There is...at least, so I believe. My love, 'tis possible," he paused, swallowing, "...that the *im*possible has occurred." He put his large hand over her belly again. "I...hear something. Inside you. I hear a beating heart. My love, I think you are with child."

"What?"

"I know this comes as a surprise," he said hesitantly.

"Oh, Fitzwilliam, are you sure? Oh, dear heavens, please be certain. I want...I want—" she broke off with a sob. Her husband cradled her in his arms while she sobbed against his chest, her dammed-up guilt and grief finally finding release.

"I am sorry," she replied at long last, her voice still tremulous. "I did not mean to—"

"Do not apologise, my love. Anyone would be shaken."

Her arms wrapped protectively around her middle. "What should I be doing? Will it be the same as a...mortal confinement? Is there a vampyre physician? A midwife?"

"In London there are vampyres who might be of assistance, who may be able to answer our questions. But we cannot risk you in travel, love. I shall write to Bingley. We shall bring someone here."

"If this is as strange as you think, who would know? Who will be able to help?"

"We will find someone, love. Tell me this makes you happy."

She twisted on his lap until she practically burrowed under his coat. "I am...oh, overjoyed seems too small a word. But part of me is terrified. Fitzwilliam, I cannot fail this child. I have to do this right, but I do not know what to do."

"Your body has been guiding you all along, sweetheart. It told you to feed often. It did not let you fail."

"But the red stones? How can those be good for the babe?"

"Very well, I admit I do not understand the rocks. But why should they hurt?"

"How? How could this be? Could I have already been with child when I was Turned?"

"I do not think any babe could have survived that," he replied. "At least, I do not understand how, or why it has never happened to others before you. Perhaps my blood, given to you in such abundance just before you entered your womanhood, might have...changed something within you, though this, too, seems unlikely. It is possible you were fertile just as the Turning took place, but it should not have made any difference. It should have been impossible."

"You said only born vampyres could father children. And that female vampyres were never fertile, born or Turned."

Nodding, he said, "We have always thought that to be true. Only de Medici House claim different, and most believe it a myth."

"There are so few females. Perhaps it is just a matter of low odds?"

He paused. "I can look, you know. Within females, I can go deep inside their...essence, and determine whether the potential for life exists. I did it for Bingley, when he determined he wanted your sister."

"You did what?" She sounded genuinely dismayed.

"I do nothing shocking, I assure you, though no doubt it seems scandalous to you. If the potential for life is within her, I get a certain...feeling, that is all. Bingley was set on marrying your sister regardless. He needs an heir, though, and wanted to plan. My point is simply that other Masters have this ability—my father taught me the skill. I can assure you, if any female vampyre had potential for child-bearing, it would have been noticed."

"You looked? In me?"

"No!"

"Why not?"

"I cannot look within *you* unless we are...already engaged in other activities. Besides, it does not matter. It was knowledge I did not need nor even want."

"I see," she said, and she probably did. Had he known for certain she was barren he would have had no argument against Turning her. But fate had decided otherwise.

"Sweetheart?" he asked anxiously, after her long silence.

She looked up at him, eyes sparkling with joy. They did not go down that evening at all, and what excuses were made to the Collinses, neither cared to know.

"Elizabeth!" Charlotte said when she joined her late the next afternoon. "I was so concerned when your housekeeper told us how poorly you felt yesterday, hoping you did not take Miss Bingley's fever. Are you feeling much better?"

Elizabeth made a hasty decision to be honest; talking about her impending motherhood seemed such an ordinary response, transforming it from distant day-dream to something more real. "I feel somewhat improved...but Charlotte, will you keep a secret?"

Charlotte looked at her shrewdly. "I knew it," she crowed. "I knew you were simply trying to keep from divulging the truth to your mother. Truly, you have been so–so different, you look so radiant, I just knew!"

"Yes," Elizabeth agreed. "We did not wish to speak too soon, but we feel that we shall have happy news this summer." She avoided putting too fine a point upon the timing. Vampyre pregnancies were apparently of shorter duration than those of their mortal counterparts, perhaps twenty-five to thirty weeks, and they had no way of knowing whether the fact both parents were vampyre would have any effect. She could not tell Charlotte any estimate of the due date without it seeming their marriage was a necessity for the reasons Mrs Bennet had once accused.

It *was* necessary to find a situation for Mr Collins, and to do so sooner rather than later. Fitzwilliam had explained his reservations, but what else could the vicar do? The only skills he demonstrated related to the amount of liquor he was capable of consuming before reaching oblivion.

"Have you thought of names?" Charlotte asked, and for the time being, Elizabeth decided to enjoy the very great pleasure of having a good friend by her side, indulging in the dreams of new motherhood.

"This is well-equipped, Catherine," Matlock remarked approvingly.

"Yes, well, I insisted it be habitable," she replied.

The cavern in which he found himself was outfitted with cushions, books, chandeliers—even though candlelight was unnecessary to creatures at home in the dark, they added an elegant ambience—and a table upon which chessboard and playing cards were already set out. He could still hear the low growls of the creature, but at least it was caged far enough away that he no longer had to endure its stench.

There was a large copper tub, an underground pool from which water for bathing might be procured—and two of Catherine's minions nearby to draw it. There was even a mapped diagram of the branches of the mine currently being worked, providing easier access to meals. "We must stay away from the ones mining silver, they taste dreadful. The leaden ones, though, are delicious," she remarked. He watched as she carefully handled a wooden box, smoothing her hands over it reverently. She noticed him following her movements and smiled, amused at his curiosity.

"'Tis a very important little item within," she smirked. Opening the brass clasp, she turned it to show him its contents.

It was a rag, brown and stiffly saturated with dried blood.

He raised a brow and she snapped the lid shut with a crack.

"The blood—'tis *hers*. I had it fetched from the hovel where Darcy Turned her. It will lead my dear creature right to her."

"So...it needs the blood of its prey to seek its victim?"

Catherine shrugged. "Anything imbued with the scent will do, but blood works best."

Jenkinson groaned from his place on the stone floor—evidently not worthy enough for one of the cushions—and began muttering. While Catherine blathered on in a self-congratulatory bliss, not paying any mind, Matlock angled himself to recover every word the wounded vampyre uttered. Though much of what the man repeated was useless, there was always the chance he would say something worth hearing. *This is why Catherine is insupportable,* he thought with contempt. *She is genius enough to conceive such a plan, yet incapable of following through to ensure victory.*

Still, he was anxious to learn how she had managed the eye-ear essence transfer, so he encouraged her gabble-mongering as well. Therefore, he almost missed the words Jenkinson spoke, words nearly stopping his heart.

"Of course, it will be Fitzwilliam Bennet if a boy. We cannot agree upon girls' names. I like the name Georgiana, after his father whom he adored. Mr Darcy favours Elizabeth, but I think it too confusing."

"What is this?" Catherine demanded, obviously listening now. But Jenkinson merely let out a little moan, and it was obvious they would hear no more. "How can this be?"

"Calm yourself," Matlock said. "For some reason Mrs Darcy pretends she is increasing. We know it cannot be so. She lies to her friend."

"Why should she?" Catherine hissed. "It is too easily disproven! Has that trull managed it? What did she do?"

"She lies," he barked. "'Tis simple. It explains her sleeping habits to her mortal friend, while gaining her sympathy. Later, she will say she lost the brat." But his excitement at the idea rose.

"Yes, she lies. And what possible difference could it make? The doxy dies, with child or not! *Especially* with child! I would never allow the shades of Pemberley to be thus polluted."

"You are correct, of course," he soothed. "Disposing of Mrs Darcy is the most important thing." He led Catherine to the thickest cushions, pushing her back among the pillows. He would tire her, and himself, and perhaps his brain would abandon the impossible, exhilarating sensation that the unattainable might be his, if only he could believe.

❧

Matlock woke at sunset, his internal clock informing him of the sun's march across the sky even though he was cocooned within the depths of the cave. Catherine still slept, a sign she gave a great deal of her blood to both Jenkinson and, he suspected, her creature. He would never underestimate her ability to waken instantly if attacked, however.

Jenkinson chose that moment to begin murmuring—and it took Matlock some time to ascertain who was speaking, but at last he determined it was Mrs Darcy's maid in conversation with the housekeeper. A mind-numbing discussion of a linens inventory suddenly segued into a topic far more interesting.

"Oh, Mrs Reynolds, we shall have to bring the nursery linens down from the attics to be washed and aired."

"I have already done so. Mrs Darcy has spoken of having the nursery repapered."

"This is so very exciting, so impossibly exciting! We...we are certain, are we not?"

"Yes, Maggie. Mark my words, by early summer the nursery will be empty no longer!"

Matlock gaped at the bloodied vampyre, and forcibly shut his mouth. How could this be? It was beyond belief! Yet, Agnes Reynolds was as honest and loyal a servant as it was possible to have, and she obviously believed.

Matlock debated leaving Catherine a note but as he usually came and went without notice, it might actually increase her distrust if he left word. She was well aware he had duties and plots of his own to nurture.

Let her wonder.

His footman was bleary and stumbling, but his human coachman was alert. With the help of Catherine's stableman, Tobias, they readied his rig quickly. After placing a powerful sleep charm upon Tobias, he drove off into the dusk. As soon as the night fed him strength enough, he left the coach and began running.

Catherine awakened with a start; though she was very deep underground, she knew sunset was not long past. A little moan sounded from Jenkinson. She stretched a little, smiling as she felt the bruises from the roughhousing of the last two nights that had not quite healed. She truly did need to feed. Devil take Matlock for refusing her—though of course she had not allowed him to Take from her either. Neither trusted the other enough to want even the slight, temporary connexions a quick Taking endowed.

She reached out across the cushions, but Matlock was gone. Likely off to feed himself, she thought. When he had not returned to her cavern by the time she refreshed herself off a miner or two, she grew suspicious. When she found his coach-and-four gone, she killed the still slumbering Tobias.

She was furious but she was not stupid. He likely intended to capture that worthless harlot and keep the supposed child for himself. For a moment, she nearly collapsed the mine simply to release her wrath. The tunnel crackled ominously, and a shower of rocks brought her to her senses just in time.

With a flash of alarm, she rushed to her creature's cage, certain he had destroyed her dear beastie in order to stop her. Seeing its growling form, she was suddenly uncertain regarding Matlock's destination. Perhaps he was away on intrigues of his own.

Well, my Lord Matlock, she thought, *there is no child. 'Tis impossible. If you are wise, my plans will proceed without interference. But if you have betrayed me...I shall have an additional kill for my dear Rosomakha!*

It took some time for her to appropriate a farm cart and horse; she had her two remaining servants load her creature and Jenkinson onto the back, making one of them drive her. The moon was high in the sky before she took her seat on the humble vehicle, sitting with her back ramrod straight, as though she were a queen.

❧

"What returns you to Pemberley, my lord?" Darcy asked politely.

Matlock clenched his teeth against the answers he wanted to spit at the younger man, affronted at the cool welcome. He did not even try to disguise the emotions swirling within him—he had no reason to do so. Frustration, fear, curiosity...and protectiveness. He was not ready to reveal all of Catherine's secrets, in case he could use them to better advantage later. But he would definitely say enough to justify his presence.

"I have uncovered details of Catherine de Bourgh's latest plot," he said tersely. "Her desire for vengeance is stronger than ever, and your wife is her target. She has gained access to...a creature, a monster. It is vicious and powerful. She is able to control it mentally. It is impervious to any of the usual—or unusual—defensive gifts with which we might foil its attack, able to savage an enemy ten times its own weight."

Darcy's expression sharpened. "Thank you for this information. I will warn my men."

"I would like to join those guarding her."

For a few moments, Darcy contemplated this. At last he said carefully, "I am honoured by your offer, my lord, but I assure you it is unnecessary. We are amply defended, and I would not distract you from your own concerns."

Matlock allowed his hurt and offence at the other man's ingratitude to permeate his aura, knowing it would scrape along Darcy's nerves. "Of course, if I am not needed, I shall not stay. But allow me to say I believe you unwise. I was on your border for several minutes before James discovered me—and I was not attempting subtlety. If James is in charge, Richard is not here. You are undermanned with such a threat as faces your wife. I would think of her first, were I you."

"I think of nothing but her. It is not that you are unneeded. It is only—" he stopped, running his hand through his hair, plainly choosing his words carefully.

"It is only...Elizabeth is in a delicate state at the moment. She must not be upset. Likely she would not be, as I am sure it was only a symptom of her Change causing her earlier distressing response to your presence. However, in her current condition, I dare not risk it."

"She has not recovered from her Change?"

"She has. Fully. Completely."

"You make no sense, Fitzwilliam. She cannot be ill!" Matlock mimicked concern.

"Not ill, no."

"Then what? What is wrong with her?"

"Nothing is wrong. She is magnificent." As expected, the younger man yielded his secrets. "And the mother of my heir."

Matlock gazed at the other man warily. "You cannot be saying... surely not, son! Why...'tis impossible!"

"Impossible, yes. But true. Somehow, true." Darcy was unable to prevent his almost boyish smile.

"And you are absolutely certain?"

"Of course. I hear my child's heart beating within her."

"Oh...oh, Fitzwilliam. My dear boy. Congratulations." He allowed his gladness, his utter glee to surface and flood the room. "You are correct. Mrs Darcy must not be upset, not for any reason. I would not have it so for the world." Carefully, he unleashed a gushing, tender concern—one of his most successful emotional 'responses'. For once, it was even truth, of a sort—he *was* deeply concerned. "But, Fitzwilliam, you must allow me to patrol the grounds with your men at night and do my part to stop Catherine de Bourgh—as I have done for you so often in the past."

Darcy hesitated, and Matlock pushed his sense of protectiveness out as far as he dared.

"I thank you, my lord. Your assistance will be greatly appreciated," Darcy said at last.

Bait taken.

❧

Catherine was two miles from Pemberley's outermost border when she ordered the cart to a halt. The horse was lathered, spooked more by the scent and proximity of the *Rosomakha* than by the pace she forced, and strained frantically against the reins. "Stupid animal," Catherine muttered. "If I wished you dead you would already be glue."

They had pulled off in a wooded section of road, so dark even the moonlight could not penetrate. The creature continued its low growls, every now and again the cage shuddering as it threw itself against its bars. Every time it did so, the driver quivered in fear, matching the vibration of the barred enclosure.

Catherine stood and, in one graceful motion, leapt into the cart to stand before the cage. The *Rosomakha* hissed and roared. Without pausing, she pushed her hand into the face of the beast. Her driver winced, convinced the thing would tear her limb off. To his astonishment, however, it permitted Catherine to stroke its oily fur.

"My poor dear love," Catherine murmured. "You do not care for that wretched cage, do you? No, of course you do not. What do you crave? What do you *need*?" She continued to stroke it as it fell back onto the cage floor, boneless. "I know what you want, my pet. You want *her*."

A new note sounded in her voice as she produced the blood-stained remnant of rug. "Is this what you want? Is this what my baby wants?"

The *Rosomakha* commenced growling again, this time with malicious intent. It began throwing itself against its cage walls, trying to reach the scrap of bloodstained wool Catherine dangled tauntingly out of reach, the cart shaking with the force of its blows until it seemed they would all capsize. Catherine laughed.

With a quick movement she unbolted it, throwing the door open. The wolverine made no frantic bid for freedom; now that the way was clear, its frustration seemed to fade. Its low growls dissipated into hissing anticipation.

"Good beastie," Catherine murmured, still chuckling. She stared into the creature's eyes; for long moments there was silence as the *Rosomakha* and its master communed. At last, she brought the fabric to its mouth. The beast snatched it with a pleased growl.

Her lips moved, though no sound emerged at first. But, gradually, her voice rose—first a whisper, then a mutter, finally recognisable words as she stroked the creature again from the top of its head to the bottom of its spine. "Head and heart," she intoned. "Head and heart. Head and heart. Head and heart." She paused, then withdrew from her pocket a shredded piece of a man's cravat. The beast growled with new interest as she held it out, as well. "My Lord Matlock, you only need fear if you have betrayed me. Now *go*." It shot into the night.

Matlock patrolled nearest the perimeter of the great castle, his sword at the ready. Would she send in the beast tonight, knowing there was a chance he was here?

Most of his thoughts revolved around the child. If it were a girl, he would not rest until he wormed a betrothal contract out of Darcy. A boy would be unfortunate, and odds were that he would be even more powerful than his father. If Darcy met with a regrettable accident, he could find a means of stealing the child for his own uses.

His attention was drawn to a noise near the walled garden. Easing his way closer, he saw Catherine's toady vicar pacing back and forth on the veranda. Mr Collins looked nothing like his former self, clutching at his head as though in the grips of a terrible megrim; Jenkinson was undoubtedly present. His presence here in the out-of-doors could only mean Catherine meant to launch her assault now, just before sunrise. Stupid, impulsive female. She ought to have relinquished the scheme the moment he disappeared.

The stench reached him only a second before the *Rosomakha* attacked.

Thirty Eight

THE CREATURE STRUCK WITH SPEED AND FEROCITY; MATLOCK drew his sword, but was unable to get in a blow before it had him down. It was bad luck that it gouged his left eye out of its socket so quickly; the spurting blood impaired the vision in his good eye. He felt its silver-tipped fangs scraping over his chest, tearing flesh open to rip apart his chest cavity.

Matlock was only just able to wrench it away from his heart, but it required all of his considerable strength to do so, and even then he could not break free.

"Bloody strong devil!" he grunted. As they tussled, he felt his muscles slowly giving way against its ferocity. It was as if the thing was *strengthened* by Matlock's struggles. *Catherine.* She fed it mentally, as her toad-eating vicar likely related every second of the contest. Could Jenkinson-Collins tell whom it attacked? The beast was atop him, his face covered by its stinking fur. Abruptly, there was a slight give in the creature's hold, and he shoved it away with every ounce of muscle he had left. The creature was flung head-over-tail into the garden wall. It thrust itself away from the bricking, and Matlock went into a crouch—this time, his sword at the ready.

The *Rosomakha* did not even pause, racing past him through the open entry into the castle.

Matlock rose to his feet on limbs that actually trembled. As he did so, he saw Collins picking himself up as well. He spared a moment for a low chuckle. The idiot vicar had tripped—breaking Jenkinson's view and Catherine's attention, giving him the opportunity needed to defend himself. Too bad the dolt had not broken his neck as well. At that moment Collins turned away, stumbling into the house after the creature.

Matlock took a moment to stuff his pocket handkerchief into his eye socket—the dashed thing bled like a sieve. Eyes always took far too long to regenerate. And then, sword drawn, he sped after the *Rosomakha.* Along the way, he shoved the vicar down the marble staircase as he passed him on the way to the family apartments. *Take that, Catherine!* He had a damsel in distress to rescue!

"What happened, darling?" Elizabeth asked when Darcy returned to their apartments.

Darcy did not answer immediately, evaluating the risks of remaining here. While the cellars were not as luxurious, certainly, there were no windows, fewer entries, thicker walls. Not to mention the labyrinth of tunnels he could utilise to hide her securely. Catherine could never touch her there. In fact, he and Matlock could lie in wait up here, perhaps trapping the creature.

His own beast growled in protest at the thought of leaving Elizabeth's side. Even the ten minutes he spent downstairs had seemed a crushing weight on his chest.

"Darling?" she said again, walking over to stand before him.

He looked down upon her tenderly. "Yes, love?"

With her hand, she reached up to softly stroke his lips with her fingers. "You were a hundred miles away," she murmured.

Smiling, he disagreed. "No. Only in the cellars. And so might we be, soon."

"What is wrong?"

"Matlock is here," he said.

Immediately her expression hardened, making Darcy feel defensive. "He discovered a new scheme of Catherine's. She has some sort of wolverine-like creature, capable of unmatched ferocity, strength of mythic proportions, and immunity to any of the offensive gifts. At least, so he believes."

"Ah. So I am to be moved to the cellars?"

"It might be best if we go below. For your safety."

"You would go with me?"

"Of course," he averred, as if he had not been considering otherwise. "I will not leave you alone, Elizabeth. I will protect you."

She stepped into his embrace. "I know you will, my love. I will be safe as long as you are near. *We* will be safe."

His hand coasted down to her belly again. He could not keep from touching her there, marvelling at the notion of new life resting beneath his fingertips.

"So..." she began, tensing a little. "Matlock...remains here?"

"Yes," he said, feeling the need to justify his invitation. His hand dropped to his side. "He is a powerful Master, useful to us. It would be foolish to reject his assistance simply because you do not care for him."

Elizabeth bit her lip, uncertain. "Of...of course. I understand we may need his help, though I truly believe you will be enough protection for me."

His smile returned. "I feel the overwhelming urge to protect you right this moment." His hands rested lightly now upon her waist, and he bent to kiss her. The kiss was tender and scintillating, slow heat and sweet burn. "Are you thirsty?" he asked.

"I just fed an hour ago! I am not that—" The next instant he covered her.

"Oomph," she grunted, taking his weight. "You are heavy!"

"Protective. Nothing can get you now."

"Except you," she smirked.

"Except me," he agreed. "What was this about your overpowering thirst? Your endless craving for me?" he asked, as she laughed between kisses.

"Mm..." she murmured, "I do seem to recall some sort of...pang."

He growled, pulling her in tightly. At that moment, he heard a noise coming from the direction of her adjacent sitting room; he had only enough time to wonder what it was, when a monster struck.

❧

By the time Matlock reached the hallway leading to the family apartments, the *Rosomakha* had already taken out the footman on guard there—Thomas, he believed; he was gutted, his heart torn from him.

He was not decapitated, and thus not dead, but Matlock did not want him recovering any too soon and calling for help, so he stomped on the still-beating heart as he ran past. *I have not much time to play the hero.*

Ahead, he saw the creature take a running leap at a door along the corridor. It was the door to Mrs Darcy's sitting room, by his reckoning, but it was a massive, solid barrier, and the thing would never breach it before Darcy was alerted to danger. Putting on an intense burst of speed, he managed to gain the door at almost the same moment, throwing it open so that the creature sailed through the entry in a blur.

Matlock rammed the door with his shoulder, breaking through it so it would appear that the creature gained admittance through its own brute force. Then he waited a few moments before following its pungent scent into the mistress's chambers.

The sight greeting him was dreadful. Darcy was wrapped around his wife, completely covering her while the beast ripped at his flesh, mauling, gnawing on exposed bones, viciously attacking any part of him it could reach, its inhuman snarling only adding to the grotesque violence. Darcy—bent on protecting his wife, could not take offensive measures—all of his efforts thrown into creating a living shield. Suddenly, with unearthly strength, the beast clamped its brutal jaws around Darcy's neck; Darcy roared in agony.

Stupid Catherine. I should have known the thing would kill the wrong victim. There was no time for dramatic swordplay. Drawing a wicked-looking dagger from his boot, with one prodigious throw he impaled the beast through the eye, piercing its brain. It did not release its ferocious bite, seizing instead around Darcy's neck. Matlock rushed in, grabbing it by the scruff and separating its body from its head with his sword. Tossing the carcass aside, he unhinged the creature's bite to free Darcy and dug its teeth out of his flesh.

As Darcy huddled over his wife, Matlock surreptitiously he licked the Darcy blood off his fingers. In the silence, he heard Mrs Darcy, muffled, ask, "Fitzwilliam?"

He straightened. "Darcy, the thing is dead. Get up."

At last, Darcy—painfully—lifted his head and set his gaze on the carcass of the animal. Black, oily-looking blood collected in a puddle beneath the severed head, ruining the rug beneath it. Elizabeth stared, aghast, at her husband—drenched in his own blood.

"Oh, my love," she said, trying to pull herself up, to see his injuries. "Come...let us attend to you."

His inner beast plainly was in charge, however, and was disinclined to release her. His eyes glowed red, then black, then red again.

"Let me help," Matlock said impatiently, coming towards him, facing Elizabeth for the first time since her Change was complete.

She dropped her eyes, clutching her hands together as though in distress, though, thankfully, she did not attack, as she had during her Change. Matlock took another step forward, and she flinched. Darcy growled. Matlock halted, his eyes narrowing. Surely, she was not repelled by him still? Undoubtedly, she was simply terrorised by the attack.

Four vampyres—Darcy men—suddenly stormed in and the situation was all taken from his hands. Surrounded by trusted men of his line, Darcy came back to himself, more or less. He waved off concerns about his own health and asked about Thomas, the footman who had been guarding the family wing.

"I passed him on my way to you," Matlock said. "The creature tore him apart."

"He must have been taken unawares," Darcy said. "He did not even sound an alarm."

"I saw him on my way to answering your summons," James said soberly. "Mrs Reynolds will have him belowstairs by now. And there was another injury. Your guest—Collins. It looks as though he fell down the stairs. Perhaps the beast knocked him down."

"Oh, no!" Elizabeth cried.

"He was not dead a few moments ago," James added.

"I will see what can be done for Mr Collins," Darcy said, nodding.

One by one, the men dispersed. One of them was sent to preserve the corpse of the creature, gruesome evidence of Catherine's crimes. Another was dispatched to ensure Mrs Collins would not realise what had taken place. James left to reorganise the property patrols.

Matlock was the last to leave. He had wrapped the bloody handkerchief around his head to form a makeshift eye patch, giving him a piratical appearance. "Catherine de Bourgh has gone too far this time," he declared. "This unprovoked attack on your property is the final insult. I shall notify the Council: she has instigated an act of war. If the human dies, it will seal her fate, but I am not inclined to wait for Council approval. I shall end this. I shall bring the Council her head, and they can debate the right and wrong of it *ex post facto*. When they hear what she has managed to do with this beast, none of them will protest too loudly. Darcy, as soon as you will, I shall want your statement."

Through a crack in the draperies, the grey-tinged light of dawn glinted. "You must sleep and feed now," Darcy advised him. "Mrs Reynolds will see to your needs, and I will have a statement for you by sunset."

Wishing to be alone with his gleeful triumph, Matlock did not argue with Darcy's command. He did not have Darcy's gifts, but even he could read the depth of the gratitude in the other man's eyes.

Thirty Nine

MATLOCK HAD NO OPPORTUNITY TO BID THE DARCYS FAREWELL. When he woke at the moment of sunset, eager to be on his way to deal with Catherine, the couple was in the cellars with the dying vicar. Matlock could take no chances that Jenkinson's eyes might still be spying. As it was, he had no idea whether Catherine knew for certain the truth of his whereabouts. While he did not believe Collins-Jenkinson had gotten a good look at him, Catherine *must* have felt the death of the *Rosomakha*, and probably knew from Jenkinson that Mrs Darcy was still alive—so she had to suspect him. Still, wondering might keep her off balance enough to give him some advantage.

He travelled in his carriage through the Derbyshire hills, towards Catherine's cavern hideaway, not bothering with stealth. If she battled him, it would not be in open countryside.

Well after midnight, his coach pulled into the wide cavern serving as a makeshift stable. He had sword drawn and every sense awake, but there was nothing to see except for Tobias's rotting corpse. Cloaking himself within the cave's shadows, becoming nothing more than darkness in dark, he darted through the tunnels. When he was just beyond the hole where Catherine made her lair, he stopped to listen for long minutes.

It was silent. He could hear nothing, neither Catherine nor the ravings of Jenkinson. Unless Catherine held herself motionless, she was not there. Which, of course, might be the case. He did a reconnaissance of the surrounding tunnels and caverns, travelling miles through passages riddling the mountain, finding no sign of her. Had she another hiding place? How much did she understand of the battle at Pemberley?

He must take her silence now as a sign that she did, indeed, suspect the truth.

Finally, he returned to her lair's entrance. If she had abandoned it, this might be a miscalculation—but he did not think she had. Rosings was surrounded, Darcy's men hunted her, and soon the Council would as well—she would be more vulnerable elsewhere. She would know herself safest here with some tactical advantage.

But such advantages would ultimately avail her nothing. Neither of them was particularly strong during the hours when the sun ruled the earth—but the Darcy blood he had managed to ingest from Fitzwilliam's wounds, and the death of the creature to which she had given so much of herself, meant he was stronger than Catherine de Bourgh. When the rays of the sun warmed the rock outside this cave, he would attack.

For hours he did nothing except disguise the sound of his beating heart in the gloom. Finally, at his weakest, he rushed into the cavern, ready to inflict death—when he was caught in the grip of a vampyre. Not Catherine. Not even a Master, and yet devilish strong...unbelievably stronger than Matlock at the moment. The little blood he had gleaned from Darcy was trumped by the veins of George Darcy's son.

Matlock amassed his powers, channelling all his considerable strength into breaking Wickham's hold by crucifying him mentally. His efforts proved unaccountably futile.

George Wickham grinned at his captive.

"You have grown curiously stronger since last we met," Matlock grunted.

"My new patroness allowed me to Take from her," Wickham chuckled.

"Checkmate," called Catherine de Bourgh, the sound of her mad laughter echoing throughout the twisting, turning tunnels of the entire mine.

One moment, Elizabeth was half-heartedly asking Darcy to attempt Turning Mr Collins, for Charlotte's sake; the next, the sound of Collins's horrific screams filled the air.

At the sight of him, Darcy went utterly still, while Elizabeth fisted her hand in her mouth.

Collins had been feverish, suffering, in pain. But now his empty eye sockets leaked blood and flesh. His head twisted back and forth rapidly, as though he were trying futilely to escape agonies.

"Mr Collins," Darcy said in his most hypnotic voice, "Be still. We will help, but you must lie still."

But the shrieks continued unabated, the man completely ignoring Darcy's call. "Impossible," Elizabeth breathed. "He pays you no heed."

"He cannot hear me," Darcy said grimly, gritting his teeth against the onslaught of Collins's torment. "And he suddenly stinks of de Bourgh. She did something to him. I do not know how or what, but probably before he ever came to us."

"Why could you not tell before?" she asked fearfully. "You examined him so many times."

"I do not know," he said again, laying his hand on the fretful man's head. Elizabeth watched as the vicar calmed beneath whatever her husband did inside his mind. When he lay unmoving at last, Darcy continued, "Whatever it was, Collins does not remember it. And the scent of her sorcery was somehow locked inside his head."

"How awful," Elizabeth said, appalled.

"Yes. I will certainly make this known to the Council. If Matlock is successful in bringing her in, this will add weight to the evidence against her." He did not want to say more, for this was the stuff of nightmares—he could scent the remains of at least three different humans amongst the matter leaking from Collins. At most, one other vampyre. Catherine had been experimenting on humans again, for which violation she had already been reprimanded.

Collins moaned, softly now. His fierce panting had diminished as well. They were losing him.

"He is dying," she said.

He did not prevaricate. "I think so, yes."

"Is Charlotte...has she been told anything?"

"We had the doctor from Lambton in and...simplified the timing and details of his memories for him. He now remembers examining a patient who imbibed too much liquor, fell down the stairs, and is presently feverish. He will relay this to Mrs Collins as soon as I give the word, and I will implant a memory of her nursing him until he dies."

"Oh, dear. I hate deceiving her."

"Mrs Collins is not the type to pick at her thoughts to find weaknesses."

"You have been telling me strong minds fight against untruths placed within them," Elizabeth said worriedly. "I know Charlotte is very strong."

"Yes, I agree. Mrs Collins is also eminently practical, unimaginative, and desires nothing more than a comfortable home of her own. She would never expend mental effort breaking down a lie that brings her peace."

"How comforting will she find the idea that her husband is dying because of a drunken accident?"

"She will not waste time judging her husband's actions. She will only want to—*need* to—have done her duty by him. Once I am able to ease her concerns about her financial future, she will accept her fate without undue distress, I promise you.

They were quiet for some time beside the dying man, not touching. Darcy despised his inability to discern her mood. Was she sorry she had entered his world?

"What are you thinking?"

"I was thinking about your mother," she said softly.

"I am sorry I asked, then," he replied, retreating into himself. If she were wise, she would leave this subject alone.

She was not wise. "She tried to kill you."

"More than once," he agreed stiffly.

"Your father fed from her for years before she became pregnant. He blocked those feedings from her mind."

"She never would have accepted it, as she proved once the truth finally became known."

"He broke her," Elizabeth pronounced gravely. "Her mind was too strong. All those lies he fed her about herself, about him, about their world…it was too much."

"I hardly think you can pass judgment upon people whom you have never met. My mother was never strong."

Elizabeth snorted. "She was the daughter of royalty. Her brother

Richard is still referred to as 'the colonel' generations after leaving the military. I am in love with her son, who is the strongest man I know. Do not tell me what she was. You did not know her until she was irreversibly broken."

"You cast my father as a brute, then."

"Of course not. He obviously did not realise the harm. But think —he would have fed from her hundreds of times. Covered up all sorts of mysterious happenings in her presence. They were only tiny moments, fleeting, simple actions and easily hidden—not huge, distressing lies he believed would be injurious. And he told her at once when he knew her to be with child, because he knew trying to hide it after that would be dangerous. But all those little secrets, caged in her mind, struggling to break free," she said softly. "It broke her, instead. 'Tis the *only* explanation. Otherwise, she would have loved you."

It was so *Elizabeth* to find a way to salvage his mother's heart and conclude he was lovable, despite his plethora of enemies and a life evidencing the opposite.

"I believe we should bring Charlotte to him, so she can nurse him in truth until the end," Elizabeth said quietly. She gently touched her cousin's wrecked face. "Do you think your blood could repair him enough for her to see him again?"

"Very likely," he said. Elizabeth was strong—still awake, though it was past dawn, and fighting her fatigue through sheer willpower—and while it was his duty to protect her, he would not repeat the mistakes of his father, treating her as though she were not. "And so could yours."

In the end, they did it together.

After the doctor relayed the terrible news, Darcy brought Mrs Collins directly to her husband's bedside. A tear trickled down her cheek as she took his cold hand. "Is he...has he..."

Darcy did not blame her for wondering; Collins's breaths were so faint as to be almost unnoticeable. "No, madam, he is still with us. But not, I think, for long. I am sorry."

Charlotte nodded, and Elizabeth went to her, putting her arm around her friend and holding her close. She laid her head against Elizabeth's shoulder briefly before straightening.

"I would like to sit with him...until the end."

"Of course," Elizabeth answered. "May we bring you anything, dear?"

"No, nothing. I can see you have not slept, my friend." Charlotte pasted a brave smile upon her face and turned to Darcy. "You must force her to rest, sir. She is too kind for her own good."

"I do not want to leave you alone," Elizabeth protested.

Charlotte put her hand out. "I would prefer it. To say my farewells."

Elizabeth clasped her hand in return. "Someone will be just beyond the door if you need anything."

With one last troubled look, Elizabeth turned and left the room. Darcy followed, but paused by the door. "Mrs Collins," he said gently.

"Yes?"

"Please remember—we leave you to your vigil for now but shall never abandon you. We are, and always shall be, your friends."

Her smile, though brief, was genuine. He shut the door softly behind him.

❧

"Hallo, George. I ought to have guessed."

"I almost thought you had, and that you would not come at all or you would bring Darcy," Wickham grinned.

"No. Darcy is at luxurious Pemberley Castle with his delicious little wife, while we suffer in a miserable cave, my boy," he said mildly. Matlock had the satisfaction of feeling Wickham's tension increase in the grip of his fingers.

"Do not let him twist you in knots," Catherine ordered. "Kill him now, fool, and kill him quickly, and then we shall take on the Darcys."

Matlock shook his head sadly. "Do you truly choose an alliance with Catherine over me, George? What does she offer you? She is as good as dead the moment she steps from this cave. Her actions have put her in opposition to the Council. Her head has a price on it."

"No!" Catherine screamed. "He lies! Every word he utters is a lie!"

"Mrs Darcy is pregnant. If it is a girl, I shall give it to you. Follow the real power, George. You have always understood who holds it." Matlock's charm, his true, terrifying ability, oozed.

Catherine shrieked her opposition. "He lies. Elizabeth Bennet is a vampyre and barren. Do not be taken in by that trull's deceit—or his!"

"Catherine could witness the birth and would still deny it. I have the truth directly from Agnes Reynolds. Just think, George—you could *own* Darcy's daughter."

"I could own her whether you live or not," Wickham snarled.

"How? Darcy thinks me his best friend, almost his Papa. I can stroll right into Pemberley at any time, while Darcy would kill Catherine on sight, even if she could get within a mile of him."

"What I cannot understand," George sneered, "is why, if he is no friend of yours, he yet lives?"

Catherine was cursing, attempting her mental attacks, but Matlock was as strong as she and could repel them while countering with his own. George could not have withstood them both, had they united forces, despite the hour. But Matlock was finished with her, and only replied, "Because I want to take the wife—and her child—alive. If she can breed pureblood vampyres, she is priceless. Killing Darcy without repercussion requires patience, which you lack. Fortunately, I have enough for us both, and Catherine has provided a lovely fortress for you here, only forty miles from Pemberley."

Wickham looked straight into Matlock's eyes, distrustful. "What if 'tis a boy?"

"Then we shall breed the lad 'til you get a girl off him. Darcy's fastidious soul will writhe in eternal torment if you own his progeny."

Wickham grinned again. "Fair enough," he agreed, freeing his captive. Matlock straightened his waistcoat.

"No!" Catherine screamed as she attempted to flee.

Wickham caught her immediately.

"Hold her for me, my good man," Matlock requested. "I am not at my best at the moment."

"Yes, sir," George replied cheerfully as Catherine's attacks pummelled them both.

Matlock withdrew the dagger from his boot. "This is what I used to kill your *Rosomakha*, Catherine," he said nonchalantly. "Silver bladed." He thrust it under her left breast, digging in, shredding whatever lay beneath as she frantically struggled against Wickham's impervious hold. He left the dagger where it was and drew his sword. George jumped away as, grasping the sword two-handed, Matlock swung it with all his might. Her head flew off, rolling lopsidedly until it hit the cavern wall, dirt from the floor collecting in her untamed hair, the flaring nostrils, and the open mouth. "Curse you," the thing hissed, before the eyes rolled back to solid whites and its tongue was stilled forever.

"Lovely knowing you, too," Matlock laughed, wiping his blade on Catherine's skirt. "My dear."

Forty

When Elizabeth wakened, Darcy was not beside her. This was unusual enough for her to feel a stirring of something like anxiety. Maggie must have been watching for her to rouse, though, because her soft voice greeted her quickly.

"I have your bath ready, ma'am," she said.

"Mr Collins? Has he—" she began.

"A few hours ago. Mrs Collins accepted a draught from Mrs Reynolds and is sleeping now."

Elizabeth sighed sadly. It was what she expected, but it pained her to know her friend faced widowhood because of Catherine de Bourgh's hatred of Elizabeth.

"Where is my husband?"

"Lord Matlock arrived shortly after Mr Collins died—after battling that despicable de Bourgh, he was grievously injured. The Master has been seeing to his care."

"Ah," Elizabeth said, revealing nothing but cringing inwardly.

She dressed carefully. Whereas before she had worn her oldest gown, now she chose one much more elaborate. *Perhaps*, she thought, *my sour responses to the man are based upon my own lack of confidence. Nerves, to a vampyric degree.* The idea was repellent. Determined to show nothing but strength and graciousness, she sought out her husband.

The sound of laughter carried beyond his open study doors; she entered to find Fitzwilliam, a glass of whiskey in his hand, toasting Matlock. Elizabeth raised a brow and forced herself to address the man.

"Good evening, my lord. I am glad to see you are recovered from your experiences," she said evenly, almost choking on the words.

"Darling," Darcy said, walking to his wife, "Lord Matlock brings us the best of news. Catherine de Bourgh is dead."

Elizabeth tried to smile, but Matlock's presence cast a pall over her ability to feel relief. Self-lectures were useless; revulsion, worse than ever before, nearly overwhelmed her from the moment she heard the man's laughter. Was she broken inside somehow, lacking in proper spirit? *No!*

"Elizabeth? Are not you pleased, my love?"

With a start, she realised her internal struggle had lasted a bit too long. "Oh...simply astonished, yes. Are we sure it is true?"

"I killed her myself," Matlock announced with relish. "I brought your husband her head. I would mount it on your front gate, by Jove, except I must take it to the Council."

Listening to his voice made her feel ill, but she tried to pretend nothing was the matter. "I am sure the neighbourhood is grateful," she said faintly.

"I am sorry, my love. You need to Take, do you not?" Darcy asked, his jubilance at de Bourgh's death diminishing as he noted her pale features.

"I...I think I would prefer to wait," she said, far too nauseated to think of feeding. She briefly turned to Matlock, looking at a spot just to the left of his shoulder rather than face him directly and cast up her accounts upon his Hessians. "Thank you, my lord, for your dispatch of our enemy. Excuse me, please." She dropped a curtsey and left the room swiftly.

Darcy made a move to follow her, but Matlock put an arm out to stop him. "One minute, Darcy. I must speak with you."

"Of course. I will not be long. I—"

"I cannot stay long. I must get that head to London before the flesh rots. Please, a moment of your time."

Darcy suppressed a sigh; he was accustomed to the other man's imperious attitude, attributing it to his strong sense of purpose. At any rate, Matlock was owed a great deal; the wounds he sustained in battle with Darcy's enemy had been vicious and, while not life-threatening, were a painful testament to his suffering on Darcy's behalf. Offending him after such valour was unacceptable; he could look after Elizabeth momentarily.

"Yes, very well," he replied, moving back to the hearth.

Matlock began to pace, his hands behind his back. "It was a near thing, Darcy," he began. "Catherine ambushed me on the road outside Matlock. I did not expect a direct attack, but she had assembled a small yet lethal force. It was quite out of character for her—and I expect she was influenced by someone else."

"You mean Wickham? Were his creatures involved?"

"Only a few and slaughtered quickly. But as you know, I have long suspected de Bourgh of abetting Wickham's escape, and now I believe she has been in league with him all along. Had he joined her at Matlock...well, the night might have ended differently—especially at dawn. I do not care to think of how close the battle was. Fortunately, I was able to outwit her in the end, but Wickham is still out there. He will not surrender."

"Neither shall I. I have men seeking him. I shall be diligent." His eyes glowed black as he considered hunting his enemy.

"This situation with Mrs Darcy...it makes everything more dangerous than ever."

"Situation? If you mean her impending motherhood, I do not see how. I will not allow anyone to hurt my family. I am capable of protecting them."

Matlock gave an impatient wave. "You have increased the number of your vulnerabilities. Between you and Wickham, there is no contest, of course. And you are well able to protect a wife, as you have proven. Now a child is coming, though. Can you keep a child as close to you as a wife? No doubt you will try...but children grow up and have a tendency to wish for lives of their own. Then what, my friend?" he asked, assuming a patriarchal expression.

Darcy shrugged, unable to think beyond his child's fluttering heartbeat.

"George Wickham understands one thing—power. He resents yours. He fears mine. If this child is a girl, betroth her to me. Let him, and the rest of the world for that matter, understand the forces arrayed on her behalf."

"My lord!" Darcy nearly shouted. "The babe is not even born! It is premature to speak of betrothals."

"It is not. It is vital for your enemies to know we are inextricably allied. I can protect her as few others can."

Darcy shook his head, bemused. He and Elizabeth had yet to decide upon names, and already there were wedding plans? Still, Matlock had a point—if the babe were a girl, she would need a powerful husband. Someday.

"Perhaps we can delay this conversation at least until the child is born," he replied at last. "If it is a boy, the discussion is pointless."

"If it is a boy, I would like to keep him at least part of the time at Matlock."

"I do not know—"

"The tradition of fostering has, sadly, faded—but do you regret your time spent in my household?"

"I am most likely alive today because of it," Darcy replied meaningfully. "But my home is a different one. For one thing, Elizabeth is unlikely to attempt the murder of our child."

"Praise saints for that. However, my powers have grown since you were a lad, Fitzwilliam. I can teach your son more than I was able to pass along to you. I can help him grow strong."

"You have always been strong, and the lessons I learned from you in my youth are priceless. But forgive me if I also believe that there is much to be gained from his father and mother."

Matlock smiled. "Of course. Yet, we both know there will come a time when a young man will listen to others more willingly than his own parents. I mean no insult, of course. I think only of the child's prospects." As this was true, his emotions were full of genuine earnestness. "I know you think me precipitate. Please, think about what I offer. Let us plan for the safest possible future, boy or girl. Your father would have expected this of me. I was his dearest friend and—as I hope I have proven—am yours, as well."

Elizabeth was his dearest friend, of course. But this man, who had defeated de Bourgh on his behalf, was a valiant and true comrade. Darcy would be forever grateful. "I am honoured to call you friend," he replied. "Rest assured, your offer will be deemed of utmost import in discussions regarding our child's future."

"I am sure that, upon reflection, you will come to the same conclusions as I about what is best," Matlock said.

Darcy put his hand on the older man's shoulder. "I would like to see you find happiness as I have," he said. "A loving marriage is a priceless gift. It is what I hope for my child, as well."

"I can safely promise," Matlock replied, "that any child of yours would mean *everything* to me."

Darcy discovered his wife returned to her chambers. To his distress, she had obviously been very ill—having not quite made it to her chamber pot before casting up her accounts.

"Elizabeth! We must have a doctor!"

"No!" Elizabeth managed. "I will be better soon. Please, leave me. Please."

"Let me help you to the bed," he said, already contemplating the express he would send to Bingley, instituting a search for *some* kind of appropriate physician to Pemberley. He lifted her in his arms despite her protests, carrying her to his bed and summoning Maggie to come clean the mess in her room.

He laid her tenderly upon the pillows, puzzled when she clambered to the furthest side of the bed. She looked pale and sweaty, and seemed to cringe when he brought her a cup of cold water with which to rinse her mouth.

"Elizabeth," he begged, "let me care for you."

"No...no...it is only...if you could..." Her voice faded as she buried her face in his pillow.

"If I could what? Name it, and it shall be done."

"If you could wash. 'Tis the blood and stench of Matlock on you. It makes me ill. *He* makes me ill!"

He took a step forward, only stopping when she began swallowing convulsively. Deciding now was no time to argue, he instead strode into his dressing room, ripping off his coats and mentally bellowing for Chamberlayne. His valet saw him hastily washed and changed so that he could return to his wife.

He found Elizabeth curled into a little ball, huddled among his pillows. She looked pale and smaller somehow in the vast acreage of the massive bed. He held out his arms. "Love," he said, when she rolled towards him instead of away, relieved that she no longer rejected his presence, though she still showed signs of agitation. "My dearest love," he murmured.

He held her for long moments, rubbing soothing circles along her back. When he felt her relax and her heartbeat return to normal, he offered her his throat. Darcy's anxiety eased markedly as she Took, as he felt her calm in his arms.

"All better now?" he asked after she had taken her fill.

"Yes," she sighed, hesitating a little before saying, "Many women have physical responses to certain foods and scents while carrying a child. Lady Lucas would not allow coffee in her house during any of her confinements."

"And you believe that Lord Matlock is like...coffee?" he asked, unable to keep the note of incredulity out of his voice.

"Perhaps he wears scent...some ingredient in it," she suggested.

"No. I would smell it if he did."

"I do not know why, then. But he was the source of my illness."

"That seems remarkable," he said, brows furrowed.

"It was not my imagination. As soon as I entered your study, I felt sickened. And then you brought him in here with you, on your clothing. I am not stupid. I know cause and effect."

"We need to find a doctor. I will have Bingley search for one."

"There is nothing wrong with me. I am well now. If, however, you wish to have a doctor in, I have no objections. How long will Lord Matlock remain?"

"He is already on his way to London with our statements. But Elizabeth, your illness—"

"Thank heavens. I know we owe Matlock a debt of gratitude...but I hope he stays away, at least until the babe comes."

Darcy decided that any discussion regarding betrothals could wait, and he would write to Bingley immediately about the need for a physician.

Another person rejoiced at the news of the death of Catherine de Bourgh: Charlotte Collins, who found herself suddenly free to return to Lucas Lodge. The papers published de Bourgh's cause of death as a melancholic fever and, after Darcy related the additional news of a tidy inheritance—which, in her pragmatic way, she did not question—she was on her way home.

Richard Fitzwilliam returned to Pemberley a week later, bringing

Dr Heberden, a Descartes vampyre, with him. Like many in that House, Heberden was obsessed with scientific studies. His research on the sorts of humans best surviving the Turning made him more knowledgeable than most as to vampyre physiology. He was a short, fierce-looking man who constantly muttered to himself.

Dr Heberden gave as his opinion that Elizabeth would deliver in early June. Fascinated by the child's pure vampyre origins, he asked endless questions regarding everything she had ingested since her Turning, as well as minutiae Darcy considered ridiculous—including how tightly she laced her corsets—while casting a beady eye and measuring glance upon Darcy's person. Darcy responded with a glare that should have incinerated the man but made no impression whatsoever. Richard had the nerve to laugh.

"Let it go, Darcy. The good doctor is impervious to anything less cutting than a sword through the heart when it comes to his scientific inquiries."

"His scientific inquiries can go to the devil. He is here to look after Elizabeth's health, and that is all."

"Good luck with that. I offer you my congratulations, Nephew. I was astonished when I received your letter. How is Elizabeth?"

"Do you truly care, Richard?" Darcy snapped, and left the room.

Darcy's response stung. Richard knew he had not done well by Elizabeth, always judging her with a prejudiced eye. Perhaps, too, he had been resentful of the loss of closeness wrought by his own actions and Darcy's marriage.

Every time he found himself liking her, he'd found new reasons to lash out again. He had been a sapscull.

Discovering her unexpectedly alone in the library that evening, he listened to his conscience at last.

"Mrs Darcy, how do you fare?" he asked.

Surprise and wariness flickered across her features, and his guilt bit deeper.

"I am well," she replied quietly.

"Colonel and Mrs Forster seemed in good spirits when I left them. I believe all is smoothed over," he began.

"I had every confidence in you."

There was an awkward pause. "That is the trouble," he said at last. "My confidence in *you* has been...lacking."

"I expect nothing, Colonel," she returned, "except your faith in, and loyalty to, my husband."

"I express myself badly," he replied. "I wish to apologise."

Her guarded look spoke volumes. "I accept your apology. Truly, 'tis unimportant what you think of me."

"It *is* important." He began to pace, frustrated by his inability to find words to fix the situation. "You have heard about my sister, I believe."

"Yes," she said cautiously.

"When Darcy was born, I knew something was wrong," he said. "Wrong with my sister, Anne. At my first visit after the birth, I discovered she hated the husband she once adored, the home she once loved, and most of all, the baby she had wished for so desperately. But I looked the other way, allowing George to soothe or soothsay me. I returned to my military duties, but I was not easy in my mind." He paced agitatedly.

"One day, I arrived at Pemberley unexpectedly, only to see a speeding four-poster, the driver lashing her cattle to urge them faster. A child lay bound on the drive, and the coach ran him over, crushing him." He met Elizabeth's gaze in remembered horror. "My sister drove the coach. It was not her first attempt to kill Fitzwilliam, nor her last."

"How...how did he survive?" she gasped.

"Vampyres are difficult to kill, and she did not have the necessary knowledge. But she hurt him, again and again."

"Why did his father allow her near him?" she asked angrily.

Richard sighed. "George was not rational about Anne. Bonded. He *had* to be with her but wanted Fitzwilliam, too. He continued hoping for reconciliation and felt a few wounds would only toughen his son." He shook his head, remembering.

"George confessed the truth. I sold my commission and moved in permanently. I kept Anne away from Fitzwilliam, taking my rest on the floor by his cot until the day she died. But his troubles were not past. Shortly thereafter, Wickham came to Pemberley—as eldest, he was George's heir. I made George Turn me, then." He laughed humourlessly. "Wickham specialised in sly, subtle torment. It was years before Fitzwilliam was safe in his own home."

He glanced at her, expecting to see disgust for Darcy's parents. Heaven knew he had felt it often enough.

Surprisingly, her eyes held the shimmering weight of tears. "Thank you," she said. "Oh, thank God for you, Richard Fitzwilliam."

"I did not tell you this to earn your gratitude," he said gruffly. "I only wished to explain...I have been protective of Darcy for centuries now. Old habits die hard."

"We would both die for him," she replied. "I hope that—"

"What do you hope?"

"His child will have your unwavering protection as well."

"His child," Richard replied, "*and* his wife. On what remains of my honour."

"I will hold you to that," she replied smilingly. He had never before noticed how sweet her smile.

Something inside him eased at last.

Forty One

THE MONTHS PASSED QUICKLY, A COLD WINTER NEARLY defeating a freezing spring. Darcy's baby grew large in his wife's belly, almost overnight requiring her to summon seamstresses for a new wardrobe. His men found clues in the lead and silver mines of Critch that they sent along to Matlock, who asserted to Darcy that he was getting close. For her protection, Darcy moved with Elizabeth into Pemberley's high eastern turret, staying near, keeping his family safe.

And in early June, an inner instinct wakened him so abruptly he sat straight up in bed. It was only a vague flicker of pain? dread? and now gone. But his beast strained within, and it had only one centre.

Elizabeth!

She lay on her side, facing away from him, much further away than when he had fallen asleep. Rising, he circled round to her side of the bed. "Love," he asked, "Are you well?"

One look at her, though, rendered his question foolish; her mouth stretched in a grimace, sweat beading upon her brow, and her heart beat rapidly in response to suffocating pain. He called instantly for Mrs Reynolds to summon the doctor.

"I...I think...'tis the babe," she gasped. "Hurts."

When the doctor arrived at last, Darcy's beast had already gained too much control of the rational man. Fortunately, Mrs Reynolds thought to call the colonel as well, who dragged Darcy out of the room while Mrs Darcy was examined.

"Come man, you must leave her," Richard said, pulling on his recalcitrant nephew's arm. "Mrs Reynolds will stay, but you must go."

Frustrated and distraught, he barely allowed his uncle to extricate him. There was no room for him to pace on the tiny landing outside the chamber door, so he made do with marching up and down the stairs, brushing off any attempts by his uncle to lure him to his study. Just when he felt he could stand it no longer, the door opened to reveal his housekeeper. Before she could speak, he dashed up the stairs and pushed past her into the room. Mrs Reynolds began a protest, but just as quickly realised it to be futile.

"The babe has dropped, but her body has not accommodated it as yet," Dr Heberden announced, unconcerned with Darcy's presence.

"How long until it does?" Darcy asked.

The doctor shrugged. "It depends. Every female is different. No way to tell."

Useless physician! Darcy thought. When he had asked Heberden about Elizabeth's bilious response to Lord Matlock, the doctor had only said, 'Keep her from people who make her ill.' At least Heberden displayed no particular anxiety now—Darcy would know.

His gift told him the moment the doctor's concern began growing. Heberden must have surmised the bright June sunshine inhibited her body's ability to accommodate the birth. But when full dark had fallen, he felt Heberden's sudden rush of frustration before the doctor quickly cloaked his emotions. And Darcy knew something was very wrong.

"Tell me the truth," he said lowly. "How does she fare?"

Elizabeth, facing a pain which never, ever abated, gripped his hand in a clasp that would certainly have broken the bones of another.

"Her body...it does not...open," Dr Heberden explained, gesturing with his hands. "It is still the same as it was from the first. The babe tries to come out but is not strong enough to rip its way through."

"What is to be done?" Darcy demanded, horrified.

"The child must come out," the doctor said flatly. "I suggest Mrs

Darcy be cut open, and the child removed. Her body would heal from that."

Darcy contemplated this for only moments. It would likely be painful, but no more painful than whatever was happening now. And most importantly, it would be over. At this moment, he scarcely cared about the fate of the babe—he only needed to end his wife's suffering. Quickly. "Very well. Do it."

"Pah!" Dr Heberden exclaimed. "I am no ha'penny surgeon! I suggest you call one!"

Darcy's eyes narrowed, blackened. "Are you refusing to assist my wife?" And then his eyes flashed red.

Dr Heberden had at least some instinct for self-preservation. "Ah...no...not refusing, but I have never done such a thing. It would be better to bring in someone who has."

"Never, Heberden?" Darcy said darkly, sensing the lie.

"Only corpses, sir!" Heberden corrected.

Worthless, worthless! Want to toss him from the rooftop and watch his bones shatter upon the stones below! Barely, Darcy kept his grip upon his own reason. "Mrs Reynolds, bring the sharpest knives we have," he said. She had already brought in clean towels and hot water. "And more towels," he added.

"At once, sir," she said rushing from the room, returning only seconds later.

Elizabeth lay unmoving now, moaning with the unending pain.

"Where should the incision be—exactly?" Darcy demanded.

Carefully, the doctor lifted her gown, flushing beneath the stare of a half-mad Master vampyre. Hesitantly, he traced a line across Elizabeth's abdomen. "I have seen it done once, along here," he said. "The female did not live...but of course, she was mortal and weak."

"This is what we shall do," Darcy stated. "I will infuse my wife with my venom. Then you, Doctor, will cut the cleanest, steadiest, least painful incision of your career, if you wish to survive beyond this hour."

The doctor drew himself up, his pride reasserting itself. "More incisions than one. The babe is inside the womb, enclosed in a birth sac, and must be freed. And then there is the birthing cord, of course."

Darcy did not even bother replying. Crooning softly to Elizabeth, he spoke to her until he was sure he had her attention, gently telling her what they meant to do. She nodded to show she understood, unable to formulate words. Tenderly he bent to her taut belly and extended his fangs to pierce the skin. He made repeated punctures, imbuing the area with his venom until he was sure it permeated throughout. Then he made a motion to the doctor, and stood back, retaking his wife's hand.

Elizabeth grit her teeth but made no other show of pain as blood spurted across her abdomen, pooling on the towels beneath her. But her eyes closed when the doctor sliced yet again—and she broke Darcy's hand with the sudden surge of agony. He made not a sound, giving her no sign, glad, even, to bear some little wound. *I did this to her*, he thought.

Then a weight was lifted from her, and they both froze.

Dr Heberden held a bloody, dark-haired infant in his bare hands, looking about as if he did not know quite what to do with it.

"Give...my babe...to me," Elizabeth managed, holding out shaking arms.

Darcy nodded once, and the doctor handed it over.

"'Tis a girl, my love," he murmured. "A sweet baby girl."

She nodded, tears trickling down her cheek.

"The babe," Darcy reminded the doctor, who was studying the placenta with obsessive curiosity. "Should not it move? Cry?"

"Heaven only knows what that child will do," the doctor said, his interest in the babe resuming. "Vampyres do not have the weakness of lung which mortal children exhibit, and its heartbeat is strong. It is as likely to live as any, I would say. Though if it turns out to be mad, my advice is to kill it while 'tis still small. The thing could be wickedly powerful." He shrugged.

"Get out," Darcy spat.

"I wish a bath and a meal," Dr Heberden announced, as though his life were not in danger of ending within seconds. "I have done enough this night." He departed, muttering to himself of arrogant Masters and his bruised dignity.

"Good riddance. You need blood, love" Darcy said, bending over Elizabeth, baring his neck to her. "Please," he said, "Take."

She did not argue. Her wounds were already healing, merely an angry red seam crossing her abdomen that would likely be gone by morning.

Elizabeth withdrew her bite, her gaze once again returned to the child who lay so still in her arms.

"Her little heart beats steadily," Darcy reassured, and Elizabeth pressed a kiss to the tiny head.

"Would you let me bathe the wee lass?" the housekeeper asked, interrupting the tender scene.

Reluctantly, Elizabeth handed the babe over to Mrs Reynolds's capable hands. Maggie and Mrs Reynolds had both vowed to help with care of the infant. Wickham must be captured before bringing another into their tight-knit household.

"I will bring our little beauty right back to you, Mrs Darcy," she said, correctly interpreting Elizabeth's anxious gaze as she left the room. "Fret not."

Darcy would allow no one else to touch his wife, tenderly wiping the blood from her skin. He exchanged her ruined gown for the clean one Maggie provided, gently lifting her in his arms to sit with her near the fireplace as the diligent maid efficiently changed the bedclothes and brought new mattresses. It did not take long, but Elizabeth cast longing glances at the door, anxious, before she was half done. Finally, Darcy laid her back on the fresh sheets—just as Mrs Reynolds returned with the infant swaddled in soft linens, wearing a gown stitched by her mother's hand.

Elizabeth reached for the babe, whose eyes remained closed. "Please," she whispered.

Darcy watched as his wife—rather painfully—sat up against the pillows, wishing she would rest and let others care for the babe until she healed from heaven only knew what damages. And yet, he also knew his tender-hearted Elizabeth could not rest until she was assured of the well-being of their child.

Their child! She looked so doll-like—he could scarcely believe she was real, except for the sound of her rapidly beating heart. Elizabeth placed her gently over her shoulder, carefully rubbing the girl's small back. The sight of them both filled his heart to overflowing, a perfect picture of mother's love. Unable to resist, he reached out to cover Elizabeth's hand with his own—still healing—much larger one, marvelling at the babe's exquisite features. Softly, he skimmed the downy, dark curls covering her little head.

Abruptly the babe raised her head off her mother's shoulder and looked up alertly, gazing right into his eyes. Maggie and Mrs

Reynolds each stifled a gasp of surprise. As he stared into the tiny, sweet face, into dark eyes perfectly matching her mother's, Darcy fell in love for the second time in his life.

"My beautiful baby girl," he said softly. "We shall call you Georgiana, as your mother wishes, for the courage, strength, and devotion of your grandfather. He would have loved you so, as I do already."

Georgiana peered back at him and smiled—as if she understood his every word and approved.

Then, as if Georgiana wished to include her mother in this important family moment, she nestled into Elizabeth's neck. Tiny fangs nuzzled against the skin of her throat, as Georgiana Took for the very first time with a soft new-born sigh of contentment.

Elizabeth's joyful eyes met Darcy's.

This is our love, given flesh, he thought—and for the first time, felt her emotions as if they were joined.

"Is her the pwettiest girl?" Darcy heard his stern, impassive uncle murmuring in a high falsetto. "Is her the sweetest wittle girl in the world?"

He entered the library to see Richard holding Georgiana so she could stand on her already-sturdy baby legs and bounce. His uncle greeted him with a nod and his next words took Darcy somewhat by surprise. "Does she ever feed from you?" he asked.

"No, never. When she is hungry, she always wants her mama—though at times I wish she would, just because I think it a marvellous thing. After all—"

He broke off, slightly embarrassed, preparing to be teased mercilessly by his uncle. But Richard surprised him again.

"How often does she Take?"

"Once or twice per day, sometimes thrice. But frankly, we think she only needs once—Elizabeth says the other times, she hardly Takes. We believe she does it for comfort."

"Remarkable," Richard replied, as though it were the most natural thing in the world for him to be discuss the feeding habits of an infant.

"I must say, Richard, your interest astonishes me. You have never been much for children."

Richard looked slightly hurt. "I say, Darcy, I was interested in you."

Darcy looked chagrined. "So you were. I apologise, Uncle. And I will always be grateful."

Richard laughed, and Georgiana joined him, sure somehow his smiles were all for her. He gave her extra bounces to show her she was correct. "Truly, I only tease. Even in your youth, you were never allowed to be a child, and I am sorry for it. No, something about our little princess makes one feel...light of heart. I find myself believing I have been off the mark, dodging all commitment. I envy you your family."

This was such a deviation from his uncle's normal cynicism, Darcy found himself speechless. But further conversation was made impossible by Morton's announcement.

"Mr Darcy, Lord Matlock is here. Are you at home?"

Matlock peered from one to the other of the two men, one with severe military bearing incongruously holding a dainty, lace-beruffled baby. His first thought was to wonder what kind of lax household allowed infants littering the library. His second, though, quickly shoved the first emotion away as he indulged his curiosity regarding the Darcy child.

His hands clasped behind his back, he gazed down at the chubby infant. "Well, well, Darcy. She is a beauty, just like her mother. I hastened here as soon as I received the news, to pay my respects."

"Thank you, sir."

"How does Mrs Darcy fare?"

"Very well. She is quite recovered."

"Excellent." Matlock concealed a covetous surge at the sight of the babe, who stared at him with a strangely serious expression, and managed to twist his escaping emotion into something resembling pride and delight. Darcy avoided scrutinising him and his emotions regardless, a neglect Matlock encouraged over the centuries. Tentatively, he reached out a graceful hand to touch the child.

Georgiana buried her face in her uncle's neck.

"She is not usually so shy," her father said apologetically.

She began to whimper. Darcy automatically reached his arms out for her, but Richard said, "I believe she wants her mama. I will take her to Mrs Darcy." He stood. "If you will excuse me, my lord." Not waiting for acknowledgement, he strode from the room.

Matlock watched him go, suppressing his annoyance. He had always found the colonel impertinent, refusing to acknowledge any authority unless it carried the Darcy name. Once he gained control of the Darcy House, he would teach the upstart a lesson in humility. Or perhaps simply destroy him.

"I brought something for her," Matlock said, putting the other man from his mind, and handing Darcy a flat, heavy case.

Darcy accepted it with a smile, but his brows rose when he opened it to see the sapphire collar glistening upon the black velvet. As he moved it into the light, the colours of the sapphire changed from blue to deep purple. "This...this is extraordinary, sir. These stones are rare indeed. We thank you."

Matlock smiled a bit ruefully. "I know you well, Darcy. You are wondering at such an offering. I obtained it in Zanzibar many years ago, and not without a cost in bloodshed. And yet, as rare as are these gems, your daughter is far more rare and precious." As he spoke, he allowed his wonder in the child's uniqueness to saturate his words. "How I wish George had lived to see his priceless granddaughter!" His sorrow over losing his best friend leaked into the conversation—though none of his guilt, of course.

Darcy swallowed. "I am honoured by this gift."

"When I received your express with news of the birth, I wept, Darcy. Hope such as I have not felt in years—centuries—filled me. And dread...I will admit to that as well. De Medicis, the Drăculeas, the Heraclians, egad, every line with representation in the Council will view Georgiana as a threat—and Mrs Darcy with her. If she could breed once, she might be able to do so again."

Darcy frowned. "I will protect my wife and child."

Matlock nodded sympathetically. "Undoubtedly. And I will assist. However, I must remind you of my earlier offer." Summoning every ounce of sham sincerity he possessed, he laid a hand upon Darcy's shoulder. "I would like you to consider this necklace a betrothal gift. A formal alliance, Darcy, betwixt your line and mine. It will send a message to every House of the unbreakable bond uniting Matlock and Darcy. All know *we* broke House de Bourgh! None will want such formidable enemies."

"My daughter is only weeks old. I am not prepared to consider her as some sort of diplomatic prize. It is far too soon to speak of this, my lord."

"I speak of her safety! I speak of her very life!" Matlock replied, with all the urgency of his desire. "'Tis never too soon to take precautions. Tell me you will at least agree to an informal betrothal. We need not do more for now."

Darcy appeared uncomfortable. "I do not believe Elizabeth would be amenable," he said at last. "She would not want her daughter's hand forced in any way."

Matlock used all of his considerable discipline to beat back his impatience. Who cared what Mrs Darcy thought? It was up to *Darcy* to arrange the vital matters of his family life to the best possible advantage. Yet, it seemed he would have to win Mrs Darcy over as well; plainly, it had not been made clear enough to her how much they owed Lord Matlock. Yet, remembering her response to him during her Change, he did not think it wise to spend too much time in her company.

"I believe I can convince Mrs Darcy, if you will allow it," Matlock said gravely.

Darcy's expression was dubious. "I do not believe that to be possible."

"I will prove to her, beyond any shadow of doubt, that I will safeguard her daughter. I shall bring her the head of her enemy and shall not return to Pemberley without it. Only promise you will do me the honour of presenting my offer in a favourable light."

"Please, do not take heedless risk. Do not attempt to bring in Wickham alone. You are under no obligation, and I cannot promise it will make any difference to your suit."

"You doubt me, Darcy? If I cannot take one man, what use am I in protecting your loved ones against the other houses? Need I remind you that I slew Catherine de Bourgh without any army of yours?" He let his affront and wounded pride out in full force, beating mercilessly upon Darcy's gift with powerful, unscrupulous shame.

"I have long felt that others on the Council shield him. I do not believe you stand against only one man," Darcy argued, looking wretchedly uncomfortable.

"All the better to prove I am a worthwhile consort. Contrary to what you obviously believe, I am ready. He has assembled a new army of creatures, and I will remove his threat, once and for all. I do not require your assistance, only your faith in my ability to rid the world of insidious evil. I trust you will explain this to Mrs Darcy?"

Darcy's half-hearted reluctance—and a lifetime of deference—could not stand against the other man's violently offended dignity.

"I will speak with her," Darcy promised solemnly, fingering the cold beauty of the gemstones he still held, "and encourage Mrs Darcy's willingness to consider the idea."

Forty Two

Darcy did not immediately speak to Elizabeth regarding Matlock's betrothal request. He would think carefully on his approach, choosing his timing prudently. He locked the necklace in one of his vaults and deliberated privately upon the idea of an informal alliance.

But fatherhood itself was his life's brightest jewel, and, to his immense pleasure, his daughter coveted his devotion. Just beyond his study, he could hear Elizabeth saying, "Papa might be very busy now. You must not be disappointed if he cannot stop his important work in order to play."

"I can spare a few moments," he said, smiling at the pair as they entered his study.

"I am sure you cannot," Elizabeth smiled back. "But the word 'no' seems to have disappeared from your vocabulary."

He threw her a heated glance. "'Yes' is a much more pleasant, fulfilling response, I think," he said, lifting Georgiana. She threw her little arms up, and he tossed her high in the air while she shrieked excitedly and made childish signs indicating he should do it again. And again, nearly to the high ceiling.

"You should trust me as Georgiana does," he said, grinning at his wife's apprehensive expression.

"Speaking of trust," she replied, "do you notice Richard has become Maggie's shadow? I am unsure how I feel about the situation."

"They are both adults, Elizabeth," he reminded, "and older than you by a bit." He could not, however, say she had no cause for concern—he felt Richard's new passion for Maggie, though his uncle did his best to cloak it.

"I know...but...Maggie... I would hate it if he hurt her, if she felt she had to leave..."

"She will never leave," Darcy said firmly. "Her loyalty to us is fixed. But perhaps I will have a word with Richard. If it is simply gallantry on his part, I shall advise him to look elsewhere."

"Thank you," she said, reaching for Georgiana. "I will take her to the nursery now—I can see she is tiring."

"I shall accompany you," he said, keeping the babe on his shoulder.

"You need not. I know you are busy."

"Elizabeth," he said softly, pressing a kiss to Georgiana's soft curls. "This is my favourite time, these moments with my girls just before dawn."

He carried the drowsy baby upstairs, then watched as his wife snuggled her tightly. Georgiana fed from her mother's vein and then she held out her tiny arms to her papa.

Darcy sang to her—ballads, lullabies, made-up nonsense songs—while her mama watched them from her chair. The nursery was a quiet, peaceful haven such as he had never known.

As he laid the sleeping Georgiana in her cradle, a potent burst of love nearly overwhelmed him. She was such a little darling, with her chubby pink cheeks and dark curls, and Matlock's words rang in his mind with something like horror. He would do anything to keep her safe; the thought of her as a target for cruelty and power was unbearable. Even the normal customs of their society would leave her a potential object of the fortune and power hunters of the vampyre world. He thought of Catherine de Bourgh, who had been both beautiful and born of a similar heritage to Georgiana's; her life had only brought misery—to herself as well as those surrounding her. He would not leave his precious daughter to such a fate. Matlock would protect her, guide her, honour her. She would be *safe*.

Resolute, he summoned Maggie to Georgiana's side, putting out his hand to Elizabeth. She took it, nodding quietly to Maggie as they passed her at the nursery's door. James stood guard, but Richard was nearby as well—he could smell him. No one would get past them, no one would harm his daughter tonight.

"Why the fierce expression, husband?" Elizabeth asked as they climbed the stairs to their chamber.

"We must talk." He followed her into the room, closing the door behind them.

"What is it?"

"I wish to discuss Georgiana's future," he said at last.

"What of it?" she asked, looking confused.

"She is special," he said. "Unique. The circumstances of her birth make her an object of curiosity and, in our world, fear. You remember Heberden's advice? That we ought to kill her if she shows signs of being more powerful than her parents?"

"And you threw him out of Pemberley. What of it?"

"Elizabeth, he is an example of the more compassionate among us. There are those who would never have allowed her to be born at all. Those who will fear that she—and you—make the Darcy line too powerful."

"You will protect us. If not at Pemberley, we will go elsewhere."

"It is not enough. We need to take our own offensive measures. Not every House is hostile to us. We must use our allies to our advantage."

"How so?" she asked warily.

"By announcing a betrothal between Georgiana and Lord Matlock. In this way, we make it clear that any action upon a Darcy brings the wrath of Houses Matlock and Darcy upon the offender."

"What? Surely you jest!" Elizabeth cried, horror clear in her voice.

He stiffened. "Not at all. We will not, of course, formalise the agreement until she is older. But this is necessary, for her safety and yours."

"You would take away her choices, her freedom, before she even knows what it is?"

"I would have her know she was protected from her cradle, that she will always be safe."

"Why Matlock, then? Is his the only House willing to form an alliance? Why not entertain other offers? Why decide so quickly?"

"Because of all the lines powerful enough to offer any protection of value, I trust him most."

Elizabeth rose. "Then we are at an impasse, because I trust him not at all."

Darcy strove to keep his voice calm. "You have no basis for your distrust, whereas I have a connexion proven over centuries."

"I cannot even be in the same room with him, Fitzwilliam! He sickens me." She physically struggled for calm. "I have given this some thought. As a mortal, I did not care for either Anne de Bourgh or Caroline Bingley. They later both proved to be untrustworthy. I feel this good...*instinct* for character was enhanced during my Change."

Darcy—just barely—stopped himself from rolling his eyes. "What you felt was jealousy, dearest. You told me this yourself. After you Turned, Caroline did not cause you illness."

"No, but I believe her self-centredness was not as malicious as, say, Anne de Bourgh's. Had I met Anne in my right mind after Turning, I believe the illness would have presented."

"Darling, you are guessing, and ill-advisedly so. You were attacked by Anne, and in your intuitive state, you defended yourself. I know you do not care for Matlock, but he is a man of strong passions. Perhaps you absorb echoes of my gift through my blood, sensing Matlock's antipathy with regard to de Bourgh and Wickham —heaven knows, his negative emotions towards them are potent and have been at the fore both times you met him since Turning."

"It does not work that way with me," she insisted.

"What can you know of the workings of gifts? You have hardly made much effort to tolerate Matlock! You are as much an infant as Georgiana in my world! Not experienced enough to comprehend the intricacies of new power," he attempted to explain.

"I *know* what I feel. I believe," Elizabeth said through clenched teeth. "I know myself."

"Elizabeth, *I* know what you feel as well. Your emotions are far more volatile, more changeable and impulsive. Like most females, you act with your heart instead of your reason, as when you asked me to Turn Mr Collins. That is not a bad thing, and I often admire it. But you must trust me to do what is best for our family," he instructed.

"Because a fickle female like myself cannot be trusted?" she asked, coldly, he thought. "Your knowledge of my feelings gives you permission to sit in judgment of them?"

"You twist my words. It is not what I said."

"It is what you meant. Answer me one question. Was this betrothal your idea, or Matlock's?"

Her intractable prejudice against the man was infuriating. "I fail to see what difference it makes, as the idea is a good one."

"Why is it that his is the only House with which the Darcys have such a close alliance? Why do not the Darcys hold a seat on the Council?"

"So, your new 'instincts' have granted you political savvy as well? Matlock holds the Darcy seat *for* me," he said, bristling and defensive. "I have not the patience for bureaucracy and endless bickering and eternal compromise."

Silence, dark and fraught with tension, filled the air with noiseless hostility. "How very lucrative this connexion with you has been for Lord Matlock," she said at last, quietly. "And now, in addition to your political power, he wants your daughter."

"It is not like that!" he gritted. "Do you know what he does, where he is, perhaps at this very moment? He faces Wickham. He knows you do not believe in him and attempts to earn your faith and trust by confronting my worst enemy. He wishes to *prove* his worthiness, by slaying our worst foes."

"Since he is part of the Council who allowed Wickham to escape in the first place, forgive me if I do not feel an overabundance of gratitude to him for finally attempting to tidy his own mess."

"A typically ignorant assumption. You do not understand. The vampyre world is populated with scoundrels of the worst sort. The Council is comprised of villains, any of who could have perpetrated Wickham's escape and some of whom, no doubt, protect him now. Matlock does not simply battle Wickham, but the powerful Masters who shield him."

"All the more reason why you should cease hiding behind him, then!" Elizabeth cried. "If the world is so bad, if the Council is so corrupt, why do you not fight to change it? Why do you give Matlock the only voice when yours is so needed? Meanwhile, he requires you hand over *your* daughter because, of the whole insanely evil vampyre world, he is somehow, some way, the *only* possible choice for her! I will not have it!" she shouted bitterly.

"And this," cried Darcy, as he stalked across the room, "is your opinion of me! This is the estimation in which you hold me! I thank you for explaining it so fully. My faults, according to this calculation, are heavy indeed! How despicable a situation in which you find yourself—married to a coward and a weakling. I suppose if I were to mould my every judgment to agree with yours, I might be worthy of your regard. Give you a bit of power, and suddenly you know more than one who has held it for centuries! Forgive me if I fail to agree with your every whim in order to win your favourable opinion!"

Cold fury marked her response. "You arrogant wretch! Your selfish disdain for the feelings of your wife reveals your inability to sit in judgment of *anything*, much less a Council of your peers!"

"You have said quite enough, madam. I perfectly comprehend your feelings, and shall not inflict my own upon you, since they interest you so little. But I warn you: *I* shall do what is best for our daughter's future using *my* best judgment, as ill as *you* may think it." Hastily he left the room, slamming the door behind him with enough force to shatter it within its frame.

What happened? Elizabeth thought numbly. One moment she had been listening to the angelic sound of Fitzwilliam's lullaby to her daughter; the next, they shouted bitter, accusing words. Where was her loving husband? Who was the haughty, disdainful man who could so easily discount her every word without even attempting to understand?

At first, she was too angry to cry, and too upset to sleep. But as the day wore on, she grew sorrowful, her fury fading into dull misery. An ache of grief filled her, until each beat of her heart seemed to pump anguish through her soul. Probably, she knew, most women would not be shocked when a spouse ignored her feelings. But Fitzwilliam had given her the illusion of friendship and respect, as well as affection. To discover she was as powerless as the girl of Longbourn was nothing short of devastating.

No! she protested. *I must be more, for Georgiana's sake.* There was something wrong at Matlock's core; even if her feelings *were* exaggerated and overwrought, as Fitzwilliam believed, he was not worthy of her daughter. She had not realised he wielded her husband's power on the Council, but she found that suspicious as well. While Fitzwilliam looked to the man as a surrogate father, she could not help believing him a master manipulator.

Unfortunately, Fitzwilliam simply would not believe her. The wife he had known for less than a year could not compete with Matlock—their link inextricably bound to his love for his father. It was not fair, she supposed, to expect it—but she *had*.

He had used his access to her deepest, most private feelings *against* her, to prove his point. Had he ripped her heart from her chest and stomped upon it, it could not have been more painful. She must find a way to protect not only Georgiana, but herself.

Darcy rode into the countryside, hoping to find peace in nature. For hours, his anger carried him, even protected him, the pain muted. But if more than two hundred years of living had taught him nothing else, he understood that words could not prick so painfully if there was no truth in them.

He *had* abandoned his duty when he allowed Matlock to step in for him on the Council. Angry at the world—and his government specifically—for failing not only to protect his father but also to avenge his murder, he had abdicated his responsibilities, allowing another to shoulder them. Even though he disagreed with his wife as to the worthiness of the object of his trust, he knew Father, for all his love of his good friend, would never have forsaken his duty and given it over to Matlock.

George Darcy had principles he held dear. Would Matlock so diligently foster those same ideals? As much as he respected the man, he understood him to be a master politician, no doubt seeing shades of grey Fitzwilliam would never accept.

It did not mean Matlock's heart was black, as Elizabeth believed! Why could she not trust her husband? Did knowing her husband shirked his duty to his government lead her to believe he would be negligent in his duty to family?

Ah, Elizabeth. You have never met any *of the collected villains, scoundrels, and rogues constituting the most powerful vampyres on earth.* Many of them had risen as Masters in their Houses by murder and blackmail. His conscience, however, forced him to admit not all of them were evil, and even rogues had their own sense of honour. Doubtlessly others would welcome more accountability from Council members.

Darcy's mount reached the top of a tall hill overlooking Pemberley. He thought of his young wife, once freely roaming the Hertfordshire countryside, and now, essentially, confined to the castle, and felt a wave of guilt and the urge to repair whatever was wrong.

Like it or not, however, she must learn to trust me to keep her—and my daughter—safe in it! he thought protectively. He turned his mount away.

Matlock approached the cavern entrance close to midnight, his powers at their zenith. With him, he carried a large, unwieldy package, hefting it easily. He was more powerful than George Wickham, but it would be foolish to underestimate a vampyre who had been slithering out of sticky situations since his youth.

He announced himself first, to ensure he appeared open-handed and harmless.

"George," he called. "I approach."

He heard no reply, but a torch flared in the darkness, the universal symbol of welcome. Plainly, Wickham wished Matlock to believe him similarly innocuous.

Matlock entered the cavernous room, not raising a brow at the large bloody splotches on the stone walls and rock-strewn floor—evidence of some very messy meals. The place stank of unwashed human, rotting flesh, and assorted rodents.

"I have something for you," Matlock announced.

"Darcy's head, I hope," George groused. He reclined, fully dressed, on the once pristine bed. Matlock suppressed a small shudder at the state of the bedclothes—Wickham had indulged in more than one breakfast in bed.

"All in good time, my boy, all in good time," Matlock said, propping his package against a wall. "It looks as though you have been enjoying yourself here rather too well," he chided.

"Enjoying myself! What a joke. Boring as the devil. I had to create a little entertainment or go mad. Turned two of the miners and let them have at each other. A bit of Gentleman Jackson in the

Peaks." Though his posture was relaxed, Matlock did not mistake the other man's watchfulness. George's sword was at the ready.

Matlock turned away from the bed, giving George his back—another gesture of trust. "Are you not curious?" he said, pointing towards the large package wrapped in brown paper.

"Hardly. What is it?" George said, shrugging disinterestedly. "The only thing you could have brought of any interest is a female. That thing is flat—thus, undoubtedly, dull. How long before we can take the Darcy whelp?"

"My plans are almost complete," Matlock soothed. "I require a few of your belongings and a crucible of your blood. I will show Darcy clues putting you on a ship to America. I have men who will sink the ship in shark-infested waters. Lie low for a few months longer. Once he believes you are fish bait, he shall be ripe for the plucking."

"Months! Unacceptable! I tell you, milord, I am half out of my mind with boredom as it is!"

"Hush, George. You will board a packet bound for Italy. A Venetian holiday will be just the thing. My agents make arrangements as we speak," Matlock prevaricated.

"Italy? I cannot. There was some trouble with the House of Medici a century ago."

Matlock sighed. "Very well then, I shall find another haven. Ought I to know about any other out-of-bounds territories?"

"I should avoid the Romanovs as well," he muttered.

Matlock rolled his eyes. "Quite. I have half a mind to return my gift from whence it came."

Wickham dropped his sulky look, eager to change the subject from his offences against the powerful Russians. "Come now, milord, don't be a mother hen. What is it you bring me?"

"Open it," Matlock said, waving an indulgent hand.

George levered himself off the bed and stood before the object, finally looking slightly curious.

"Allow me," Matlock said, and, producing a knife, slit the brown wrappings and string. The paper parted to reveal a life-sized portrait of a female.

"Mother," George gasped reverently. "You had her portrait enlarged." He reached out to caress the brushstrokes of the beautiful woman pictured. "I miss her so," he moaned. "If only Father had not refused to Turn her, she would be with me still."

"It was cruel of him," Matlock agreed.

"I did not mean to hurt her. I never wished to hurt her. I only wanted to keep her with me, forever. She is the only one who has ever loved me." He bowed his head in remembered grief.

"She knows that, George. You had never Turned anyone before, and you were so young. There was no way to know your blood would Turn her into one of your—" Matlock stopped.

"Abominations," George said shortly, a tear trickling down his cheek. He lifted his eyes again to the portrait. "Oh, Mother, I am so sorr—"

But whatever words of apology he planned to say were lost as the silver blade Matlock held slid with lethal force directly into George's heart, splattering blood all over the painted canvas.

"Wh–" he sputtered, struggling against Matlock's hold, futilely trying to grasp the knife twisting, shredding the organ in his chest. When George was sufficiently weak, Matlock grasped his hair, withdrew George's own sword, and cleaved his head from his neck with a mighty thrust.

Matlock peered at the vanquished head, noting with displeasure his own favourite waistcoat was ruined.

The head stared back, accusingly. "D-D-Darcy's man," it stuttered.

"Oh, no, dear boy," he replied, as the whites of its eyes replaced the brief gleam of censure. "Matlock is, and always has been, solely for Matlock."

Forty Three

Elizabeth went to the nursery immediately upon rousing from slumber. She found Maggie and Richard playing a game of 'Toss the Baby,' and her daughter giggling joyfully. "Throw her this way, if you please," she said.

"That is all for us, Mags, we have been replaced," Richard announced.

Elizabeth lifted a brow. "'Mags?'" she enquired.

Maggie blushed. "How did you sleep, Mistress?" she asked, plainly hoping to change the subject. Then she looked alarmed, as if she had broached a forbidden topic.

Elizabeth wondered whether everyone knew her husband had not shared her bed. Probably. There were very few secrets when it came to the Master of Pemberley. She decided to be blunt. "Do you know where my husband is, Colonel?"

It was Richard's turn to look uncomfortable. "He was riding most of the day but is returned now. In his study at the moment."

For a time no one spoke, Maggie obviously wishing to escape, Richard wanting to probe. Elizabeth decided to let Richard have his way.

"What is your opinion of Lord Matlock?" she asked.

Richard shrugged. "Decent enough chap, I suppose. After my sister died, he spent a lot of time cheering George. I appreciated that. He was good to Darcy after George was killed. Truthfully, I seldom give him much thought, but he has always been a friend of sorts."

"Fitzwilliam wishes to betroth Georgiana to him, over my most strenuous objections. I do not expect you to take sides—or rather, I do not expect you to see my side. I only say this so you know why my husband and I are at odds. I feel the need to stay close to Georgiana at the moment, and I wish to be undisturbed."

"Of course, ma'am," Maggie said at once, eagerly turning for the door.

"I say, it does seem a bit early to be talking of betrothals," Richard said. "But I am sure he only has Georgiana's best interests at heart. You must talk to him, Elizabeth. He will surely see your point of view once he has time to think on it."

Elizabeth refused to argue with him; after all, if her husband would not listen to her, what were the odds of his people doing so? "I daresay," was all she answered.

"I am sure—"

"Richard!" Maggie hissed. "The mistress wants her privacy." She grabbed his hand and practically shoved him through the door.

Once again, Elizabeth's brows rose—first, at Maggie's boldness with Richard, and second, his meekness in allowing it. Perhaps she ought to caution her—and then laughed bitterly. Maggie was far older, while Elizabeth had no particular talent for dealing with difficult men.

Georgiana clamoured to get down, immediately crawling towards a large pile of painted wooden blocks in the corner. To Elizabeth's delight, the infant began piling them, building colourful stacks with her tiny hands. Astonished, Elizabeth's first impulse was to fetch Fitzwilliam, so they might marvel at her great intellect together. The urge was quickly followed by a sinking in her belly, a heavy grief reminding she was no longer on good terms with her husband. Had she ever been? Or had she simply never disagreed?

Self-pitying, weepy thoughts were useless. Consciously she drew instead upon the creature existing within her, that creature who had been hissing and growling with fury ever since her husband offered up her daughter to her enemy. What she needed was a plan.

This new instinct whispered: if she could shut her feelings away from Fitzwilliam just enough, if she could elude him long enough, if she were prepared to move often enough and hide well enough...he would collapse into a grave-like state of near-death until she either fed him or died herself, at which point their connexion would sever. Permanently.

At the thought, even her creature howled in pain and distress; she promptly burst into tears.

❧

That was how Darcy found his wife, face buried in her hands, racking sobs nearly choking her. It was all he could do not to race to her side and enfold her in his arms—but he was the *cause* of her distress. Georgiana was not so hesitant; she pulled herself up using her mother's skirts, staring at her weeping mama with puzzled interest.

Not wishing to startle either, he tapped gently upon the open door. Immediately, his wife turned her head away in a futile effort to hide her emotion. Georgiana was happier to see him, giving him her widest grin.

He could not resist the urge to pick her up. To his surprise, instead of her usual indications that he play, she buried her face into his cravat, snuggling tightly against him and wrapping her chubby arms about his neck. Suddenly, it was all he could do not to weep himself.

For several moments he rocked his daughter, trying to think of what to say. Elizabeth surreptitiously used the corner of her sleeve to swipe at her eyes. She was blatantly emotional, and yet...while he stood there, wordless and awkward and over-full of love for both wife and daughter, he made a terrible discovery.

Because he was unable to penetrate Elizabeth's emotions at will, no matter his powers, he had thought her *unfathomable* without their intimacy. Perhaps, once, this had been true. Nevertheless, somehow, subtly, living with her, loving her, sharing his life with her, he had grown to know her. Intangible senses had become attuned to hers.

But now...*now*, though her sorrow was plain enough for any simpleton to see, she was as closed to him as she had ever been. Shut away, locked and barred. Impenetrable, as she had not been in months.

He could only stare at her with gathering grief and dawning fear.

Heaven have mercy, he thought...*what have I done?*

Richard barged into the nursery, bursting with barely repressed excitement. "Matlock is here," he said. "He must see you at once."

Darcy turned back to Elizabeth, whose expression hardened when she heard Matlock's name. She was unreachable, would not listen while her hatred for their visitor created a barrier between them.

"Here, my sweet," he said to Georgiana, placing her in Elizabeth's arms. Elizabeth clutched the babe to her as if she was afraid, turning her face away from him without speaking. His senses incessantly sought and failed to find some hidden, formerly accessible entry. With painful effort, he forced himself away.

"Matlock is severely injured," Richard explained. "I have Mrs Reynolds attending him. Despite his wounds, he brings welcome news."

Darcy followed Richard into a second-floor room. Matlock lay propped up on pillows, looking frail, the entire left side of his face disfigured, though the flesh was already knitting together. His right arm was only a stump. It would likely take him a day or two to fully heal from these painful injuries.

"My lord," Darcy said, holding out his hand.

Matlock grasped it with his remaining one. "Darcy," he whispered hoarsely from his wrecked throat. "Almost I did not believe I would ever see you again. A welcome sight."

Darcy covered the weaker hand beneath his. "As are you."

"Richard...the bag," Matlock ordered, with only a trace of his usual imperiousness.

Richard stooped to pick up a canvas sack and opened it.

"Wickham," Darcy murmured, as Richard pulled the head from the wrappings. "So...it is finished. At last."

"At last," Matlock said huskily, "my old friend has been avenged." A piercing sorrow filled the room; Darcy knew Matlock too injured to suppress his potent grief.

"Thank you," Darcy said softly, "for all you have suffered on behalf of my family."

"All...is well?" Matlock asked.

"Yes," Darcy said. "I shall let you rest now—it will be full light soon and you must sleep."

"Good, good," Matlock murmured, his eyes already drifting shut.

Darcy left the room carrying the head, Richard following close behind. He went into his study, setting the gruesome trophy upon the marble hearth. Richard poured two glasses of port, handing one to Darcy. "A toast to Matlock," he said.

Darcy drank, but swiftly set the glass down.

"I thought you would be happier, Darcy."

Darcy stared ahead moodily. "I thought I would be, as well," he muttered.

"Are your poor spirits related to this disagreement with your wife over Georgiana's betrothal to the wounded earl?"

Darcy glanced up sharply. "Elizabeth told you, then. I suppose she thinks me a monster?"

"I do not know what she thinks. She did not plead her case or defend her views."

"What do you think, Richard? Am I wrong to wish for this alliance?"

"Not wrong, no. But it appears to me that in making the one, you risk losing the other. I suppose you need only decide which you prefer—an alliance with Matlock, or the one with your wife?"

"I simply fail to see why I cannot have both! Why will she not be reasonable?" In complaining to his uncle, Darcy knew he only nursed his grievance. But his pride had taken a beating; he hoped for sympathy.

Instead of answering, Richard rubbed his chin thoughtfully. "I wonder," he said finally, "whether the bonding can survive the severing of your minds and wills. Perhaps death need not be the only answer—only the death of your desire for unity."

Darcy grit his teeth. "Unity has nothing to do with it. My mother certainly had none with my father, once she learned the truth."

"It was not your mother who was bonded, Darcy. Neither is it Elizabeth."

Darcy froze in a cold wave of dread. Richard had a point. Though he did not believe Elizabeth precisely *un*-bonded, she could survive without him. Her need, her love for him was not compelled—it must be nurtured, nourished. Shuddering, he recalled those recent feelings of expulsion from her essence.

How had he forgotten? Where was the man who had been willing to die rather than horrify her by drinking from her? He cared deeply about Matlock's feelings, true—but he had not vowed to love, honour, and cherish Matlock.

Bonding instinct or no, he—the man as well as the beast—loved her madly. Even if this decision cost him an old friendship—and he did not believe it would—it was a small price to pay in comparison.

"I have been a fool," he said, sighing.

Richard chuckled. "I have come to recognise that the sacrifice of a bit of pride is a small loss in return for the respect of a good woman."

Darcy looked at him curiously. "Maggie?"

Richard grinned rather sheepishly. "Perhaps, someday. She does not yet see me as a potential..."

"Lover?"

"I was going to say, 'mate.'"

"Oh! It is like that, is it?"

"Yes. It is like that."

Darcy smiled. "I only wish your happiness, and hers."

Richard nodded, standing. "Do you mean to seek out Elizabeth, or will you stay here and sulk?" he asked bluntly.

"I fear she has no interest in seeing me at the moment. No, I will speak with Matlock first. Perhaps she will be kindlier disposed once she sees I have taken her reproofs to heart."

It was a sign of how much the colonel had changed that his only departing comment was, "Best of luck with the grovelling. You shall need it."

Darcy spoke with his men patrolling the grounds, informing each of them personally of Wickham's death rather than simply communicating via thought. The celebratory spirit he lacked, personally, was in strong evidence amongst his cadre; though all swore allegiance to him, more than half had been his father's. While some remained on duty, he reduced the day patrols, when they were least vulnerable to attack and most gathered back at the castle where Morton hosted a revelry.

Finally, he rode alone to the Pemberley cemetery. The monument erected in his father's honour was a simple one, and he stood before it with his hands clasped behind his back, his heart heavy.

"Father," he said. "Rest peacefully."

He stood for several more minutes, hoping to find tranquillity in the quiet afternoon. None was forthcoming. Perhaps because his father—even after everything—would have wanted Darcy to find a way to redeem his eldest, rather than see him destroyed. There was, truly, nothing to celebrate. Squaring his shoulders, he let it go.

It was midnight before he returned to Matlock's room. The difference in the other vampyre was obvious; dressed in his usual finery, he was seated before the fire with a tray of meats beside him, a glass of brandy in his good hand. His arm had regenerated, though still in a sling.

"My lord, it is good to see you so recovered," he said, smiling.

"It is good to have both limbs again, though this one is still fairly useless," Matlock said, nodding at his sling. "I had forgotten the pain of limb regrowth. It has been many years since I was so careless with one."

Darcy nodded. "Were any of your men fatally injured?"

"Two. Good men. They shall be missed," Matlock replied, making a mental note to kill two of his men and bring Darcy to the funeral. The guilt would be good for him. "I took very few with me, as speed and surprise were vital."

"I am sorry. If either has a family, I will of course pay reparations."

"You need not worry about that. I always take care of my own."

"Yes," Darcy agreed, but somewhat absently.

"You seem very sober tonight. I thought you might join those who took the festivities to the tavern in Lambton."

Darcy sighed. "I wished to speak with you instead. Doubtless you will find me very ungrateful, but I must refuse your offer of a betrothal to my daughter." He withdrew the case containing the necklace Lord Matlock had presented for Georgiana, holding it out to the earl. "I am honoured you considered it, but regrettably, it is impossible."

A wave of surprise and fury washed over the other man before he could suppress it, though it was quickly gone. He made no move to accept the jewels. "I admit to some astonishment, Fitzwilliam, that you should decline me out of hand." He controlled the rage, allowing his offense to shimmer brightly, and was pleased to see Darcy look abashed. "I thought you might at least do me the courtesy of giving the offer serious consideration."

"I did," Darcy answered quickly. "Indeed, I have thought of little else. But 'tis impossible."

"And this is all the reply which I am to have the honour of expecting! I might, perhaps, wish to be informed why, with so little endeavour at civility, I am thus rejected. But it is of small importance."

"My reasons are my own," Darcy replied quietly. "I understand your affront, but I am determined to give Georgiana more choice in her future."

For a time, they sat in a seething silence. "When she comes of age, will you allow me to court her then?" Matlock asked.

"We will allow no one to court her until we are convinced she is old enough, and wise enough, to make her own decisions. We intend no formal or arranged match. We will teach her to defend and protect herself, to think for herself. If she wishes to choose a mate for dynastic reasons, the choice will be her own. However, we will encourage her to wait for a mate she can love, and who will love her and cherish her."

Matlock did not bother to hide his absolute contempt for these sentiments. "Devil take it! The girl will be murdered before she reaches adulthood, if that sop is your idea of good sense. You cannot believe such drivel. Your father would be ashamed to hear it."

Darcy's jaw firmed. "How timely, this reminder of my father's wishes. Because we both know I have, indeed, been ignoring them. He always meant for me to take his place on the Council. We discussed it many times—my duty, should anything happen to him. I do not mean to continue failing him. I appreciate you carrying my burdens, but it is time for me to shoulder them myself."

"You mean to take my seat?" Matlock gasped. He had not seen this coming, no, not at all, and shock nearly overwhelmed him.

"I am sure I need not remind you—it is my seat to take," Darcy warned. "However, Catherine de Bourgh's has not been filled. I will support your bid for it wholeheartedly. The alliance between Matlock and Darcy need not suffer in any aspect. Your enemies are mine."

Matlock expended every ounce of his superb self-control to resist murdering Darcy where he stood, not allowing his rage to leak from behind the barriers where he kept it carefully hidden. He had sacrificed *everything*—his best weapon, his ultimate revenge—for this mawkish fool! Plunging a knife in Darcy's heart would be delicious, but he would never escape Pemberley alive if the colonel and his men sensed an attack on their master; of course, in his current weak state, even the element of surprise might not conquer Darcy's inherent strength. But he had not gained his depths of power by making rash decisions. No, he would take everything owed him, and he would not wait centuries—or even decades—to possess it.

"You realise I only have been looking after your best interests," he said coldly, not attempting to disguise his displeasure.

"I know that," Darcy replied, eagerly now. "You have my undying gratitude and loyalty for how you have helped me, guided me, and fought for me and my family. I believe that together, we can do much to prevent the de Bourghs of our world from gaining power. By creating new alliances, we will encourage those with honour to eschew violence and bloodshed, establishing laws to make the world safer for both mortal and vampyre. We will root out the self-interest currently guiding the Council as it stands, giving every citizen a voice rather than merely those who have a mighty House. The world is changing, and we can change with it—make it better."

"High ideals," Matlock managed to say, hanging onto his fury by a thread.

"Are not they the very ideals you pledged me when you assumed the Darcy seat—to continue my father's fight for the rights of all?"

Matlock, the consummate politician, knew he must now tread carefully. He had much practice—George Darcy had frequently mouthed such tired rubbish but, fortunately, enjoyed debate and philosophy far more than determined action. His principled son was more dangerous. "Of course—which is why both Matlock and Darcy vampyres have the freedom to leave our estates and establish themselves elsewhere. But we both know most think more of their next meal than matters of State. We care for them far better than they could care for themselves."

"That is true of some Masters, but sadly, many neglect their constituents in favour of greed and power. We can make a difference together, sir. And regardless—for honour's sake, it is our duty to try."

Matlock made a decision. "Ah, you make me feel young again,

Darcy." He sighed gustily. "Keep the necklace, my friend. If not for Georgiana, as a token of my esteem for your lovely bride. I will give what you have said much thought. Perhaps we might discuss it over dinner tomorrow night? I prefer to have the use of both my hands when I begin speechifying," he said dryly.

Darcy chuckled. "Yes, my lord. Dinner tomorrow it is."

Forty Four

When Darcy finished his conversation with Matlock, his heart was immeasurably lighter and his mind firmly focused. It was time at last to find his wife.

Elizabeth.

He found her in the nursery, of course, and wondered if she had slept at all. She had penned a letter, using a little chest for a desk, keeping one eye upon Georgiana even as she wrote. She looked paler than usual, and he realised she had not Taken—from him, at least—in a day and a half. While Elizabeth met Georgiana's needs, he had insisted upon giving to her daily. Some intuition told him, however, that she would not agree to Take if he offered. She had thrown up walls and would not be interested in allowing him within them. She said not a word in response to his tentative greeting, only barely nodding in his direction.

His daughter, at least, was once again eager to see him, allowing him to pick her up and hug her tightly. Quickly, however, she squirmed to get down, crawling to a corner where she had her towers stacked, brick upon brick, in colourful piles. "Did you build these? What a brilliant girl!" he praised.

Joining her on the floor, conscious of Elizabeth's eyes upon them, he built stacks of his own. When Georgiana gleefully knocked his down, he smiled at the sweet giggles and could not help stealing a glance at his wife. Her countenance had softened slightly, and he seized his chance.

"Have you heard the news? Wickham is dead."

"Yes. Maggie told me."

"I wonder...would you walk out with me? It is a lovely night, and at last we have few worries of skulking enemies."

"I-I would rather not, thank you. I write to my parents, informing them of Georgiana's birth. I suppose it is time."

He closed his eyes briefly, absorbing the blow of her rejection. Slowly, he turned to face her, though he remained on his knees. "Please, Elizabeth. Please."

"Do not, Fitzwilliam."

He stayed at her feet. "Only a walk. I wish to show you a place you have not yet seen. And then I shall not disturb you again."

A long moment passed before she nodded once, briefly.

"I shall summon Maggie for Georgiana," he said, and she nodded again.

Both Maggie and Richard answered his call and joined them in the nursery. Darcy shot Richard a look. *Will you ensure the men who went to Lambton return by dawn?* he thought to his uncle.

Of course—you do not expect to return soon?

Darcy caught the thread of amusement in Richard's query. *I profoundly hope not,* he replied, with no amusement whatsoever.

They walked side by side, not touching. Elizabeth was glad, after she was beyond the castle walls, that she had agreed to come. A slight breeze ruffled her hair, bound in a loose braid over her shoulder, ruffling the skirt of her simple dress. She cared little that she looked more like a country maid than mistress of Pemberley; after so many months of confinement, there was a lovely freedom in the hillsides. She felt the calming of an unrecognised tension, and gradually—though against her will—the harshest edge of her anger dulled. Her hurt, however, was still a bruising pain within her chest, and she used it to remind herself of the necessity of maintaining her guard.

Darcy led her to the same outlook he had visited the previous day; the view was even more beautiful to a vampyre by moonlight. The castle was a series of ivory pinnacles, the quiet village picturesque, the hillsides sparkling from within their shadowed greenery. Silently admiring the beauty in the stillness, she startled when he spoke, as though she had been drowsing.

"I wish to apologise to you, Elizabeth."

She looked at him.

"My father taught me many valuable lessons in life. He was, as I think I have said before, all that was amiable and benevolent. However, I am just beginning to understand that his love was selfish. He preached the value and worth of the lowliest vampyre in his line, but in practise, cared for few beyond his own family circle. He taught me correct principles, but allowed, encouraged, and almost expected me to be overbearing in their application. Thus, I have had a certain example in my mind as to how a family is to be managed, but in point of fact, it is not an example I wish to follow."

"I do not take your meaning," she said.

"I mean...if I lose you, I am empty, a heart that beats to no purpose." He took her cold hand in his. "I should never have disregarded your feelings towards Matlock or treated them as unimportant simply because I do not understand them. I do not have to understand. Perhaps you see a fate one hundred years in the future that I cannot, but truthfully, it matters little. I ought to have protected your feelings as I would your life. You had every right to expect it."

She spoke defiantly, hardly trusting these words, but finding the courage within his apology to be honest. "I doubt my feelings towards him will ever change. I will oppose the alliance you wish and thwart your objectives, if it is in my power to do so."

He looked at her with earnest intent. "My truest objective is that Georgiana know the same love with her future mate that I feel for mine. That she grows to maturity secure in the love of her family, and with the education and choices she requires in order to achieve happiness. It is plain this goal cannot be achieved with Matlock. How could she have the support and love of all her family if I were to do something so divisive? I have already informed Matlock that the betrothal can never take place. There will be no alliance by marriage," he pronounced firmly.

"You-you told him?"

"I did. I beg forgiveness for not considering your feelings with the same respect I gave the earl's."

Elizabeth inhaled a large breath of the bracing mountain air, trying to accept the strange idea that her husband would reverse himself. She could not help but look for the trick, the catch in the argument.

"What did he have to say to that?"

"He was not pleased, of course. I did not think he would be. But you were correct in everything you said, Elizabeth. I *have* ignored my duty. My father may have ruled our family imperfectly, but he at least did not wholly shirk his responsibilities and obligations as I have done. When you challenged me regarding my seat on the Council, I believed myself perfectly calm in refuting your argument, whereas now I am convinced I spoke in a dreadful bitterness of spirit. In my heart, I knew you were right." He brought her hand to his lips, kissing the soft skin. "I have informed Matlock that I will assume my own seat, while supporting him in a bid for the de Bourgh seat. I told him there can be a powerful alliance between the Darcy and Matlock Houses, but it will be political in nature—and is contingent upon his assistance in creating change for the better in our world."

This was astonishing—even, incredible. As she contemplated his words, she felt a certain easing in the creature prowling within so strongly—as if it, too, sensed his earnestness. Her natural protectiveness towards him began to reassert itself.

"The Council," she whispered. "Have I goaded you towards danger, more peril?"

"Ask rather, what else ought I to do? Where else should I serve? You taught me a lesson, hard indeed at first, but most advantageous. By you, I was properly humbled. You showed me how insufficient were all my pretensions to please a woman worthy of being pleased."

"I never thought you pretentious."

He smiled. "No, I believe you thought me an arrogant wretch."

She sighed. "I was unciv—"

"You were honest. You could have called me much worse. All I want—no, *need*—to hear is your forgiveness."

Elizabeth bit her lip, looking up into her husband's sincere expression. It was hard to meet his gaze. Something within her had withdrawn from him and she felt the distance between them as though it were physical miles separating their hearts. For the first time since the argument, she began searching for a way to overcome it.

He still did not believe in her feelings against Matlock. Regardless, he had refused the earl what he wanted. Fitzwilliam was a proud man, and she had rejected his decisions utterly; nevertheless, he had taken her words to heart, even to the extent of resuming his seat on the Council. Though her heart quaked at the thought of him taking up dangerous duties, she grew conscious of a fierce pride in his ability to subject himself to earnest self-examination.

"Of course, I forgive you, Fitzwilliam," she said instantly. "And I thank you. You honour me with your decisions."

Carefully, he drew her up into his arms, the first time he had touched her since their quarrel. His touch was gentle, tender, brushing his hands across her back and shoulders. While she did not resist in any way, an anxious distance remained and she did not understand how to let him back in.

"I would show you something else," he said. When she agreed, he took her hand and led her down the hillside, entering a forested part of the property. There did not seem to be a pathway, but Darcy walked without hesitation. For perhaps a mile, the only sound was of forest creatures disturbed in their habitats, many of them loudly protesting the vampyric presence.

At last they reached a clearing where sat a snug cottage, a smoking chimney puffing into the cool night air, the windows alit from oil lamps within.

"Who lives here?" she asked.

"It once belonged to our gamekeeper," he replied, opening the door. "No one uses it now."

She looked around the tidy one-room space. A fire burned in the hearth, and there were several colourful rugs strewn across the bare wood floor. A table occupied one corner, laden with several covered dishes. But pride of place went to a large, sturdy bed covered in sumptuous coverings and enough pillows to satisfy a maharajah.

"The gamekeeper had unusual taste in furnishings," she said wryly.

"I made a few alterations," he murmured. "Sit down, please, and allow me to get you a plate."

Elizabeth was not truly hungry for meats and cheeses but was eager for diversion from the prominent bed. However, she quickly realised there were no chairs in the room. Sighing, she kicked off her shoes and piled a few pillows against the footboard of the bedframe.

"Here, love," Fitzwilliam said, handing her a plate. She picked at the offerings in a desultory fashion as he filled his own.

"I spoke to Richard about Maggie," he said, after a long, awkward pause.

"Oh? Did he say anything of his intentions?"

"Much to my surprise, his intentions are honourable and...permanent," Darcy replied.

"Truly? And yet, she seems the opposite of the type for whom Richard would—," she broke off mid-sentence.

"Richard has changed. It is due to you, naturally," he stated matter-of-factly.

"Me? I cannot imagine why you think so," she replied, dumbfounded.

"Because you are beautiful and good and kind. You make me so happy, any man who sees it grows envious. So unsurprisingly, he began searching for a woman who has similar traits. It will take time, I am sure. Maggie does not entirely trust that Richard knows his heart, and hers is well protected. But I do not doubt his success."

"He does not...feel a bonding instinct with her? What would it do to her if he somehow bonded to someone else later?" she asked curiously.

He gazed at her meaningfully. "Very few males *ever* bond. And no matter what you may think, Elizabeth, there *is* choice involved. Had I left Hertfordshire last year and never returned, as I intended, I would have stayed free. However, I searched for any excuse to see you again. Physical intimacy was required to bond fully, and it completed because my heart was uncommitted elsewhere. Richard's heart is no longer his own. She need not fear that he will stray." He paused. "Do you fear I will ever regret our bonded mating?"

Her expression grew pensive. "That is not what I fear," she answered. "Your access to my feelings gives you so much more of me than I can have of you. There is such an...inequity, in this connexion of ours. I wonder if I am able to bear it."

"Do you...does it hurt, that I know so much of you?" he whispered, staring at his feet.

She set her mostly untouched plate aside. In sudden decision, she reached for him, giving all, as he met her lips in eager kiss—her love for him, her care and affection, her desire, her anger and her hurt. And, too, a certain sad acceptance, that this sharing was all one-sided.

"Not at all," she replied, leaning back. "I only wish I knew as much of you."

As much of you. The words echoed in his heart.

He had felt her sorrow. It was so small, curled there amongst the other emotions he preferred. It had been there, he realised, for a long time...almost from the first.

She knew him better than anyone on earth ever had or ever would—and he did not read her mind. Yet, he invaded something equally private: her feelings. One could not argue with them...feelings simply *were*. They were even more dangerous than thoughts; logic did not govern them. One could get past them but not always over them. They welled at random, engulfing, occasionally hurtful. He did not care about that—he would rather know how she felt, so he could understand.

It was the most natural thing in the world, that she should wish for the same.

I can take but cannot give, he nearly said. But was it true? In his lifetime of despising his gift, had he ever considered any capabilities it might give him beyond pain? Was it possible that the door to his emotions *could* be opened?

He took her in another kiss, so they were linked, and fixed his mind upon his power, on the feeling of their joining. He identified his feelings, where they existed within his mind and heart—and he reached for her. Extending both his feelings and his gift, he went searching for whatever barrier kept them sealed off, separate and apart.

It was surprising how effortlessly he discovered it, a massive door, thick and iron-strong—and bolted only on his side. But would he open it? Could he bear it? Suddenly he was aware of a horrible vulnerability...this was his most private, secret self...a primitive beast, ugly at times, only half-tamed. With staggering understanding, he finally recognised what he had stolen, from their very first kiss, was an enormous imposition, a violation of privacy so immense it could not be quantified.

And yet—she had never denied him, never resented him except for the one time he had used that intimacy against her. She was the most giving, accepting woman on earth. How could he not offer her the same, even if his feelings were coarser and less worthy?

He pulled back from a kiss grown suddenly wild. "Come inside me, Elizabeth. Feel me like I feel you. Know me like I know you." And then he unbolted the barrier between them, exposing his naked soul.

She made a tiny noise of surprise...and then...he felt her feelings about his, and it was the most excruciating, blissful experience of his life. Their gazes met as they merged—and in an exchange of excitement and heartbreak, epiphany and wonder—she knew him as he knew her.

"I did not realise," she began breathlessly, laughing joyously between kisses.

"How much I love you? Surely I have shown you," he said, completing her sentence, putting his mouth to hers again.

She gasped. "That, as well. But I did not—quite—understand how much you need me," she managed breathlessly.

"You could not have. There are no words." Words became superfluous. She had always, it seemed, understood and believed in him. Now, faith was replaced with knowledge as her feelings intertwined with his.

They came together with the perfection of rhythm first experienced dancing at an assembly in an insignificant village in Hertfordshire. The intensity of the sharing spread throughout their bodies, their blood, their minds, and their hearts until the oneness coalesced in shimmering heat.

Their souls reunited, and it felt like coming home.

Elizabeth slept with the dawn, but he did not—he was too happy, wanting only to watch over his precious wife while she dreamt, making plans for an impossibly bright future.

Thus, he was wide awake when Richard's scream of agony pierced his mind.

Forty Five

By the time Richard found the last celebrating straggler, dawn had broken over the village. Not so very long ago, he would have been one of the revellers. Now, he preferred to stay in the nursery with Maggie and Georgiana. Astonishingly—to himself, at least—it was sheer pleasure, watching Maggie, talking with her, sharing the care of his niece, and, of course, savouring the occasional kiss she now allowed him. He smiled at his own besotted foolishness—to trail a pretty woman all evening long in exchange for a kiss or two! Not since his fourteenth year had he behaved so much like a green boy.

Entering the house, he nodded to James, who was still on watch. "I will look in on the nursery, and then relieve you," he said.

"Miss Georgiana is with her parents," James volunteered. "Lord Matlock took her for a walk in the gardens as she was a touch fussy and he said Maggie wished a moment to herself. He sent a groundsboy back with the message that he met Mr and Mrs Darcy while walking, and they now have the child. The babe was a trifle upset, when I've never seen her do aught but smile."

Richard frowned. It was out of character for Maggie to weary of caring for Georgiana, and for Matlock to take an interest in an unhappy baby. The hairs at the back of Richard's neck rose, instinct telling him something was amiss.

"Matlock did not return?"

"No—I thought he decided to join the rest of the men in Lambton. He asked where the celebration moved."

"Odd. He did not go to Lambton." With a feeling of deep unease, he took the stairs to the nursery five at a time, moving with preternatural swiftness. He smelt the blood before he reached the end of the corridor and burst in to find a macabre nightmare. Maggie's head, its silver-blonde hair now stained red, stared back at him from a pool of blood on the nursery hearthrug. Her decapitated body was pinned to the wall with a silver sword—did it pierce her heart? He ran to her, a battle cry issuing from the depths of his soul.

"Something is wrong at the house," Darcy said sharply, jumping from the bed and grabbing for his breeches.

Elizabeth's eyes flashed open. In one seamless motion she was out of bed, running for Pemberley. Nude.

"Elizabeth!" Darcy cried, snatching her dress from the floor as he chased her. Though he was far stronger, he did not overtake her until she reached the outer wall of the castle. Her eyes had gone red; indeed all civil thought and action were seemingly gone as though they had never been. "Put this on!" he said, throwing the dress over her head as she fought to free herself, stitches ripping.

He had no time to button the front placket before she was off again like a startled doe. "Devil take it!" he cursed, chasing after her. She ran directly for the nursery. The smell of blood once they reached the third floor lent wings to Darcy's feet, however, barely managing to shove her behind him as they reached the nursery door.

He was poised for attack, but there was only Richard holding a headless Maggie, with Mrs Reynolds kneeling beside him and James cradling the decapitated head. Richard met his gaze. "Matlock did this," he said, his voice low and vicious. "He has Georgiana."

"Carter has already found a scent trail," James said.

Darcy turned back to Elizabeth, ready to hold her, to say *something*. But she was already gone.

"Elizabeth!" Darcy yelled, though his wife did not slow or even acknowledge hearing him. Though he paused to hastily dress and gather a few necessary items before giving chase, even he was amazed by how far she had run. When he finally captured her, she fought like a banshee to escape.

"Elizabeth!" he shouted again, trying to reach her through her beast who had control. It was only because, ultimately, her beast had submitted so often to his, that he was able to penetrate. "Listen to me!" he said, shaking her a little.

"Must reach her," she managed. "Maggie...Georgiana...no!" she screamed, loudly enough to echo throughout the countryside. There were blood and tears enough in the sound to break his heart.

"We will find her," he said. "You are heading away from the scent trail. Away from Matlock."

"I move towards my baby," she stated unequivocally, determination in her flickering eyes.

Darcy considered her solemnly. Internally, his soul pulsed with the need to give chase, and he knew the scent trail was likeliest. But Elizabeth showed every sign of following an instinctive scent—and new vampyre or no, she had been correct about Matlock, had she not? He shoved aside the pain of that betrayal.

His beast, while not as close to the surface as Elizabeth's, was ready to fall in with hers, fall in *behind* hers, eager for the first time in its life to *follow*. Perhaps it was time to put the man's trust in her, as well.

"Take these," he said, holding out sturdy shoes. "Never go into a battle situation without your shoes if you can help it—your body will expend too much energy constantly healing your feet."

She did not argue, but immediately dropped to the dirt to push them on. He knelt beside her, lacing one boot with firm, unwavering hands and then pulling her up when she finished the other. The act of doing something so mundane seemed to have recalled Elizabeth to herself, and while her eyes glimmered with shadows of her beast, they were undoubtedly her own again.

"Can you scent Georgiana?" he asked.

"No. I only know in which direction she will be found. My heart tells me."

"Then we need not stay close to the ground. Come," he said, opening his arms.

Unhesitatingly Elizabeth stepped into them, and before she knew it, they were in the air. "We have to go high," he said into her ear, "so we will not be seen." He prayed he would have strength enough to bear both of them for as long as was needed. He was gifted in flight, but the talent was a draining one; his wife was not heavy for a vampyre but was far more muscular than a mortal of her size. Truthfully, *any* additional weight would be exhausting, and to do this in broad daylight was asking for trouble. Still, he could feed from her if necessary, even in the air.

"It will be cold," he warned.

Elizabeth nodded her acknowledgment. Her hair blew from its loose braid and flew out behind her, tangling hopelessly in the wind, while she closed her eyes to feel the direction they should go. It was not a perfect compass—she could not see the way, she only knew if they strayed too far from it. With nudges she directed her husband, and he altered their route accordingly. The inner guide to their daughter grew strong, then faded, then grew strong again.

"We are going in circles now," Darcy said. "I think we must be at our destination." He flew them lower over the area, a rocky peak fading into stony cliffs, not seeing any signs of life.

Landing them on a hilltop, he had a good view from all sides—with no visible ambush points. Matlock would not have phenomenal strength while the sun shone so brightly, but he was always stronger than Elizabeth, and may have set traps. Amazingly, Darcy felt as fresh as he had before they started—utterly replete. Perhaps his rage fed his strength.

"How far have we come?" Elizabeth asked. She sounded calm, though her eyes again flashed red.

"Perhaps forty miles."

"I am surprised we did not overtake him."

"He can run like the wind at night. With the start he had, and given the time he likely left Pemberley, he probably was here for over an hour before dawn. And I believe I know where we are," he said, with sudden realisation.

"Where?"

"It is a silver mine. I am almost positive this site was among those leads on Wickham I sent to Matlock. He either discovered Wickham's hideaway and adopted it for his own or—"

"Or he was hiding Wickham all along," she finished.

"Given your perceptions of the man, which have proven flawless, I think we must assume so."

Elizabeth clutched his hand. "Never have I wished so much to be wrong."

He gave a brief nod; his grief was great, but his guilt ate at his gut like gunpowder, and fury burned its fuse.

Together they sought an entrance. As they reached a lower elevation, they found well-travelled pathways, evidence of frequent usage, though no one was in sight. And not long after that, Darcy caught a wisp of scent of his prey.

"We must search now, while the sun is high. Even in the caves, daytime will affect him negatively. But when I say we must leave, we leave immediately. Due to our flight, none of my line will be able to track us, and we need everyone if we are to have any success capturing him at night. For all we know, Matlock has lieutenants stationed throughout. However, they will all be worse during the day than he is, to our advantage. He will not believe he has been followed so easily," he said. "Faith, *I* can scarce believe it, but I can scent him."

"Georgiana...can you scent her as well?"

"No. But the presence of silver makes all more difficult. This is not his first visit here, I think."

"Are there mortals inside?"

"Miners, you mean? Difficult to say. No one breathes near us now, and there are no fresh human scents, but there are working mines throughout these hills—lead, silver, other ores, and minerals. No doubt the various mining tunnels intersect. I can conceal you from mortals, however."

They made their way through several low tunnels leading downwards in seemingly random patterns. In some places the tunnels were obviously weak, and even their light, careful passage sometimes brought down showers of rubble. And then Elizabeth stumbled and fell.

"Elizabeth!" he whispered. "What happened?" Her vision should be as clear inside the deep earth as it was in broad daylight, and since Georgiana's birth, her daylight weakness had diminished significantly. For the first time since entering the mine, he looked at her carefully; he could see she was pale and sickly.

"I do not know," she said. "Something affects me ill."

"Could it be Matlock? I do not scent him yet, but the silver would inhibit—"

"No," she disagreed immediately. "'Tis not him. I feel...dizzy."

"I am a sapsculled idiot," Darcy said. "It is the silver, of course. You are too young to have any resistance, and if the veins are rich...we must return. We shall get the others and—"

"No!" she protested. "If I slow you, go ahead, but as God is my witness I will not stop searching." She heaved herself up determinedly. "We can cover more ground separately."

"Out of the question," Darcy said sharply. "We continue together."

Again, he forged ahead, holding Elizabeth's hand to reduce the silver's incapacitating effects.

Darcy opted for one of the larger branches when the tunnel they were in petered out. They travelled another hour before he halted suddenly, holding up one arm, his nostrils flaring.

"Georgiana," he said. "I have her! We are on the right path!"

The scent grew stronger until Elizabeth, even, could smell it; Darcy pointed to a single drop of blood on a stone amongst many upon the rock-strewn floor.

He picked it up. "Dried," he whispered.

"Georgiana," she cried softly.

But after that—nothing. The scent was gone once they were out of range of that solitary drop, though they followed the tunnel to its dead end.

"We have passed other tunnels," he said, returning the way they had come. Without a word, she followed.

They found another passageway and followed it—and shortly thereafter startled a cavern full of bats, followed by an arduous, steep downward slope. Darcy caught Georgiana's scent again. And once again, they found a single drop of blood.

Darcy picked up the stone, both of them staring at it. They picked their way through to another dead end. And then they turned back, trying yet another branch, a long shaft into nowhere.

It was perhaps half an hour later that they found a third droplet. Darcy picked up the stone.

"Do you scent Matlock at all?" she asked.

"No," he said, "but the presence of silver overwhelms everything and would aid the diffusion of scent. Likely, nothing short of blood leaves much odour in this place." He turned to look at Elizabeth, brushing the rock in his fingers. "I believe we waste our time."

"What? No!"

"Think, Elizabeth. Matlock arrives at a predetermined hiding place somewhere within these tunnels shortly before dawn. He feels safe, for he has left a false trail sending us in an entirely different direction while cleverly managing to disguise his scent leading here. However, he is both sly and cautious, knowing I will eventually remember these mines. He uses what little night he has left to take a small amount of Georgiana's blood and place drops in random tunnels and caverns, hoping to confuse any pursuit. Doubtless, come nightfall, he plans another web of false trails to confound us. All the blood tells us now is that we go in the wrong direction."

Elizabeth nodded her frustrated agreement. "But why leave any evidence at all? Why not allow you to believe he has gone to ground in London, or even left the country?"

Darcy's jaw firmed. "He does not believe we will begin searching here for some time and does not plan to stay here long enough to be caught. He wants me to spend hopeless years buried in the earth, searching futilely."

"I will find her, wherever he takes her," Elizabeth vowed.

"And yet, this is our best chance. We must bring the others, Elizabeth. We know he is in here, somewhere reasonably close, within our grasp. He has not deployed his plans for escape. For one thing, he will require the assistance of his best men. He knows I will immediately surround Matlock, and his minions will be vulnerable to attack once they leave his keep. He may have acted upon impulse, though doubtless he has been considering a kidnap for a long while. I do not believe he expected me to refuse his suit at all, much less so categorically. And when I informed him of my plans for the Council seat, it confounded him utterly. Of all things, I believe he felt that seat was securely his. But for you, it may have been."

At that moment, they heard the distant sound of voices, and realised they must have wandered into an active part of the mine. Darcy immediately shoved Elizabeth behind him, backing them both against the tunnel wall. "They will not see us," he muttered over his shoulder. His eyes glowed black.

The miners talked in a desultory fashion, a lit candle affixed to each helmet. Darcy used his illusory powers to obstruct their view—to any human, the pair would blend into the rock wall. The group was nearly upon them when Darcy caught a brief spurt of panic. Since none should feel they had anything to fear, he examined each closely as they trudged past. The silver affected his senses, but not enough for him to miss that the last male in the line was vampyre.

Darcy waited until the vampyre was alongside him before making his move. Lightning fast, he grabbed him. The other vampyre, evidently prepared for his ruse to fail, attempted to flee. But he was no match for Darcy, and the brief, silent scuffle was over almost before it began, the miners never even realising anything had happened. The short-lived fracas appeared to have drained all the strength from the vampyre hanging limply in Darcy's clutches.

Darcy moved them further into a decrepit, abandoned tunnel. Elizabeth touched his arm. He turned to her.

"I believe I recognise his scent," she said. "I cannot be certain, because the memory was from before I Turned...but I think he is the one who brought me to Wickham at Kympton. I did not have a good enough look at him then to be sure, but there is something about him."

Darcy's eyes glowed red, fury filling him. "Tell me your name and your master!" he ordered in a low, deadly tone.

The other vampyre stared back sullenly. Darcy seized his fingers, twisted, and wrenched the hand off as easily as if he had been pulling a grape off its stem. The vampyre let out a sharp scream, which ended quickly when Darcy tightened his grip on his throat.

"Listen well," Darcy snarled. "To me, you are nothing more than a collection of worthless body parts. You are dead, and doubtless know it. Only one choice is left to you: how quickly you die. I can make it swift and painless, or I can take years—decades, if need be—during which time you will beg for death as the blessing it would be. But you will decide right this moment how it goes. Look at me and tell me if I deceive you."

The other male met Darcy's eyes, reading the resolve written there. Any remaining resistance drained, and he slumped in Darcy's hold. "Me name be Jenkinson," he said slowly. "I were lately of de Bourgh's House, but I been wif Matlock since 'e kilt 'er."

Forty Six

JENKINSON, ONCE BEGUN, ENJOYED BOASTING OF HIS ROLE. "They coudna done it wifout me," he bragged. "Crawled right up yer castle wall. Ain't no one better at sneakin'."

"You forgot your skills this afternoon, then," Elizabeth muttered.

Darcy tightened his hold on the vampyre, eliciting another groan of pain. "When you stole Elizabeth for Wickham, were you working for de Bourgh or Matlock?"

"I were de Bourgh's man," he admitted. "But they was innit together. Mostly, Wick'am listened ter Matlock."

Darcy glowered so fiercely, the air burned, and Jenkinson felt the urge to add something useful. "But 'e kilt 'er after 'e kilt 'er beastie, when milady were usin' me eyes an' ears for the vicar. That 'urt somepin awful, I tell ye. Milady thought Matlock were innit wif 'er, but 'e does as 'e pleases. I bin Matlock's man ever since. Matlock trusted me ter rough 'im up after 'e kilt milady an' Wick'am, ta make it look as if 'e fought 'em instead of tricked 'em. I can lead ye to 'im."

"Does he have Georgiana?" Elizabeth broke in.

"A wee babe is wif 'im."

Darcy took a small leather-bound notebook out of his pocket, along with a scrap of pencil. "Draw me a map showing where he hides and where he posts his sentries. Do not attempt to deceive me, or I shall know it."

Jenkinson, muttering curses, took the notebook and roughed out a sketch, leading from a different entrance than the one by which they had entered. The route to Matlock's hiding place was complicated, and it took the vampyre four pieces of the paper in order to map it out, including the placement of a small retinue of guards. It was located deep in the heart of the hillside, with a cleverly concealed entrance.

Darcy examined the map and then examined Jenkinson, plunging deep into his feelings to discern whether the vampyre lied. He found fear and hatred, frantic, futile attempts to communicate mentally with Matlock—all blocked by the mine's silver—as well as an obsequious desire to ingratiate himself in order to live, but no evidence of deceit. Darcy supposed he could try to use him, but the risk of betrayal was too great.

"When does Matlock expect you?" he asked.

"By nightfall," Jenkinson answered. "But 'e knew I might 'af to 'ide meself if yer men were too close," he added. "Matlock 'adn't time ter esplain 'is plan, jest sent me to warn 'em."

"How soon do his men join him?" Darcy demanded.

"They 'as to sneak away, travel one at a time, careful-like. I 'spect 'twill be a night or two afore they'll begin arrivin' into the upper tunnels."

"Very good," Darcy nodded. "Jenkinson, you have admitted to participating in the kidnap of both my wife and my child, as well as my attempted murder. Because you have been honest in confession and provided valuable information, your end will be far swifter than deserved." With a motion faster than the eye could see, he pulled a short silver double-bladed sword from a scabbard at his waist and plunged it through the other vampyre's heart. Before Jenkinson could so much as feel pain, it was withdrawn. Astoundingly, the blade caught fire, Jenkinson's blood blazing upon its razor edge. Drawing it back in a smooth arc, Darcy sliced the blade through Jenkinson's neck like a hot knife through butter.

"I believe there is adequate silver here to cover his scent, if we cover the body deeply enough in this rubble," Darcy said, wiping the blade upon Jenkinson's coat. Immediately the edge cooled, and he replaced it in its scabbard. "And there is abundant debris to bury him." He began throwing rocks over the corpse, rapidly covering it.

"That is an impressive sword," Elizabeth said.

His expression lightened. "It is the oldest Darcy treasure, a gift from Saint Lazarus, father of my House. It is only to be used when our line is threatened. Once it tastes the blood of a combatant, its every blow is lethal." He finished the makeshift grave and dusted his hands off upon his breeches.

"It is nearly eventide. We must leave at once."

"No!" Elizabeth protested. "I cannot leave this place, knowing Georgiana is here somewhere with that murderer. Do not ask it."

"You *must*. We know where he is, but Matlock did not grow to his age and strength by stupidity. There is not time to reach him before he achieves his full night-strength. You heard Jenkinson—Matlock will wait until tomorrow evening before he grows anxious. We must retrieve the others, who will be frantic, wondering what has become of us. At first light, we attack, when the posted guards will be at their weakest."

"Will his guards not warn him? Georgiana will be in grave danger if he knows he is under attack."

"Not if we seize both guards at once and kill them before they even know their peril—which is why we need others. They are vulnerable with daylight as well. We must go now, Elizabeth."

The sun had just fallen below the horizon when they returned to the point where they landed that morning. Darcy held out his arms, but Elizabeth put a hand to his chest in a staying gesture.

"No...wait. Please...say I may wait here, concealed near the entrance Matlock uses as his exit. If I am well hidden, he will not see me, but then I will at least know if he makes an escape attempt. I cannot bear the thought of his disappearance while we are gone."

"No, Elizabeth. I know you. If he tries to leave, you will attack and he will kill you. Matlock is a hundred times more powerful than you. Likely he would scent you the moment he exited."

"Then I will go higher up, to that peak up beyond. I will be too far away to do anything except note whether or not he departs."

Darcy grit his teeth. While her plan had merit, he did not believe she would not try something foolish if Matlock attempted to flee. He despised leaving Georgiana behind as well, but he firmly believed that Matlock would not hurt the child, at least not yet. He had no such reassurance regarding the man's intentions towards Elizabeth.

As if she could tell her husband's thoughts, Elizabeth said, "I swear to stay concealed, Fitzwilliam, on the blood of my child. Trust me to do as I promise."

He made a sound of frustration, knowing he could not claim he did not trust her. Time was of the essence, and they had little of it enough without standing here, exposed and bickering. Sweeping her into his arms before she could protest, he flew her up to a tall outcropping far up the mountainside. There was scrub enough for concealment and yet still an adequate view of the cavern entrance, at least for one of vampyric vision.

"You will remain here. You will not make a noise or movement until I return. Upon Georgiana's soul."

"I swear," she promised fervently.

He sealed it with a swift, hard kiss, feeling her honesty, and shot into the rapidly darkening sky.

❧

Darcy had not yet flown half the distance before he bitterly regretted his decision.

I cannot, he realised. *I cannot do this.* It was *wrong.* Even knowing his people would be deeply anxious, he turned back, cursing.

By the time he reached the small patch of land where Elizabeth waited, the exertion had drained him, as the flight there had not. He dropped down lightly beside Elizabeth's hiding place—and was startled when she jumped him, pinning him to the ground before he could softly call her name. Her eyes glowed red.

With his superior strength he flipped her to her back, trapping her against his chest and holding her still. "Elizabeth," he hissed as she struggled against his weight. "Elizabeth!"

She recognised him at last, and he could tell she was forcibly regaining her control. "You...scared me," she managed, when she could speak. "I...did not believe you would return so soon."

"Neither did I, but Elizabeth...you must return with me to

Pemberley. I need to bring our men here, but I *cannot* leave you here alone. Please...I beg you."

In his absence, however, her beast had gained too much the upper hand. She began struggling again.

"We do not have time for this," he said, and in one massive thrust, heaved them both into the air. "Pray I make Pemberley with my remaining strength," he muttered.

Hurtling through the sky in rapid ascent, even Elizabeth's maddened beast seemed to realise that it must stop fighting and hang on instead. They were nearly to Pemberley before she truly came to herself, her grip slackening and the tension leaving her body; she gave a little defeated sob, her despair echoing through her frame and his. He held her tightly, protectively, coming to a gentle landing just inside the castle walls.

"All will be well, love," he whispered. "We will return very soon. Please, try to understand."

Obviously, his men had been watching the skies and spotted them, for Richard immediately tried to communicate mentally. Ignoring him, Darcy tilted Elizabeth's chin up so that he could look into her tear-filled eyes. "I need you to be my warrior," he implored. "We must join forces in order to reclaim our daughter."

A sense of rightness filled him as she nodded her agreement, straightening, summoning her strength. He heard the approach of several men rushing through the gardens to meet them; at the same moment, he realised that the fatigue he had experienced in his abbreviated solo flight had disappeared once he took Elizabeth in his arms. He could have flown a hundred miles further without discernible effect.

Joining forces. It was the answer to everything.

"The blackguard," Richard growled. "If I get my hands on him, I shall peel his skin off in layers and feed it to the dogs."

"You will not sink to his level," Maggie said. Richard's vicious expression softened as he turned to look at her. "Let the Master deal with the likes of him," she added.

"She does not care so much for *my* soul, Uncle," Darcy snorted. He and Elizabeth had joined Richard in the room where Maggie rested while she underwent the lengthy healing process—Darcy noting it just happened to be the chamber nearest Richard's apartments. Matlock had missed piercing her heart by the tiniest fraction of an inch.

"Elizabeth and I will fly back to the caves just before first light," Darcy said. "Where is James? I asked him to bring writing materials—ah, there you are, James. I will draw a map to the cave, and another to Matlock's lair entrance." He began sketching rapidly while he spoke, referring occasionally to Jenkinson's drawing. "There is only one tunnel leading to the lair, and the guards he has stationed must be within this area to be useful," he said, pointing to an area on his map. "So even if Jenkinson was lying, which I doubt, and despite the fact that his information is several hours old, it makes no sense for Matlock to position them elsewhere."

Richard and James both nodded their agreement. "Richard, your task is to clear that tunnel. Matlock's men must not have *any* opportunity to warn him of danger. I believe the silver present will inhibit communication, but we cannot count upon it."

"I will take Carter and two others with me," Richard agreed. "They will be in hell before they know what happened."

Darcy explained his theory regarding Matlock's plan to confuse future pursuers by using Georgiana's blood. "He will likely spend these night hours spreading hints of her presence throughout various tunnels and caverns. Ignore any scent indicating a different direction than these maps. The silver will disguise yours, and I removed ours. He does not have most of his personal cadre. I believe he acted impulsively when he stole Georgiana, and his men, *if* they can even get past those you have sent to surround his estate, should not begin arriving until tomorrow night. However, he will begin to be anxious when Jenkinson does not return, and you must be vigilant. We have no certain means of ensuring he returns to his lair at daybreak—'tis only our best guess. And if he finds Jenkinson's body tonight, he will flee immediately, and all must give chase.

"James, take Nigel, Andrew, and Thomas and leave within the next quarter-hour. Set a watch on each exit, here, here, here and here." He indicated the various points on the map; James nodded. "Keep this drawing with you. I will do another for Richard and his men. They will coordinate their entry with you. No one is to enter the caves before dawn."

James accepted the map, and without another word, disappeared.

"Richard, Elizabeth and I will enter the caves thirty minutes after you and your men. When the tunnel is clear, try to communicate with me, but do not worry overmuch if you cannot. We will trust you to be successful. Whatever you do, you are not to engage Matlock. That pleasure belongs solely to Elizabeth and myself."

"Darcy—you cannot mean it," Richard cried. "Keep Mrs Darcy safely here with Maggie and allow me to assist you in the taking of Matlock."

Elizabeth began a protest, but Darcy held up one hand in a silencing gesture. "No. This is something Elizabeth and I must do together. If we fail, you are to call all my people in from all my lands and raze Matlock." At the pained expression on Richard's face, he smiled—and there was something lethal in the expression. "You need not fret, Uncle. I have discovered that together, Mrs Darcy and I are a deadly combination."

Darcy gathered Elizabeth into his arms just before dawn, relieved that the waiting was over. It had been torturous for both, but especially for Elizabeth; he did not need any gift in order to feel her burning anxiety to be doing *something* to recover their daughter. He was proud of her, though; not once did she break down or succumb to the rage of the beast flashing bright within her eyes.

It was still dark, so there was no need to fly in the higher altitudes. Darcy kept an alert eye out for non-Darcy vampyres in the area, seeing nothing out of place. But this time, he paid attention to something else as they soared—his internal perceptions of his own strength and power—and confirmed that using his gift while holding Elizabeth did not drain him of energy; instead, it actually increased. It was as if he fed from her while they flew.

"Does flying seem to weaken you? Do you find it tiring?"

She shook her head in the negative. "No, not at all."

Astonishing. Their beautiful experience together in the gamekeeper's hut had shown him that while in intimate contact with her, his own gifts were multiplied beyond reason. After being renewed while using the exhausting gift of flight the evening before, he had remembered Anne de Bourgh's capture, and his sudden ability to turn Anne's gift back upon herself. He had been holding Elizabeth when it occurred, though she was mortal at the time. It was all Elizabeth!

Mortal or vampyre, she empowered and strengthened him, perhaps even allowing him to take upon himself the gifts of those around him. Almost inconceivable. He would have to test these astounding possibilities. Dissect her powers meticulously...when there was time. It was sheer madness to go into this desperate situation depending upon an untried talent, but his heart, his instinct, whispered his course.

Besides, he could not prevent Elizabeth from going to Georgiana, no matter what powers he did or did not possess. If he attempted to leave her behind, she would destroy Pemberley trying to go to her baby.

He landed in a sheltered copse not far from the cavern entrance. Although he could not reach Richard, mentally he confirmed with James that his men were in place guarding the exits and that Richard's men had entered not quite thirty minutes before.

With gentle hands, he cupped Elizabeth's face. "Matlock, to the best of our knowledge, is still inside. We must face him together, my love. That means you must take my hand, or at least keep your touch upon my person."

Her brow furrowed. "Why is that? I do not yet have your daylight vigour. I may slow you."

"No. You strengthen me. Do not let him separate us, no matter what."

"You are already the stronger," Elizabeth contended. "At dawnbreak, you will have many times his power."

"We are stronger together. Never underestimate him," Darcy reminded. "And even during the day, his powers are greater than yours, though his strength is diminished. Promise me you will not let go of me, no matter the provocation. Swear it on Georgiana's life... because it might well mean our deaths, or hers, if you forget."

"I...I swear it."

He bent to kiss her, long and deep, feeling her terrors, her determination, and her impatience to begin. He opened the barrier to his own feelings, so she would know he felt the same. "Give me of your strength," he murmured, his beast pleased by her immediate willingness to feed him. After, he gave her his neck. "Take from mine."

They would both go in with all they had to meet their enemy, conquering—or dying—as one. As the first fingers of sunrise separated darkness from dawn, they slipped into the cavern. Together.

❧

They walked swiftly, their path unimpeded by human or vampyre. Elizabeth could not truly say she was afraid, at least for herself—her terrors were all for her daughter. Death could not frighten her, but the thought of her innocent, helpless baby in the hands of a conscienceless scoundrel such as Matlock was horrifying. If Richard had failed in his task, they might be marching straight into death, but Fitzwilliam did not hesitate—and neither would she.

Finally, they reached the entrance of Matlock's lair. It was not until they nearly reached the access point that she heard a sound causing her heart to move to her throat—the sound of a tiny wail. Jerking forward—she was halted by Fitzwilliam's hand clutching hers. His eyes glowed red and black, boring into her with his feelings of resolve. The hardest thing she had ever done was drop back, stopping her headlong charge to her daughter.

Jenkinson had warned of a stone barrier blocking the lair's entry —added after Matlock killed Wickham, apparently. There would be no way to accomplish their aim by stealth. Briefly, Darcy let go of Elizabeth's hand—after another intense look, silently reminding her again of their plan. The baby's cry did not sound as though it were directly in front of the entryway. A good thing, she reminded herself. She nodded to show she understood—and stepped away.

In the blink of an eye, Darcy had withdrawn to the other end of the passage...and then he hurtled towards the barrier with vicious speed. Just before he reached the blockaded opening, he threw his body at it, feet-first. It was a dangerous plan, giving Matlock the upper hand for a few moments.

The barrier shattered against the force of Darcy's collision, startling even Elizabeth who expected it, the noise like a gunpowder explosion. If Matlock attacked quickly...

But as the dust settled, she saw her husband, unhurt. He stood, arms akimbo, at the centre of a large cavern. Remembering her instructions, she sped to Fitzwilliam, locking her arm in his, feeling tension thrumming throughout his body as if it were an electrical storm, the unholy stench of evil nearly choking her. Matlock stood several feet away. In his arms, he held Georgiana, who appeared unharmed.

Unless one counted the silver dagger pricking her small chest directly over her heart, a tiny drop of her blood welling at its tip.

Forty Seven

"AH," MATLOCK SAID CALMLY. "I SEE YOU HAVE DISCOVERED MY little hideaway. Jenkinson?"

"Jenkinson, in part," Darcy replied, restraining the beast within. "We bumped into him, so to speak, in one of the upper tunnels. We would have discovered you, regardless."

"And Lionel? Pelham?"

"Since they did not halt our progress, let us assume they did not survive their encounters with Richard and his men."

"Forgive my curiosity, but how did you discover me? I took great pains to cover my flight from Pemberley. By all rights, your men should be eagerly tearing apart London by now." Matlock sounded only mildly inquisitive.

"Elizabeth's love for her daughter is far stronger than your little schemes, my lord. There is nowhere on this earth you could keep Georgiana hidden."

"What do you know of love? I loved you, Fitzwilliam. I cared for you, nurtured you as a boy when everyone else in your life ignored or rejected you, helping you whenever you had a need. Two centuries of care, and how am I repaid? You should have allowed the betrothal, son."

"Was it love when you had my father murdered?"

Matlock's brows rose, plainly debating whether to lie—how easily

Darcy could read him now!—before deciding against it. "How did you learn the truth?"

"Jenkinson revealed Wickham was in *your* pocket, not de Bourgh's. It was obvious if you protected Wickham from capture, you must have helped him evade the death penalty he ought to have received in the first place. I always knew he could never have murdered Father without the assistance of a greater mind than his own," Darcy said. "I do not understand why you acted, however."

Elizabeth clutched his arm more tightly, lending her strength and support while he spoke. It steadied him, keeping his voice from trembling with gathering rage and power.

Matlock smiled coldly. "Poor Wickham had *such* useful gifts. I admit, I was tempted to renege on our little agreement and let the Council slaughter him...but of course, Catherine de Bourgh thought she shared control of him, and it amused me to allow her the illusion."

"I am sure both Wickham and de Bourgh came to regret the alliance."

"Perhaps. I regretted the necessity of killing your father, but truly, it was your own fault."

"An interesting conclusion. How so?"

"As long as George was alive, you would not settle down to fulfil your duty to your House. Your father was determined never to reproduce again, and I *needed* a Darcy bride. I did everything I could to encourage him to change his mind, but he refused. A man can only be so patient." He smiled at Elizabeth. "And was I not correct? Within a few short years of his death, you were married and a father. This little beauty was born for me—she would not *exist* without me. She is mine by *right*."

"My marriage had naught to do with my father's death. My heart awaited Elizabeth."

"Pah! *Your heart!*" Matlock spat contemptuously. "This is what is wrong with you, Fitzwilliam. You learnt *nothing*. All those years in my care, and *this* is the result. Such a disappointment. You rely upon weak emotional ties in the place of purpose and the acquisition of power, never comprehending the meaning of strength. For instance, I know *your* pathetic heart would quail to see this silver blade plunge. She is so young, I might not even need to sever her head in order to truly kill her," he added conversationally. "I am willing and able to do whatsoever is necessary. The heart, you see, is only useful insofar as it gives you power."

His wife stirred at Darcy's elbow, a slight movement only, conveying immeasurable distress. When they discussed their plan, Elizabeth had been fixed upon their necessarily noisy entry as the most dangerous time, but he had always understood that it would be this—for her, who could barely remain upright in Matlock's presence, to be forced to stand helplessly and simply watch, and for himself, his raging beast burning to cut down his enemy with the sword of Lazarus!

But *any* battle of blades would put Georgiana at grave risk.

No, their plan was best, now more than ever.

Elizabeth's fingers dug into his sleeve with enough force to tear the fabric of both coat and shirt, the skin of her bare hand touching the skin of his bicep. The skin-to-skin contact helped his attention; he could feel his powers gathering, gaining strength as never before as her gifts boosted his. *Must keep him talking, distracted.*

"Tell me, my lord...why did you go to the trouble of saving me from de Bourgh's creature?"

Matlock showed his first sign of annoyance. "Because I supposed you had a capacity for gratitude! I *saved* you! You should have understood your daughter would be in good hands with someone who could rescue even *you* in the face of such danger."

Darcy watched the other vampyre carefully, but Matlock's knife hand never wavered. "Since you were in league with de Bourgh, I imagine you could have prevented the attack in the first place," he said, forcing himself to continue the conversation.

Matlock shrugged. "It benefited my objectives to encourage it. Catherine wanted the child dead. I did not. Our alliance was at an end regardless." His expression grew sly. "As a matter of fact, I opened the door to your room to let the creature in. What good is a saviour if he has no one to save?"

Elizabeth's hand dug into his arm hard enough, almost, to make even Darcy wince. His beast clawed at his control. He need not glance at Elizabeth to know her eyes glowed red.

"I suppose you could also have prevented Elizabeth's kidnaps, had you wished?"

Matlock's smirk grew vile. "I *planned* the first kidnapping, you fool. But once again, I thought only of you. I showed you how strong your feelings were, at a time when you spoke of a white marriage! I gave you the opportunity to play the hero to this mousy little *nothing*. Catherine was responsible for the abduction that ended with her Turning." He glared at Elizabeth—the loathing only she once sensed now obvious to all.

"I wish Wickham had obeyed Catherine," he shouted at her, the first fissures showing in his control. "He was *supposed* to kill you at once. Had he done so, *none* of this would have been necessary. I wish I could have watched him humiliate you, use you as his toy. I would have allowed it, you know, before Darcy managed to escape his silver chair. I would have applauded him while he did it," he spat viciously.

Elizabeth made a low growl, but it quickly turned to a tiny noise of anguish as Matlock delicately pressed the blade a fraction closer to Georgiana's heart; Darcy could not take his eyes off Matlock for even a second, but the beast within grew ever stronger with every moment of her distress. Darcy harnessed their rage and betrayal, throwing all the potency of their combined powers into his gift.

Matlock was a master at shielding his emotions—the man had been deceiving him for *centuries*—but Darcy also knew he had never attempted to penetrate Matlock's defences. No, Darcy had spent his life hiding from this particular ability. Matlock had been the first to discourage him from looking too deeply, stressing the dishonour above all else. *Irony.*

"Ah, but this 'mousy little nothing' produced the miracle child you have risked everything in order to seize," Darcy said, his tone imperturbable. "You pretend she is not good enough, while without her, Georgiana would not exist."

"All it proves is that I am fated for my little princess," Matlock said, his tone suddenly switching to a cajoling warmth. "Had I not spared Wickham from justice, you would not have Turned her. You should be thanking me, not threatening me!"

Darcy shook his head, still keeping his rage contained from Matlock's senses. "Do you even hear yourself?" he asked. "Can you recognise your madness? You are so full of arrogance, you have grown stupid with it. Did you drink from Wickham, that you believe your own lies, as he did?"

"Ungrateful wretch! Why do you resist the truth? She is my fate!" Matlock cried, losing his calm once more. Though his dagger-hand remained perfectly steady, his pupils dilated and a fine film of sweat sheened his forehead.

Just a little longer, sweetheart, Darcy thought to his child. *Papa is here.* To his surprise, he felt a delicate touch within his mind, baby-soft. There were no words...but he knew—knew!—it was Georgiana, seeking him out, in search of the familiar haven of her parents' love. She was not precisely afraid, but she was hungry, angry at the wrongness of the arms holding her, and gripped by an instinct that kept her still and silent even so. His beast—his *soul*—yearned to snatch her away from the cold hands threatening her. He spared just a bit of his power to flow a gentle stream of love and comfort through the connexion they shared.

"Fate has different plans," Darcy said coolly. "God gave this child to parents who shall never allow her to be used by the likes of you. You are a worm who cannot earn respect, so steals it. You are a coward and a leech, a rat scrabbling for crumbs. You are overpowered and outnumbered. It all ends now."

Matlock's laughter was laced now with panic. "So you believe, Darcy. But I warn *you* now, unless you allow me to walk from this place unharmed, I will plunge this blade into the child's heart. And then you have the worm, but not the fish, eh?" he cackled.

"Set the babe down, and you may leave," Darcy said calmly. He felt Elizabeth sway beside him, in illness, terror and protest, all three. A little more time was all they needed. Just a little...

Matlock snorted with contempt at this offer. "I would be dead the moment I raised the point of this knife away from her blessed little heart."

"Perhaps *your* word means nothing, but mine still does. If you put her down and go, I vow you may leave without interference from me or mine." He made the offer easily, knowing a man who judged others by his own moral fibre would never trust it.

"Pah! Richard awaits me beyond that passage, we both know."

"Richard will obey me. We will hunt you, but you may leave if I so decree. I will grant a five-minute start."

"Forgive me if I do not accept your sincerity," Matlock sneered. "Now, my friend, it is time to leave. Rest assured, as long as you and yours leave me be, dear Georgiana will be entirely safe. Her life is only at risk if mine is. I promise you she will be well cared for...very, very well."

The time for distraction was gone. From the first moment they entered the cave, Darcy's senses had invaded every aspect of Matlock's emotional terrain—the peaks and valleys, the rocks and rills, every hill and escarpment. Darcy did not simply measure and weigh Matlock's feelings—as was his habit, if he bothered with his gift at all. No, he searched, studied, explored and exploited, wrapping his senses around every stray thought, every exposed nerve, every care, fear, doubt, and distress, his wife's intangible power enhancing his every ability.

Matlock, of course, had thick emotional walls bounding every spare feeling he possessed—but no wall was impenetrable to a gift flaring bright as a comet and strong as the sun at noonday.

When Darcy's power surrounded each feeling, he began demolishing the ramparts sheltering them.

Unconsciously, Matlock had resisted the subtle intrusions. He was uncommonly strong, and perhaps at some level, his keen sense of self-preservation sought escape. But he could not truly resist what he did not feel, and Matlock had numbed his finer sensibilities centuries before.

"We go now—" Matlock began, stopping mid-sentence with a horrified gasp. He clutched the knife desperately in a hand suddenly trembling.

Darcy's power besieged Matlock's innermost feelings like creeping ivy, tendrils wrapping around each brick and stone, overwhelming the decayed mortar and shredding them to dust. Until, at last, every feeling was exposed, raw, like the new flesh under a burn.

❧

Elizabeth channelled...herself. Her power could not be described; what she possessed was a devotion to her family permeating the marrow of her bones, the blood in her veins, the beat of her heart.

Centring herself upon it, though she could not see it nor feel it as other vampyres might their own gifts, it nevertheless existed the same way love existed. Though it could not be seen or even properly explained, like love, it was strongest when it existed for the care and nurture of others. She fixed it unreservedly upon her husband and her daughter, all that she had, all who she was.

Slowly, she absorbed a subtle change in the balance of power, a lessening of her overwhelming illness. As she grew stronger, she *knew* he must be weakening. Matlock's rocklike discipline began to crack; it started in his eyes, in his skin, and she was desperately afraid he would realise he was losing control and plunge his dagger in a final act of vengeance. But he waited too long—by the time he aimed the knife in a downward slash, Fitzwilliam had taken control.

"Dear Lord...what am I...what am I?" Matlock screamed, as his every sensitivity, every finer emotion buried over the last four hundred years of evil plots and misery came rushing to the fore. The shame he believed crushed, the conscience he supposed was ground to dust...they were intact. Virtue and decency were not simply nice ideas, but the foundation of the soul; they could be numbed but never destroyed. Matlock had erected a bulwark covering the acknowledgement of his own evil, but Darcy shattered it, and Matlock could do nothing except face the sordid, repellent creature he had become.

He dropped Georgiana, not seeing her any longer, his eyes locked in a sickening true vision of himself. Elizabeth caught her before she hit the ground. "My baby," she murmured, tears trickling from her eyes, falling onto Georgiana's soft skin as she curled herself around her daughter. "My poor little girl."

Darcy placed one hand upon Elizabeth's hair while she rocked their child close, his wife no longer noticing the man now writhing on the floor, frothing at the mouth, feet drumming, trying desperately to stab himself in the heart.

Richard joined them. Darcy glanced at him from the corner of his eye, still keeping most of his attention upon Matlock.

"What in blazes did you do to him?" Richard exclaimed.

"By and large, he acts upon his own will now," Darcy replied as Matlock managed to gouge out his own eyes. "He has been made to look truthfully at himself. Plainly, he does not enjoy what he sees."

"Saints and angels," Richard muttered, shaking his head incredulously. "'Tis a bloody Judgment Day."

By the time Elizabeth finished feeding Georgiana, Matlock was a shattered mess of exposed wounds and mindless screaming. She stood, clasping the babe tightly in one arm while brushing the cavern's dirt off her skirts, finally casting a glance at the thrashing figure on the floor.

"How long do you suppose he will continue to inflict such punishment upon himself?" she asked.

"I am not convinced he punishes himself so much as tries to end it all. He does not have the control to finish it, however. If his soul is as black as I am persuaded it must be, he could be at it for years." Matlock punctuated Darcy's words by ripping open his own throat, tearing at the jagged edges of his flesh, peeling it from his body in an effort to reach his heart.

"No," Elizabeth said matter-of-factly. "It ends now. We are finished with him, and it shall be God's decision how long in the eternities he suffers for his sins. Richard, will you see it done?"

Richard looked at his nephew. "I heard, Darcy. I heard him admit to killing your father and more. Revenge is your due."

Darcy let out a long sigh. "Revenge will not bring my father back. I only want justice...and peace. I wish to go home with my family. Elizabeth is correct. Will you do this for us?"

"Gladly. Will you advise those who watch the exits? James is at the end of this passage, but the rest are in sunlight now. I might be some time," Richard replied.

"Of course, but how long can it take to finish off this wretch?"

"Oh, two slices of my blade, mayhap a second or two. But I am not so good a man as you, Nephew. I am happy you are satisfied, but I shall stand guard until I calculate he has atoned for Maggie's fear, pain, and suffering. And your father's. And Elizabeth's. And Georgiana's. And all of those who love and care for you and yours. I should be satisfied in an hour or so. Perhaps two. Possibly three. If I am a long while in returning, you need not be concerned."

Darcy looked at Elizabeth. She shrugged.

"Very well," Darcy said, drawing his arm around his wife and pressing a kiss to a sleeping Georgiana's head. "Enjoy." With his family close beside him, he headed back towards the light.

Elizabeth emerged from the cavern into a sunny morning, blinking at the bright light of day. It seemed impossible so little time had passed; it felt like lifetimes to her. She clutched Georgiana even more tightly to her bosom as she sensed the approach of another, calming only when she recognised James. As he drew near, her husband nodded to him and whatever communication they exchanged was silent. After James departed, she asked, "Where does he go now?"

"He will wait near Richard. The rest will return to Pemberley."

A Pemberley carriage awaited them, standing ready in a clearing. One of Pemberley's mortal coachman held the reins, while Andrew stood guard. Elizabeth passed Georgiana to Fitzwilliam, allowing Andrew to help her in, settling with some relief onto the soft cushions, exhausted. Darcy climbed in easily, sitting beside his wife. She immediately held out her arms for the baby, as Andrew shut the door behind him.

For some time, they travelled in silence; she was peaceful, but she knew her husband suffered. "Are you well, my love?"

For a moment Darcy did not answer, his attention on some point far beyond the small carriage window. "Elizabeth..." he began at last. "You are very gracious in not demanding straightaway the tremendous apology you are owed for my mistaken judgment of Matlock." He shook his head, adding quietly, "Apology seems too small a word, too insignificant in the face of my mistakes."

Her brows knit. "You apologised already."

He gave a mirthless laugh. "Yes, I apologised. I apologised and then left our daughter alone in the house with a madman. By trusting him and my judgment, I withheld a part of my trust in yours. After everything, I still trusted him—even knowing you did not. You cannot know how much I regret it."

She snuggled in closer to him. "You did not recognise what he hid, Fitzwilliam. You are not omniscient, and he had more than two hundred years to practise his deceits upon you. Your father did not see it either, much as you respect him. And even though you did not understand my feelings, you supported me in them. You chose me over him. I never believed he would do such a thing either. No one could have predicted this."

Darcy shook his head in disbelief. "Have you not even one 'I told you so'?"

"It gives me no pleasure to cause you pain. And you fixed everything, love. You saved Georgiana."

"*We* saved her. I could not have done it alone. Elizabeth...without you—" His voice broke on an anguished sob, and though he swallowed and stifled it immediately, the effort left him shuddering.

Elizabeth understood. It was all too much. His misplaced trust in the man whom he had loved like a father, the betrayal, the truth behind his father's death, Georgiana's kidnap...even a powerful Master vampyre such as her husband could not easily vanquish such incredible pain. Fortunately, she knew where comfort was to be found.

Sitting up, she carefully transferred Georgiana's precious weight from her shoulder to his. In her sleep, Georgiana stirred restlessly until she nuzzled directly into his neck. Instinctively, her tiny fangs extended as she sought and found the arterial connexion. Before many moments passed, she was Taking from her father.

"Egad," Darcy whispered. "Elizabeth, she is...do you see?" He held his daughter to him, plainly terrified to move lest he disturb her. "She must think I am you."

"No," Elizabeth whispered gently. "She knows it is her Papa. But she was frightened and needs extra reassurance. She knows, deep within, that Papa will never let anything bad happen. He is big and strong and he will shield her."

"*We* will shield her. After what you helped me do...there are no words. I believe you will not only sense those with stained souls but will be drawn to those with the best. You will discover those of the finest character, I will work to destroy those who have none. Together, we are unstoppable."

"And to think, at first I thought you an angel," she mused. "How foolish of me."

"You would have no use for an angel," he averred. "A warrior such as you would eat angels for breakfast."

Elizabeth smiled, adjusting herself so she was nestled beneath his other arm. "All will be well, my dearest love," she whispered. With that, she closed her eyes and within a few moments was sound asleep.

Darcy squeezed his eyes shut against tears until he was sure he had himself under good regulation. For the rest of the journey home, he held his girls tightly within the shelter of his arms—knowing that, though he grieved, his most priceless treasures were wholly protected. There would always be dangers, and the infant he held was so terribly vulnerable. His House needed leadership and strength, or they would be at risk. His world needed change so that the weakest amongst them were never left at the mercy of evil. All must be kept safe, for all to be well.

With Elizabeth by his side, he had no doubts he—*they*—could make it so. Together.

ABOUT THE AUTHOR

Julie Cooper, a California native, lives with her Mr Darcy (without the arrogance or the Pemberley) of nearly forty years, two dogs (one intelligent, one goofball), and Kevin the Cat (smarter than all of them.) They have four children and three grandchildren, all of whom are brilliant and adorable, and she has the pictures to prove it. She works as an executive at a gift basket company and her tombstone will read, "Have your Christmas gifts delivered at least four days before the 25th." Her hobbies include reading, giving other people good advice, and wondering why no one follows it.

In addition to *Tempt Me,* Julie is also the author of *The Perfect Gentleman* and *Lost & Found.*

ALSO BY JULIE COOPER

The Perfect Gentleman

Georgiana Darcy has gone missing. Lizzy Bennet knows just what to do to find her

'Tis no secret that Lizzy Bennet has dreams. The uniquely talented daughter of a woman with a dubious reputation, Lizzy knows she must make her own way in a world that shuns her.

Fitzwilliam Darcy carries the stains of his family's dishonour upon his soul and only by holding himself to the strictest standards has he reclaimed his place in society. If his fifteen-year-old sister cannot be found quickly, her scandal could destroy years of perfect behaviour. Lizzy is willing to join the pursuit to get what she wants but will Darcy be willing to trust her with his secrets? And what will they do when the search for Georgiana reveals what neither expected to find?

This *Pride & Prejudice* variation is two stories in one book. Volume 1 starts in Ramsgate with the disappearance of Miss Darcy and follows the adventures of Elizabeth Bennet as she seeks to find her. In Volume 2, our favourite couple has recognised their feelings for one another but more surprises and challenges still await them at Pemberley.

Lost and Found

Sisters. Chaos at home. A father who isn't paying attention. A powerful hero, whose behaviour is anything but heroic. Sound familiar? Some of our favourite characters from *Pride & Prejudice* star in this story set in Fairy Tale England, where enchantments—of the magical and of the heart—meet.

Once upon a time, there lived two sisters. Jane was fair, with mild blue eyes and hair the colour of corn silk. Elizabeth had long, dark, thick curls and eyes the startling green of a spring glade. Soon after the arrival of an evil stepmother, the girls found themselves starving and alone in the woods.

Their fairy tale ending is not easy to accomplish as one sister disappears into the home of a witch and the other sister—the valiant Elizabeth—is set to work as her slave. Wickedness is all around, and only by working with, and trusting, the cursed master of Pemberley can she break free of her captor captor, and release her sister and her beloved Darcy from the spells cast by the witch.

Q
Quills & Quartos
PUBLISHING

ACKNOWLEDGMENTS

With grateful thanks to Lisa Sieck for so many readings and encouragement to write the story in the first place, Jan Ashton for her editorial genius, the many encouraging readers and commenters at AHA so long ago, Kristi Rawley for additional editorial repairs, Amy D'Orazio for kindly indulging my cover vision disorders, and everyone at Quills & Quartos for professionalism, transparency, and supportiveness.

Made in the USA
San Bernardino, CA
10 August 2020

76802159R10275